JOURNEY

C.N. Eisenbruch

TO

ARI

who wears the ring

Table Of Contents

Chapter	Title	Page
Chapter I	Girl	1
Chapter II	Society	19
Chapter III	Souls	34
Chapter IV	Bullseye	50
Chapter V	Holvir	65
Chapter VI	Pasture	83
Chapter VII	Ambition	101
Chapter VIII	Sun	118
Chapter IX	Champion	139
Chapter X	Union	155
Chapter XI	Whispers	163
Chapter XII	Prejudice	178
Chapter XIII	Life	190
Chapter XIV	Ambassadors	204
Chapter XV	Morning	222
Chapter XVI	Mortals	240
Chapter XVII	Courage	250
Chapter XVIII	Blessed	265
Chapter XIX	Unity	280
Chapter XX	Divided	295
Chapter XXI	March	313
Chapter XXII	War	324
Chapter XXIII	Death	348

I

GIRL

A slim young girl, her high cheekbones framed by locks of soot black hair, walked slowly toward the golden throne. Though many eyes stared at her upright figure, she kept her own firmly fixed upon the wizened, yet keen gaze of the woman who sat before her. Elgitha, Grand Master of the Guild of Tooth and Claw.

The throne stood tall at the end of a long gallery. Eyes- some hostile, some curious, few kind- all watched her. No grief written on that clear brow, no pain bowed her limbs. They waited for her to falter, betray weakness, anger, emotion, something. But they waited in vain. When she reached Elgitha, she took a breath. Holding out her hand, she spoke clearly, her youthful voice carrying to the furthest corners of the hall.

"My brother is dead."

The words, irrevocable, resolute, dropped like a thunderbolt among the company. And into Elgitha's lap dropped a small object also.

A signet ring, featuring the profile of the god Bahamut.

Arya stood motionless before the throne, fighting back the dam of emotion that threatened to burst forth. Her mother's words rang in her head. True power is in only letting them see what you wish, not what you feel.

Your feelings mean nothing, they serve no purpose. You are a T'ssama, of the long line of paladins and Ladies who upheld the might and greatness of Bahamut.

My brother is dead.

She winced, but regained her focus quickly, hoping no one had caught her moment of weakness. The woman before her stood motionless, staring at the ring in her lap, silver brows betraying as little emotion as Arya's black ones. Arya wondered at what point she would be dismissed, already loathing the thought of returning to her mother without even so much as a single word to report about restoring their family's favor. Elgitha hadn't moved a muscle, save to clasp the ring dropped in her lap in her scarred, palsied hand; the same one that had placed the ring upon her brother's finger all that time ago.

But suddenly she noticed something else gleaming on the woman's hand. A tear.

"All of you. Go now." Though she had her face still turned downward toward the ring in her hands, her voice rang through the hall. In an instant, every member of the audience present vanished. Arya tensed, wondering if the woman had meant her too.

"My child," whispered the woman. Her normally stentorian tones were querulous, almost unintelligible in her grief. She looked up at the girl with her eyes, said to possess the power of turning a daemor to stone with the force of their gaze, swimming in tears.

For him.

For her brother, the man whom the guild she led as Grand Master for half a century had thrown out and then relentlessly persecuted. Arya didn't know whether to shriek in anger or in anguish. What right had this woman to cry when she, the sister who loved him more than any other, could not?

"Yes, Grand Master?" she answered, marshalling the tones of her voice into flat obedience. She would leave no opportunity for her mother's criticisms today.

"Will you keep this?"

Arya looked at the woman, shock not quite completely hidden by that expressionless visage. She felt the weight of the ring Elgitha had placed in the palm of her hand.

"Grand Master Elgitha," she said, her tone still passive, "what are you saying?"

Her brother's signet ring. The tie that bound him, the child of prophecy, to the guild that betrayed him. For years, Arya had envied that ring on his finger, chafing at the very different destiny she'd faced throughout her childhood and adolescence.

The future Lady of Wheelspoke could never become a paladin of Bahamut.

Her eyes grew wide. This certainly wasn't the forgiveness her mother had expected, and yet here was a choice she could make, all of her own free will.

What would it mean to wear that ring?

"I'm saying it is time you join us. You do not want the burden of your mother's legacy, I know," Elgitha murmured, a crooked smile breaking through her tears.

"If the gods were kinder, it would be your brother himself who would offer this ring to anoint you as a novitiate of Tooth and Claw. Alas," she said, with a fearsome bite to the words, "men and women think the kindness of the gods means less than the advantage taken of them."

The words had a meaning that didn't escape the shrewd child. Though her mother, the Lady Arianna of Wheelspoke, spent as much time as she could wrapping her daughter in the stifling wool of her own persuasions, Arya had her own methods of discovering what the guilds were up to.

And the discoveries honestly terrified her.

—

"We shouldn't have to barter for our safety," Masa Riquelme, the imposing red-haired Lord of Dragon's Hill, spoke with disdain, not caring whether the tones of his voice carried to the ears of the Lianorran envoy who waited in one of Wheelspoke Manor's comfortable offices. Though facing his rival and cohort, Lady Arianna of Wheelspoke, he minced no words in his speech. *"Si nos lastiman a cualquiera, nos lastiman a todos."*

Rivals or not, they were all asafolk of Beausun, and their god's glory shone upon them all.

"It's not a barter, Lord Riquelme," she replied, her tones only barely audible to the perked ears of Arya as she sat demurely out of sight in one of the manor library's many shadowy alcoves. Allegedly studying a dry and tasteless tome of law, Arya was not about to waste the opportunity to observe the altercation unraveling before her. It was rare her mother let her into her father's old library, now used as the Lady's quarters for public council. And rarer still during this, a meeting of two of Beausun's most powerful leaders. Thinking perhaps her mother had simply forgotten about her presence, she remained motionless as the marble statues of her dead ancestors that lined the wall intermittently and lent such grandeur to the space.

"We already report to the great nobles of Lianor," Lady Ari continued, a thin finger propping up her fragile, yet gracefully sculpted chin. The sheet of black hair that draped from the crown of her head to the balls of her feet betrayed not a single silver strand or roguish curl. "*Era sólo cuestión de tiempo*. Our individual precedence no longer means anything to them."

"And you think this will bring you greater strength, do you?" Masa hissed, expressing his family's famed temper as though to melt the Lady's icy reserve. "I just don't see what's in it for you, for surely you must see the more power they wield over us, the weaker we- *our* people- grow. How much must we hand over to these... these outsiders?"

"The nobles have lived here for generations," she replied dismissively, "and they have since brought us nothing but peace and prosperity. I see no danger in trusting them now, when the strength they offer is finally being put to the test."

"*No lo quiero*! I'll have none of their strength!" he responded explosively.

Arya winced. No one had ever raised their voice to her mother like that. Asafolk always listened to Lady Arianna; though she faced nothing but disagreements every blessed day, it never took long for dissidents to see things the way the Lady wanted them to.

However, despite his volatility, Lady Arianna T'ssama refused to react. She simply folded her hands and smoothed her visage, peering at the irate Lord through half-lidded, expressionless eyes. "You'll do what they tell you, or you'll perish. Your daughter has already defied the guild once. Do you think they'll just let that go? Our ways don't matter to them anymore. The guilds offer protection. Our faith and our strength, when allied with theirs, will be unparalleled. Resist, if you wish," she said dismissively, waving a white hand carelessly. "But Wheelspoke stands with the guild. Our doors are shut forever to traitors."

The conversation made little sense to Arya at the time. She took it as simply one of the many altercations her town had with their powerful neighbors, the quixotic mages of Dragon's Hill. The rumors that passed through Wheelspoke were always shared in whispers, and Arya, a budding youth who had yet to initiate into the triumphs and tribulations of adulthood, struggled mightily to first hear those whispers; and then, to understand them.

In fact, she had almost forgotten their exchange entirely. Until the news broke, shortly after, that an unknown scourge had descended upon Dragon's Hill and reduced the entire town and all who didn't manage to escape to a pile of charred rubble.

Now suddenly, she faced the most powerful aesir in all the realms, telling her that the throne upon which she sat was built on lies, while simultaneously offering her a chance to win it as her own.

"My whole life," she responded slowly, trying to maintain a stern command over herself but unable to keep the taste of venom from her words, "I have longed to hear these words spoken. But..."

The years spent sparring against her brother at every given opportunity. Hours spent hiding from her mother, studying the history of the great paladins of Bahamut. Moments with her father, before his death, seeing the light of pride in his eyes over the destiny of his son and resigned to the fate of his daughter. Her memories flooded, the words struggling to swim to the surface and rise to her tongue. Since the first moment her mind had grasped the concept of becoming a paladin of Bahamut, Arya had known that was what she wanted more than anything else life could possibly offer. And here it was, extended in the wrinkled palm of the Grand Master herself, over the sacrificial altar of her brother's soul.

Forgiveness at a price, a secondhand gift. A betrayal of his memory.

"I don't know." She could almost hear the disappointment and anger of her mother ringing in her ears, "I don't know if I believe in a guild that could... could treat my brother, the great paladin Seth T'ssama, the way it did. I don't know how you could ask it of me, either, Grand Master."

There. She'd said it. Might as well not even go home. Her mother was going to kill her.

A strange sound arrested Arya's attention. Elgitha was... laughing?

"Oh, you beautiful, noble soul," chuckled the Grand Master, wiping her face with a sleeve. "It stands to reason your family has such renown. What a hero you will be, my child!"

Arya screwed up her face, uncertain if the Grand Master understood her. "But... hero? I'm turning you down. I don't want this," she said, turning the ring over in her hand before tossing it back into the woman's lap.

"I heard you. If you did, I wouldn't think as well of you as I do. Come, Arya," she said, rising from the throne. "There is much you need to know, but too many ears around to hear it."

Confused, but eager to prolong her audience with the imposing woman (and avoid returning to her mother), she followed wordlessly as they made their way from the hall, through a side door and hallway out into a glorious garden. Roses of every hue and size permeated the garden with their aromatic and colourful sprays, drinking in the golden light of an afternoon sun. The great Cathedral of the Golden God, the guild's home in Lianor, possessed a timelessness and tranquility that transcended even the dread and fear dogging the realms since the advent of the undead scourge. Footsteps echoing across the stone told of labyrinthine passages around and below her. The sparkling, colourful stained glass bearing the sigil of their great god shone overhead, reflecting a myriad of rainbow light and filling the space with an aura of calm hope and grandeur.

The Grand Master led her to a bench, patting the seat beside her. Arya sat. Was she supposed to cross her knees? Or her ankles? Ugh, Mother was going to be furious. Absolutely furious.

"It is no mystery to me," Elgitha began with no preamble, "that the guild has begun to act beyond the reach of my own considerable grasp. And I am old," she said petulantly, "too old to command what I once was gifted in the respect and admiration I held of them all.

But I am still Grand Master. And it is a tenuous, ever-changing seat I sit upon."

Still no hint of expression marred the stoic look with which Arya had been trained since childhood to maintain. But internally, she writhed in incredulity. Arguably the most powerful woman in the realms, wielding greater might even than the nobles of the city in which her guild resided, sat before her complaining about the weakness of her position. *I'm fifteen and this is the first time I've left Wheelspoke alone. What does she expect me to say?*

"I don't understand. You mean..." she took a breath, wondering if she should trust her understanding of the rumors with this woman, "you know about the evangelizers? You know... what the guild has been doing?" Arya arched a dark eyebrow aggressively.

"Of course I do, child." No question, or judgement, passed with that statement. Arya breathed easy- and with a little more faith in her eavesdropping abilities. "But what you don't understand is what I have done about it. I had meant," she spoke softly, the querulous note returning to her voice, "for your brother to succeed me. In every way he would have been the most able and qualified Grand Master this guild has ever seen. His abdication, his abandonment, while it broke my heart, served to justify that only he truly deserved the honor I wanted for him. But it left me in something of a dangerous position."

Arya's eyes widened as she realized what Elgitha meant. Without a named successor, at her age, Elgitha was indeed almost powerless. She couldn't rule forever. And meanwhile, the guild simply grew more and more corrupt with the power from the convenient advance of the unstoppable horde and gold promised by Lianor nobles.

"The other Masters… the ones who defy you, and abuse Bahamut's name," she said, trying to clarify the dawning comprehension, "did they threaten you?"

A cheeky smile spread across Elgitha's face, and in it Arya could see vestiges of the resourceful and cunning woman chosen by Bahamut to act as the Cathedral's monarch a lifetime ago. "Not in so many words. I am still Grand Master. To depose me in any way short of natural death would visit the wrath of Bahamut upon the guild. As long as I sit upon my throne, the wayward squires and Masters who seem to think of our religion as a means to fill their own coffers must remain in the shadows, or risk outing themselves as traitors and be excommunicated completely. But I am old," she said again, "and with Seth left the only successor I could name. All the others are either sitting in the pockets of those corrupt malingerers, or dead."

The finality of that last word struck the young girl. Dead. An entire generation of paladins, questing against a *daemor genirae*, disappearing without a trace; a single survivor, the ambiguous and cutthroat Master Gareth.

He's still here. Seth is not. She sucked in a breath. *Do the gods really decide our fate?*

"So you're stuck," Arya mused, "you can't call them out, because to do so would weaken your own position… a Grand Master is responsible for her followers, after all. But without a replacement, the guild is doomed to fall into their clutches. And that…" she trailed off, suddenly annoyed, despair and frustration at both the Grand Master sitting before her and the god whose word she supposedly commanded tinging her calm words with acrid spite, "that's why you want me to join? Just so you have someone else to replace my brother?"

And without warning, there they were. The tears that never fell. Not when a small, silken package bearing his ring and a note telling of his death mysteriously appeared on their doorstep; not when her mother held a solemn, candlelit vigil "to guide his soul into Bahamut's goodly light" as she called it; not even when she spotted James, the man who loved and had been loved by her brother in their wild and adventurous youths, his face a deathlike pallor that shone out amid the pews of the curious, the grim, and the malicious.

One by one, unbidden tears spilled down her crimson cheeks and filled the soft grey eyes that could sparkle like mithril or thunder like a summer storm. She collapsed, sobbing helplessly into Elgitha's lap.

"No one could ever replace him. Not my Seth. I could never… I will never be as good as him."

Elgitha stroked her tousled hair, softly caressing the poor, broken-hearted girl whose stormy passions had finally broken the boundaries imposed by her mother. As the sobs subsided, she put one hand on each of Arya's cheeks, holding her tear-stained face and pointing it toward her own.

"Of course you could never replace your brother. You were never meant to," she said, her tone reminding them both of the traditions that governed the realms. No soothsayer had blessed Arya's cradle. Yet here she was, on the brink of a destiny she'd longed for, regardless.

"You are a T'ssama. You are your own spirit, and the strength of it will make those cowardly vermin who forsake their souls for filthy lucre tremble and obey. I would never ask you to replace the irreplaceable. But will you, Arya T'ssama, daughter of Arianna and Sethisto, accept the novitiate I offer you to become a Master and paladin of Bahamut? Will you forge your own path, and restore the honor of his guild that was too weak to save him, too lost to find him, and too ready to let him go?"

A shaft of light, a dazzling beam of glorious golden sun, sifted through the bowery garden and alighted on Arya's face. She felt the warmth of her brother's touch, heard the depths of his laugh, and saw the ferocity of the thrust of his sword. Her whole life, she had longed and prepared for this, a dream that refused to fade even as misfortune after misfortune befell her family. Enduring her father's death, her mother's manipulations, and her brother's disgrace would be worth their suffering.

I am my own soul. My successes are my own, as are my failures, and none belong to my family anymore.

"Grand Master Elgitha," she said, kneeling and sliding the ring upon her finger, "I pledge myself, Arya T'ssama, to uphold the might and glory of Bahamut, and serve as a goodly paladin of the Guild of Tooth and Claw."

A summer breeze blew through the arbor and scattered a shower of petals, as of golden scales, raining them down upon her.

--

"It's true then?" whispered a disembodied voice in the darkness. "The paladin is dead?"

"I heard his sister bespeak it with my own ears,"

replied a second, deeper voice.

A light gleamed forth. The strike of a match, tossed carelessly into a brazier that flamed to life, displayed the supple and feline physique of the Lady Astore. Accompanying her was a man whose powerful build belied the plainness and simplicity of his garments that bore no sigil or mark of guild. Both looked into the brazier as it flickered and danced with a fiendish glow.

"Tell Cleric Qu-lan. Now the paladin who banished him is dead, Makarh can return to our mortal plane and join the Lich King's army as our greatest general. We must make haste, though," she whispered, toying with a dagger-shapped pendant slipped deep between her breasts, "before Atosa manages to engage the pantheon."

The man's eyes had travelled to her lithe fingers, distracted by their play. She smirked, running a pink tongue along elongated teeth.

"What part of haste do you not understand?" Her arms pressed under her chest, amplifying the curves of her figure seductively. The man caught his breath.

"Were I a daemor, Astore, I would teach you the meaning myself," he jibed, before sweeping away from the woman and making his way up the gloom of the staircase.

Lady Lilithen Astore rolled her eyes and returned to the brazier. Asafolk were almost too easy. Since childhood, the calculating woman had known the power of wielding her body like a weapon. This knowledge, carefully cultivated, she used both as a tool for intrigue and a release for tendencies that grew more vicious as she grew more insatiable. And it had elevated her from one of many hopeful novitiates to the patroness of the mysterious and insidious Cult of Naszer. After the timely death of her autocratic and dispassionate father, her own skills as a *sacerdhosa* continued to grow- due, in part, to the licentious interactions she partook of with the beasts of the Abyss.

Indeed, asafolk were far too easy. Daemor posed a much more satisfying challenge.

Left to the silence of her summoning chamber, Lady Astore could feel the lingering presence of the being to whom her entire cult devoted their undivided allegiance.

"My Lord," she murmured, bowing to the essence of the despised Celestial of Darkness as he materialized slowly before her.

"No fear from you, Lady Astore?" The fallen god hissed softly. "No anger at the loss of your precious son?"

She remained completely still, impassive, as the specter drifted around the room, testing the boundaries of his material form. Ghostly hints of Razan, the assassin who had sacrificed himself to destroy the Lich King's possession over Princess Katarin's mind, lingered in the figure standing before her. Surrounded by a mist of inky blackness, the body within was mostly obscured, the only distinction being bright red eyes that glittered evilly in his long face. Not quite daemor, not quite Celestial, not quite aesir. This being who manifested from every plane had been nothing but a whisper of an idea for centuries before being discovered by the Cult of Naszer in the vacuum of Atosa's venture upon the Material plane. Decades of devotion and unholy alliances among daemor and *sacerdhosse* alike caught the dread Lord's attention, and his powers promised much of the chaos the fiendish beasts reveled in.

More than that; his summoning marked an epoch in the Cult's careful climb from obscurity to unquestionable power among the deeply devout asafolk who roamed Faie.

Though swift to obliterate any challenge to her reign, Lady Astore knew that unquestioning loyalty to the chaotic god would be a necessary sacrifice in the face of what she stood to gain. Destruction of the pantheon would completely obliterate the goodly guilds and lay waste to any obstacle that faced the opening of the Abyss to the Material plane.

But what idle obeisance these men demand, she thought idly to herself.

"Caution, *sacerdhosa*. Your thoughts are as clear as words," he rasped, his mocking voice like nails on slate. "You think I care about your allegiance? Your predecessors meant even less to me than you do. But I suppose I could owe you thanks, at least, for being the one to bear my host."

Lilithen snorted at that. "I do not desire thanks, my Lord." *Only the power your existence promises. Only the destruction of the cursed pantheon and the gods that grant these worthless asafolk their pathetic powers.*

"You have it, regardless, and you'll be glad for it," he responded curtly. "What of my army?"

"Atosa's... presence... has posed some challenges." She arched a delicate eyebrow expressively. Despite spending decades manipulating the goddess-child Princess Katarin, using her and her power to trap Atosa in a monstrous mortal form of a dragon, the Lich King ultimately proved unable to destroy the goddess. Since the events in the chasm of Naijor, her freedom allowed her to continue to thwart his attempts at amassing a powerful enough undead army to completely subjugate the soulful population of Faie.

"A minor setback. So long as the rest of the gods continue to ignore her, she won't be able to maintain the strength necessary to restore the balance of Life and Death."

"Hmm. You seem so sure of that," Lilithen spoke, but quietly. "At least your efforts to influence the guilds have proved more successful."

The Lich King laughed outright at that, a harsh noise lacking any mirth. "Ah, yes. Though I no longer have the control I once possessed to insinuate myself into any willing victim I desired, that one proves most easy to manipulate, even in this new form."

"You find your strengths better suited to enacting your own will, as opposed to exploiting the wills of others?" Lady Astore's cold lilac eyes were almost a challenge, daring him to try those professed powers on her.

"What need have I to exploit your will? You do exactly as I desire without such frivolous waste of my energy," he replied dismissively. "You and those repulsive daemor of yours. Bearing the mortal son of aesir and daemor both," he hissed suggestively, "has put you highest in my good graces. Do with that what you will."

His words mocked those sacerdhossa who'd gone before her. Attempting to mate with the beasts of Abyss and birthing their spawn had led to many untimely deaths among her cult.

Her lips pursed, and silence stretched between them. She almost wondered why she defied her god like this; his avatar, so like and yet so unlike the son who failed to escape his daemoric fate. With his sacrifice, Lady Astore's cult had finally done what her father could never do: summoned the glory of the Lich King. A move that promised to destroy the pantheon once and for all, beginning with Atosa and Sh'nia, Faie's twin sisters of Death and Life.

If she didn't know any better, she could almost accuse herself of resentment for that sacrifice. Though Razan had made his hatred of his mother and their hellish family clear, the man had his uses, after all. But she shrugged to herself. In the grand scheme of things, her feelings both for the loss of her son and her disdain for the being who stood before her didn't matter. So long as the Lich King left her to her devices, they could work in tandem to reach their shared goal.

Her father, her mentors, all underestimated her. They lived only long enough to see how wrong they were to do so.

"I will see to your army, my Lord," she bowed gracefully. "The Cult of Naszer has ever existed to serve you."

Without a word, he withdrew, his presence vanishing into the deep labyrinth below.

The only sound to break the stillness of the room was the crackling of the lit brazier. She stared into the flames, seeing not their dance but instead the swirling machinations of a war decades in the making. The chaos promised by her dread Lord's presence tantalized her, and she broke into a fiendish, mirthless cackle that rang through the empty chamber.

The Lich King's army would not be made up of merely legions of the undead. She casually removed her silken garments, slipping languorously from them as they pooled upon the floor. The mention of daemor had been irresistible. She must deliver the news herself. Hissing a guttural chant that awakened the portal to the Abyss, spoken in its inhabitants' own tongue, promised her a visit both of power and pleasure. The trace of the Lich King's presence evaporated in the roiling aura that poured forth from her, here, in the realm that suited her fiendish appetite beyond any other.

"After all," she said, stepping forth naked into the devouring flames, "Lady Arianna T'ssama was not the only one to lose a son."

II

SOCIETY

A sweet, familiar lilt filled every nook and cranny of the imposing clock tower with sound, carrying its own kind of magic to mingle with the mechanical machinations that made the building such a marvel. Goodly faiefolkr packed the rooms, alcoves, and balconies. The crowds rendered it unrecognizable to its emptiness the night a party of friends, escaping from the ilmaurte hordes, had stayed in its vaulted rooms.

"Can ye imagine the look on Timmet's face were he to see this?" A grizzled older woman, with arms like corded adamantine, smirked at a mountain of a man who let loose a familiar and ringing laugh.

"Almost wish he would. The sight may stop his heart, assuming he even had one," the blacksmith, Yori Magi, replied, returning Berta's grin.

Most of the audience, listening and talking amongst themselves, were the original settlers who remained, despite adversity, to defend Ljotebroek against the advancing scourge. But others appeared among the audience as well. Shy holvir huddled together in pews; refugee asafolk, returning from the ilvin forests to homes burned and farms razed, mingled among one another. Resigned to their fate, and ready for the guidance of the gods to help them recover. Even a small contingent of durgir hovered in the lofts to hear the news of the wide world which had been so disrupted.

"Rowan's twice the magistrate he ever were, anyways. We're lucky he finally stepped up to the plate," Michelle, the blacksmith's wife, replied through pursed lips. She kept her gaze riveted to the spectacle of two holvir standing upon the dais, the closest thing to a godly hall Ljotebroek possessed.

But the divine magic in the gears and cogs that moved the structure, much like religious fervor of the town's citizens, had dwindled near to nothing.

"Some sour apples you weren't asked, love?" Yori elbowed his wife with a charming smirk on his face. She stuck her tongue out at him.

"As if I could manage you *and* the town. We'd be in ruins in days. No, it's in better hands with him, though..." she trailed off as she narrowed her eyes at the holvir again, "I... question his taste in allies."

"Give 'em a chance, Michelle," Yori's tone was light, but serious enough. "Give 'em a chance."

On the platform, surrounded by a soft haze of light filtering through the mullioned windows, stood Ginni and Tjena, the holvi bard companions of those two heroes who passed through the doors of death after facing and defeating the mortal dragon form of the goddess Atosa. Diminutive yet commanding, Ginni's voice lifted in song and Tjena's hands coaxed a mesmerizing melody from their instrument, bow flying with grace.

"Did you ever think, Tjena," Ginni mused before they took the stage, "that we'd be, I dunno, heroes?"

Heroes. Tjena (who sometimes went by Tjen) barely qualified themselves as a person. "The absolute state of Faie, I guess," they joked with that half-smile Ginni adored. Even the Lich King couldn't take her lover's crooked grin.

"Yeah, you're right. Reflects more on them than it does on us. Ah well, we're here now," she took a deep breath, balancing first on the balls of her feet and then rolling to the tips of her toes. "Time to make some music."

There's nothing quite like universal adversity to bring the blighted together with the oppressor, thought Tjena as they surveyed those gathered before them. Their mind went back to the pair who had welcomed them on their adventures, granting them a respect and an affection unknown to the holvir in general and to this unlucky pair in particular. McKenna, the durgirn monk who'd left Mount Oer to find her beard, certainly didn't owe them anything. And Seth, the aesir paladin-turned-rogue she'd managed to trick into accompanying her on her quest, descended from a race known to go out of its way to oppress and subjugate them. Yet they both put themselves in considerable personal danger to save Tjena's sight, restore them to their kin, and fix the curse placed on the realms.

Considerable personal danger was an understatement. Technically, they were both dead.

As far as Tjena was concerned, these beloved heroes had died for them. The least the holvir could do in return was sing for them. Beg, beg with all the humility and grace of their downtrodden race, to make sure their lives were not spent in vain.

All they could hope was that the rest of the realms were listening.

*"Time anew for a tale of Faie
Twin sisters join our humble lay
One, princess in ilvin bowers slept
The other, durgirn monk her kin left
The ivory child knew her destiny
But ebony daughter only mystery
While one from towers high did claim
Honor of mother's immortal name
Humility did her sister guide
To quest among those in divinity divide
Though different were the goals of each
Together were forced to enter the breach
A journey together through doors of Death
To save their loves, restore their breath
Lost to the Lich King's horrific rise
Atosa's gift, her children's prize
Good faiefolkr who live on this land
Please grant the honor of your hand
Do battle with evil beside your brothers
Hide not from fear of one another
As we join our might to destroy his reign
Only strength combined defies Lich King again
The immortal gods who see our plight
They too are begged by Atosa's might
Our world, our selves, our culture, our life
Defined by choice, preventing our strife
Believe in the sisters who offer all to love
And believe in each to bring strength from above."*

The whisper of melody charmed the audience, soothing a measure of their fevered hearts that had so struggled against this seemingly unbeatable foe. Though the idea of cooperation with the other races antagonised the fibers of their very beings, worse still was the prospect of their homeland being annihilated by the advance of the Lich King's army.

Luckily for the holvir, their audience numbered mostly those who had suffered at the hands of the Lianor nobles and the godly guilds, betrayed by their own kind and forced to flee to beg refuge from the ilvir. While prejudice ran deep, gratitude runs deeper. And the refugees were willing to listen now to those whom they would normally turn a deaf ear.

So far the feeling went unspoken. But a man stood in the crowd, saluting the little pair. His finely trimmed whiskers may be a little greyer, but there was no mistaking Rowan of Ljotebroek, militia master and Lord magistrate of the town that lay on the edge of the realms.

"We don't really do 'deities' in this town. We don't fight the battles of the gods, any more than they fought for us. But," he lifted a genial eyebrow and swept into a courtly bow, "you and your companions saved our home, and reminded us of the loyalty we have for one another, and the friendships we built within these walls of brick and rhoditum. We owe you a debt we mean to repay. I believe your story, little holvir," he continued, head still lowered before the pair, "and would give my everything to keep faith with you."

At his words, others in the crowd stood in similar salute. The booming laughter of the blacksmith followed, unable to help chuckling at the solemnity of the militia master's words. He stood too, and raised an eyebrow at his petulantly seated wife, who rolled her eyes but couldn't help a grin as she inevitably rose with him.

"I thought I'd be too old to discard old prejudices," she said, her accented voice reaching the ears of the holvir she'd snubbed so many moons ago. "But what Rowan said is right. You did us a favor. And for the glory of that righteous woman, I pledge myself to fight this evil king."

The holvir in the pews, nervous but determined, cast a grateful smile toward them. As Michelle spoke, another couple of asafolk stood from a small group. The first, a woman with features marbled by vitiligo, accompanied by a bear of a man whose gaunt face had clearly looked upon the depths of despair.

"We are the asafolk of Wheelspoke," Katherine's musical voice rang out merrily through the crowd. "In Seth we lost a brother, a friend, a lover, and our village's greatest hero. We refuse to let these false rumours told by the guilds spread, and we refuse to let him die in vain. Together," she said, and cast an eye upon each of the goodly creatures before her, "we pledge to honor the sisters' quest to restore him, and we too will fight for the cause."

The asafolk around them mumbled in approval. Some stared curiously around the intricate machine in which they sat, while rubbing pendants bearing the sigil of Beausun's patron deity, Bahamut, hanging from their necks.

Most sat still, uncomfortable; with the awkward rigidity of those who lack conviction in their actions but were determined to do what they believed was right. Little did they know they represented the truly devout.

Little did they know, if it weren't for such devotion, their journey to Ljotebroek through the undead-infested wastelands of Beausun would have been impossible.

Finally the durgir from the balconies chimed in, their words like an avalanche tumbling down the mountainside.

"We fight no battles of aesir nor god. We live our lives in peace, guarding the stirrings of secrets kept locked beneath the mountain. But we, too," the duergi, robed in the garments of a head Priest of Malfaestus, paused and took a ragged breath before continuing, "we too have lost a hero ter this scourge. We cannae hide no longer, whether the world moves without us or no. I pledge," Pabble held a small golden hammer high above the heads of his brethren, "the strength o' my kin, the honor of our god, to seek our bright star - and in her honor, and her name, wipe this evil from our land."

The durgir surrounding him stood, grim, silent, but resolute.

Ginni clasped her hands and held them out, beseeching the audience with her charm and her pure, loving spirit. Though she'd travelled far and wide, in the company of her beloved Tjena, never before had she the courage to attempt any such feat as this. A unity, a reconciliation, amongst representatives of cultures who had long ignored and despised one another.

"We are small. But we are mighty. Gods and magic have divided us for too long. Together we can make new discoveries they could only dream of. Please believe me when I say, I have faith in us. I know you don't like us, that the holvir have been always an outcast race. But for the respect and affection you hold for McKenna and Seth, and the honor you have for each other, you have to trust us. The Lich King has risen and his army of undead march upon the realms. Only together can we stop them."

The audience grew still. And then, united by a single purpose, let out a cheer that rang in the rafters of the clock tower.

The crowd packed Ljotebroek's tavern as the evening wore on and filled the space with their laughter and camaraderie. Holvir sang and danced, durgir told ribald jokes and asafolk entranced each with stories of their harrowing pilgrimage from the groves of Meliamne. At a long table in the center of the boisterous crowd sat Ginni and Tjena, beside their friend Rowan and the blacksmith and his wife.

Michelle extended a hand toward Ginni, who took it with a smile and a wink. Tjena tuned their instrument with a new set of strings gifted by Yori, woven of fine strands of the same black adamantine metal that decorated the town's architecture.

"Thank you for the goodness of your hospitality… again." Ginni was saying to the magistrate beside her. "If it makes you feel any better the woods were much easier to get through this time!"

"I would hope so," he responded with a grin. "After you left, Yori outfitted the entire militia with weapons of mithril that made short work of any marauding ilmaurt."

"Ah, give me less credit," he boomed, clapping the back of the white-haired woman beside him. "Berta managed the most of it. Were it not for her getting that magic from McKenna's guisarme, they would've been just as useless as stone pitchforks."

"You uh... you kept her blood?" Tjena asked, slightly dumbfounded.

"Gods no, ye heathen. We melted down the mithril when we rebuilt the blade. I just... err, borrowed some of it," Berta replied defensively.

"You melted mithril? How in the realms?!" Ginni's jaw dropped. "I thought only the durgir could do that!"

"Not completely true," Pabble's voice carried into the conversation as he leaned over from the bench behind them. "Only Malfaestus can melt mithril. Ye've a powerful blessing, lass," he winked at Berta, who blushed, and buried her face in a foaming mug.

"It's the least I could've done for such a charming... er, duergi, did she say?" The crowd laughed chummily, but sombered quickly at the grim and heartbroken faces of the contingent of durgir around them. "I hope that woman returns to us soon."

"Atosa won't let her lose her way in there," promised Ginni, her eyes shining and full of hope. "Think of it like a... practice run. She's a demigoddess after all, she's just testing out the territory!"

"Luckily she has better taste in friends than just ilmaurte," mused Tjena. "She promised to release all the trapped souls from the Material plane, after all."

The tale of McKenna's journey with Katarin through the Doors of Death, though the guilds of Lianor were choosing to treat it as an incredible and unbelievable rumor, traced its source in the little holvir who had determined to travel the furthest reaches of Faie to tell it. After climbing free from the chasm, they sought refuge with the orgir upon the wide savannah that bordered Naijor. Urtha, filled with joy at the return of their beloved goddess and the story she had told of the fallen heroes, made sure the holvir knew all of what Atosa shared.

"You little wanderers, who came back now twice from death," she chided, waggling a finger in mock consternation at them. "You seem to have left someone behind."

She presented Ginni with a small, silken package brought by the goddess - a signet ring of Bahamut, nothing more. Ginni's eyes filled with tears.

"I hoped… she's a daughter of Atosa after all, and the Doors of Death were right there. I thought maybe she could, I don't know, sneak Seth's soul back without anyone noticing." Tears tracked silver trails down her and Tjena's cheeks. Urtha put a hand on the little holvi's chin, wiping one away with her thumb, her normal calm smile quivering. None knew better than orgir the perilous path taken by the living in search of the souls of the dead.

"It doesn't work that way, little one. It is up to the will of the gods that McKenna's journey with her sister be not made in vain. But…" she hesitated, remembering the aura of the demigod, and the obvious and heartfelt devotion that existed between her and her paladin, "if any can bring him back, it is her."

As the Magis and Rowan continued to banter lightheartedly with the Hammardin clan, the holvi bard stood, making her way to a corner where she recognized the faces of Katherine and James. Katherine had a look of concern and concentration on her face; while James stared, unseeing, into the crowd before him. He had a mug of ale in his hand, but the dissipating foam indicated he had forgotten all about it. Ginni laid a soft hand on the man's leg, and smiled into the slow start of surprise that shifted across his face.

"If anyone can bring him back, it's McKenna," she offered. "She's scary when it comes to protecting her friends."

Katherine responded with a cheery smile directed at both her silent friend and the holvi. "I believe in her. Before Arya left, we talked about her visit, and the rumors the guilds were spreading. They're not..." she grimaced, "particularly nice."

James huffed, then quaffed his beverage and wiped his mouth with the back of a trembling hand. "I hope Arya knows what she's doing, joining the guild her brother betrayed. I thought better of her than that."

"You don't know everything, James. You're biased and you know it. Elgitha adored Seth. She'll see Arya comes to no harm."

Ginni knitted her brows in confusion. "Arya? You mean, Seth's little sister joined Tooth and Claw?"

"Yes," Katherine cut off her friend before he could launch into a less than complimentary diatribe. "She went to the guild's stronghold in Lianor to announce her brother's death."

"Did she say anything about how they found out?" Tjen asked quietly.

Katherine eyed them sympathetically. "I never told her. Or her mother. I didn't want them to even think about trying to blame the holvir."

Because of course it would only be too easy to pin the mysterious death of her disgraced son on an outcast holvir village, on the farthest borders of the realms. Tjen shook their head, sipping resignedly at the pewter mug full of ale.

"I wish we could have told Arya the truth. She deserves that," Ginni muttered quietly under her breath. "Seth deserves it, too."

"You did the best you could to protect them both. And your caution made it easier for us to drum up support, bring those who dissented with Lady Arianna and the guilds here with us. I know what danger you put yourself in, to not only bring the ring to us, but to retrieve it in the first place. We owe you more than we could ever repay, Ginni. But that won't stop us from trying," promised Katherine, with a hand over her heart.

The *Spokirres* weren't the first to reach Ljotebroek. Rowan and the Magis remembered and welcomed the holvi couple who sought to unite the goodly faiefolkr. The moons since their journey from Naijor were spent collecting as many as would listen, and the asafolk of Ljotebroek, despite the controversy of their town's inception, proved far more convincing to the homeless refugees of Faie than the guilds that initially abandoned them.

Of all the towns we could save, she thought with a rueful grin as she remembered their deadly battle against the ilmaurte, *it would be the one that ended up helping us the most.* She almost begrudged the races their gods, who could work in such mysterious ways.

"Bah. Just gives us more food for song. So go on about Arya then. What convinced Lady Arianna to let her leave home?" Ginni bantered with a blush. Gratitude was still a novelty, and one she hadn't mastered how to accept.

"I assume her mother made her do it so she could restore their family's favor and get out of house arrest without, you know, actually having to admit to doing anything wrong." Katherine mused. "Of what was actually said between Arya and Grand Master Elgitha, I haven't the faintest idea. But what I do know is she stayed, accepting the nomination as a novitiate. Thanks to her heritage and the popularity of her family, she could reach Master in a few short years. And that, I'm assuming, is Elgitha's plan. Elevate Arya T'ssama to Master, then nominate her to the ascension of Grand Master before she dies."

Ginni whistled. "Good grief. Isn't Arya, what, fifteen? That's a lot to ask of a teenage girl."

Katherine laughed. "I see you didn't spend much time with their mother. Arya would put up with a lot more than that for the chance to escape Lady Ari."

Remembering the aura of the autocratic woman and the fingers of insinuation that emanated from her, Ginni couldn't help but agree. "So, what about these rumors? About McKenna? What could they possibly have to say?"

"Basically, the same thing they were saying before she disappeared. Mysterious daughter of Atosa, summoning ilmaurte to try to overthrow her mother and control the realm of Death." Both Katherine's tone and face were mocking, and she took a deeper draught than she normally would as though to drown the bitter taste the words left behind in her mouth.

"Oh. Lovely. So it wasn't just Razan making stuff up. That's... reassuring," Ginni replied carefully. "She was so mad when he came to us, touting all this intrigue about how she wanted to challenge her sister for the mantle of goddess, blah blah blah. But then she'd just broken up one of the most beautiful fights I'd ever witnessed, so maybe she was just piqued."

Snorting, Katherine nearly inhaled the contents of her mug and choked on both ale and laughter. "I'm assuming you mean Razan of Onyx Blade?"

"That's the one," said Ginni.

"Those two couldn't be within a league of each other without drawing blades. I would've paid to see that."

"Ahh, it was beautiful, but alas, McKenna's such a prude. She cut them off just as it started getting really good." Ginni pouted mockingly, and snuck a sip from the listless James' mug which he'd forgotten again.

Or thought he had. He nudged the mug away and playfully flicked the holvi's nose. "I'm paying attention. Sorry. It's all still so… fresh," he winced.

Humming a soft little melody under her breath, the charm of the bard's voice recalled the free and wild adventures of the youth he shared with the fallen paladin. He sighed again, but smiled, this time without a trace of bitterness. One didn't simply forget the love of a man like Seth. Though only a squire- and an uninitiated one, at that- the paladin hadn't let James' position reduce the affection and trust he'd had in him since they were boys. To the point where he wouldn't let James abandon their hometown when he defected.

"Stay, and protect my family," he'd begged the squire on their last night together. "Don't let my disgrace destroy the name we built for ourselves."

What is a name after all, James thought in despair. *You're dead. And I'm here alone, fighting a battle I could almost wish to lose.* He screwed his eyes shut tight, then exhaled slowly.

"Though I owe her one for replacing me," he said with a rueful grin, "my faith is with McKenna. Whether she returns with or without him, I am forever in her debt. To see him smile like that again," his voice lowered, pitched with emotion, "she can have anything from me."

Katherine raised her mug, standing tall upon the bench. "To McKenna! May she return, and with her sister restore the balance of life and death!"

"To the sisters!" cried the chorus of voices in the tavern, once, twice, thrice.

III

SOULS

A perpetual twilight spread its charming lavender gloom over the land upon which the two sisters walked. The air - was it air? or simply the absence of denser matter? surrounding them felt light, cool, unassuming. The ground beneath their feet shifted constantly; a velvet carpet, a gravel walk, a bed of moss. Each step brought them closer and further from any direction they tried to move.

McKenna couldn't believe that of all the roiling emotions threatening to overpower her, the only one standing out right now was annoyance.

"This is ridiculous. You're a sorcere, right? Can't you make this… I don't know, less magical?"

She wrinkled the nose set in her dark face, coils of copper crowning her amber gaze. The woman beside her scoffed, tossing her own thick sheet of moon-bright hair and rolling her amethyst eyes.

"Sure, you want me to summon a daemor?" Katarin replied sarcastically. If one listened closely, they could hear the sarcasm thinly covered an unspeakable depth of pain nearly impossible to bear. "I'm not some crackpot magician. Sorcery is no simple magic of illusion and trickery. Just as foolish would it be for me to ask you to call down an oath of Malfaestus, here where he has no presence."

McKenna groaned, pressing the heel of her hand to her forehead. Navigating the realm of Hel shouldn't be this difficult. They were both demigods of death, after all, left on Faie as babes by the goddess Atosa upon her return to the pantheon. Surely they should have some edge over this not-quite-material plane beyond the Doors of Death. But all McKenna could discern was that, while they were clearly no longer in the land of the living, this still didn't have the sense of being the realm of the dead, either. It didn't have much sense of being particularly somewhere, to be honest. It seemed more like the absence of being anywhere.

A pang tore at her heart at the thought of losing Seth to such blank chaos. Staring off into the distance at the slowly undulating vista marred occasionally by patterns and ghostly images, McKenna could only sigh, her amusement marred by bitterness. She wasn't used to such a feeling, this weakening, anxious dread that descended every so often along their journey through this chaotic plane. Nothing had prepared her for the pain of the paladin's loss. Every fiber of her being alternated among denial, anger, and a sense of futility that soured every breath and dimmed every bright thought. Death was somewhat of a novelty to her. All of her peers among the Hammardin clan's monks had been fairly young by durgirn standards, and she was as much a novice to grief as she was to the love that so inspired it. In the near century she'd lived under Mount Oer, only two durgir of their clan had passed on. And their deaths, like that of all durgir, had been a celebration.

Other than theirs, the only funeral she'd attended had been that of an aesir woman.

"They be worshippers of Malfaestus, or something?"

the novitiate had asked as durgirn pallbearers marched mournfully past, bearing the unassuming coffin draped in willow branches and lilies. The entire funeral procession had been made up of durgir, filling the hall with their gravelly song. Only two asafolk accompanied the casket. A man, bent with labor and grief, holding the hand of a tiny girl child who seemed confused by her surroundings.

"Nae, girlie, but the family be… friends of our clan," Pabble had murmured, hands clasped around a small mithril hammer that glowed with the blessings he prayed into it. As the casket passed them by, he tapped the hammer lightly upon the lid, and beams of light began to scroll along the wood, burning into it a beautiful pattern of Clan Hammardin's crest mixed with that of the sheaf of wheat and bundle of hops that marked the Clan's favored ale. The hammer, embedding itself into the wood, continued to glow, pulsing fairy light along the coffin and transforming it from a humble wooden box into a work of glorious art.

The lifeless body at the bottom of the gorge would see no such procession, no funeral rites, no noble burial.

Shrugging up her shoulders at the memory, McKenna swallowed hard, forcing the frustration and hopelessness past the dryness in her throat. *You'd think being goddess of death would grant me some kind of immunity to this feeling.* Calling upon Sha'vasana, the martial discipline of her monkhood, to calm her mind and spirit she peered at Katarin through the corner of her eyes. *We're together, at least,* she thought to herself, thankful for her sister's presence. *Neither of us has to do this alone.*

"I still can't believe you fought a dragon… and won." Katarin's voice was tinged with awe. "How did you do it?"

"Uh. There was a lot of... magic, involved," stammered McKenna, as she remembered the deathly aura emanating from her. "Also, I'm impervious to fire, so I guess that was lucky."

"You're impervious to- oh," as she studied the inky runes on the monk's skin. "Malfaestus. Of course."

"Yep. Could definitely tell she was annoyed about that," laughed McKenna, wincing at the memory of the dragon's sharp claws and spiny tail. "I'll give her this- I don't think Atosa had any idea who I was. If it weren't for the mirror, she probably would've eaten me eventually."

At least McKenna had broken the curse; the curse cast by Katarin upon Atosa, trapping their divine mother into the mortal form of a dragon. At least the battle, and its aftermath, meant Seth's death was not in vain.

"You sound so casual about it," her sister replied after a moment's pause.

It's hard to fear death when life promises greater pain, winced McKenna, as she felt Seth's hand slip from hers, and watched him plummet into darkness.

Though she didn't quite understand it at the time, McKenna could only be thankful their mother had sent both of them through the Doors of Death. Perhaps a measure of guilt had guided the goddess. It was Atosa's absence that caused the rise of the Lich King, after all, and the sequence of events that had led to Seth's fall and Razan's sacrifice. Or perhaps she meant it to bring the sisters, who had for a century been strangers to one another, together.

McKenna couldn't be quite sure. But it eased her heart to see the figure beside her, sharing the same lineage, the same untested and mysterious powers.

That is, until the woman suddenly disappeared.

"Wh- Katarin? Hello?"

Well, everything disappeared, really. It seemed almost as though the concept of appearance had simply been removed; all sensations remained, aside from the visual. Mentally throwing her hands up in vexation, McKenna willed herself to remain in place until the plane shifted back to something more akin to the Material. Or at least, something even vaguely functional.

"McKenna?" Her sister's soft tones trailed through the space, seemingly from a fair distance, though McKenna could sense she wasn't actually very far away. "You still there?"

"You still not a 'crackpot magician'?" the monk chuckled in response.

She heard a scoff, the only response she really expected from her slightly less humorous twin sister. "Come on, Princess, it's just a joke."

At the word "joke", vision suddenly popped back into place for the both of them. The same undulating nothingness surrounded the two, but at least they could see each other. McKenna took an agitated breath, repeating a guttural chant used by the monks of Malfaestus for guidance and patience. Malfaestus had no domain here, but the familiar sounds were soothing anyways.

"Kind of curious about that, actually," Katarin had her hand to her chin, staring thoughtfully into the nothingness. "You mean you weren't a princess, too? You really had no idea who you were?"

A cackle of laughter triggered a sparkling light in the space, that faded along with the sound of McKenna's stifled snorts. "'Princess', that's rich. I was raised by durgir. They don't have princesses. They have a Jaerl, but that's kind of a misnomer, really... I think the title just sounded nice, and they pass it around to anyone who decides they want it. Keeps things interesting. But otherwise durgir are pretty straightforward about..."

Katarin raised a ghostly eyebrow, interrupting McKenna's tangent. She cleared her throat apologetically.

"Sorry.. anyways, no, I was not a princess. I was just adopted. And then I joined the monks of Malfaestus, and the rest," she held her hands out from her sides with a shrug, "didn't really matter. Until this quest." *Pabble is getting a bed full of sand when I see him next.*

Katarin appeared to accept that, a thoughtful look softening the haughty lines her face usually settled in. "That's... unfortunate. I could only imagine how much of a shock it was when you found out."

McKenna's eyebrow shot up so fast it threatened to disappear into her hair. "When I 'found out'? You mean when your assassin lackey started a fight in my campsite and accused me of unleashing an ilmaurte scourge upon the realms of Faie? Yeah, I guess you could say it was a *shock*."

"He said what?!" replied Katarin, pivoting in place to stare at the monk.

"Oh, you mean that wasn't your doing? How kind of him, then," she replied flippantly. "I guess he thought it was a warning." Truthfully, it didn't matter. The enigmatic assassin's attempts to turn her from her path backfired on him. That was the reason Katarin was here, after all.

"He was supposed to get the mirror. Although I'll be honest," her voice was heavy with guilt, "I didn't exactly instruct him to pull any punches either."

McKenna turned to regard her sister, a cheeky grin pulling at the corner of her mouth.

"Oh, he didn't fight me. He fought Seth."

"Seth," Katarin paused, and seemed to ponder for a moment. "You mean Seth T'ssama? The disgraced paladin?"

McKenna's eyebrows- both of them this time- took flight again. After spending so many decades under a literal rock, it still baffled her every time those who should be complete strangers professed knowledge of each other. "*You* know him? How?"

"Haven't you realized by now all the heroes tend to know one another?" Katarin answered with a crooked smile. "Razan was NOT pleased to have lost against him once. He wouldn't shut up about it for weeks. I can only begin to imagine the vigor with which he fought that paladin again."

"All I've realized, honestly," McKenna huffed, "is that my time spent studying the pantheon, the eternal Lore of Faie, really meant nothing in the grand scheme of things.

The realms are so large, so impossibly vast. It's a mystery to me how everything is so connected, how faiefolkr all seem to know everybody's business but their own, and yet despite that, they're still... I don't know," she trailed off in frustration, "fighting each other."

The sorcere felt a sympathetic current run through her. She'd seen a century of life among the faiefolkr; witnessed firsthand their slow migration away from one another, the insidious distrust and evil manipulations that shattered a once unified population into fragments. She felt guilty again, realizing afresh what it meant for her sister to have grown up ignorant of everything. Especially in comparison with how she herself had abused the knowledge her mother had misguidedly left with her.

"I can... only imagine how frustrating it must have been, to realize who you are," she said again, but with a measure of empathy that struck the monk as deeply sincere. "I don't know what our mother was thinking. But," she held her hands out and gestured at herself self-deprecatingly, "you can clearly see how well that turned out for me. Maybe she actually did you a favor."

One breath, two. Her nostrils flared slightly, but McKenna had to admit, to herself at least, perhaps her sister was right.

Raised in obscurity. But at least that meant I got to make my own way. While the monk could curse the innocence that left her so vulnerable to these moments of ignorance, she could only be thankful for it, too, that it protected her from the weaknesses and foibles that characterized the quixotic and variable aesir race.

She stared over the woman's head, digesting these new ideas. Suddenly, she knit her brows in confusion.

"I can't believe how different we are," she mused.

Katarin seemed to shrink within herself, wincing. "To be honest, it surprises me you could even… travel beside me. Or choose to listen to our mother when she told you to trust me."

McKenna's expression of confusion shifted as she realized what Katarin was getting at. "Oh. Oh you mean the whole 'possession' thing. Nah, I just meant you're short."

Katarin stared at her in bafflement. "Are you serious?"

"Well, yeah. I mean, just look at you, you come up to, like, my shoulder, and yet we're supposed to be twins-"

Katarin tried to bite back a snort, but failed. She dissolved into laughter. "You're incomprehensible. I thought… you would hate me."

Her sister looked at her quizzically. But she put a hand out, hoping despite the shifting material on the plane that she could grip Katarin's shoulder.

Of all the identity crises McKenna had suffered, and the blossoming of a love for someone she watched die, and the development of her innate abilities as a demigod; it was the discovery of a sister, of a person with shared blood, shared heritage, and shared history, that affected her the most.

"Look. It's because of you, the man I love is dead. But then, it's because of you the man you love is dead too. I can't begin to pretend to know what that's like," she said, locking her gaze with Katarin's own. "But I also can't pretend to know what it was like growing up as you did. You're right, I was mad enough when I found out that I was supposed to be some goddess' child left with durgir. Durgir! Of all the faiefolkr!" she cried, shaking her head in disbelief. "You knew you were a princess, and what your destiny should have been. You can't be held accountable for trying to keep faith with the expectations you were born to, any more than you can be held accountable for the manipulations of some... what did Ginni call him... 'smelly old ilmaurte god'."

Though tears had begun to form in her eyes, a chuckle escaped from Katarin. What a woman this sister of hers was. She could almost forgive herself, when she saw how wholly and unconditionally McKenna did. But she felt compelled to honesty, refusing to absolve herself of guilt for the role she played in the Lich King's return. "I thought... I thought his voice was my own. I thought I was listening to the desires of my own heart, despite what I had to accomplish to fulfill them. And that is what makes my actions so unforgivable."

Watching your love die. Nothing quite like killing him yourself. And simply becoming a demigod, when all my life I demanded divinity. She deserves better than this, but... do I?

"Unforgivable, maybe. But Katarin," McKenna squeezed her shoulder for emphasis, nearly sighing with relief that the gesture returned a tangible response to senses that had long since given up on the strange realm in disgust, "they're forgettable. We move on from our mistakes. We allow them to teach us but we do not allow them to control us. If we hold ourselves accountable forever, can we really be better? He controlled your past and yet you still prevailed. If you let him control your future too, you're lost indeed."

The sorcere took a breath, but seeing the utter sincerity reflected in the depths of her sister's kind and compelling amber eyes, smiled and nodded. While she couldn't completely absolve herself, nor really even agree with her sister, it was impossible to ignore the sincerity of her words and the relief given by her unconditional empathy.

"Fine. I will do my best. And I thank you," she curtsied prettily to McKenna, "for honoring and teaching me, too."

McKenna reached out her arms and the women hugged, for a moment thankful each had found the other, to learn life's lessons together. At least, McKenna thought it was a hug. From some perspectives, Katarin's hands were floating aimlessly off into the distance, and her own body decided to manifest itself upside down and about several steps to the left of where her presence firmly believed it currently was. This place was madness.

"Okay. Now that's sorted, how can we get this place to stop… doing… ACK!"

With a flash and a pop, a sparkling soul had crackled into appearance suddenly before them. "Oh! Oh dear. I'm sorry about that. So rude. I should've… agh, well, it's too late now."

McKenna and Katarin stared dazedly at the apparition. Did it just… talk?

"Of course I talked. You're in our realm, mortals. We have voice and form, same as you, when you walk the Material plane to which you belong. Now, why are you here? Wait. Wait a minute."

The soul flitted around them for a second, then returned to hover in front of them. "Oh my gods. Oh my goodness gracious heavenly gods it's Atosa. But there are two of you. Why are there two of you? Isn't there only one Atosa?"

The women blinked. Katarin responded, slowly, "We're her... children. She sent us here."

They both observed the spirit narrowly, unsure how to address it in its own realm. Neither sister had spoken with souls as they would other mortals on Faie, though both had experienced the phenomena of encountering denizens of the afterlife. Katarin cast an expressive glance at McKenna, who shrugged and indicated she'd rather not be the one to continue this unnatural conversation.

"You're the princess, after all," she whispered, nudging her sister while scooting back a step.

Katarin sighed, then squared her shoulders and regarded the soul with all the imperial might she'd been wont to express in Meliamne. "Can you help us?"

Were it a faiefolkr shape, McKenna could almost see the soul shifting from one foot to the other, remaining pensive and seemingly distrustful.

"I don't think you believe her," she said, peering shrewdly at it. "But why in the world would we lie?"

The soul pulsed and shrank quickly. McKenna could sense it almost seemed ashamed of itself. That was new. How could she know what souls felt? Thinking about Seth's inscrutability, she could almost laugh to herself- the skill certainly didn't work on asafolk.

"Hmm. You're right. I'm sorry, I shouldn't have judged so quickly. Of course, her children. Why are you mortal, then?" it asked, inquisitively, yet not unkindly.

Katarin and McKenna looked at one another and shrugged. "We honestly have just been asking ourselves the same question. To be fair, I don't even think Atosa herself could answer that."

"Atosa was mortal when she bore us," added Katarin. "Could have something to do with it."

"Then how is she still a god?"

"McKenna, please, I'm going to get a headache."

The soul seemed to accept this. "So am I. Well, anyways, you're mortal, so you shouldn't even be here. Yet here, you are. So I bet you're finding it hard to be here, in the here and there, neither here, nor there, aren't you?"

McKenna's jaw dropped. Wasn't that gibberish what she'd said about the souls in the mirror? Was it a spell?

"Ah! That's right! You have the mirror? Oh, oh that's much better. Just look in the mirror. You see what's in there? What's in there, that's what is here!"

The soul's words made absolutely no sense to the sisters, but McKenna just shrugged and pulled it out, holding it so both she and Katarin could get a clear view.

"Perfect. Just like that. Anyways, you want to see the true nature of this plane, don't you? Well, all you need to do is ask!" The soul seemed to enjoy bossing them around.

McKenna frowned at their host, then turned her concentration back to the mirror. Unable to keep the catch from her throat as she spoke the runes she had first learned from Seth, she thought to herself- *What harm could it do?*

"Asone mal'dhenna mak lahde."

In an instant, the twilight gloom grew dark, then brightened. The ground resolved to the kind of soft spongy grass that could be found on the edges of a springtime forest. Overhead arched what passed for a glorious afternoon sky. And what was once an ephemeral vapour with a voice shifted and became the figure of a man. A figure that looked oddly familiar...

"Uhm. Excuse me, and I do hope I'm not offending you," McKenna asked, heart beating in her throat as she addressed the curious specter, "but are you... Seth's father?"

Katarin stared at her, then back at the spirit. He bowed, the wiry bristles of his tawny mane bobbing in the light breeze that skirled through the newly established atmosphere.

"Sethisto T'ssama. At your service, my dear child." he replied, with a kind smile. "I do remember seeing you in the mirror, now. Time seems to work strange miracles here, so I'd completely forgotten. And you recognized me, too! How pleasant."

So, the mirror's scrying alerted its target, did it? She wondered if he had been able to sense Seth's presence as well, but decided now probably wasn't the best time to ask.

McKenna laughed. "I don't remember you being so…"

"Annoying?" he offered, with a self-deprecating grin.

"I was going to say joyous," she finished. "Your son described you as having the charm of a… bugbear."

Sethisto's laugh carried through the rippling pasture. "He would. I guess I just never had patience or tolerance for most of the ignorance around me. Much easier to just pretend to be the unapproachable and aloof Lord than try to talk down to everyone. That was my wife's job. She sure was good at it too." He paused, and looked ponderous for a moment. "I hope he didn't inherit too much of that from me."

He peered questioningly at McKenna, who blushed and held up her hands. "Oh no. Don't ask me. I called him grim once and I don't think he'll ever let me live it down. But I think," she said, her voice softening, "I think you would be proud of him, for all that."

Sethisto took her hand in his. "I already am, my girl. I am so proud of my boy it hurts."

McKenna swallowed hard, then turned to her sister, who had a very familiar look of empathy on her normally cold and imperious face. The expression suited her. "Sorry, excuse me for not introducing you. This is my sister, Katarin."

Katarin curtsied, then raised an eyebrow curiously at the man. "You know, I think I may have met you. At a joust."

Sethisto studied her for a moment, then dropped low into a courtly bow. "Princess Katarin! Princess of the Starflower- how your silver beauty shone down our golden girls in the stands. But... that had to have been, what, four decades ago? How you... haven't... aged."

She laughed, and shrugged at McKenna's bewildered look. "See, we told you," she replied charmingly. "We're really the children of Atosa."

"Mortal, but with perks," McKenna enjoined, unconsciously echoing the words of Razan.

Mortal, yet able to occupy and traverse the land between life and death. Able to speak to souls long dead. Left with durgir, left with ilvir, then thrown into a war. Untapped and untrained potentials that could be more dangerous than any Lich King or daemor. The monk was beginning to understand why she'd sent them both into this realm... and also resent restoring Atosa from her cursed state as a dragon. *She almost seemed too eager to send both her children into another plane of existence...*

He smiled again, taking their hands. "Forgive my distrust. In exchange, you have my company for as long as it benefits you. So now, why exactly are you here?"

Feeling her sister's concerned gaze upon her, McKenna took a breath to steady her voice.

"We're looking for your son."

IV

BULLSEYE

"Ugh. *Qué es el propósito*? A waste of time... no wonder they let so many novitiates go along."

With unerring accuracy, a crossbow bolt struck the heart of a target midway down the range. Occupants filled every stall; with a few along the ends haphazardly erected for the overflow of eager young marksmen.

Arya took a deep breath, pausing diplomatically as her friend vented her ire. Hearing *Besonne* spoken in Layne's irritated tones always made her homesick, though the ancient language had been all but forgotten in Wheelspoke during her mother's inflexibly Lianorran reign. She nocked her own bow, taking a deep draw that let fly an arrow across the grassy paddock and alighting near the center of another target.

"Proper form while questing is almost as important as the quest itself," she recited, easing another arrow from the quiver slung over the post beside her. "Just because we didn't actually engage with any of the ilmaurte doesn't mean the whole trip was pointless."

"Ah yes, forgive me. How could I forget the absolute necessity of learning exactly how to pitch a tent, or how deep to dig the hole for the commode," Layne shot back sarcastically. With shoulders thrown back aggressively and an almost comically loose stance she let fly a bolt without even looking that sailed into a target at the furthermost reach of the range.

The moons of training passed quicker than Arya could believe. A temporary relief from the advance of the horde passed through Faie, and though few of its common citizens knew why, they also decided they really didn't want to question it. The Guild of Tooth and Claw benefited from this period. Explosive growth within both its ranks of squires and its tithe-paying converts for a time simmered the resentment between it and the rest of the realms. Rumours of those mysterious events in the chasm of Naijor made its way through the guild-protected Eastern stronghold of Lianor by word of mouth from discerning masters to eager novitiates, who took it upon themselves to sell the news indiscriminately to city herald after city herald.

Rumours with no source make the best kind of headline, after all.

"You're probably the only person in all of Faie complaining about a lack of ilmaurte right now. *Besonnen* are finally able to come home, and rebuild their cities. Isn't that something to be happy about?" Arya leaned on her bow, fixing her companion with a thoughtful look.

"*Bahamut bendiga*," grumbled Layne, rolling her eyes.

Those tales told of a tetherless undead army, led by an unknown figure said to be the daughter of Atosa. The guild of Tooth and Claw claimed the woman was still at large, but in hiding, and her army driven to near extinction by the tireless efforts of the paladins of Bahamut. Though one Red Solstice, and then another, had come and gone since then Besonnen refugees had only just now begun to make the journey back from the ilvin groves of Meliamne to the ravaged towns scattered across

Beausun's plains. The scars left by the horrifying specters may never fully heal, but the resilience of the aesir race promised progress and a successful season in which to rebuild.

Arya, with a discernment marked by her lineage, took all stories with a grain of salt. It was bad enough being a T'ssama. Everyone either despised her or dismissed her as just a victim of nepotistic favoritism. Not that it held her in any particular shadow. Corruption in the guild went so obviously deep the girl often debated giving up in disgust. It wasn't until she'd finally had a chance to join the occasional goodly quest to extinguish undead marauders, and a chance to prove her worth and her conviction in the wide realm, that she truly came to terms with this somewhat sordid destiny.

My first lesson, she often thought to herself, *seems to be making a name for myself instead of just living up to the one they've made for me.*

The novitiates who trained beside her made that easier as time went on. Though none offered anywhere near the soul-deep understanding and bond she shared with her brother, being around those of her own age and station had subconsciously helped to develop the little spitfire.

Her closest in both age and accomplishment currently stood beside her at the shooting range, wielding a crossbow to deadly effect. Elena Riquelme, a child of prophecy from Dragon's Hill and youngest daughter of Lord Masa Riquelme. Each bolt fired by the tall, crop-haired girl struck the center of its target, no matter how quickly or carelessly she fired.

"Hey Layne, could you stop showing off for like

maybe thirty seconds and give me some idea of how in the world the rest of us can fire so well as you?" Arya sighed exasperatedly.

Layne laughed, loading another quarrel that struck the heart of Arya's own target. "*Piensas demasiado. Piensas demasiado en todo*, Lady Arya."

"Ugh, I'm literally going to kill you if you don't stop calling me that," she groaned. "And can you ease up on the *Besonne*? I'm rusty."

"What? I'm just reminding you where you'll end up if you don't become Grand Master," the girl replied mischievously, firing several more bolts toward the targets.

"You're so annoying. Don't you want to be Grand Master too? We're the same age. It's likely only one of us could actually be nominated, you idiot."

"Why in the worlds would *I* want to be Grand Master? Absolutely no thank you. Sitting around on some throne while people pay me lip service before going off to sneak deals with Golden Eye, or the Noble's Council? Not my idea of a good time." She paused to lick her finger and stick it in the air, before shooting the last of her bolts into the center of the targets in rapid fire succession.

Several eavesdropping novitiates shot them sullen, disapproving glances. Arya lowered her eyes demurely before casting a furious look at her companion, and shooting an arrow toward the target that shivered a couple inches to the left of her friend's.

"Layne, *deja de hablar asi*," she hissed uneasily, hoping their homeland's tongue remained mostly unknown to the other novitiates.

"No I don't," the girl replied clearly in faiefolkr Common, seething through clenched teeth and refusing Arya's bait. "I hate it just as much as you do, Lady Arya. Do you know how hard I had to fight my family to let me join, despite my prophecy? The guilds exist to protect our land, to spread the joy and strength of Bahamut across the plains to all who sought or needed his help."

Trying to diffuse her friend's mounting ire, Arya smiled apologetically and held out her wrists in peace. "I didn't realize you were so devout," she teased.

Layne snorted, slapping Arya's proffered palm and rolled her eyes again, though unable to completely stifle the grin creeping across her face.

"My family's been worshipping Bahamut since before your family climbed out of Sh'nia's Gamorren mud flats. Don't act like you've all the righteousness, Lady Arya."

Realizing she'd never live the nickname down, Arya simply sighed. Lowering her voice slightly and hoping Layne would take her lead, she continued. "Why blame the Grand Master, then? We're all here to represent the same Golden Dragon, after all. And not all of us," she raised her eyebrows, indicating to herself, "pay our undivided loyalty to every move the guild makes. Why do you think so many faiefolkr are here?"

"You're going to make me sick, Arya. Why do you think they're here... honestly! Half of them are trolls hired from gods knows where, and the rest were probably forced by families who gave the guild every last penny they had for protection," she retaliated. "You say we're so great, that we all love the same god, yet here they are, evangelizing left and right, sticking their greedy hands into every town left standing by the scourge. Dragon's Hill lost everything- everything! Just because we refused to cast out the refugees who came to us. My family all but forbade me from joining Tooth and Claw. But I told them, it was my duty," and she shone with glorious purpose, "my duty as a child of prophecy, to restore the goodly might of Bahamut, and to stop this corrupt rot that threatens to undo us."

Arya gulped, looking at the brilliant aura surrounding her friend. Her red hair shone like fire, and the freckles across her copper-hued face were a constellation of the heroes she spent her whole life admiring. Child of prophecy, indeed. No soothsayer needed to choose Layne for this path. She'd have walked it, backwards and blindfolded, regardless. The girl swallowed, then pulled another arrow from the quiver.

"Fine. You're right. But I swear to the gods, Layne, if Master Gareth assigns us library cleaning duty again..." she threatened, before training her bow at the target opposite.

The arrow she loosened quivered triumphantly beside Layne's.

"I mean, at least we're good at it at this point," Layne joked a few hours later when, inevitably, the girls found themselves surrounded by the spiral of bookcases and straight backed chairs of the guild's library, carrying buckets of mineral water and a sack of rags.

"I am so mad at you right now I can't even speak," grumbled Arya, rubbing her wrist in agony as she keenly studied the wood and marble table she'd just shined for any mark or grime.

"Huh, that's funny. Isn't speaking that thing you're doing with your mouth?"

"Layne, I'm going to light your bed on fire with you in it if you don't shut up."

"What!" she laughed, tossing her own sodden rag at the grumpy Arya. Arya dodged, then immediately regretted it as the grimy cloth instead slapped a streak across her pristine tabletop.

"Ugh! You are the worst!" she cried exasperatedly, but ultimately unable to escape the infectious laughter of her friend.

That seemed to be Layne's talent; driving Arya's subdued passions too high to remember the draining housework, the ache of disapproval from her mentors, and the agony of loss that still stabbed her at every opportunity. Part of Arya felt guilty that she could find such solace in the company of this girl she just met, and the rest of her defied any such negativity. Tooth and Claw, even just in the time she'd been there, had shown demoralization at almost every turn. Priceless artifacts went missing, destroyed by resentful novices or stolen outright by opportunistic ones. The general atmosphere of the halls had turned sour and unwelcoming. The novitiates, though allied by their inexperience and determination to save their individual homelands, found it difficult to truly find trust in one another.

Yet here was Layne. Unapologetically devoted, determined, and clearly blessed with gods-given talent, to remind Arya to not lose all hope. That they were to be paladins, who rode for the glory of Bahamut, and all his goodly might to bring peace and joy to the surrounding realms.

When they finished, the two stretched amiably before the embers still casting their light and warmth from the fireplace. They shared a tome before its meager light, and an apple the redheaded novitiate managed to smuggle from the mess. "You know, I think we may have something of an edge, doing all this cleaning in here," said Layne through a mouthful of fruit. "We get so much extra time to study."

Arya, nose deep in the book, nodded and held out her hand for the apple Layne offered, taking a distracted bite. "Ah yes, extra chores *and* homework. Exactly what I hoped for in my novitiate."

"Didn't your brother warn you about how thrilling and full of excitement it was?" Layne joked in response.

The hand on the book quivered, but the voice that responded was steady. "He... wasn't really home much during his novitiate. James told me lots of stories though. Probably to annoy my mother, who tried to prevent me from talking about the guild as much as she possibly could." The firelight flickered in Arya's grey eyes as she stared into its depths. "Drove her absolutely batty when she'd catch me practicing fencing in the library."

"You fenced in a library? What did books ever do to you?" cried Layne in mock horror, pulling the tome shared in their laps from Arya's reach.

"It was the only space large enough where I knew no one would bother me!" she replied defensively. "Now give me that back, you can't even read it."

"Rude! I can... read most of it..."

The page before them contained a myriad of languages and alphabets from ancient cultures across the realms of Faie. Thanks to her unorthodox education, courtesy of a father who put no embargo on learning regardless of source, Arya could interpret almost all of it. The particular passage they were translating was especially convoluted. It was a poem, written in alternating lines of the five ancient languages of all the races - ilvin *Venir*, durgir *Chesel*, Beausun's *Besonne*, orgir *Nath'tar*, and holvir *Yboura*.

"I didn't realize holvir had a language. I always thought they were, you know, like goblinoid creatures before they met asafolk," remarked Layne as Arya slowly recited the poem aloud.

"Don't you dare tell a holvi that," Arya warned. "Their kind are older than asafolk, older even than orgir. They're so short lived, they probably evolved out of their more ancient and natural cultures faster than we did. I just don't think asafolk ever really... listened to them."

Chastened, the girl slowly repeated the words first in their native tongue and then translated along with Arya into the faiefolkr Common speech adopted by all beings across the realms. "I've never actually met a holvi. Did they come to Wheelspoke often? I don't remember seeing any the few times I visited."

"My father loved spending time with them. Invited as many as he could to stay at the manor, and help him write down all the stories and myths their bards like to share," she replied wistfully, reminiscing about long evenings spent before the large fire in her father's study, sitting in her brother's lap and listening to the songs and stories shared by the diminutive folk. "That is... 'til my mother finally got fed up and banned them from the house. She said it was...unseemly, to have them visit like guests. They were welcome to play in the taverns but not 'sit among us like family or respectable visitors'" she drawled mockingly. "Of course, this was just before Seth was about to leave for his novitiate. I can only imagine the pressure the guild put on her to rebuff them. Not that she really needed their encouragement to be racist."

A satisfied smirk crossed Layne's face. "That doesn't sound like you, you suck-up."

Arya stuck her tongue out at her friend. "Look. Being a paladin didn't change my brother. He stayed as open-minded and generous as he'd ever been, even when he joined the rank of Master. And I don't... think..." she hesitated, the words on the page, representing a unity that once existed amongst the fractured races, "it will change me, either. I hope it doesn't."

An unsettled feeling of unease filled her, almost making her queasy. *Could I become as insufferable as my mother? As intolerant?*

Layne put a hand on Arya's book. "*Quieres esto? Realmente?*" she said.

This is why she kept Layne around. The girl had a keen sense attuned toward her feelings, something her mother actively tried to suppress and even her brother, separated as they were by age and disposition, couldn't quite figure out. She only hoped she offered as much to the girl whose friendship and loyalty grew more dear by the day.

"I do, Layne. I want this more than anything." Arya set the book aside to grab her friend's hand, massaging the palm calloused by archery and excessive cleaning. "Even before… everything, I wanted to be a paladin. Just like him. I thought maybe at first, I only wanted it to impress him," she said, a faraway look on her face, "but then I realized that it was a part of me, the deepest and truest part of my nature yearned for the glory of battle and deeds done in honor of our goodly god. And as it turned out, I never needed to prove myself to my brother." She remembered McKenna's words, and the hand clasped to her shoulder in solidarity and belief of the woman she could become. "He loved me regardless."

Layne blinked, then squeezed Arya's hand and smiled. "Of course he did. And so does Grand Master Elgitha, and so do I."

The book lay forgotten as the friends embraced before the fire, sharing a moment of solitude and appreciation for the strength of one another. A crackle from a log shook them from their reverie.

"I wonder if Clint even knows how to read," Layne mused aloud.

"Doubtful. Did you hear him yesterday during our philosophy session? He confused himself about six times. My father would be rolling in his grave to hear his ideas on the ascension of Nahariel. No wonder our guild is going to the dogs... children of the prophecy aren't what they used to be," Arya responded, shaking her head in mock despair.

"Says you, the first novitiate elected by a Grand Master and not a soothsayer in, what, a hundred years?"

"More or less," replied Arya cheekily.

Layne smacked her and returned to the book, turning to the next chapter. "How do you even follow half of what this is saying, anyway? I can barely focus!"

The chapter open before them detailed a complex and ancient description of the development of Lianor. The book, a dusty text titled *Unitye and Graciousnesse*, wasn't a particularly popular one. Arya'd found it on accident, stuffed backwards and upside down in a haphazard corner of the "maps" section of the library. What she'd actually been trying to find was an original blueprint of the Cathedral of the Golden God. Despite the moons she'd spent in the Cathedral, constantly losing her way from the practice halls or the barracks was getting old. But as she pulled the battered book from its ignominious hiding spot, she felt a thrill of recognition that distracted her from her original purpose. Her father had this book, and as a child, it fascinated her.

Mostly because her mother forbid him from reading it to her.

"Unbelievable. You mean to tell me holvir built these roads?" Layne asked in awe while Arya translated some of the more difficult runes halfway down the page.

"No, sorry - that was the durgir. Holvir designed them, and drew the layout for this whole city. Didn't you know that?"

"Durgir?! You're mad! Durgir barely tolerate asafolk, they wouldn't go out of their way to actually work for them!" cried Layne in contradiction.

Arya studied her with an fathomless look on her face. "You sound like my mother. Don't tell me Dragon's Hill parrots the same garbage about the other races that

Wheelspoke does?"

"It's not garbage," muttered Layne defensively, in a tone that clearly meant I-can't-believe-you're-right-about-this-but-I've-learned-not-to-question-you-by-now, "at least, it didn't sound like garbage. Have you ever even met a duergi? Or a holvi, for that matter?"

"Actually, I've met both," replied Arya smugly.

She had to quickly stifle the shriek of laughter that burst forth at Layne's bewildered face.

"It was recently. It…" she winced. It had been the last time she saw her brother. "My brother came home, and he had some friends with him that he'd met on the road. A married holvir couple and a six foot tall duergi woman."

Layne mouthed the words "six foot" but didn't interrupt. Arya giggled again.

"Well, she said she was a duergi anyway. In your defense, I've never met any other, so I can't compare them."

"Let me get this straight. Your brother dumped the Guild to shack up with some duergi and a couple of… of holvir? Arya, that's insane! He's insane."

The apple rolled to the floor along with the book as Arya stood up in a fury. "Stop being so racist! They're faiefolkr, too, you know that? Just because our kind choose to pretend they're better than anything else that walks these realms, doesn't mean we're right about it. The holvir have family, the durgir have stone, and the ilvir have… have…" she foundered in her fury.

"Magic?" the conscience-stricken Layne offered.

"Sure. Magic. Whatever. The point is, this book," she pointed at its battered binding, "my father, and our history, our real history, all spoke one truth. That we all belong on Faie, that we all deserve our own place, and that we all, at one point, worked together to make this world. It would almost make sense," she thought pensively, before sitting back down beside her chastened friend, "that the undead were sent as a sort of… of punishment, for our kind's hubris. If we really think we're better than the world that raised us, it's time to put that conviction to the test."

She stared moodily into the fire, unaware of Layne's intense, almost worshipful, consideration of her profile. It wouldn't be the first time.

The penitent novitiate grabbed Arya's hand and squeezed it. Arya returned the caress, knowing she couldn't just blame Layne for the upbringing every single one of them shared.

"I'm sorry," she said, staring into the girl's bright green eyes. "I shouldn't have lost my temper on you. It wasn't fair."

Layne made a face of disgust. "Stop being so noble. You make it hard to be righteously indignant."

"There is nothing righteous about you and you know it."

"I'm righteously attached to you. Does that count?" Layne laughed, then yawned. "Anyway, this is exhausting, and we both have early Mass tomorrow. Can we go to bed now?"

"Depends. Where are my matches, I promised to light your bed on fire."

"You're so mean!"

"I know."

Groaning as they uncurled themselves from before the warm fire, Arya stretched and yawned, thankful the eternal and exhausting day was finally over. She made a mental note of the page they had left off on. She had every intention of finishing that book, and that lesson, with her less enlightened companion.

I am nothing like my mother. I won't let her intolerance guide me, and I won't let whatever's happening to the guild do it either. I know better than that, I always have, and I always will.

With that, the girls tucked the book back on its shelf and, dragging out the embers until they were nothing more than smoke, dimmed the lights of the library and swept off to bed.

V

HOLVIR

Soft footsteps disturbed the peace of the pearly grey dawn as Ginni made her way through the forest and out to the open plains beyond. She heard a low whistle and turned toward the sound, a smile lighting up her face at the figure of Urtha reclining against a tree.

"Urtha! You found us! What a relief," said the little holvi, hugging her friend's knees in delight.

"I am better at searching than you are," she chided. Sitting cross-legged on the forest floor she patted the ground beside her. "How goes your sing, that so inspires the sluggish hearts of men?"

The confidence the two women shared always granted a measure of joy to the cheery bard. Urtha, by orgir standards, was the most powerful and important person in the realms. And yet Ginni had won a space in the orghi's heart that often made her the source of communications the rest of the soulful races wouldn't have a chance to ever know... if they even bothered to waste half a thought on the doings of holvir and orgir, that is. While holvir earned a begrudging acceptance among the other races as long as they remained subservient, the fierce, and often violent, independence of the orgir kept those lines aggressively drawn.

Without Urtha, Ginni would never have learned the truth about their friends' fates in the chasm. Though loathe to share the secrets of death, Urtha recognized her tribe's impotence. Especially when it came to actually talking to anyone not an orghi, she relied on her garrulous and trustworthy companion to be a voice for the voiceless. And the bard appreciated that more than words could say.

"It went great! I think we really have a chance. Turns out, when you abandon people to the mercy of an ilmaurte horde, they're less likely to blindly trust you." Her direct tongue-in-cheek reference to the persecution of the guilds brought a smile to the corner of Urtha's mouth. About time asafolk got a taste of the treatment they wrought on their neighboring races.

"At least… I think they believe us," she continued, beaming at the memory of the united faiefolkr standing in solidarity with the two sisters. "We're hoping we get large enough to train a proper army. Lianor has kept its gates closed for too long."

Urtha nodded, her expression as ever an enigma to the bard. "Hmm. That could be so. But, my holvi friend, you and your partner will have another quest, I am thinking."

"Another... quest?" Ginni's tone faltered. The united army of Beausun was still just an idea at this point. Would they be able, or willing, to stay their course without the holvir's inspiration? "What have you heard?"

She leaned back against the tree while gumming her pipe, little eddies of smoke trailing from between her teeth. "Atosa seeks the assistance of the grater pantheon, but the gods will not hear her. As long as she remains at odds with her sister, they say, why should they fight her battles? They, like you, rely on the power of the guilds and their might to do away with this hellish horde," Urtha snarled, then spat in distaste. "And without Sh'nia, Atosa is not so strong as she needs be. She needs her sister, just as Katarin and McKenna needed each other."

The memory of the friends she lost momentarily checked the holvi's fervor. She lowered her eyes and covertly wiped a tear from her cheek.

"So… what can we do? What can I do?" she said, looking up into the kind, ethereal eyes of the chieftainess.

"You must do what Katarin did. Summon Sh'nia, and make her listen," replied the orghi.

"Wow. Oh yeah, I'll just, you know, get right on that. Give me about thirty years to become an accomplished sorcere and oh, maybe another century or two to devise the spell that took an entire contingent of ilvir to manifest," Ginni said dryly.

Urtha stared blankly at her, then laughed until the leaves above them shivered and shook. "You little imp. There are better ways than that to summon a goddess," she said, drawing out her pipe and taking three short puffs.

The clouds that billowed forth glowed a brilliant crimson and gold. The dawn of day, glorious in contrast to the dim and foggy wood, expanded in breathtaking splendor. Among the clouds leapt tiny figures, crawling and snarling and sifting amiably and aimlessly throughout. Ginni watched in entranced fervor as the smoke manifested trees and the enormous, curious creatures seen only in storybooks.

"Gamorre. You want us to visit the Sun ilvir?" she

asked, the light of the display reflected in the pools of her hazel eyes.

"They worship Sh'nia with a devotion rivalling that of the Moon ilvir's for Atosa. If anyone can reach the Goddess of Life, it is them. And if there is anyone in the wide, wide realms that the Sun ilvir will listen to, it is you."

"Me?" screeched Ginni. "What? Why would they listen to me? I'm just a holvi."

Urtha narrowed her eyes almost angrily at the assertion. "You are not 'just' anything, my friend. You and Tjena have journeyed twice to the pits of despair, looked death in the face and yet felt no fear."

"Oh, we felt fear all right," interrupted Ginni with a shiver. One didn't just forget the blight of their beloved partner. Or the fiendish horrors of the Lich King.

"But you did not let that fear deter you," continued Urtha. "Your souls, linked as they are, stand testament to the unity of all our goodly creatures. Together, I am sure you will reach the realms of Gamorre. And with your song, charm them as you have charmed so many already, bringing unity to a people long estranged from one another."

Overcome with emotion, she listened in rare silence. It touched her to the heart to hear Urtha's confidence and praise. Sighing, she stood and pondered the road before them.

"Oh boy. Tjena's going to be thrilled. They got their sight back just in time to go stare at the rising sun," she huffed, attempting to disguise the bubbling joy at the chance for adventure to which her soul thrilled.

Urtha laughed again, and stroked the holvi's bouncy red curls. "You will make it far, child. And let this be known- when your hero's souls make their final journey, I myself will escort them through the Doors of Death."

Ginni laughed. "I mean, we don't exactly like, have those. But you know, I appreciate the offer all the same." Holding out her arms, she swept into the orghi's fierce embrace. Then, before the rest of the town could rise, Urtha disappeared in the tall grass that so characterized the vast prairie of Beausun.

"How in the world am I going to convince Tjena to do this," moaned the holvi, wringing her hands and shaking them at the impartial gods who left mortals to do their bidding.

A tenday later found the pair back on the road, accompanied by a durgirn party making the trek from Wheelspoke to the great durgirn stronghold of Bristendine. The wind whistling across the prairies promised hope, and Ginni loved watching those rolling waves of amber grain. She turned to Tjena, kissing her beloved on their forehead.

"So I'm guessing you don't miss being blind, then?" she joked, aching with happiness at the sight of Tjena's green eyes hungrily devouring the landscape before them.

They sighed. "You know, I couldn't tell you. There is so much beauty in this land, it's true," they said wistfully. "But also so much ugliness. When I was blind, I could feel more; sense the nature of faiefolkr and things as they passed me by. And you, too," they smiled at their partner, "you're much prettier when I can't see you."

Their sharp "OW!" startled a family of nesting doves from a bush alongside the road.

Great paved roads, wonderfully engineered by resourceful holvir and pounded into place by burly durgir, made their travel smooth on the backs of carts laden with northern goods. Waypoints every dozen leagues or so marked distance, and broke up the monotony of the more remote camping the holvir generally experienced on their solitary travels. The durgir sponsored taverns and rugged hostels along the route north from the days when they managed trade with their mountain kin from the north, before enterprising asafolk waylaid their prejudice and opened their gates to durgirn metal and coin. But without a member of the guild to sponsor them, the holvir were just as unacceptable to those comforts as they often were to the towns in between.

Most of the asafolk villages that dotted the byways still stood empty, burned out husks completely ghosted by the undead horde. But the occasional post of duergi or lucky trader offered them company, good drink, and most importantly, a stage for singing.

News carried by bards tended to be more welcome than the other, more official kind. For most, it was easier to hear and acknowledge the tragedies of the West when sung plaintively by Ginni's sweet, honey coated voice accompanied by the masterful twanging of Tjen's instrument. And for others, especially this far south, the grating tones of northerners and their nearly illegible notices written by assuming and pompous heralds drove any sort of interest or empathy far from their minds.

The holvir had seen it all before. All they could hope was that, with the inevitable advance of the horde, this time the others would listen.

Some distance between two waypoints, the caravan stopped abruptly.

"Huh. Wonder what that's about, Tjen, should I go ask?" Ginni peered around, her view obscured by the walls of the cart.

"No. I think you should duck."

"What?"

"DUCK!"

Throwing themselves on top of her, the two holvir narrowly escaped being pegged by a hail of arrows that struck the sides and the bed of the cart. Scrambling from their perch and diving beneath its wheels, Ginni squinted along the dusty road while trying to prevent herself from hyperventilating.

"What in the gods is going on? Ilmaurte don't use arrows??" She crawled toward the front of the cart, hoping she could make her way toward the tightly knotted durgirn shield wall that had formed around their party.

"Garble! Who is it? Not undead?" Her voice carried to a sunset bearded duergi, who answered in a growly undervoice without turning to regard her.

"Nay. Aesir."

Tjen groaned. "Asafolk? But why? Do they think

we're ilmaurte?" Ginni demanded, sneaking closer so she could stand beside the duergi and steal glimpses of the still empty road between the chinks in their shield wall.

"Ye feel like goin' and askin?" Garble responded gruffly, wincing as a few more arrows and a wobbly javelin bounced off the heavy wooden shield.

Setting her tiny teeth, the little holvi bristled in frustration. "There's a real threat to this stupid realm and yet we're still fighting each other. This has got to stop."

With a pitched voice, she wailed out a banshee cry that, as she cunningly reflected it off the curved shields, fell harmless on their ears but tore into the hidden attackers like their own arrows. A man- a boy, really, barely of age to hold a pike- stumbled out of the tall grass and fell in a dusty heap on the road. Two others, an older woman and a girl about his age, quickly jumped out behind him. They tried dragging the prone form back into the brush, but as soon as they removed the fingers stuffed into their ears the battering ram of Ginni's powerful voice drove them to their knees.

"If you don't want durgirn martial law enacted on you right now, I suggest you tell us exactly why you're here and what you think you're playing at, firing at a trading party with no provocation," she demanded, each word falling from the sky to strike her listeners like hailstones.

"Alright, alright, we surrender! Gods bedamned, silence that harpy!" shrieked the boy from the ground.

"Harpy? How dare... ugh. You want to talk to them, or should I continue?" Ginni turned an aggressive eye on Garble.

"Ye kin try first. Ye're supposed ter be peacemaker, after all," he replied with a shrug.

"I'm coming out, and I swear on the Faie Mother herself if you shoot an arrow at me I'm going to kick you in the shins."

She slid between two interlocked shields, and approached the bedraggled party with her wrists exposed. She kept her ears trained toward the brush, where lurked signs of other attackers. None came out to accost her, though, so her focus remained on the group before her. They cast her sullen glances, shock not quite able to hide the disgust on their faces as they realized what she was.

"A holvi?" The boy spat.

"Yes, and if you think my voice was bad from there, you can't even begin to imagine the damage it'd do to your eardrums at this range. What are you doing here? Why are you attacking durgir? Not only is that a stupid idea on a good day, it's completely uncalled for under these circumstances."

"You're bold for a holvi," the older woman interjected. Several others clambered from the dry brush, bows in hand, but hesitant at the sight of the heavily armed durgir behind the Ginni.

The little bard's nostrils flaring as she took several deep breaths, eyeing the crowd ranged before her. *You've been to Hel and back, twice. You can deal with some good old-fashioned intolerance.*

"I have the might of an entire Hammardin envoy

behind me and the invitation of Bristendine's Head Priest to welcome me. You would do well to respect that, even if you don't respect me. Now, do not make me ask again. Why did you attack us?"

Some of the older men cast each other wary, hard looks. None chose to speak, but tightened their grips on their weapons.

"Looters," said the boy unexpectedly. "We thought... we thought you were looters."

The prairie moaned as a breeze rifled its emptiness. Racking her brains, Ginni could just barely recall the desolate remains of a village, left behind several leagues past. Standing before her were clearly the remaining villagers, returning home, she supposed, after taking refuge in Meliamne.

Still though, their aggression grated on her, and a fire kindled in her hazel eyes. "You fired on an armed party of durgir? Based on a rash assumption? Under what circumstances could you ever think that was a good idea that would end well for any of you?"

His eyes dropped in defeat, and his shoulders slumped as he could make no answer. As mad as she was, Ginni suddenly realized that their bravado may actually be a symptom of desperation.

"This isn't a time for vigilantes," she said, the edge taken out of her voice and infused instead with the soft, sympathetic tones that came more naturally. "It's a time for healing. I understand your situation, probably much better than you would ever give me credit for."

"How do you expect us to believe that? Your lot

haven't any home," spat one of the villagers.

"What devilry you done to yonder durgir that they protect you, anyway?" snarled another.

As the general mutters grew louder and more vicious, Ginni could only watch and keep her composure as well as she could. Backed into a corner, thrown to the mercy of the elements, as their homes were destroyed and they could only watch helplessly. Ginni, though sympathetic, couldn't help but be annoyed at the irony of these asafolk who could still treat her the way they did even after experiencing the exact same tragedies as her race.

And I have to convince these people to fight for us. Urtha is crazy.

"Listen, fine, whatever. You don't like holvir. It literally does not matter what you think, though, because our entire realm, all of it, and everyone in it, is still in danger. We've *all* suffered from the horde, and from the guilds, too. Your home may be gone," she turned towards the boy, who despite the incensed mutterings of all the others watched her with a guarded, but not hostile, look on his face, "but if we all work together, trust each other, and protect each other, we can rebuild it. And if you don't have faith in us, then..." she shrugged helplessly, looking back at the unmoving shield wall, "at least just let us pass, without violence."

He nodded, and turned to regard his mother and sister. The girl curled up on herself sullenly, but a measure of curiosity eased the rigidity of her features. The older woman's face simply crumpled and great tears began to leak from her eyes.

The rest of the group slowly began to slink back into

the brush. But though the girl tugged on her brother's shoulder he remained behind, staring curiously at the holvi woman without speaking.

"I can't make you like me," Ginni smiled, infusing charm into her singsong voice. "But if you promise to behave, I bet I can help you join our envoy. The durgir of Bristendine have pledged to help Beausun rebuild. It's been slow going, for," she gestured at the retreating forms of the aggressive villagers, "obvious reasons. But they honestly just want to help."

"Appreciate your offer, truly I do," he replied quietly. "But you go on. I just stayed to say... sorry."

He rose manfully and bowed, a display that nearly knocked the breath from the bard. With a solemn salute to the durgir, he turned, and followed his family and the rest of the village refugees through the dense underbrush of the quiet prairie.

After a moment of shocked silence, Ginni shook herself and returned back to the still defensive line of durgir. She knocked pertly on Garble's shield, who pulled it back with a bemused look on his face.

"So... talkin' worked, then?" he raised an eyebrow at the asafolk retreating quakingly behind her.

"Talking worked! I mean, yelling started it. But talking finished it. Come on," she sighed in relief, a musical note dispelling the tension in their group, "we've still got a long way to go."

In more ways than one, she thought to herself, as the memory of the villagers' hostile faces rose up before her.

Soon enough, the looming cairn under which Bristendine's mines and forges rang with goodly durgirn song rose into view. As their cart rumbled under the massive gates and into a deep tunnel, Ginni turned pleading eyes and voice to all who passed them. Her ditties charmed her durgirn protectors, some of whom had ties to Hammardin and remembered McKenna.

Unlike their secretive and aloof brothers to the north, the Bristendine mines were a wide open market of commerce among all the goodly races. Holvir sold and bartered their goods in the underground bazaar, asafolk heckled with durgir over the patent rights to tools and designs, and even a gnommi could be seen tiptoeing furtively through the crowded, thriving space in search of precious minerals and metals. Ginni and Tjena drank in the sight, reveling in the various natures of those around them.

Evening found the two atop their favorite stage- a bar, ranging the length of a mead hall and stacked high with kegs full of the honeyed drink. Eager to earn enough coin to outfit the remainder of their trip, and mindful of their responsibility to the army of Ljotebroek, the holvir duo performed again the ballad that charmed the refugees and converted them to decisive action.

They didn't expect much. In this closely guarded keep, the ilmaurte existed only in the form of night terrors, and the name Atosa simply a segue into spouting the glories and greatness of Malfaestus. But they weren't the most esteemed and talented bards of their tribe for nothing. By the end of the night, they'd gathered around them a crowd of eager, loyal listeners ready to serve against the Lich King's advance.

"No tendrán suerte con esos guilds, *¿Ya sabes?"* spoke

a man from the crowd, his fiery hair and pierced ears giving him a somewhat rakish look.

"Charlot... *cállate*. Give these two a chance, will you?" sighed a woman at his elbow, rolling her eyes at her contrary partner. "Your sister belongs to one, after all."

A look of loathing crossed the man's face. "Elena... excuse me, *Layne*," he sneered, "is a glory hog. As far as I'm concerned, the moment that signet ring went on her finger, she was dead to me."

Ginni watched the two volley back and forth, then slipped off the bar to engage in their conversation. "Forgive me for eavesdropping. You know what they say about big ears on little pitchers."

The woman laughed again, her dark hair bobbing merrily. "I do indeed, I do indeed. With whom do we have the pleasure?" she offered a slim brown hand to the holvi, who bowed over it gracefully.

"Ginni Willow and Tjen Oak, of the Padfoot tribe, good lady. And yourself?"

"Lady María Riquelme, of Dragon's Hill. My charming companion here is Charlot, of the same goodly town."

Ginni wracked her brain for a moment, trying to place the town. "Dragon's Hill? Surely you're quite far from home?" she said, peering curiously at the pair. *Explains the Besonne. Didn't know anyone still spoke that.*

"As of right now, 'home' doesn't exist," the man replied bitterly, sipping from the mead before him.

"Ah, but it will again. We're here on a diplomatic mission, to beg the aid and investment of the Bristendine durgir to rebuild our town, destroyed by the horde."

"*And* by Tooth and Claw," Charlot interrupted. María rolled her alluring brown eyes.

"Just drink and be merry already," she flicked him, then turned back to the holvi.

"I don't know, my lady. I think I'm on Charlot's side," agreed the bard, casually swirling the contents in her own mug. Dragon's Hill had a reputation for being as fiercely devoted to Bahamut as even Wheelspoke, rivalling the greater town in heroic deeds and distinguished paladins. She could easily tell why the guild's defection had such an effect on their morale, but what she didn't understand was why they didn't go along with them as Wheelspoke had done. "We haven't heard much about Tooth and Claw that was complimentary, either." Ginni hesitated, wondering how much she could trust these strangers. "You say your sister joined a guild? Which one?"

He grimaced. "Our town is called *Dragon's* Hill. I'll give you one guess," he spat.

A child of prophecy, disowned by her family for joining the guild that betrayed them. Sounded like allies to her.

"Well, at least it wasn't Golden Eye," María jockeyed. "Even I would've disowned Elena if she'd joined that bunch of stuck up-"

A boisterous laugh interrupted her less-than-savory remark. Ginni flinched, then noticed the source- an innocuous band of durgir, attempting to fling one of their own into an empty keg barrel.

"Tooth and Claw, huh. If you don't mind me asking, why exactly is that a bad thing? Are you saying your town refused evangelizers?" she said bluntly, watching mesmerized as Maria toyed with a cherry stem plucked from her drink.

"Boy, did we ever. *¿Qué tenemos que demostrarles?*" She shook her head apologetically.

"Bah, our clan has lived for Bahamut since he walked the land as a mortal dragon. Our lances shattered the shields of those *Lianorres* before their town had walls. And now they come and demand of us, that we turn our own out into the wilderness, because we bear magic they don't understand? Pay them a tithe for protection we never asked for and didn't need? What would you do?" snarled Charlot.

The man literally shook with fury. Maria put a hand over his to calm him.

"She's a holvi, Charlot. If any knew suffering at the hands of those ungodly bigots, it's she."

The bard swept another mesmerized look over the woman. Ginni was impressed.

"So, despite all that, your sister left and joined Tooth and Claw, motive... unknown," she added diplomatically. "I wonder if she knows Arya."

"The T'ssama girl? Who doesn't know her?" replied María. "Rumor has it she's next in line for nomination to Grand Master, as soon as she completes her novitiate."

"A truly lawful good paladin earning the nomination? *Sí claro, y yo soy Bahamut mismo*," grumbled Charlot.

"Elena adores Arya. The two are inseparable," María continued, ignoring him.

"How do you know?" scoffed her brother angrily.

"She writes to me, you dolt."

"*¿Para ti? ¿Por qué?*"

"Because no one else in your family will write back!" she cried, actual anger kindling under her former mirth. "You Riquelmes have all such a temper. Holding her personally accountable for the actions of a guild she had no part in yet… you're stubborn and foolish, and you don't deserve her."

Ginni watched them bicker bemusedly. "Well, I guess it's a good thing they've managed to initiate some actually decent people recently. We were beginning to worry the corruption spread too deep, and your goodly guilds were doomed."

Charlot muttered under his breath, but didn't push the argument. María nudged her empty mug and he rolled his eyes, then got up to get more. She leaned in confidentially toward Ginni.

"I will make sure Dragon's Hill seeks your heroes from Ljotebroek. We suffered heavy casualties from the horde's advance and the guild's negligence. But our kin are strong," she declared, a sparkle in her eye, "and we will always have faith in the goodness of each other. Take care, young holvi. When next I write to Elena, I will mention the tales you bring from the west."

A genuine smile lit up the holvi's face, as she toasted the fiery woman and returned to the bartop.

"Well, that was interesting," remarked Tjena, rosining their bow nonchalantly.

"I'll take what I can get. I sure hope I get a chance to visit Dragon's Hill. They don't make women like that anywhere else!" she sighed enviously at the woman's voluptuous figure and warm, chocolate eyes.

"My love, you're drooling."

"Hush."

VI

PASTURE

No matter how long they walked through the strange realm of not-quite-death, the day grew no shorter and the smooth turf no softer. It seemed to roll on, monotonously and without end. Katarin couldn't help making a comment to their guide.

"Is this limbo, then?" she asked, peering at the emptiness surrounding them.

"Hmm. Yes and no." replied Sethisto, continuing to forge along. "This is the pasture. Where the shepherds bring their flock."

Sure enough, now McKenna and Katarin knew what to look for, they spotted the silver-lined auras of orgir mingling among the vapoury forms of spirits. Some waved to Sethisto, and peered curiously at the corporeal forms that accompanied him.

Without warning, Sethisto suddenly flickered, then vanished from sight. But before the sisters had time to blink, he was back again.

"Excuse me for a moment, if you please," he said breathlessly, "I'm being - oh dear."

With a faint pop, he disappeared again.

"Huh. That's... unsettling," Katarin offered, as they

began to realize just how lost they were in the strange realm without their helpful guide.

Several of the slowly moving figures began to take notice of the sisters as they stood uncertainly in place on the shimmering, somewhat grassy path. McKenna grew uneasy; as she knew all too well, orgir tended to be aggressively territorial. And two mortals wandering through their most carefully guarded domain ranked a bit more invasive than simply starting a fire on an open plain. Though she may hold no grudge with Katarin for the role she played in Atosa's capture, she doubted the orgir would be so forgiving.

Katarin seemed to think like McKenna. She edged closer to her sister, hoping the monk's sheer size would screen her from view.

"I've never met an orghi before," she whispered. "Have you?"

"Yes, a couple times," McKenna whispered back. "I've even met Urtha, Chieftainess of Kumbo's tribe. Ginni introduced us."

Katarin stared perplexedly at her sister. "A holvi introduced you to an orghi? Preposterous."

The monk raised an eyebrow, shifting her weight to one bare foot. "You need to leave your ivory tower more often, Princess. If there's anyone who can empathize with another, it's the orgir and the holvir."

A smile tugged at the corners of her mouth as Katarin scoffed, mouthing the words "ivory tower".

"Fascinating how they manage to shepherd every

soul to limbo though. Or, what did he call it? Pasture? What's the difference?"

"Beats me," mumbled Katarin.

"Perhaps you could ask us and find out," a voice over their shoulders announced.

Both sisters started, freezing in place. They turned to address the speaker who stood a few paces behind them, scarred arms crossed and an impassive expression on his alien features.

Fierce was the first word that always came to mind when McKenna faced an orghi - not a unique reaction by any stretch of the imagination. Nomad plains dwellers who roved as much of Beausun that the ever-migrating asafolk left free, they often engaged in loud, violent war games and feats of wild strength, like chasing down dire beasts bare handed or, more frequently, evicting entire tribes of invasive goblins and kobolds from their territories.

The one before them proved no exception to the stereotype. The breadth of his shoulders eclipsed the small cloud of souls hovering shyly behind him, and his flinty black eyes met even the top of McKenna's lofty head with ease.

This was good. It meant she had a moment to slide between his gaze and her sister's before she managed to finish looking up at him. Fixing her own eyes below his collarbone, she nodded politely, waiting a beat for him to speak.

"For someone who knows not of orgir, you greet this one well." The hint of amusement in his voice was a relief. Katarin shifted uncomfortably behind her, but stayed put.

"The light of life is... humbled, before the bringers of death," McKenna mumbled, frowning as she tried to recall the difficult orghirrish greeting. The one who stood before her bore an aura of importance and power that rivaled even Urtha's. He was no mere grunt or hunter, that was for certain.

"Hmph. So formal. But I will let it pass," he said, touching a long finger with a sharp black fingernail under her chin. "For daughters of our goddess, Kumbo will let much pass," he smiled, "though I wish she taught her children better."

His tone now had a mournful quality to it, and McKenna, though exasperated by the constant deference to her celestial mother, bit off her retort in sympathy. After a moment, she felt her chin tilting further as he lifted it, gently, allowing her to see the eyes that searched her face hungrily, almost reverently. Now that she'd faced Atosa herself, she could understand just how her mortal face, so like and yet unlike the immortal goddess, affected him.

"Kumbo?" Katarin's voice, though curious, was almost a whisper. "You mean... are you the orghi god, Kumbo?"

"He is long dead, child, his lucky soul departing to pasture and the astral planes beyond," replied the orghi, without looking at her. "I am N'dari, merely one of his flock."

"You're an avatar?" She persisted, and McKenna tensed at the imperious quality of her sister's questions.

The hand that held McKenna's face dropped, clenching into a fist. "Did you think yourself one?"

His voice carried. McKenna could hear the challenge in it, and she hoped her sister would too, and stand down. *The last thing we need is a fight... though, we're not even corporeal, as far as I can tell. Wonder what would happen if-*

Suddenly Katarin buckled, her shape seeming to crumple and twist in place. In a moment, she was on the ground, clutching her chest and breathing heavily.

"Stop that!" McKenna stepped protectively over her prone sister. "What in the realms are you doing? How dare you attack a child of Atosa, here in her own domain?" She demanded, aura blazing wildly in her fury.

"I was testing her, to see the purity of her soul," N'dari responded casually, an expression of mildly impressed curiosity on his face. "I expected her to be weaker."

"She was possessed," McKenna insisted urgently, stance spread to shield the sorcere from the potentially hostile attention they were beginning to attract. "The same Lich King who kidnapped Atosa and closed the Doors of Death had her under some kind of mind control. And so she's here, under my protection," her eyes flashed a challenge at the orghi, "the child of Atosa who defeated the dragon and restored her to her godly form. You fight my sister, you fight me," she finished, crossing her arms and drawing herself up to her full and considerable height.

For a moment, it looked as though he meant to take

her up on that challenge. His chest swelled, and jaw flexed as fists clenched in preparation for a fight.

A soft murmur interrupted him. The souls that huddled behind his back, attracted to the women's energy, shuffled around making noises that barely registered as audible in an attempt to investigate them. Thankful for the interruption, McKenna held out a palm toward them. They swirled around her, seeming to dance and pulse in the aura that radiated from her- the aura of death, that she'd summoned upon fighting the dragon form of Atosa.

"These souls..." she spoke slowly, chin still set in defiance, but tone soft and inquisitive, "were they from the chasm?" She strained to hear the voices, plaintive, murmuring as they swirled around her extended arms.

N'dari cast another hostile glance at Katarin's shivering figure, but couldn't keep his attention away from the spectacle of his flock hovering adoringly around McKenna and the power emanating from her.

"No." He watched as they floated in a loosely rhythmic dance, treating the auras among the three like eddies and air currents. "These ones managed to evade the enchantment inflicted by him and his sacerdhosse. Now the Doors of Death are open again, I'm able to bring them home. But the souls stolen by Nezheer are beyond our reach."

Nezheer. The name was unfamiliar, but at the sound, the mourning sounds that emanated from the souls grew a little louder. "The Lich King... he's called Nezheer?"

"It is an ancient name, for an ancient evil. The Likirricanthe- what you call Lich- is only a fragment of this. Regardless, the hold it has over the realms of Faie is beyond the help of mortals," he replied, his voice grown less combative. The tension began to leave his frame, and McKenna breathed a little easier. He eyed her in amusement, huffing through his full lower lip. "Come on, goddess-child, would not you relish a battle?"

Katarin coughed weakly, casting an incredulous look at the two of them. Every so often the outline of her prone figure would wobble, as though the fibers of her soul were being plucked by an invisible force. This didn't exactly answer whether or not they had a corporeal form in this limbo between life and death, but it gave McKenna a better idea of their composition and abilities in the strange realm.

"Not at the expense of my sister, I wouldn't," she answered, resting a hand on Katarin's head and frowning in concentration. Her sister's soul seemed blended with her aura; and McKenna, drawing from her experience with meditation, found herself able to harmonize the energies that the rogueish orghi manipulated.

Seeming to think like the monk, Katarin flexed her long fingers and blinked, concentrating on the faculties newly restored to her. "Does this mean we can't die here?" She asked bluntly, though not really expecting an answer.

"Let's hope we don't find out the hard way," McKenna responded anyways, helping the woman to her feet. She turned to face N'dari, summoning an almost regal firmness of manner that took her sister aback.

"Will you let us pass?" The force of her words made the souls surrounding them shudder slightly, and N'dari narrowed his eyes. Suddenly, he crossed his arms before the sisters, and bent his neck in submission.

"I will honor the children of Atosa so long as they fight alongside the goddess, and not against her," he replied, with a poignant glance at Katarin. "For it is true that we face the same foe. Nezheer will stop at nothing to destroy death itself. The souls he commands in his undead army are but a small fraction of the true damage he could do, were he left to roam unchecked on Faie. Now he has a body, and access to mortal and immortal magics," he stared off into the soft lavender gloom that surrounded them, the black depths of his gaze unfocused, "there's no telling what evil he can control."

And with that warning, N'dari vanished.

"Well. That was. An experience," blinked Katarin, as the souls slowly began to fade from sight in pursuit of their otherworldly guide. She shook herself slightly, as though still feeling the effects of the malignant spell he'd cast at her. "Are they all like that?"

"Katarin, for the love of the goddess, could you please watch what you say," replied McKenna exasperatedly. "Not all orgir are the same, not all ilvir, not all asafolk."

"Sorry... you're right."

"Of course I'm right. Now... where did Sethisto go?"

They both peered into the gloom, but saw nothing other than the faint pathway undulating through the celestial grass. McKenna wondered idly if she could summon spirits, though a bit shy at the thought of such an intrusive and presumptuous effort. She cast a furtive glance at her sister, who stood beside her with her arms crossed and a slightly piqued look on her face.

"Not used to being outranked, I'm guessing?" McKenna offered in a humble tone. The edge went out of Katarin's posture and she sighed through pursed lips.

"It's a... learning experience," she admitted with half a smile. "Of course, I had masters in the Guild of Moonbow, but they were more like... instructors. None assumed any actual control over me or my actions. I guess that's what led me here," she shrugged noncommittally, swiveling languidly in place. "And I can tell what you're going to ask me to do next. It's written all over your face."

"Well, like you said yourself, you're the summoner after all..." the monk wheedled.

"You just don't want him to see the truth, do you?" Katarin's words were blunt, but in the depths of her amethyst eyes McKenna could see sympathy lurking. "Are you afraid he'll hold you accountable?"

"Accountable for what?" The voice of Sethisto preceded his figure, which resolved itself suddenly out of thin air as he resumed his place upon the path before them.

"Gods, will you stop doing that?" McKenna wheezed, clutching her chest as the heart that skipped a beat resumed normal operations.

"Sorry! Sorry! I don't realize I'm doing it!" The spirit bowed apologetically. "I hope you two didn't have any trouble while I was away?'

He looked from one guilty face to the other, and smiled benignly. "Never mind, you don't have to answer that. Now, where were we?'

"Honestly, I still don't actually know the answer to that question. We're not dead. We're not alive. We're not in the Material or Celestial planes... and yet, this isn't truly Hel, either. So, what exactly is this place?" Both sisters looked expectantly at the spirit, whose unfathomable expression made the back of McKenna's neck prickle. He looked almost mournful, and the emotion was so discordant with his jubilant personality that she longed to comfort him, but had no idea how.

"I told you. It's Pasture. The realm between realms."

"So… limbo," muttered Katarin under her breath.

"Time means nothing here," Sethisto was saying, as they continued to amble at a mediocre pace. "You may make your way back to the Material plane and find years have gone, or only minutes. There's really no way of telling. But considering you both are on something of a hero's journey, I'd wager to bet the gods will bring you back just when you're meant to. Spirits don't usually stay here for long. Most leave almost instantly, ascending to the Celestial plane as soon as they can. But others, who choose to linger for loved ones or unfinished business, can stay as long as they want, really."

His tone remained utterly neutral, and the shimmering vapors of his form hid his expression. She looked at her long, dark fingers, the runes tattooed up her arms, the tattered skins she still wore even here beyond the mortal realm. Stuck in the here and there, neither here, nor there. Though she really had no idea how long they'd been wandering this realm, it wasn't nearly as long as he'd done. She could only begin to imagine the toll it would take on any soul spending day after day, year after year, in the quixotic realm.

"Convenient. But now I'm curious," McKenna pulled the mirror out again, "when I summoned the souls to the mirror, did that send them here?"

Sethisto contemplated the mirror for a moment, and McKenna wondered again how he managed to exist for so long in this strange limbo. *It's good time means nothing,* she thought to herself. *I've been here for who knows how long and it already feels like an eternity. I can't imagine not knowing when, if ever, I'd get free. I wonder if he's the "waiting for family" kind or the "unfinished business" kind.*

"Unfinished business, my child. Though my family are infinitely dear to me, I'm fully confident in their ability to find their way to Bahamut's hallowed halls without my guidance."

McKenna started guiltily. She'd forgotten the spirit's uncanny ability to read her mind.

But he was smiling at her. "I wonder just how much my son told you about my death."

She flinched. "Only that it was... untimely."

He got a faraway look on his face, one that McKenna felt deep within her and one that Katarin couldn't even look at. With a shock, McKenna realized the woman's lover must have taken his own life before her eyes, explaining her struggle to face a victim of the same end.

And in an instant, she understood exactly what it was that held the man here.

"There are so many lies we're taught..." she spoke hoarsely, but gained confidence with each word. "No one should be left with the burden of truth, as you were, without the relief of sympathy from anyone else. If I had the gift," she held out her hand toward the spirit, holding it over his heart like a benediction, "I would free you from the guilt that holds you here against your will. Death comes for us all, and it is not for anyone to say they know better when or where."

Something did happen, though none of them had the chance to notice it. But it's not every day demigods discover innate abilities that have lain dormant within them since birth.

He nodded deeply, and McKenna's breath caught in her throat as the ghostly visage flashed an expression she'd seen so many times before.

"I couldn't tell you the fate of the souls in your mirror," he replied, studying the clear glass and runes etched in its beveled edge. "The orgir have several theories as to how he's been able to steal so many. Not the least of which, their own excommunication from the plains of Beausun- the slow migration of their kind away from the rest of Faie's soulful beings. Hard for souls to find Pasture when the shepherds are driven away," he said with an ironic grin. "But once the Doors of Death were closed, and Atosa trapped, it was easy for a necromancer to both harvest and enslave them."

"That chasm is still permeated with souls. Do you think they were freed to the Pasture as well?" Katarin asked.

Sethisto looked grim. "I'm afraid not. Some powerful evil magic settled there when you caused that rift, and those souls are all trapped in its thrall until the Lich King can be destroyed."

McKenna knitted her brows. "But I freed some of them... the souls in my mirror were stolen souls I collected from all the ilmaurte I defeated. If they came from the chasm, doesn't that mean we can free the rest?"

Sethisto paused, putting a hand to his chin. "Hmm. It looks like your celestial powers can act as a blessing, similar to Atosa's, and break the Lich King's curse. They're trapped on the Material plane until the mirror releases them to Pasture, and once they're here, they're stuck again until they are blessed with passage to Hel."

McKenna stared at Katarin, and could tell the woman was thinking along similar lines. Even if those souls could be restored to the Pasture, what would stop the Lich King from stealing them back now the Doors of Death had opened and providing limitless fuel for his undead army? Dispelling them to the pasture may be only half the battle...

"But if I remain behind," spoke Katarin, a decisive edge to her voice, "I can bless them when they appear here, and free them."

McKenna looked concernedly at her sister. "But... you don't know how long you'll be stuck here for. It could be ages before I manage to collect all the souls, or defeat the Lich King."

As if something suddenly broke within her, Katarin slumped, putting her head in her hands. McKenna dropped instantly beside her, gripping her sister's shoulders softly. "What is it? What... Katarin, what's wrong?"

"What if Razan doesn't come back?" she whispered.

"What if I can't save him? His heart belongs to the Lich King now, and his soul…" she gasped, a sob bleeding into her voice.

"Sshh, it's okay," murmured McKenna. "We… we'll try…"

She was right, though. At this point, they had no way of finding Razan's mutilated presence. If his spirit hadn't appeared by now, was it lost forever among the thousands trapped in the chasm? Or worse, did his sacrifice destroy the soul within him?

"Without him, there's no reason for me to return," finished Katarin. A rigidity enhanced her features, as she watched the orgir advance and retreat with souls clinging to them. "I feel it is my duty to remain here, as long as I have to, and bless the souls that come. As my penance for thinking I could assume our mother's mantle, and sacrificing the only love I'll ever know to my hubris."

The monk remained silent, unwilling to question the determination she heard in the sorcere's voice. She stood and pulled her sister to her feet, wiping tears from both their cheeks. Again that pang of empathy for this unknown sister filled her heart. Katarin didn't ask for this any more than McKenna had. Limitless potential as a child of an immortal goddess- zero accountability, guidance, or even companionship. McKenna needed to have some severe words with the ilvir of Moonbow, if she ever got the chance.

Noticing Sethisto watching them with a curious, but concerned, look McKenna couldn't help but wonder how he knew where to find Seth. The realm surrounding them echoed a sameness that had the monk lost as soon as she stepped through its doors, and it grew no more familiar even as she felt the stirrings of her own dormant powers. She understood a measure of the orghi chieftainess' otherworldly charm, that she spent so much time in this realm that defied the logic and order of theirs.

If I'm not careful, I'll start seeing them all, their dreams, their final moments, their deaths. Is that how Mother sustained her divinity? She is no mere individual; the goddess of Death, a collective of all that have lived and then passed on. It's easier to understand how we two were lost in the millions she's seen before or since. I guess I can't blame her for that.

Suddenly a bright, golden glow lit up the horizon. It stood out clearly from the unvarying, soft light of the sky they walked under, casting its own shadow against each blade of grass, and each hair of the pelt draped across McKenna's form. It grew so dazzling, she could barely make out the outline of Sethisto as he advanced toward it. Without a word, the figure came to a halt, and McKenna stood silently behind him, awaiting further instruction.

"You are a monk of Malfaestus, yes?" he turned, studying the runes inked along her skin. McKenna stared at him blankly.

"You're asking me this now? Of course I am," she replied proudly, but with some trepidation as the spirit's sudden worry became clear to her.

"Hmm. I wonder if the dragon will see you, then."

McKenna recalled the lithe shape of the golden god, guarding Seth's spirit as it moved from hers. She remembered his bow, and smiled humbly.

"He's waiting for me, I think." The monk glowed in the light of her god, but that did nothing to dim her in the presence of his. Sethisto contemplated her, the crown of her shining hair and the strength of her powerful limbs and the nobility of her heroic soul. He bowed, and smiled.

"Yes. I think you're right. You know," he said, suddenly stern. "I wanted to be angry with you. Were it not for your interference, my son would still be alive."

Katarin gasped, staring first to McKenna and then to Sethisto. McKenna stood as though rooted to stone.

"I wanted to be angry with you, but I couldn't. You showed my son the truth," he whispered, staring at the mirror held limply at McKenna's side. "You showed him what he never would have believed on his own - that he had the strength to succeed where I had only the weakness to fail. I want to hate you, but all I can do is be thankful for you, McKenna of Clan Hammardin, child of Atosa and monk of Malfaestus. Thankful that you saved his soul once, and," he said, beckoning them onward toward the great golden castle that lay before them, "thankful you have returned to save his soul again."

With that, he vanished.

"Well. That was… different," Katarin offered after a few moments of stunned silence.

McKenna made no response. Her heart beat frantically in her chest, though it did nothing to dim her purpose.

His father. His father, who died ultimately from a weakness he couldn't overcome, had watched for years as his son seemed to walk the same path. The monk couldn't even begin to imagine how agonizing that must have been. Then to see him finally free of that peril, in a heroic death that earned him a place beside his god - and still, without hesitation, walk the woman responsible for that noble death directly to the keep where he could remain in eternal glory, for no other purpose than to drag him back to the realms where he lived so despised and disgraced. A measure of awe settled over her, and she bowed her head in benediction for the soul of a man who would so learn from his own mistakes.

After all, what right have I to bring him back? Is this not a fool's errand?

Katarin peered at her, trying to read the words unspoken on her face.

"I don't have to go with you, you know. In fact," she said, turning back towards the pasture, "I don't think I even can. Bahamut does not recognize me, and I have a duty to the souls trapped in limbo. You go your way, my good sister, and I will go mine," she held out her wrist to the rigid monk. "Let us hope we meet in the middle."

McKenna looked first at her sister's hand, then her face. Without blinking, she swept her into a fierce embrace, which Katarin returned in equal force.

"Be well, sister. We will find and save them both. I promise," whispered McKenna into Katarin's ear.

"Good will always triumph over evil." she responded, with her eyes downcast almost in reverence.

They parted, Katarin sweeping back toward the pasture, and McKenna, shoulders thrown back, ascending through the gates to the realm of the dragon god.

VII

AMBITION

Forward thrust, step back, block high. A dance of swords, a calm, principled stance, a-

"NOVICE! Was that a strike or a love tap? Show respect for your sparring partner, or leave the lists. Disgraceful."

-another wasted effort.

Arya inhaled quietly. Her loose, expressionless stance betrayed no disappointment, no anger. She'd pierced Clint's guard, by her count, enough times to fell six of him. So far the closest he'd gotten to the same was the snap of wood striking wood as she blocked the only thrusts close enough to her to bother blocking.

This isn't discipline. This is torture.

Those who observed them couldn't even begin to gauge the combatants' levels of enthusiasm and comprehension. Arya T'ssama's reserve and poise had grown legendary already in her time among the guild, while Clint Achor, her rival opposite, simply had no emotions to express. Arya often wondered if he were part goblinoid. There was no doubt in her mind whatsoever that his father, Master Gareth Achor, descended from the subfaiefolkr creatures. He stood not far off, spitting criticisms like venom at the girl, burning each move with acid words and counting each point against her in acrid spite.

The Achors are nothing to the T'ssamas, echoed her mother's voice in her head as she bowed before Clint, preparing another offensive. *Not even worthy to squire our pigs.*

But Lady Arianna had succumbed to the guild's decrees anyways. Lip service from the woman whose ambition and direction kept Wheelspoke running with legendary perfection.

Her father agreed- but not in so many words. Her father preferred subtler censure. Like training his son to never back down from his conviction, and reminding his daughter that their noble heritage only carried them so far, anyway.

"Anyone can fight, Arya. Anyone with anything worth protecting can pick up a weapon and use it to their advantage. You have to show something more than that. You have to want to win. You have to want it more than anything- more than your opponent, more than your pride."

But Sethisto never got what he wanted. His ambitions ended in death.

She closed her eyes slowly, drinking in the light filtered through the high windows, the echoing clatter of practice bouts surrounding her. Did she want it, really? Or was she a hypocrite, like her parents?

"Again!" The Master's voice rang through the hall. Clint advanced listlessly, arms held rigid, blade at an awkward angle.

Well. I certainly don't want to lose to that.

She stepped backwards, setting a pace for the boy to follow. He shadowed her slowly, his face still blank, lank locks of dirty blonde hair scattered haphazardly across his pale brow. Her blade swung outward, a strike intended to draw his arms across his chest. He followed, easily parrying the weapon Arya was sweating to keep steady in its slow motion. She raised her attack higher, cutting toward his unprotected cheek, but she followed the move with her body, providing a clear opening for him to counter. A dull light kindled deep within the sullen boy's gaze as it slowly dawned on him what she was doing.

If his father won't train us, I guess I have to.

Keeping a solemn face as he went for the opportunity, Arya dodged nimbly, increasing her pace with every step and encouraging the same from her opponent. Other novitiates begun to slow in their own repetitions, watching in awe at the normally peerless girl painstakingly attack, miss, dodge, and counter. Some cast furtive looks at the Master, wondering if he understood her actions, wondering if he would intervene.

Clint pushed through a lunge, and with an almost dexterous twist managed to cut within Arya's tight guard. With a start, she raised her blade to parry but, in the heat of his unexpected closeness, pushed hard against his strike. First dropped blade, then dropped knee, crashed to the hard stone floor.

"Halt! Foul!"

"A *what*?!" She shouted back in frustration, then clapped a hand to her mouth.

Not fast enough.

"Insolence. You are dismissed," Master Gareth seethed, then motioned for another novitiate to attend his fallen son. Clint pushed the girl off grumpily, casting a confused look at Arya. But another dark scowl from his father made him think better about opening his mouth.

Rigidity enhanced every feature. Her eyes were dark, fathomless, cold. She turned and bowed first to Clint, then to Master Gareth. Grabbing both practice weapons and sheathing them on the racks without a word, she marched out of the hall.

"Well, Lady Arya has a voice after all," rasped Layne in amusement at her elbow. Glowing with sweat from her own practice, the girl followed her into the darkness of the Cathedral's corridors.

"I shouldn't have spoken back to the Master like that. It is my duty to fight, it is his to judge," Arya replied, with more conviction than she felt.

Truthfully, her composure surprised her. She wanted nothing more than to break every single piece of bloody pottery lining the walls.

"*Bahamut bendiga*, you lie as prettily as you fight," laughed Layne, draping a shoulder over her more diminutive companion. "Come on, we stink. At least getting dismissed early means we have dibs on hot water."

Arya knitted her eyebrows. "You got dismissed too? Why? I missed that. Would've been nice to see someone else chewed out for once."

"Turns out, calling the Master's son a spineless coward is frowned upon by His High Holy Judginess. That boy's never done anything better with a blade than stumble, and you actually managed to get him within your guard. Yet he still won't stick up for you to his father? Worthless," she seethed, eyes snapping along with her white teeth. "When the others started mocking your movements and he did nothing but stare, I lost it. However, I'm less of a target than you, so I just got a hand wave. You know the one," she threw her head back and assumed a haughty, high browed look of disdain, loosely flicking her wrist and sneering in a fair imitation of their unfair Master. Arya snorted, then laughed outright along with her shameless friend.

Steam rose in lazy swirls from the marble baths sunk every few feet into the flagstones. Nose hovering just above the surface, Arya closed her eyes, soaking the sweat and disappointment from her skin and her soul.

Katherine did warn me it would be like this. Deserters receive no quarter. Their disgrace is visited upon the entire household. Mother would be ashamed of me, thinking I could set this right myself.

She blew bubbles idly in the mineral water. Its tang stung her tongue. They didn't have water like this in Wheelspoke, just the clear, cold springs that drained from the high hills dividing their valley from the plains of Beausun. Of course, her mother expressly forbid playing in them, not that that stopped her. Lifting her onto his shoulders, her brother used to get in wrestling matches with James and Katherine in the largest brook that meandered lazily outside the city gates. James matched Seth for strength, but Arya more than matched poor Katherine in agility. *Always game for it, though. I miss that woman.*

"Huh, I always thought you had to bribe the divine maidens if you wanted bubbles."

Arya started as Layne plunked a towel down next to the bath, lounging casually while draped in one of her own. Rolling her eyes at the lack of modesty so prevalent in the novitiate from Dragon's Hill, she stood from the bath and wrapped the soft cloth closely around her.

"You know, they used to say the waters here were blessed by Bahamut himself," she mused, wringing the water from her short dark hair. "Bit weird though, did he like, know we were gonna bathe in it you think? Or were we supposed to just drink it?"

"You idiot, you can't drink this stuff. You'll puke," Layne laughed, toweling herself off vigorously. "It's got sulphur and ashvine in it. Great for your skin, terrible for your guts."

"How do you know?" Arya pressed.

"Because Bahamut did bless this water. It's the same as what's in our reservoir back home," she shrugged. "It shifts the ground a lot though, kind of a pain, likes to open sinkholes and all sorts of fun projects that keep our civil engineers busy."

"Really? Why? Can't you guys just move dirt with your mind and stuff?"

"Oh my gods, Arya, you are so dense. We're not telepaths, we're just… attuned to nature."

"Hmm. Sounds fake, but okay."

"You're so annoying!" Layne spun her towel up and flicked it at Arya's shoulder, the crack echoing through the empty chamber followed by an enraged squeal of pain.

Their damp, bare footsteps dismissed the silence of the corridors as they headed back to the bunks. The journey seemed to drag on, though each ignored the sensation, assigning it to simple exhaustion. But a few wrong turns later, Arya began to realize they'd been deliberately led astray. A tapestry that once hung above the alcoves had gone missing, converting the well-known path to a hopeless labyrinth of dim stone hallways.

"You think we should try and find it? How does a tapestry just disappear?" she said begrudgingly as they retraced their steps for the third time.

"Well, we can't get any more lost," Layne replied, looking around in despair. "Here, this looks nice and suspicious. Let's check through there."

The "there" Layne pointed to was a conspicuous opening in the wall. The girls advanced toward it, but suddenly stopped dead, staring furtively at one another and breathing more heavily than usual. Though still warm from the baths, an eery chill raised the hairs on their arms, and the air grew heavy. It seemed as though a dank curtain of dread hung in the darkness before them.

Heart pounding, Arya took a step back, putting a hand on Layne's elbow. She felt something, like a spark, kindle deep within her. If she didn't know any better, she thought she could see golden eyes staring mournfully at the vacant space.

"This is…" she breathed quietly.

"Evil. This is evil," finished Layne, her warm copper skin blanched ghostly pale behind the shadow of freckles that spread across it.

Arya had to agree. "But… we're in the Cathedral of the Golden God. Bahamut is a good dragon. You said it yourself, everything within this space is blessed. So how…" she trailed off, again feeling that spark, those mournful eyes, from within her.

"I don't know. But I can't even think about trying to find out." Her words, usually carrying with them the bright vivacity of a burning campfire, now sounded almost brittle, breathless with unease. Arya nodded, grabbing the girl's hand and leading them both away from the curious and ghastly corridor.

It wasn't until they were tucked together in the bunks that Layne's voice came back to normal. The experience still left Arya's own reserve shaken. She contemplated bringing it to Grand Master Elgitha's attention.

"Best of luck to you," murmured Layne sleepily. "Elgitha barely knows which way's up anymore. Unlikely she'll know the source of a deadly and evil aura lurking somewhere outside the lavatory."

"Don't talk about her like that," snapped Arya. "She knows more than she lets on… it's just… it's complicated."

Layne rolled over, locking eyes with a deadpan expression on her face. "Complicated. She's ruled this guild for half a century, Lady Arya. This guild that's spent the better part of these past few years terrorizing converts and abusing its own members. There's nothing complicated about it. She's old and complacent and desperate for you to grow up and replace her."

Grand Master. That's what I want. I want it more than anything.

Layne studied her with an unfathomable expression. "You're so cute when you're flustered, you know that?"

"Flustered?! I am not flustered, Layne Riquelme."

"I can feel your face from here, Lady Arya."

"Shut up and go to sleep."

"As my Grand Master orders, so I will obey."

"I can't believe you!"

Somewhere deep in the cathedral, a door swung shut.

—

Rain drenched the streets of Lianor for a tenday. Alternating patrols from the guilds often found themselves called to save property, even people, from being swept into the arroyos that crisscrossed the stone city. Tavern patrons, raising their glasses and their eyebrows, couldn't remember such a storm.

"Streets not fit fer living," mumbled a tall, grizzled aesir wrapped from head to toe in curious furs.

"Speak for yourself," mumbled a voice at her elbow, nursing an acrid concoction and draped in finely woven, mud-stained garments. "Faiefolkr beg to be let into our city, crawling out of their backwater slums hand over fist."

Nobles didn't often patronize this tavern. Enid's, at the bottom of the canals, found itself a harbor for the poorer and quieter civilians that populated Lianor's streets.

But old habits die hard. And he hadn't been a noble long.

The woman in the furs turned and looked down a crooked nose at the man, eyes snapping. "They shouldn't have to beg, you disgusting hypocrite. We built this city for everyone, not just the ones with gold burning holes in their pockets."

"We? Who's this royal *We*, now?" the drunkard challenged.

"I'm a builder, from the Hand Over Fist, as your bleary eyes could've told you if you'd bothered to look," she responded, jabbing a gnarled finger at a threadbare crest on her coat sleeve.

"You're a liar and a fraud," slurred the leathery old man, pointing his own crooked finger at his table mate. "Just like everyone from Hand Over Fist, claiming they built near all the cities in Faie. Bet you've ne'er been further North th'n Wheelspoke."

"Bah, as though you Norrn'ers know anything that doesn't shine like metal or grind like stone," she scoffed in return, shaking her half empty mug. "My guild built this town shoulder to shoulder with the durgir of Bristendine and the holvir of the wastes, long before you nobles-"

Before she could finish, the door to the tavern swung wide, admitting two novices streaming with wet into the dim and crowded space. A sudden hush descended upon the patrons, some sullen, most covertly curious.

"Pardon us. We're looking for a missing child," Arya's voice carried clearly, as it always did, through the smoky bar. It possessed those calm, but compelling tones she inherited from her mother. With her words though, the compulsion made itself known, pulling on the better nature of her hearers instead of insinuating itself without their knowledge. A woman carrying a brace of mugs turned, a concerned look on her face.

"You mean the Wheelers' girl? They were in here, not an hour ago. No child seen, I'm afraid," Enid, the bar's owner, offered.

Layne spoke up. "They here often? Does the child tend to play anywhere nearby?"

The woman set her mugs down, puzzling up her face in contemplation. "I'm afraid they come here less than before… times are harder, it seems, and drink's not cheap."

A few of the sullen looks cast themselves more directly at the paladins, who realized with a start the bar was full of Besonne refugees from the plains. The sigil of Tooth And Claw, emblazoned as it was on the tunics they wore over their quilted armor, did them no favors here. Their expressions seemed more fiercely directed toward Layne, whose red hair and towering stature clearly recalled her heritage from Dragon's Hill. A man with a bandaged eye sneered and turned into his mug.

Layne's face remained neutral, hewn from stone. With a sinking feeling, Arya understood. "We're not here for collections. We want to find that child. Thank you for your help," she said, and untying a small pouch at her side placed it meaningfully on the bar top. "Dinner and a round is on Bahamut tonight. Our god promised to protect you," she spoke soulfully, and with enough conviction her hearers couldn't help but believe her, "and we intend to keep that promise."

With that she and Layne bowed themselves out of the establishment and back into the pouring rain.

"Novice!"

The woman had followed them to the door.

"I know you mean no harm. I didn't want…" she bit her lip, not meeting their eyes. "The girl. She sometimes plays down by that canal," she stammered, pointing off to a stone channel swollen with rainwater. "I do hope she's not…" she trailed off, then without another word turned back into the tavern.

Angry brown water tumbled viciously along the arroyo, occasionally splashing over the lip and onto the pavement. The space seemed completely devoid of any sign of life- any sign of anything, really, since the torrential downpour had proved to be quite talented at sweeping away all in its path.

"If she were in that canal, she'll be plummeting over White Face into the sea at this point," Layne spoke dully.

Layne hated rain like a cat, which meant they'd been appointed patrol almost every night since the storm broke. "Makes a nice change from the library," she'd joked weakly as they'd made their way out of the Cathedral for another interminable round.

"Please," Arya winced at the thought of the deluge that ran from their city by the sea heartlessly dragging the poor victim along. "Let's just look for... I don't know... anything."

"Does that count as anything?" Layne pointed at a bright object somehow still resting determinedly on the flagstones.

It was a toy, a painted wooden and clay figure shaped questionably like an animal. Somehow it had lodged itself between two paved slabs. Arya began to pocket it, but then thought better of it. Hovering her hand above the object and muttering an oath to Bahamut, she sought any kind of clarity, or history, from the discarded doll.

"Oh! It's hers, Layne, it's the girl's!" She cried excitedly, turning frantically in place as though hoping its owner would appear out of nowhere.

Layne turned around too, and emitted a sound somewhere between a growl and a cry. Arya turned and followed the direction of her gaze, then watched in shock as her companion suddenly bolted for the canal and lept in.

"LAYNE! Are you crazy?! What are you- oof!"

A grappling hook struck her where she stood, tied to the end of a sturdy cable. Arya pondered it bemusedly for a moment and then took hold with a grip of adamantine as she realized Layne, tossing the lifeline with the unerring accuracy she perpetually demonstrated at the range, drifted somewhere under those deathly rapids at the opposite end of it.

"You… can't… strong… agh! Bahamut, bless me with strength!" She cried in frustration as the cable cut into her palms, vying for release.

Layne burst to the surface, gripping tightly to a dark bundle. Below them, in a small chain of pockets carved into the stone canal, lay the girl - trapped first by the rapids, then spun out of them as her haven slowly flooded. She now clung, gasping and frightened, to Layne's shoulder.

Now would be a great time for that blessing, Arya thought desperately, as she strained against the flow of the current, throwing all her strength hand over hand to pull the victims from the arroyo.

The effort was brutal. Her palms grew raw and bloodied, but with a final heave, they reached the lip of the canal and Layne managed to lift herself and the girl out.

Arya plopped down next to her, breathless, and grabbed her friend's face. "If you ever do that again so help me Layne Riquelme I'll-"

"You'll what?" She retorted weakly, then turned to the little girl who lay limp at her side. Arya noticed with some surprise the distinct lack of blood left on Layne's cheeks, and looked down at her shredded hands.

Not a scratch remained.

Better late than never, I guess, the girl thought begrudgingly; then straightened in shock as a very alien, and very smug, feeling flooded her. *What the…*

"Alright then, lass? You've got your breath now?" Layne was wiping the girl's face, pulling at her eyelids to check for delirium and her ears for debris from the brackish water. The girl nodded shakily, then noticed the toy tucked in Arya's belt. Her eyes went wide.

"Oh? This yours, right? You went to some trouble to save it-" her words caught in her throat at the sight of the girl's face, shying away from Arya as she approached with the toy. She caught sight of the child studying the symbol emblazoned on her tunic, and noticed with chagrin that she considered her with fear, and not with hope.

The faiefolkr in the tavern looked at us like that too, she thought in silence as they walked the girl back to her parents. They thanked the paladins fervently, but Arya could keenly sense the wariness underlying their gratitude. It cut her to the core, even as she could spot their small reliquaries of the dragon god, to know they worshiped with their words and not with their soul. *Why bother?*

The alien sensation, once smug, now mournful, could only agree.

"No, you don't have to pay us anything. We're just a patrol, your tithes pay it-" Layne was explaining to one of the men. The other held the girl tightly, casting fearful looks around the tiny apartment. The tension grew palpable and finally Arya snapped.

"Please. I don't understand," her eyes, soft as a grey dawn, turned toward them pleadingly. "Why do you fear us? You can speak before me, I promise," she held out her wrist, baring it in a sign of peace and goodwill. "I know you are... newer, to faith, but it doesn't matter. Our god will protect you. *We* will protect you. Why do you doubt this?"

The man speaking to Layne drew himself up. He had considerable height- a Northerner from Bread Basket, Arya suspected, which he confirmed with his own words.

"Faith, you say, just like the others of your guild. They told us to come to Lianor. They promise protection. But like most, we purchased security with liberty. Our home in Illusen," he swept an arm wide at the bare room, the paltry space, "were filled with all manner of beautiful things. We trade with the durgir for generations, and yet now this scourge is upon the land suddenly our ways are no longer acceptable. No longer righteous. We must give up our livelihood, our home, for this? For the boot of oppression ever upon our necks?"

Arya began to speak, but Layne held up a hand.

"I come from Dragon's Hill. None of my kin answered to Lianor, to the Guild of Tooth and Claw. When the horde came..."she choked, then swallowed. "They destroyed my home. They murdered our citizens, my family, and the guild watched as we burned. You think we don't know? You think we are as blind as them?"

That's right. That could have been us. Mother was protecting us. But at what cost?

The man holding the rescued child spoke mournfully. "I'm sorry for your loss. But you don't know. We'd rather have lost everything than be left with this, our cowardice; the weakest of our kin who ran without a backwards glance."

Layne bit her lip, then turned and stormed from the building. They were left with Arya- a pillar of inscrutable poise once more. The T'ssama girl, raised as a Lady, alone to restore their family's legacy.

They nodded apologetically in return to her icy bow.

The storm passed that night.

VIII

SUN

The echoing slap of stone against water reverberated across the lake. Though their flat surfaces made crossing the water easy enough for stones, doing so would prove much more daunting for the holvir. Somewhere beyond that wide expanse lay the wilderness of the Gamorren jungle, boasting creatures and inhabitants unknown to most of the world at large. The home of the Sun ilvir was a mystery even to the two well-travelled and experienced holvir.

"You sure Urtha said we were the only ones for the job? You don't think she's just spent too much time mooning around with the dead?" mused Tjena out loud.

"That's what I told her. She laughed so hard I think another rift opened," moaned Ginni. "But someone's gotta do it. Why not us?"

"Hmm. We do seem to always stick our noses into things we have no business sniffing. And we always make it out in one piece. Err, mostly. What's up with that?"

"Divine intervention," scoffed Ginni, with a scowl into the heavens.

It's not that she particularly hated gods, not really. She just had no use for them, or they for her. Other than to either convince people they were better than she was, or worse- give them the power to prove it.

"Preternatural luck is more like it."

Reclining against a mossy stone, Ginni closed her eyes against the early afternoon sun. Her thoughts wandered off, into a not-too-distant past when first the holvir's paths crossed those of Urtha's and her tribe.

—

The sounds of thundering hooves and beating wings echoed across the vast, windy moors. The normally golden prairie seemed desaturated; blanched by the banks of clouds that roiled overhead, threatening rain but not quite committing to it. Dark figures darted along the horizon, some aback shaggy bovrin- beasts of the Beasun plains that resembled cattle- some astride wild horses. Most were simply on foot, fleet and swift as any of Faie's creatures.

Orgir called these war games. Feats of strength and wit in battle, that tested their might and their abilities and kept them feeling alive when they spent too much time in the realms beyond the Doors of Death.

Ginni watched in fascination as a squadron of hardy asafolk emerged from a swell of heath, rolling a wooden and metal war machine up to the front lines. Orghi archers let fly smoldering arrows, coated with a resin instead of pitch, so that they would catch the wood on fire but extinguish if they hit the dry tinder of the prairie instead.

For the war games were just that- games, meant to ape the vigor and violence of battle, but not the bloodshed or the wanton destruction that such events tend to generally encourage.

The arrows whistled through the air and Ginni could hear dull thuds as they peppered the side of the war machine. Asafolk, ducking under shields, reached up with pikes and polearms to knock the burning arrows free before they did any real damage.

With a mighty blast from a horn, the machine began to unfold. A pendulous arm, attached with thickly woven cable, tilted back to fill with a strange phosphorous substance. Before Ginni could react, the operator released the cable and the arm jettisoned forward, flinging its load into the sky. An aesir, stringing a flaming arrow to his bow, let fly and the phosphorus exploded in the air, driving back the advancing orgir in a flurry of activity.

"Hang on. Is that fair? Can they do that?" Tjen watched in fascination as the wispy smoke dissipated quickly and the asafolk took advantage of the cleared space to advance.

The whooping orgir, sounding their horns and cheering at the unexpected but brilliant assault, seemed to answer that question. The holvi shrugged.

"War games. What will they think of next?" cried Ginni in exasperation.

The orgir seemed to have no defense against this explosive weapon. Though they tried to navigate dexterously around or through the line of attack, the aesir stood stalwart, releasing a load of effervescent phosphorous every time they drove too close to the front. The fluttering flag of Bahamut, bearing beneath it the standard of Garden Gate, stood atop a small hill to the east of the advancing asafolk. And they drew ever closer to the wind-whipped standard of Kumbo, the painted flag that rose from behind the orgir.

Suddenly an unnatural whistling sound pierced the din of sounding horns and hoof beats- and in a split second, all the air seemed sucked out of the clearing.

Ginni's heart beat once. And then an explosion, brighter than the immortal light of the gods, rocked the moors.

"Wh- what was... Tjen? Tjen, are you okay?" groaned Ginni, shaking her head as she propped herself up on her elbows. The blast had knocked them both off their feet and onto the soft ground, where they had laid in a daze for a minute.

"Yeah. I think so. Everything still attached," replied the holvi, as they wiggled their fingers gently, studying each one as though to reorient themselves.

"Wow. Do you think they meant for that to happen? If it hit us this hard so far out... what happened to the asafolk?"

A wail carried across the moors. Slowly, the shaggy figures of the mounted orgir stumbled back to their feet and advanced quickly to the epicenter of the blast - the smoking, hulking wreckage of the strange war machine.

"Oh, Faie Mother preserve us, that was NOT supposed to happen, Tjen, we have to help them!!"

Taking off at a run, the holvir arrived just as two orgir had managed to extricate a body from the twisted metal. Ginni had to look away. She'd never seen a corpse so badly mutilated as this one. She heard retching behind her. Another aesir, wiping her mouth, gasped in terror.

"The war game is forfeited," spoke one of the orgir- a female, a head taller than the other beside her, with severely cropped hair and an aspect of otherworldly nobility. Ginni almost felt herself inclined to bow, but shook the sensation off. Holvir didn't bow to orgir.

Suddenly the sound of pounding hooves arrested them. A small contingent of asafolk, arriving on horseback, approached at a breakneck pace. Their leader reigned up, a proud-looking man with a tunic bearing the crest of Bahamut worn over his plate armor.

"Oh no. A paladin," groaned Tjen. Ginni, who had leaned down beside the sick woman and was singing softly in her ear to ease her discomfort, paled.

"Put down your weapons, you bloodthirsty bandits," the paladin ordered, brandishing his pike imperiously at the orgir. "You are all under arrest. Resistance to comply will be met with force."

The orghi woman bristled, the ferocity and fury in her eyes unfathomable. Seeing the explosion had left the aesir squadron- those that survived the blast, that is- too dazed to do more than blink. Tjen stood up, bowing deeply before the paladin.

"Well met, Paladin of Bahamut," they said, wrist exposed and deep obeisance granting them the right to speak to such a high-ranking aesir. "On what grounds do you arrest these folk? This is a war game, and their leader already declared forfeit."

The paladin's lip curled. "Holvi. Of course the orgir

wouldn't speak for themselves. The magistrate of Garden Gate warned us that bandits were roaming the outskirts of the city, threatening war."

"It... it's a war game, Master," Tjen expressed no emotion whatsoever, though even Ginni had to choke back derision. How had this aesir never heard of a war game? Were Lianorrans truly so sheltered?

"This?" The Paladin pointed to the mutilated corpse, and the shell-shocked asafolk scattered around the blast site, "This is a game to you, holvi?"

"We were witnesses. The orgir had nothing to do with the explosion. You'd have to ask whoever designed this machine what happened, because there's no way the orgir could have-"

"I've heard enough from you," spat the paladin with disgust, his black eyes flashing with ire. "You're all to come with me, on pain of death."

The orghi snorted, the first sound she'd uttered since the approach of the paladin. All turned to regard her.

"We declared the war game forfeit. The laws of asafolk have no claim on us. Should you wish to challenge us with violence, do so at your own peril, paladin," she spat the word, but looked with concern at the scattered aesir forms surrounding them as Ginni worked feverishly to dress the wounds of some and sing the consciousness back to others, "but I am thinking you have more important matters to attend to, for their souls are not long for this world otherwise."

"Is that a threat, Urtha?" he hissed, even as he gave a signal for the rest of his squad to attend the fallen asafolk.

"It is the truth, Master Achor, but then that matters little to you after all," she replied dismissively. She emitted a low whistle, and the orgir that lined the rise of heath retreated quickly, leaving only her and her companion to the mercy of the paladins. Two novitiates clapped them in chains, and, loading the wounded onto makeshift litters, they returned to the town of Garden Gate.

"Urtha. Did he mean... is she really the chieftainess of the tribe of Akan? Did they really just arrest the most powerful orghi in Faie?" Tjen whispered to Ginni, who paced alongside the litter of the woman she tended.

"It looks like it. What could have possibly possessed her to come quietly? She looks strong enough to take them on singlehandedly," Ginni mused, stroking the poor woman's forehead. She had wrapped a tourniquet around the woman's thigh, desperate to staunch the flow of blood. Her leg, from the knee down, had been completely shredded by shrapnel from the bomb. Ginni didn't have a knife sharp enough to amputate it, so all she could do was sing softly, distracting the woman's mind from its frenzy of pain.

"I think she was really worried about not getting the survivors home quickly. Orgir take their war games seriously. No one, not even an enemy, dies in a war game."

"You're right. But how do we convince the magistrate the orgir had nothing to do with this? He should already know better," she said with a frown. "What magistrate would let a village participate in orghi war games without knowing death is against the rules?"

Tjen screwed up their face, thinking deeply. "One who's trying to start something with the orgir, maybe."

"You're starting to sound as cynical as I do."

"You're a bad influence."

They made it through the gates of the village. Ginni made to follow the wounded, but Master Achor stopped her.

"You, and the other holvi- you come with me. Your word may not be worth much, but since no one else is capable of telling us what happened, it looks like I've got no choice but to present you before the magistrate."

"Urtha already told you what happened," Ginni replied, trying to keep the sarcasm from her voice. "Why didn't you listen to her?"

"Because an orghi's word is worth even less than a holvi's," he replied ruthlessly. Ginni blanched, her full lips pursed in a thin marble line. "Garden Gate's healers will tend to the wounded. Your services aren't needed. Come with me." Without waiting for a response, he dismounted and, handing his horse off to his squire, strode towards the magistrate's hall that lay in the center of the village.

With a musical huff that belied her annoyance, Ginni followed, Tjen close behind.

They might as well have not wasted their breath. Lord Milton, upon hearing the word "orgir", bristled and demanded justice for his murdered kinsman.

"Murder... it's not murder to die in a war game,"

insisted Ginni. "Something went wrong with that... that war machine. The orgir had nothing to do with it!"

But the man wouldn't hear them. With a dismissive gesture, the holvir were ushered out of the building, without even get a chance to hear the fate of the orgir currently held prisoner by the paladin's guild squadron.

"Well... we did what we could," shrugged Tjena as they hustled down the high street and back toward the gate. "Should we just leave? Something tells me we'll get in a ton of trouble if we try to..."

They trailed off at the look on Ginni's face, as she stared winsomely toward the makeshift gaol that held Urtha and her orghi companion. Two red-faced novices stood at attention on either side of the metal cage, but the orgir were otherwise unguarded.

"Ginni. You're going to get us killed," Tjen said matter-of-factly; almost resignedly, as they realized what their partner was scheming.

"No I'm not, Tjen, not if you know how to use that *naiti*," she countered with a sly grin.

Holvir voices were powerful by any standard. Gifted holvir, like these two, could charm, coax, or coerce almost any soulful creature into whatever state they pleased. Though the novices had divine oaths for protection, their guard was lowered around holvir. Because despite their abilities, they were just holvir, after all.

This was not the first time asafolk underestimated the diminutive race.

Leaning nonchalantly against the metal bars, Urtha

watched in amusement as the guards, charmed and lulled into lethargy by the bards' powerful song, leaned forward and then collapsed into heaps in the dust. Ginni knelt and deftly swiped a bundle of keys from one snoring guard's belt, and opened the gate wide, releasing the orgir inside.

"Little holvir," Urtha said, as she waved her companion off to alert the tribe of their freedom and prevent an attack on the unsuspecting village, "you have saved many more lives than you realize. I will assume the debt of each one, for it is known," she said, a flash of light shining in her strange silver eyes, "that you will do much more than this for our tribe, in a future you do not yet see."

"That's... cryptic. But we don't really have time to riddle it out," Ginni replied, as Tjen whistled under their breath from their scouting position up the road. Master Achor and the magistrate had ended their conference and left the hall.

"This is true. Run, holvir, and I am sure you know better than to return to Garden Gate. But when next you find yourselves upon the open savannah," she insisted, "you will find the tribe of Akan, and we will speak again."

With that, she bolted after her companion, and the two holvir ducked out of sight and departed down a separate trail.

They never did go back to Garden Gate. But word travelled fast. Lord Milton declared war, real war, on the orghi tribe of Akan, banishing them forever from the moors. And from that point on, the already deteriorating relations between asafolk and orghi were no more.

But the holvir's daring brought them the honor and respect of Urtha. And the road that, it seemed, had ultimately led them here.

To the banks of Lago Entrasol, the gateway to the realm of Gamorre and home to the ilvir of the Sun.

Hiking through misty cliffs and hanging forests, they arrived before the great lake bed that shimmered under a sun amplified by the blueness and clarity of the sky above. According to directions given by their durgirn hosts, their destination lay at the base of a waterfall found somewhere along its banks. However, they had failed to mention the lake's seemingly interminable vastness-something the holvir quickly discovered to their dismay.

"It's going to take just as long to walk around this thing as it did to get to it. We should've hired a boat," moaned Ginni, her flat stone sailing across the expanse, sinking with a splash just shy of Tjena's.

"What, and carry it a hundred leagues from the mines to here? You're not thinking, Ginni," replied Tjena, whipping another to slap across the still waters. "We should just follow the path around. We're sure to run into something if we do."

"Something that may not want running into, you mean," she retorted. "I'd rather take my chances on the water. At least I can swim."

"So start swimming then."

"You're not helping!"

Tjena couldn't help but laugh, agitating the frustrated bard even further. Grumbling disconsolately, Ginni retreated along the beach in high dudgeon, ransacking the underbrush for any kind of logs or vines to fashion into something that would float. Though boat-building did not fall under any general skill set of holvir, she figured they were small enough to make something work.

Her reward came swiftly. Buried in a thicket, under the broad leaves of a tropical tree, she spotted the prow of what was unmistakably a boat.

"Ah! No way! I wonder who left this here... must've been an old fishing boat or something that drifted from its mooring." She tugged as hard as she could, but the boat didn't budge. "Hey, Tjena, come help me with this," she cried, pushing branches out of her way and digging at the edge of the little canoe.

Tjena slipped in beside her and, with an almighty heave that sent the two holvir sprawling, tugged their prize free. Rising and dusting off the clinging brambles and wet sand, they moved forward to investigate the spoils of their effort.

And nearly tripped over each other in an attempt to run away.

"AGH! A BODY! A BODY?! HELP!" Tjena cried, clinging behind Ginni.

"Wait! Wait Tjena, it's... Faie Mother preserve us, he's moving. Quick, quick, help untangle him!"

The debris and the clinging vines didn't give up their prize easily. Ginni, thinking quickly, hummed a little tune of rejuvenation, reaching out for any vestige of life or spirit left in the forlorn figure. To her great surprise and relief, she sensed a small but definite return in the spark that clung to her voice and her words. Focusing on singing it free from stasis as she and her partner worked the body out of its trap, they finally managed to stabilize and animate the life again within him.

The boy, younger even than they, coughed weakly and stirred. Thick locks of gold hair framed his sunburnt face, bright enough to catch the light of the sun and shine with a lustre rivalling the metal itself. Ginni noticed with some curiosity that his features were striped- as in, literal shadows of dark discolouration sliced cleanly across his face, not unlike those of the fabled dire tigre.

Her song, accompanied by the low, coaxing sounds of Tjena's instrument, continued to nourish the feeble life returning to the child. With a hand gently under his head, she tried plying him with a skein of water. At first he lay still, comatose and insensible to their attempts at restoration. But finally his eyelids fluttered and he sipped, then began gulping desperately. Ginni had to pull the skein quickly from him before he shocked his dehydrated system. Both holvir supported him as he struggled to sit up.

"I'm... I'm alive. Blessed Sh'nia preserve me... the gift of life is granted again!" he cried softly, reaching out his hands toward the sun before focusing again on the two who saved him. "My good friends, I owe you the very air I breathe. To whom… do I offer payment for such a debt?"

The child's formality bewildered the bards. "Uh, well, this is Tjena, and I'm, well, I'm just Ginni."

Tjena whistled along the strings of their instrument, echoing her words with a sound of agreement that softened the heart of the boy even further.

"Your song... I've never heard anything like it. Not even the kulning of Sh'nia herself could whisper back a soul passed so far through the Doors of Death as mine had been. How ever did you do it?" he demanded.

"To be honest, we wanted your boat. The rest was just luck, I guess?" offered Tjena with a smile.

"My boat. You are welcome to my boat, my bounty, my life; my preservers! Take of me anything you will!" he replied magnanimously, before coughing weakly.

"Woah, slow down there sunchild. We're already handfasted. Appreciate the offer, though," giggled Ginni. "I think we're right in guessing that you're one of the Sun ilvir of Gamorre?"

He nodded, rubbing his yellow eyes with a striped arm. "'Sunchild'. I like that. It's close enough to my own name, even."

"Oh my gods, we didn't even ask. How rude of us. What is your name, then?" she asked hastily, offering up the skein again to the child while holding his wrist to test the pulse that, though sluggish still, quickened with the life restored to him.

"Siberne. Siberne of the Tigre, gentle Tjena and... just, Ginni. It is indeed a pleasure to meet you, for not many of your kind make it so far as to see my home. What brings you to the jungles of Gamorre?"

"Atosa. Well, the orgir asked, but it was Atosa," she replied.

She would have no accusation of trickery or intrigue

heaped on her and her partner. If the ilvir of Gamorre despised Atosa in their love for her sister, it wouldn't do to enter too far into their realm on her errand.

Luckily, they were spared any repulsion. Siberne beamed. "Ambassadors! What a lucky sunchild I am indeed! Left to perish on the lake, yet the very breath restored to me I owe to great and omnipotent ambassadors of the Sister of Silence!"

And to Ginni and Tjena's absolute horror, the boy actually bowed to them, the tip of his long, feline nose nearly touching the wooden planks of the floor of his boat.

"Oh no, no no no. Don't you start that. We're *holvir*. No one bows to us. Look, please, I know you're very appreciative and that you think you owe us your breath, or whatever, but honestly. We... we're atheists," she continued pathetically, hating the debasement of her race that so alienated them from the other goodly creatures of Faie. "We are blessed by no god, we just do what we can to make our way. And right now, what that means is we need to get to the Sun ilvir of Gamorre and summon Sh'nia."

Siberne opened his mouth as though to retort, but closed it at the look on the holvir's faces. The expression that crossed his own reminded Ginni so much of McKenna the little bard was hard put to stifle the tears welling up in her hazel eyes.

Though the holvir pair had travelled wide and travelled far, so few offered them the respect and honor their departed friends had gifted them unasked and unconditionally. And yet, here was a stranger, both of person and of race, willing to provide the same. The boy's candor touched Ginni to the heart, and she put out a hand to grip his shoulder.

"You honor us, truly you do. Now, will you please help two homeless holvir find the clerics of your city?"

"I will ask their bounty for you myself," he declared, his yellow eyes glittering benignantly.

Insisting, however, that the three of them make camp by the coast and offer Siberne a few more hours' rest, the three found themselves ranged before a small fire kindled as the sun began to dip toward the horizon.

"So, what happened to you, Siberne?" queried Tjena, weaving flowers plucked from the hedge into Ginni's coppery tresses. "How did you get stuck?"

"I was kulning. But I must have annoyed a vine dryad. One minute I was floating along the shore, the next I'd been knocked out cold and bound tightly by those brambles from which you pulled me free."

"'Kulning'. You've said that a few times now. What exactly is it?" they prodded.

"Ah! You are bards, are not you? You have no kulning in the northern lands?"

Tjena looked down at Ginni, who shrugged. "Evidently not, and we've been almost everywhere."

Siberne stoked the fire thoughtfully. "It's a song. Or I guess, the closest any animal noise could get to a song. Here, listen,"

From the boy's slender throat came a low, almost

imperceptible tone. As he breathed, the sound grew, vibrating the very air surrounding their camp. It warbled to the pitch of a jungle cat's scream and mellowed to the bass of a dire lion's roar. Ginni and Tjena were entranced by the elasticity of the boy's voice. And even more so when the forest around them echoed back his cries. Sharp trill of bat, the yelp of a yote, and even a gurgling splash of a kelpie accompanied Siberne's calls.

"That... was magical," breathed Ginni.

"Why don't you try it?" he offered. "It is a call of the wild. Focus on your spirit, the brightness and the form of the life within you. You say holvir have no gods, but you are alive, are you not? To every life there is a pair; a wild mate without the intelligence of our soulful races, but with the eyes that see and mouths that feast on this world's bounties. Search and find it, and then, call out to it."

Ginni closed her eyes, feeling the nature of Faie on which she called when she sang her ballads. Shifting that sense inward, closer and closer to the mud and rock that made up the holvir's own form, was a more difficult challenge. What did holvir have inside of them?

She opened her eyes. Siberne was frowning slightly at her. "You are so... careless of yourself. You seem to think yourself less than you are, Ginni. But if I can see the greatness in you," he smiled, a warm smile that lit the fire of Ginni's very being, "Then so should you."

Sighing, she looked at Tjena, who stared into the fire in the same kind of reverie they often assumed when they were blind. Calm, quiet, composed. A call of the wild, to the being within her that spoke not with words, but lived and breathed with the life of Faie. Attuned to these thoughts, she found herself reaching in for the warmth drawn forth by their ilvin guide.

A shape took form. A long, feathered tail, short, sharp beak, bright, beady eye. A hoarse caw, a raven's cry, more melancholy than music.

A low trill, the normal sound she made as she drew breath to sing her strongest, mellowed out into a chirrupping, rollicking tune. She whistled, she called, she chirped a sweet twitter and then- she sang.

The forest, that stirred to life at the kulning of the ilvin lad, burst forth in a torrent of chiming song as every bird in the surrounding area let loose a cry in response to her calls.

Tjena had pulled forth their instrument, plucking and twanging music to match his partner's voice, and the reverberations melted into a delightful melody accompanied by birdsong. The warmth that Ginni had noticed grew, strengthened, brightened as her voice echoed among the trees. Siberne laughed, a hearty sound that transmuted into the kulning of his own voice. Feral growls and purring roars blended in harmony with the holvir. At last, breathless, Ginni wound up the kulning with a sweet melody written by the eldest of her tribe.

"Far and gone, the wind blows
Swift and soft, but oh so strong
Fall on me, I'll catch you
We'll follow where they go
Far and gone, I see you
Silhouette against the sun
As strangers we part,
And friends we align
Oh so far and gone"

The yellow eyes of Siberne danced in merriment, pleased at his newfound friends' skill. "You are bards after all! What luck, what skill, what power you two have! And to join a kulning so seamlessly… the harmony of your souls must be strong indeed."

Your souls, linked as they are, stand testament to the unity of all our goodly creatures. Urtha's claim- that their bond's strength broke the Lich King's hold over Tjena, and that their seamless cohesion served as a testament to the unity of all goodly creatures, echoed from Siberne's words.

The animal sounds died away as the twilight deepened over the forest along the banks of the lake, and she realized the orghi may have been more right than she knew.

"Thank you for the lesson, Siberne," she said lightly, smiling at their host.

Then she laughed outright. Sun child, indeed. Once the sun disappeared entirely below the horizon, the boy had fallen deeply asleep.

"Shouldn't be too surprising. He almost died, after all." Tjena remarked at the sound of Siberne's soft snores.

"Who did you see, while kulning?" Ginni asked quietly, a soft expression in her light eyes.

"A raven. Just as you did," they replied, plucking softly at the strings of the naiti.

"Copycat."

Dawn lit the horizon in shades of blush and

mandarin. After crossing the lake and diving under a roaring, misting waterfall, their ilvin guide led them deeper into the jungle.

An absolute cacophony of color and sound surrounded them. Bright beasts with fangs longer than Ginni's arm; small, starry flowers creeping along vines that snagged on Tjena's vest; and the constant, flute-like kulning of the Sun ilvir summoning their queer animal companions.

"I hate to be trite, but your forest is so full of... life," she said, as they stepped nimbly along a narrow path lined with wildflowers waving overhead, bearing starry buds in purple and gold.

"It is the gift of the goddess. So long as we pay her homage, she gifts us with life. Every day brings new souls in the forest, though lately," he frowned suddenly, "their birth rate has seemed to drop. Almost as if the souls which renew them are simply... gone."

Ginni and Tjena exchanged looks. They knew about the chasm, where lay the souls bound by the Lich King's evil necromancy. If those souls were part of a cycle...

"They're trapped," replied Ginni. "It's a long story. Do you want us to tell it to you now, or should we save it for your Masters?"

He pondered for a moment, then shrugged. "I suppose I could wait. We are here."

He swept aside a canopy of vines hanging like a curtain, and the holvir gasped at the view he revealed.

Below them lay thousands of brightly colored domes

made of blown glass that sparkled and shone in the sun. Creatures of every size, shape, and color wandered among them, barking and cooing and crying and yelping. Threading through it all were the kulning sounds of the Sun ilvir, a wild race who stood almost thrice as tall as the holvi pair. All bore marks and designs upon their skin similar to Siberne's. Spots, stripes, speckles, patches- the curious designs made the ilvir almost blend in with the creatures following them. They stared curiously at the holvir, but greeted Siberne with a cry of joy and a rapturous hug or kiss. Consequently, the progress they made through the ilvin city was slow. But that wasn't a bother. There was so much to look at.

Ginni tried her kulning again, releasing a simple melody of little chirrups. Suddenly she found herself faced with no fewer than three peacocks, six sparrows, two eagles, and an inquisitive dire raven almost the same size as her. She laughed helplessly as the birds began to flutter and flap, causing a gale that whipped the other animals into a frenzy. They subsided at the sound of Tjena's instrument, cooing softly and dispersing almost as quickly as they had come. Save for the corvid, who hopped resolutely behind Ginni even unto the threshold of a giant blown glass structure.

"Welcome to the great Hall of Gamorre, home of Sh'nia's most devoted druids and the Guild of Sunbeam. Our High Druid, Master Llen, will hear your story," murmured Siberne, as he bowed the pair through the portal into the shimmering dome.

IX

CHAMPION

Panoplies of gold draped from every inch of the castle. Their vibrance and profusion stunned the monk as she solemnly made her way through its towering marble walls. In the distance she could hear shouts and cheers, though the hallways and chambers immediately surrounding her, surprisingly, stood empty. She wandered through the stone maze of the building until finally she traced the source of the din to a large, open field.

Before her lay quite an amazing sight. Stands surrounded a pitch, rippling green and gold under the midday sun. Ephemeral forms packed each riser, full of cheers and jubilance and resounding joy. She'd never seen a tourney in person before, only in the illustrated pages of aesir histories she'd stumbled on during her studies. The images often surprised her, and she'd skip over them, scoffing at the idea of such glamour, such romance, existing anywhere in the wide realms. Let alone existing exclusively for a series of battles where perfectly good warriors, for seemingly no reason at all, tried to seriously injure one another.

The jewel tones of the garb upon lord, lady, and in between, the luxurious materials used in constructing the pavilions, the lists, and the shining armor worn by the combatants, and the bright, boisterous music, cheering, and sighing proved beyond a doubt that her books had seriously understated the majesty of the event.

And to crown it all, upon a throne at one end curled the large, imposing form of a golden dragon. He smiled and smoked benevolently, gazing at the spectacle before them.

Within the lists, two figures sat astride powerful destriers who stamped and snorted, each prancing in their corner and waiting for the drop of the kerchief. McKenna watched in breathless fascination as they wheeled their magnificent steeds and, with an almighty crash, met with such force that the lances held by each shivered into infinitesimal splinters.

So perfect was the control over their horses it seemed as though the riders had no mount at all. A resounding cheer broke from the crowd as heartily as the lances of each rider. As far as McKenna could tell, the warriors' move had pleased the audience. They stood at the ready in the corners of the pitch, their squires fitting shields upon their shining pauldrons, and at the flutter of the kerchief they spurred into action to meet in the middle again.

This time, the knight whose shield bore a sigil of a hammer speared the shield of his opponent, bearing the sigil of a rose, upon his lance. Though both riders kept their seats, the draconic referee awarded the point to the lance of the hammer. The accolades of the audience grew louder as their champion circled the pitch, directing courtly bows at the lords and ladies filling the stands. He removed his helmet, and McKenna almost fainted from shock.

Nerveless fingers reached out. Trembling feet stumbled, then tripped, then ran. And a soundless voice made its cry heard above the din as she reached the gates barring the audience from the lists.

"Seth!"

In an instant she was in his arms as he vaulted over the fence from the back of his horse to land nimbly beside her. Her whole body felt as though it were on fire. Every nerve of hers felt every inch of him: the edges of his mail digging into her chest, his hand in her hair, his hips pressing against her thighs.

Of course this wasn't limbo, she remembered thinking giddily to herself. This was *heaven*.

He murmured something unintelligible into her dark coiled locks, cupping a hand to the small of her back as he drew her as close to him as possible. Audience or no audience, god or no god. She was here, in his arms, and he would defy anyone to take her from him.

Her scent- that intoxicating, ethereal aura that drew in his senses, filled him with bliss. *My goddess, who never gave up on me, who refused to leave me to die with disgrace for a legacy.* What a miracle she was.

After what felt like simultaneously an eternity and an instant, they broke apart. The audience around them had grown silent, watching bemusedly at the spectacle of their champion embracing this wild looking woman who appeared from nowhere on the edge of the pitch. Many turned toward the dragon, wondering how their heavenly host would react to such an interruption.

But the gaze of the dragon was invariably wise, and calm, and kind.

Seth grabbed her hand, and led her toward him.

Though she had seen Atosa's immortal form, still she felt dazzled by the godly being before her. Every inch of his shimmering scales scintillated with a might and such magnificence that she finally understood why so many fought in his honor. Not a single negligent or malignant sensation came near. He was all good, all benevolent, all glorious. As she dipped low in a bow to the mighty god, he held out a clawed foreleg, and bowed his own head before the pair.

The stands rippled in murmured shock. They had never seen or heard of such a display. A god, bowing before a mortal?

"These are no mere mortals," spoke Bahamut, his voice echoing through the courtyard and chastising the questioning crowd.

"McKenna, daughter of Atosa, though you honor my rival Malfaestus and not myself, you ventured forth to restore the soul of my greatest champion. You dwelt so long in caverns dark and dreary, seeing the light for a brief time only. And still you forwent your freedom to save your mother and the land upon which you walked. Your hero's journey has only just begun, my child," he said, blinking slowly at the monk clutched tightly to Seth's side. "You may be mortal now, but who knows? The gods are old. We turn away from the Material plane, our envy and desires blinding us to the needs of our people. What kind of gods are we," he continued, now looking directly at his champion, "who let our brightest heroes leave our light in favor of those who would defile our name and seek their own glory?"

Seth nodded deeply, his eyes locked to his god with as much determination as the arm he kept around McKenna's waist.

"And now, Champion," the dragon said, raising his voice to address the audience surrounding the pitch. "Have you chosen your prize, for the goodly feats of prowess this day that so marked you victorious?"

"I have," he replied, cupping a hand under McKenna's chin and sweeping her into a long, slow, lingering kiss.

She put a hand to his cheek, savoring the sensation, thankful that the gods did not let their omnipotence temper their benevolence.

"Our champion has chosen!" roared Bahamut, and the stands erupted in cheers and cries. "Look upon your mirror, monk, and it will guide you back through the Doors of Death."

She took a deep breath and held out the mirror, locking eyes first with Seth. Her look seemed almost shy, inquisitive. He was a champion, after all, enjoying the glories of his god in the afterlife. Would he give that up to return with her?

His golden gaze spoke more than words ever could. Together, they looked into the depths of the mirror, and spoke the runes that lined it.

"What do you always see in a mirror?"

"Yourself."

With a start, she realized the ground beneath her felt hard and gravelly, not like the soft turf upon which she'd walked for so long. Her eyes were screwed tightly shut. Opening them, she peered into the murky silent gloom.

And then she heard a cough.

"McKenna?"

She turned, and where had once been a cairn, built in honor of the fallen warrior, lay the recumbent form of Seth.

And he was breathing.

Her knees quivered as she sank beside him, crushing him in a bone-destroying hug. He coughed again, stroking her back and winding his fingers in the locks of her hair. For a moment she could barely breathe. The pain of losing him, though she had carried it with her on her entire journey through the Doors of Death, seemed almost as fresh as the first moment she'd held his lifeless form in her arms.

And the agony that, perhaps, she had been wrong to retrieve him in the first place made its venom known.

Finally they broke apart, dusting themselves off and adjusting to the environment of the chasm. The dissonance between the absolute silent stillness of the cavern floor, compared to the vibrance and cacophony of their voyage in the afterlife, almost disoriented McKenna more than her first steps in the pasture.

The dead would not let her forget them, either. As the feeling faded she began to hear with greater and greater clarity the whispers of those trapped souls buried in the rock around them. Guiltily, she tuned them out by burying her face in Seth's shoulder.

Just a moment, please. Let me enjoy him for a moment

longer.

"I'm not going anywhere, McKenna," he said, stroking a finger along her jaw. "We're in this together. All of it. Come what may."

She nodded, holding his hand against her face. Taking a deep breath, she pulled out the mirror and held it toward the walls. Sure enough, she could hear the whispers grow louder, see the motes of light grow brighter.

"My sister and I-" she started, then stopped at the look on his face. "Oh boy. You've missed a lot."

He laughed incredulously, then took a seat cross legged upon the fictile floor. She sat beside him, and briefly as possible recounted the events since the tremors and his plummet into the chasm- her mother's return, the restoration of Tjen's sight, her forgiveness of her sister, and the Lich King's rise. He flexed at that, clenching his teeth in a grimace.

"We can't fight him. He's almost a god himself."

"I think Atosa… I think she means to fight him. She said she would gather as many of the gods as she could get to destroy him. She said it was her fault, that the vacuum she left behind when she became mortal was what allowed him to rise in the first place."

He nodded in agreement, motioning for her to continue her story.

"I had to take Katarin with me. We had no idea what lay in wait on the other side of the Doors of Death. And she… she said she lost someone too." McKenna trailed off, remembering the stricken look in Katarin's eyes. "Razan. He must have sacrificed himself to the Lich King-"

"Good riddance," scoffed Seth.

"Be nice. I don't think he meant it. There was something strange… some sort of dissonance about him. I couldn't understand it," she screwed up her face in concentration, remembering the daemoric light of those blood red eyes. "And we couldn't find his soul, either. Not in Pasture."

"Yeah, well, you know what they say about the Cult of Naszer," he countered, still unwilling to sympathize with the dead assassin.

"Actually, I don't know, but do tell," she quizzed him.

"Ugh, please don't blame me for being the bearer of awful news," he replied cryptically. Then, seeing the inquisitive look in her eyes refused to quell, he sighed. "They consort with daemor."

"Oh, Ginni told me about that. But I don't really get it."

Seth cringed, then continued. "Razan, most likely, has literal daemoric blood."

She knitted her brows in confusion, and then the dawning look of comprehension that descended upon her features drew a deep belly laugh from the paladin. She wrinkled her nose in disgust and smacked his arm. "Ugh! You can't be serious! You're serious? How does that even happen?"

"Nobody knows, and nobody, I'm assuming, is brave enough to ask," he replied with mock solemnity.

She mimed retching, and he laughed harder. "My sister... and my sister travelled through the Doors of Death for *that*! She's insane. Well, I mean, I kind of already knew she was, but now I REALLY know. But wait," she stopped, realizing the implications of what Katarin and Seth had said regarding the mysterious assassin. "If the Lich King has his heart, and part of his soul is daemoric, would he even be able to find Pasture? Do you think maybe he... he's lost to the Abyss?"

"I have no idea. I guess it depends on the will of the gods, and the measures he took to establish his personhood over his heritage. I don't hold out much hope," the paladin said frankly, his words still tinged with disgust.

McKenna pursed her lips, not so ready to assign such a permanent dissolution of the love of her sister's heart.

Their journey had really given her a measure of empathy toward the sorceress, and she hoped they would meet again. Perhaps if Katarin rejoined Sethisto-

"Oh, that's something else I forgot to mention. We met your father."

He started, staring into her face. "My father? How? I..."

His face downcast, his words came out no more than a whisper. "I couldn't find him in Bahamut's palace, and I... I feared the worst. I feared the nature of his death... meant that Bahamut disowned him, that he would be lost in limbo forever."

McKenna remembered the man's words about the souls who remained in pasture, her blessing and her sister's touch bestowing a power unrecognized.

Unfinished business, he said.

"I… don't really know if I can answer that, Seth," she said quietly, her head bowed. "But I don't think he minded, really," she smiled at the thought of his quixotic questions and answers while in their company. "I think he really enjoyed learning all there was to know about the realm of the Doors of Death."

"Sounds like him," chuckled Seth.

"He also said he was proud of you," she continued, smiling into his face. "Just like I did. The mirror told the truth. He believed in you, and was thankful you saved yourself from his fate."

Seth bowed his head as though in silent prayer. McKenna, her hand in his, closed her eyes alongside him in mute gratitude that she had the opportunity to meet the person who had so shaped the man his son would become.

She felt a finger stroke her cheek, and saw his golden eyes gazing upon her reverently.

A happy sigh escaped her. He came back. He came back with her.

"So what's next then? Where is your sister?" he asked.

"She stayed behind. This chasm," she said, placing a

hand on the wall of rock, "is saturated with souls trapped in the Lich King's thrall. As long as he exists, he can keep them here or steal them from Pasture and use them to fuel his army of ilmaurte. But… we discovered that if I summon the souls into the mirror, Katarin's blessing on the other side will allow them to ascend, free from his clutches."

The size of the chasm, the pressure of all the entrapped souls, nearly overwhelmed her. "But there are thousands and thousands here. I don't know if I can even free them all by myself. If we face the horde on the field of battle, and we destroy his army, his hold will weaken and the souls can be freed of their own accord. Plus, he has to have some kind of… of refuge, now that he's left Naijor. There must be someone else he's controlling now that Katarin is safe. But where? Who?"

Seth thought for a moment, then sighed. "There's only one place I can think of. We have to travel to Lianor, and convince the guilds to turn out the Cult of Naszer."

"Ew. You mean the group that mates with monsters?" she replied, disgusted.

"I really have no other suggestion. Naszer is the only guild with the power and the ability to reach into the Abyss. The Lich King is a daemoric presence. Which means either they can find him, or it's clear they summoned him. But don't worry," he said, kissing the tip of her nose. "I find you far more attractive than any daemor."

"Oh, that's reassuring. I can put your soul back, you know."

He laughed and swept her to her feet. Together, they

began the long ascent to the top of the chasm, ready to face what peril or triumph the day may bring.

"While I have you here…" he said, when they'd crested the lip of the chasm and returned to the sweeping prairie beyond, "there aren't any, you know, burly durgirn significant others I should worry about… should I?"

Amazed, she turned to study the paladin as he shifted uncertainly from one foot to the other. She couldn't tell whether or not he was joking.

"Seth… I can't return home from a beard quest until I grow a beard. Why would it matter?"

"I just, you know… wondered if…" he started to redden, and she noticed his eyes wandering along the wide curves of her body. Suddenly she understood, and whispered a number into his ear.

The brightness and heat emanating from his face rivalled the stars that floated mischievously above them. While he choked on his words, McKenna, breathless from laughter, rolled on the grass beside him. When she started gasping for air, he smacked her playfully on the thigh, and with difficulty she swallowed her hearty laughter and sat up. Giggling and wiping her eyes, she turned to the paladin whose crimson visage had faded by now to a more becoming hue.

"If I'd known that would be your reaction, I wouldn't have asked," he huffed fretfully. She bit her lip quickly and placed a hand on his knee.

"Asafolk, I swear to Atosa… you act like you're the only beings to walk these realms! How do you think the rest of us are made, Paladin?!"

He shrugged defensively. "Once you're in a guild, you don't just go wandering. And I mean, you're not exactly... I mean, you weren't..."

"Born?" she said, with an eyebrow raised quizzically at him. "I can assure you, I absolutely was, Seth." She settled against him, trying to not get distracted by his golden gaze, illuminated as it was by the moon and stars. "Atosa became mortal, in every sense of the word."

"How do you know? I thought you were taught about her metaphorical children," he countered.

"For starters, Katarin mentioned it, while debating whether or not we would even be considered mortal. And as for the metaphors... durgir are pretty particular about the myths they pass down. They had no real proof that her children were real. Pabble may have suspected who I was, but she didn't exactly leave a note. Plus..."

She got a faraway look in her eyes as she thought of her adoptive family, and he sought her fingers, "I think he may have been trying to protect me. Give me as normal a life as possible, let me come into my own, as I would."

"And that involved pretending you were just a tall duergi?" he pressed. "Doesn't that seem a little... I don't know... manipulative?"

McKenna pursed her lips, unable to answer in so many words. She'd had her battles with her identity already in the time they'd spent on this adventure. But she could tell Seth truly just worried about her, and about her finding a place in the world he knew.

"I think perhaps we both have had our own sort of manipulative upbringing, in one way or another. Things are never as they seem, when they're told by people of authority to those of ignorance. You know?"

He nodded, but seemed unconvinced.

Regardless, she wasn't about to let the opportunity pass by. The prairie unrolled silent before them, the chasm from which they climbed innocuous despite the arduous journey they'd just experienced passing through it. She swept a lock of his hair behind his ear, exposing the rigid line of chin that never could quite fully relax, even in her presence. Her sudden movement did nothing to reduce that; she felt tension ripple through the man's figure at her impulsive caress.

"I saw the way you and James looked at each other. I know you're no less a novice to this than I," she whispered, sliding a hand along his waist and teasing the clasp of his belt buckle. He exhaled and grinned, but made no move; enjoying the closeness of her, disciplining every muscle in his body to absolute stillness. The sudden change in his breathing and the slow swelling below his belt was all the encouragement he would give her.

Her hands paused their exploration to undo several strategic knots in the garment she had tied haphazardly around her. The pelt, clean, but worn from its time on the road, fell away; revealing the woman as she had looked when she walked from the mines of Mount Oer.

He bit back a gasp. He'd caught sight of her on occasion, when they'd passed enough water to bathe in- she wasn't shy- but somehow, surrendering herself like this, disrobing for him, and he alone, struck him with a pang and a longing he'd never felt before.

He caught her scent and released himself to her, to the body and fiery soul that danced upon him before the world.

A soft breeze rippled the grass that hid them. She paused, feeling the primal energy of the land and the sky meet with their own, a glow of spirit communing with spirit. Together they stared into the sparkling abyss, feeling the blessing of the life they were granted again. Together, like this, they could conquer anything. As a shudder from the tips of her toes to the crown of her curly head began to unroll itself within her, she could feel the release of his own control. She cried out against his mouth, her voice wavering with pleasure, and she felt his hands tighten against the small of her back and at the nape of her neck. The moment went fast; the moment lasted a lifetime.

Who needed death? Who called on gods?

She placed her hands softly against his chest while the aftershock, the sudden release of muscles held too taut, passed through them and left him gasping for air. Climbing from his lap, she rested his head against her chest, stroking him softly and whispering words unheard into his hair.

There was nothing in the form she held that she feared anymore. Who would have thought the first person she met outside the mines would come to mean so much? That despite the difference of their paths and the shape of their goals, they could choose to walk them together?

She may not know how to ask the question, but he would always await her answer.

X

UNION

Relaxed against a brittle moss-covered hollow of stone, her languid, scintillating form quivered anxiously. Few would consider the blood red sky or misty chill of death permeating every inch of this place - the Abyss, the daemoric Plane, whatever name it took - idyllic, yet it filled Lady Astore's senses with undeniable bliss. Though mortal, the daemoric energy granted her by her ancestry suffocated with every excess moment spent on the Material plane, and expanded eagerly as soon as she set foot in the sulfuric realm of her birth. The Cult of Naszer insisted that all the most prestigious of their followers gave birth here, certain that it made their sacerdhossa more powerful, their control over daemor summoned to the Material plane more consuming.

They were wrong more often than right. Astore had been an exception.

With her, the Cult of Naszer had risen from ignominy and impotence to the deadly powerhouse that existed today. Despite the disappointment she suffered with her firstborn's defection, she found ample compensation in the promising young mages she'd raised since. And no power in all the realms could stop her from trying to beget another heir. Currently, every nerve of her body sang out in pain and pleasure from her infernal union with Makarh, yet she already ached with longing for the dread daemor's return.

The walls of the Abyss hissed and hummed with the thrill of thriving evil creatures. All knew better than to disturb her. She may be a mortal, and normally a denizen of the Material plane, but her very spirit and magic emanated an energy not to be trifled with. Even a daemor genirae, passing by lazily overhead and spotting her succulent naked figure reposed invitingly, knew that to descend unless at her own express invitation would invite the wrath of her powers, rending the very fiber of his daemoric soul as painful as a dousing of Celestial dew.

The beast continued on and the sacerdhosa, eager to resume her licentious fornication, sought again her intended mate's vile and vigorous form. She settled into a state of suspended animation, sensing it finally amidst a horde of chattering daemoric creatures with whom he was embroiled, augmenting and organizing them as the army to accompany his inglorious summons to the Material plane. She sighed in frustration, for she knew his occupation would last for some time, and cast a wider net for some other willing sport.

The return shocked her upright. How could it be?

Out there, in the mists and smoke, floated the blood of her own body, the child of her own womb.

She cast an enchantment towards the daemoric spirit, summoning him to her side. To her surprise, the spell worked.

As he approached, her eyes widened in the shock of recognition. Livid veins latticed his normally smooth, invariable black skin. The rust colored eyes that had pierced McKenna's vision were blood red, lit in a perpetual frenzy of evil and spite. The hands, so skilled with blade and soft with Katarin's touch, were topped with talons, streaked with the blood of underworldly creatures that dared to cross his path, to challenge his might.

"How curious. Despite his protests, he had the making of a true daemor after all," she muttered to herself.

The idea piqued her curiosity- while her affinity for the daemoric transcended that of all her clan, she still only possessed the merest trace of daemor blood. And though she could mate with the filthy creatures, their differing biology made reproduction impossible. The best she could do was absorb their essence, disseminate their power and carry it back with her to the material world while she found a more compatible mate. And so far, the experiment had only worked once.

Had she actually managed to produce a living daemor?

Lady Astore had to quickly stifle a questionable feeling of arousal at the vision. He was *perfect*. But she understood with sudden clarity, what he had become. No flicker of animation, no quip or personality, remained of the aesir he had once been. He had flung himself whole into the pyre as a sacrifice to the Lich King's rise.

But it looked like the only thing the Lich King needed was his heart.

Astore watched as her prodigal son stared her down, impassive, awaiting instruction. *I could make him do anything I wanted. I could make him bury himself in me and slit his own throat. I wouldn't have to waste a single ounce of energy to do it, either - he is of my blood, my bone, my body. He is mine entirely, and he will make sure my will succeeds in this*

He bowed deeply. "No reason to hand them all the cards. With your leave, I will prepare a missive and deliver the information myself."

"Granted. There's no need for you to hang around so much as you do already. Alert the sacerdhossa. We mustn't lose any time. The novitiates, as best they can, must be prepared to take orders and ascend. Makarh keeps his end of the bargain, and we would do well to keep ours."

He eyed the sparking brazier, his face dispassionate. But knowing her prowess and her affinity with the filthy Abyssinians, he simply bowed and left the apartment.

A seeping, insidious darkness filled the space in his absence. She turned, and behind her appeared a swirling blackness that slowly resolved into their master himself- the Lich King.

She swept into a low bow. "My lord. Your generals are prepared."

"Generals?" he hissed, drawing out the sibilance of the unexpected plural. "How is it that you bring me two?"

Astore, without raising her head, let out an Abyssal chant. The daemor Razan stepped forward, impassively studying the vile being that inhabited his mortal body.

"Lady Astore, you surprise me. Is this him, then?" chuckled the Lich King, as he circled them. "The pitiful soul who cast himself into the flames for me to devour?"

Astore hesitated before answering. She had no idea

battle. Oh, my child, you tried to escape your fate, she thought with a malevolent grin, *but you ended up right back where you started. Pitiful.*

"Razan," she whispered, the evil grin matched on both faces. "Won't this turn the tables."

The grumbling form of Cleric Qu-Lan could be seen shuffling down the spiral steps, just as Lady Astore stepped from the brazier. She glanced around carelessly for her discarded robes, and he held them out to her while absently gazing into the flames of the brazier.

"Was your journey a success, then?" He asked disinterestedly, noting the bruises on her neck and casual lacerations visible on her dark flesh as she slipped the silken garments over her bare skin.

She flashed him a feral grin. "Makarh is eager to once again taste the joys offered by our Material plane with his hellish army, if that's what you mean."

Qu'lan nodded, arms crossed in study at the figure before him and the brazier behind her. Lady Astore's fiendish tastes in pleasure aside, she was the most powerful sacerdhosa boasted by their cult. If she could reach and ignite the fury of the daemor genirae, the Lich King's might would be unparalleled.

"Most excellent. I hoped the news of your son's sacrifice had not impaired your abilities. I see you speak true when you say he means nothing."

Her eyes glittered, and again that grin curled her seductive features, casting in them a look almost repulsive in its sadism. "Oh, good Cleric, that is where you're wrong. My son means everything to me."

She hissed an incantation, the runes surroundin[g the] brazier sparking to life. With a clap of fire that swir[led] around the cleric's robes, he could feel the energies [she was] summoning. He raised a hairless eyebrow in intere[st. She] was summoning a true daemor genirae, not just a f[iendish] imp or demodand, with almost as little effort as if s[he] were chanting a simple spell of illumination.

Only years of strict discipline and utter respect [for the] powers she commanded kept him rigid, and stopp[ed him] from interrupting her cast. And an actual gasp of s[urprise] escaped him when the unmistakable form of Raza[n] stepped from the brazier, emanating a pure evil au[ra that] rivaled even the might of Makarh.

"You see?" she whispered, as the cleric's gaze [turned] to the daemor genirae. "He's perfect."

Cleric Qu'lan couldn't help but agree. Lady A[store] had outdone herself this time. She was hissing at [the] figure in the guttural language of the Abyss, ensu[ring the] summons bound him to her irrevocably. Though [it] sapped the life force of the summoner, drawing fr[om to] power the energy necessary to walk the Material [plane,] her control over Razan was effortless. He wonder[ed if] their daemoric heritage, or simply the bond of blo[od they] shared, made the summons so simple and irrevo[cable.] She whispered something else to the daemoric pr[ince] and he melted into the shadows.

"I see. I shall see to it Master Gareth is inforn[ed of] Makarh's readiness. He'll be pleased to know of [your] progress."

Astore stroked her chin thoughtfully. "Will [you tell] him what else you've discovered?"

how both body and soul could exist simultaneously, and an edge of doubt troubled the normally audacious and assured sacerdhosa. Had she erred in summoning her son forth?

"He will prove a fine warrior," she said, confident despite her misgivings. "Half my blood runs through his veins. I need give him no more life to sustain his march upon the Material plane than when I birthed him so long ago."

A second daemor genirae is just the edge I needed. Our Lich King has no power over me. I know he resents it, and resents that he is reduced to manipulating those other weak fools. But he knows too that, without our strength, his own would be overpowered easily by those goddesses of Faie. Without the Abyssinian legion, his own horde is nothing.

Silence echoed in the empty halls, the clamor of daemor clawing for release still yet to descend. Chaos balanced on the razor sharp edge of the knife. Her face, impassive, cold as the blood that ran sluggish in the daemor genirae's veins.

You will not so easily manipulate this power I have sacrificed everything to wield, god or no.

"Hmm. I hope you are right, Lady Astore. The daemor Makarh will be difficult enough to direct. I would hate for your spirit to be torn apart and tossed in pieces into the Abyss by these hellish creatures for which you have such marked... taste."

She cast a cold, but provoking, glance at him. He chuckled.

"Turn not your tastes to the omnipotent gods,

mortal," he spat. "It would be your undoing."

With that, he vanished.

A low growl emanated from Razan. Lady Astore studied him for a moment, then dismissed him back to the labyrinthine bowels below the guild. While she held seamless, unchallenged control over his essence, the thousands of daemors that made up Makarh's legion posed another challenge entirely. They could not afford to move too quickly, not when their own guild numbered so few. Though she despised the assumption of authority the Lich King posed, she couldn't help but acknowledge his warning. She breathed a sigh of relief, staring deep into the smouldering embers upon the dais.

"As if there were any pleasure you could give me that I could not give myself," she muttered, and with a snap of her fingers extinguished the brazier.

XI

WHISPERS

The ghostly corridors swam before the novitiates' tired eyes. Most of the rest of the cathedral's occupants had long since retired to the barracks and sleep. Yet here they were again, on the familiar path from the sparring hall to the library. Arya could barely lift her arms.

"Ouch. My bruises have blisters," groaned Layne. "Is that even possible? Look at it, do you think it's gonna get infected?"

She held her palm out hopefully toward Arya, who lifted an eyebrow. "What? You want me to kiss it better?"

"Maybe. Or at least take pity and not make me do grout this time."

"You should've thought of that before you tried throwing a hammer at my shield."

"What!! You blocked it, didn't you?" the red haired girl laughed, jostling Arya's aching bicep. She hissed and wiggled her arms weakly out of the girl's reach.

Some of the drills the girls practiced on each other, late into the night when all the masters and most of the other novitiates left for bed, would raise eyebrows and almost certainly condemnation.

But Arya hadn't been the annoying little sister of one of the guild's greatest masters for nothing. She pressed drill after drill, balancing her favored wooden practice sabre lightly, jabbing it expertly at every opening provided by Layne's wide, sweeping hammer thrusts. While Layne could outshoot every single member of the Guild, Arya's fencing and melee skills outranked her at every turn.

Arya counted herself lucky they matched up so well. Most of the others either snubbed them or found themselves cornered by bigger and meaner novitiates if they didn't. The ranks seemed to have an unspoken alignment- while they all paid lip service to Elgitha and her divine aids, Master Gareth commanded the true power among novitiate and master alike. Arya's notoriety of favored and family did her no good, and the general eccentricity and disgrace of the citizens of Dragon's Hill isolated Layne.

She wouldn't let it bother her. Being raised for diplomacy, she begrudgingly admitted to herself, gave her more of an edge that she realized.

Eventually she'd thank her mother for that.

"Come on, we're almost there."

Layne looked around confusedly. "How can you tell? Wasn't there a vase here before?"

Both inspected the empty and dimly lit plinth. It took them a couple moments to process, realizing with a start the whole hallway, once richly decorated in all matter of ornamental weapon, tapestry, and priceless pottery, stood nearly bare around them. Layne ground her teeth.

"Still stealing from their own hallowed halls. What low will they sink to next?" she growled. Arya knitted her brows in concentration, muttering a spell over the few items remaining.

"Layne, this is weird... these things left behind, they have no attunement to Bahamut. They're blank. Everything else," she motioned around them, hands vibrating lightly as they hovered over the vacant plinth, "these were all blessed items. Why would they take just the gifts from our god?"

"Maybe they want to make sure he can't see inside anymore," Layne muttered caustically.

"Is that how those work?" Arya thought to herself out loud.

It struck a discordant note deep within her, and an almost overpowering feeling of sadness came with it. The god knew. The god was not pleased.

But he was just a god. What could he do?

Tears sparkled in her summer storm eyes. She clenched her teeth and swallowed hard. A hand found its way into hers, and she could see the depths of empathy looking back from Layne's own green gaze.

"Come on. Let's get to the library," was all she said. Arya sniffed and nodded, and the two took off down the darkened hallway.

Less than a moon left before both were elevated to the rank of Master and here they were, stuck spending evening after evening buried under dusty tomes and draining housework, elbows deep in suds and dust like fledgling novitiates.

"Aren't you supposed to be Elgitha's favorite? Why do we have to keep doing this?" whined Layne.

"Elgitha's not allowed to have favorites. She hasn't spoken to me for almost an entire solstice. Though to be fair, I don't think she's spoken to anyone. There's so much going on right now, so many rumors… and she probably has to be careful with which ones she chooses to listen to and share," replied Arya thoughtfully, unwilling to doubt the omnipotence of their enigmatic Grand Master.

She had buried herself particularly deep in a crinkly and worn old scroll, training her focus on the inconspicuously blank margins running down the sides of the script. Years and years of notes scribbled by past novitiates lay hidden, effaced from the pages by simple persuasion spells. And there was nothing Arya loved more than to read the words of those who'd gone before.

These spells were second nature to most guild novitiates. Good candidates for paladins were born with an innate affinity for persuasion and charisma magic, and those who weren't, either learned quickly or became squires instead. Making the scribbled notes vanish from the sight of future readers was a fairly amateur spell, and one that took a trained and intuitive mage to reveal.

Of course, persuasion magic was second nature to Arya, who'd had it used on her since she was an infant. And spent her childhood training to resist it.

This particular text showed ancient paladin oaths that had been buried for years in the dusty old library. Considering the wear and tear of the vellum, Arya could only assume some of her bolder forebears tried most of them, and so wasn't shocked when her own brother's crabbed scrawls appeared among the others. Rolling further down the scroll, she came to a small text conspicuous only in the fact that it had no notes whatsoever. Frowning, she focused harder, training her persuasive powers to uncover any whisper of magic, frown deepening as nothing revealed itself.

This can't be possible. This oath isn't... oh, here we go. Her face relaxed as a faint outline, Seth's writing, again appeared on the page.

"By request of Grand Master Elgitha, I have cleared all previous commentary from this oath. No paladin in the history of the guild has been able to successfully call down this power- and on pain of excommunication, none else shall try."

Arya snorted at the formality of the words, scribbled as they were almost incomprehensibly by her brother's hasty hand. Curiosity peaked, she reviewed the contents of the oath itself. Though short, its implied power slowly became more and more alarming. As Arya began to experience dawning comprehension into why Elgitha might have banned this particular oath from practice, another note revealed itself in the margin.

"I bet Arya could do it."

Hands suddenly limp, the scroll dropped ignominiously to the table. The noise caught Layne's attention, who looked over at Arya in concern as she tried to subdue her sharp, shallow breathing.

The girl cradled her chin on Arya's shoulder, knitting her eyebrows over the painstakingly difficult text. "This is... you can turn into a what, now?"

Arya puffed, disturbing the soft lock of hair that fell across her forehead; a tiny sigh of relief. Layne couldn't read her brother's note. "If I told you, you'd be mad."

"What, it's not like you're going to try it or anything."

The novitiate remained silent.

"Arya."

She laughed, then rolled the scroll back up. "What! Like any Master in a thousand years could call down a blessing strong enough for this oath."

I bet Arya could do it.

She winced, then continued. "Let alone a couple of novitiates so lowly they spend each night elbows deep in dust and dirt on the floor of the least used room in the Cathedral."

"Well, at any rate, we'll be the cleanest Masters the guild has ever seen. Probably the most well-read, too. Do you think anyone has even opened some of these?" Layne struggled with a book sealed shut by the pressure of the others surrounding it, and huffed as she tugged at the stubborn binding. Finally giving it up as a bad job, she left it on the table, idly browsing the rows for a more forgiving read.

After scanning the oath one more time, committing as much of it to memory as she could, Arya took a last look at her brother's old handwriting, then sighed and rolled the scroll back up, sealing it into one of the many beeswax tubes that lined the walls of the library. Over the course of her novitiate, Arya had found her way into the contents of almost all of them. Much to the annoyance of Layne, who preferred to simply pull them out and put them back into the cubbyhole while dusting.

"I'm never trading back for grout so don't even bother asking," Arya declared once in response to Layne's cry of protest. After a long night of scrubbing the stone floor and ready to call it a night, she'd looked up to see Arya buried in a pile of uncapped scrolls, dusty honeycomb of bookshelf untouched behind her.

"You just don't like chapped hands because you think it affects your marksmanship," Arya jibed back.

That had been ages ago, Arya mused to herself as she tucked the scroll back on its shelf and returned to her bucket and rags. Several hours of silence crept by, nothing interrupting their solitary vigil in the lonely library.

Finally, Layne groaned and crumpled dramatically next to Arya. "We should call it a night. Everyone has to be asleep by now. How much longer do you think we have to stay in here for-"

"Shh!" hissed Arya, holding up a warning finger at her friend. An unfamiliar sound echoed through the library's high ceilings. Footsteps, and the glittering clangor of maille and mithril.

The two stared at each other, uncertain who at this late hour would be browsing for a bedtime story. They both paled as a familiar voice reached their ears. Master Gareth, accompanied by an unknown figure.

Their situation seemed perilous, and they weren't sure what to do. Master Gareth must have known they were in there. It was he, after all, who constantly assigned the two novitiates to this most despised duty in the first place. It wasn't even hard to figure out why. The marksmanship of Layne and the intellectual and strategic prowess of Arya constantly eclipsed the Master's son, Clint. And were there not even a question of Elgitha's preference for the T'ssama siblings, Gareth and Seth's rivalry had been legendary amid the halcyon days of their own novitiate. Arya, while loath to blame Clint for the prejudice of his father, chafed under the biased treatment each received under the paladin's training. And since that day in the lists, she thought guiltily to herself, she really didn't bother pulling her punches with him either.

Footsteps, and then the drag of chairs against the wooden floor, echoed from the vaulted ceilings. She winced. Those scratches would take ages to buff out.

"Are you certain this chamber is empty, Master Gareth?" spoke the unfamiliar voice, with the faintest hint of a lisp slurring his words.

"Hmph. Those obnoxious brats probably snuck out long before now. But you're right, I'll check," Gareth replied, subsiding into a muttered incantation.

Acting quickly on impulse, Arya whispered her own standing meditational prayer to Bahamut, a spell to suppress her and Layne's aura and render them innocuous as the shelves of books among which they hid. She heard a similar whisper behind her, and smiled at the thought of her friend so seamlessly echoing her thoughts.

The oath worked. The proddings of the Master's incantation hovered around them, then dissipated as it sensed nothing amiss.

"Clear, then. I should have known they'd sneak off

early. I'll punish them for it later. But now," the chair and table creaked as he leaned forward, "to your most urgent news from the other side."

The stranger unrolled a parchment, fiddling with the scroll and whispering his own incantation to reveal the words hidden upon it. Behind the stacks of sizable lexicons, neither Arya nor Layne could see the parchment. Luckily, they didn't have to. The man read it aloud.

"That goddess-child of the durgir, McKenna- she has returned to the Material plane. She seems to be heading for the company of that pathetic holvir tribe living on the banks of the Styckes."

"Good. The perfect cover for the advance of the horde," murmured Gareth. Arya raised an eyebrow at Layne. McKenna, responsible for the ilmaurte invasion?

"So that is the line the guilds take, still?" The whispery man spoke with a shrug in his voice.

"Yes. While it was easy enough to point the finger of blame to her sister for their release, the ilvir of Moonbow are not so easily silenced. They know, from their own seances, that the princess remains in limbo between the Material and Celestial Plane. The Lich King's hold on her is broken, but she served her purpose well," he hissed quietly.

Layne's grip on Arya's shoulder tightened. Did they say Lich King?

"But her sister roaming free on the Material plane, and the disruptions of Atosa among the pantheon, makes a perfect cover for Makarh's legion." He paused briefly, nonchalantly picking at the side of the missive. "Speaking of which, there are rumors she did not return alone. Your rival, that disgraced paladin, accompanies her."

A scoff drowned out the stranger's soft fidgeting sounds. "Impossible. Seth T'ssama must be dead. If he were not, Makarh would still face banishment from this plane, yet he has been summoned by Lady Astore herself. While I wouldn't put it past the cult of Naszer to try and break the bonds of banishment, there is no mortal strength on Faie with that power."

There was a pause. Arya could imagine the man shrugging, not confident enough to question the veracity of the rumors.

She could hear the rushing blood of her beating heart. Seth was alive?

"Perhaps Bahamut's blessings are more potent than you realize, Master Gareth. There is no telling what the gods are capable of. I just thought you should be aware. Elgitha is old, and she has ever favored the goodly family of T'ssama. It wouldn't do to have both siblings challenge your son's nomination, would it?"

Gareth grunted in distaste, but summarily dismissed the warning with a wave of his muscular hand.

Luckily, both women had the presence of mind to keep absolutely silent. But that didn't stop Layne's eyes from expanding to the size of silver coins, and Arya's jaw from dropping nearly to the floor. Clint Achor, nominate for Grand Master? Who was Gareth kidding?

"Whether this is true or not, nothing will absolve his disgrace within the guild. It's been years since his banishment. And meanwhile, Elgitha grows no younger.

She waits to nominate the T'ssama girl, but if she dies before the child reaches the level of Master, I alone possess the influence and rank necessary to make a nomination in her stead. Seth T'ssama is too late," he hissed, "and too weak, to save his legacy from dishonor or his sister from the eternal servitude that awaits her."

The low growl emanating from the girl beside her could be felt, rather than heard. The force of Layne's deadly gaze as Arya turned to regard her nearly knocked her flat. She thanked all her lucky stars that her friend's crossbow lay locked in the guild armory. The woman looked ripe for murder. Though touched by her friend's loyalty, the fierce expression slightly terrified her too.

"It grows late. I must return, the Lady does not like to be kept waiting." Again the chairs screeched against the floor as both figures rose, their bustling noises drowning out their final exchange.

"Go forth with speed, Qu'lan. It is only a matter of time before the Lich King can unleash the full might of his army. And with any luck, our goodly guild will be there to pick up the pieces that lay in the path of their destruction."

Without further words, they both swept from the chamber. The sound of the library door swinging shut broke the stillness in which the two women sat, dumbfounded by all they had just heard.

My brother is alive.

Layne whispered another spell, deadening the noise of their steps and breathing. Pulling Arya to her feet, they left the library to regain the darkness and privacy of their own bunks.

"A Lich King. So the rumors were true," muttered Layne. "But who are these sisters? What do they have to do with Atosa?"

Arya puzzled this over for a minute. "McKenna. She travelled with my brother. If she is sister to Princess Katarin, that makes her a child of Atosa as well." Suddenly the pieces fell into place. "She… I can't believe it. She must have entered the Doors of Death. She must have gone to bring my brother back."

Excitement raced through her, elevating her pulse and her breathing. Layne knitted her eyebrows, putting a hand on the girl's shoulder.

"Arya, you have to calm down. We don't know for sure. And besides, we've got a bigger problem. Why is Gareth working with this... this Lich King? What about him nominating Clint for Grand Master?"

Arya rolled her eyes. "He's got no chance in Hel. I mean, it's not just Elgitha who nominates Grand Masters, right? You have to be confirmed by Bahamut, and there is no way in all the realms that Bahamut has even noticed Clint is a paladin, let alone would bless him as Grand Master."

They were silent for a moment. Master Gareth had been the center of a controversy legendary in the guild's recent history. While on a quest with seven of the guild's greatest Master paladins, all but he had disappeared without a trace. The Master had returned to the Cathedral, mute and barely breathing, and once restored to his faculties unable to remember the events that lead to the disappearances- and presumed deaths- of the Guild Masters. Though even then he'd made more rivals than friends among his peers, Grand Master Elgitha pardoned any accusations and allowed the man to maintain his status. His reputation had suffered ever since. But to collude with a clearly evil entity, no matter what his reasons, threw up a huge red flag to the discerning women.

"We could just be biased. I mean, he hates us, but he seems to have plenty of other loyal followers..." Arya tried to reason. "Maybe he's trying to learn more about the undead horde?"

Layne snorted, raising an expressive eyebrow at Arya's equivocation of the Master they both despised. "Would make more sense he's trying to undermine Elgitha's power by trying to ally with this Lich King, so he can destroy all the ilmaurte and look like a hero."

Biting her lip and frowning, Arya had to admit a measure of what her partner said was true. Master Gareth wasn't talking like an innocent man. Secret meetings in unused corners of the Cathedral bespoke more intrigue than a righteous campaign.

Elgitha's bitter words rang in her ears, and the empty mournful halls of the Cathedral swam before her. The guild had drifted far from its goodly course, in bids for greater power and influence in their ever-evolving society. "My brother..."

"Is dead, Arya. Has been dead for like three years now." Layne returned bluntly.

"But..." she trailed off, desperately recalling the details of the conversation. "That man said he'd returned from the realm of death..."

"Yes, but don't you remember? They seemed to think that because they summoned this… this daemor, whatever his name was, means he's not alive."

"Makarh." The name filled Arya's heart with a deep, deadly loathing. The quest on which Seth had gone, to slay the daemor rampaging through the goodly towns of Beasun, nearly took him from her. Though he managed to defeat Makarh and banish him to the Abyss, the encounter left a physical and mental scar his sister didn't think would ever completely go away. "I'm not so sure about that. Seth *did* die, so if the Cult of Naszer managed to summon Makarh before he returned, technically that broke the banishment, right?"

Her friend pursed her lips and made a grunt of neither agreement nor dissuasion.

"I don't get it, Layne. My brother could be alive. Why are you so against this?" Arya whispered, not able to understand her friend's hesitation.

Layne paused for a moment, and then suddenly the dam broke. "Do you know what it's been like," her voice trembled, then grew fiercer as each word rushed forth in a torrent, "to train beside you… to watch you grow, in strength, and courage, and determination, for these past three years? I remember when I first met you," her voice softened at the memory. "We were both stuck in the library, and you were crying over a book. Some dumb list of jousts that probably no one has ever bothered to look at. When I came in you closed it and tried to wipe your face, but I could still tell. That's the last time I've ever seen them," she continued, putting a hand to her cheek. "The last time I've ever seen the sparkle of tears in your eyes. Ever since then, since meeting me, you've been able to focus on your own power, on your own greatness, and stopped focusing on what he would have done, what he would've wanted you to do or be. I just... I just don't want to see you lose that, Arya."

Her voice tightened, and Arya bit back a gasp. Was Layne... crying?

"You belong in no man's shadow. You may love him, but you are still a champion in your own right. And I vow to let nothing, absolutely nothing," she said, the deadly light kindling again in the depths of her emerald eyes, "stand between you and your nomination to Grand Master."

Arya gulped. Suddenly she could understand her friend's caution. Should Elgitha become aware of Seth's return, what would stop the Grand Master from nominating him in his sister's place?

She put her hand over Layne's, squeezing it tightly. "I honor you, Layne Riquelme, champion of Dragon's Hill. I promise, I will not let your loyalty be in vain. I have not trained beside you these three years," she smiled into the woman's face, "to let my brother take my chance at greatness."

Layne wiped a hand across her face and, with a watery grin, enveloped Arya in a fierce hug. Together, the girls snuggled into the bunk, and slept with hands bound together as tightly as their vows to each other.

XII

PREJUDICE

The quiet prairie rolled endlessly before the army, occasionally giving way to copses of trees and farmsteads that dotted the landscape. Each member, from nervous holvi to burly duergi to stalwart aesir, walked with dignity and determination to succeed in the face of fear. Their destination lay to the east- Lianor, a massive marble cliffside stronghold bordering the sea.

Rowan, leading the slowly marching column, took note of the sun that sank behind them and reigned in his sprightly dappled bay. "Do you think we should make camp here? It's still a fair distance to Lianor, and they bar their gates in the evening," he said, turning toward Katherine as he spoke.

Their numbers, and specialized weapons endowed with the spell of McKenna's protective blood, had so far turned most of the ilmaurte and unfriendly beings in their path to dust. Still, it wouldn't do to leave themselves unprotected at night. Especially so close to the hostile fortress.

She pursed her lips thoughtfully, then nodded. "Not on the road, though." Riding up to one of the league posts that marked the distances along the highways, she noted the letters and numbers carved into its side and, unrolling a small map, consulted both for a moment.

"We should be within the borders of Dragon's Hill. Illusen is gone, I know," and she winced, staring off toward a twisted copse of trees that descended into a low valley from the ridge they marched upon, "and it was my understanding that Dragon's Hill, too, fell to the scourge. But they were larger, and more prepared. If any remain, they might be able to shelter us."

The march had been a grim one. Where once stood thriving communities and farming villages now lay smoking, twisted black ruins reminiscent of the Abyss itself. No signs of life remained. Only the vestiges of death and decay. It surprised the party that they encountered no more refugees than the ones who had already made it to Ljotebroek. Until scouts reported the remains of a ilmaurte horde milling along the dry riverbed of Styckes that ran from Faie's coast to the great chasm in Naijor, barring any sort of passage to the western realms.

As she reviewed the road before them, her heart beat in her throat at the sight of the gathered company. Nothing like it had ever been seen in the history of Faie. An army united under a single purpose, of all Faie's soulful creatures. While perfect accordance and harmony had yet to be achieved, so far, the time spent both gathering more recruits and travelling from Ljotebroek had been a successful one. Occasional word from the holvir duo travelling to Gamorre often came accompanied by new recruits who, though slow to overcome the prejudices that divided them, ultimately acknowledged that Beausun's army promised fairly.

Katherine knew they had to keep that promise. When missive after missive to Lianor returned, scorned or unheeded, they decided their next and only action was to march.

The ivory walls must come down.

A scout appeared on the path before them. "Dragon's Hill, dead ahead. The town is a ruin, but looks like some of its residents have returned."

The leaders exchanged furtive glances. "We should investigate first. James," Katherine called, searching for the mountainous form of the squire, "will you come with us?"

He nodded, shouldering his shield, and together the three ascended the path pointed out by the scout. Ruin was no exaggeration. Nothing even resembling a building or wall remained along their road. They came to the outskirts of a blackened town square, draped with strings of tattered colourful lanterns and curious ridges of stone that crisscrossed between buildings, and peered around for the signs of life intimated by the scout.

"Hail, citizens of Dragon's Hill! We are the goodly army of Beausun, and seek shelter and companionship among you," cried Katherine, her soothing tones reaching far in the silent space.

The ground shook slightly. The three travelers stepped back quickly, and before them materialized a flamboyant figure with a shock of dark red hair and dashing whiskers. He surveyed them for a moment, then bowed deeply and gracefully.

"Ah! Travelers! *Qué sorpresa*," he said, taking first Katherine's hand and kissing it, favoring the two bemused men with a smirk and a wink. "Forgive our shyness. As you can see, it's been some time since we've had any... welcome visitors. *Porque estan en nuestro pueblocito?"*

"We kind of just told you, didn't we?" grumbled James, leaning nonchalantly on his shield that bore the T'ssama crest. Katherine elbowed him.

"Vamos en Lianor," she replied glibly in *Besonne*. *"Y necesitamos su ayuda."*

"So you are *Spokirres*." The man, a spark kindling in his eyes as he used the old *Besonne* term for residents of Wheelspoke, put a pensive finger to his chin. The two towns had been rivals for generations. Something Katherine had hoped would be irrelevant in today's trying times.

Until she noticed the crest of a spiny flower against a shield embroidered on his quilted gambeson.

"Usted Lord Masa? Masa Riquelme?" She gasped in surprise.

"Si, señorita. Usted sorpresan?"

"We... we were told you died," she whispered. "My name is Katherine, and I am indeed from Wheelspoke–"

"Did your Lady send you here?" His charming tone had disappeared, and he buried his smile in a single contraction of his fiery brow.

"No, no, Lady Arianna has no idea we are here. In fact, if she did, she'd probably be furious, and close her gates on us faster than ever she did you," Katherine rushed to speak, sensing an explosion and hoping against hope to be able to diffuse it. "Please believe me when I say our magistrates' response to the plight of

Dragon's Hill and Illusen was something many citizens of Wheelspoke, including myself, and James," she waved a hand at the squire, who had thankfully dropped his aggressive pose and was instead focused on translating their conversation for Rowan, "resisted as much as we could. We are not all like our leaders, Lord Riquelme. My companion and I, along with the rest of our party, all were either chased out of our own homes by the horde, or chose to leave our towns who closed their doors to those in need. We see the damage Lianorres and the guilds have done to our kindred, and we want to fix it. It's not just asafolk of Faie who suffered. Our goodly company boasts all races affected by this blight."

"You would say you travel with…" he trailed off, investigating them keenly.

"Holvir, durgir, the faith-free of Ljotebroek," she responded, nodding to Rowan, "lend aid to our enterprise. We have united under one banner, which we call the United Army of Beausun. Our division has left us weak and ripe for destruction. Only in unity can we find peace."

Masa inhaled deeply, his black eyes trained on the earnest countenance of the healer. Then he smiled, white teeth shining in the sun. "Katherine of Wheelspoke, you speak with more grace than I am wont to hear from *Spokirres*. You are welcome, sincerely, and we hope we can help."

That evening the travelling army, thankful to find shelter from the dangers of the open plains, transformed the town square; decorating the rubble with fluttering pennants and the sounds of ringing metal and cheerful song. The asafolk of Dragon's Hill took a break from their recovery efforts and joined the party, spinning tales of their town's destruction and their return from Meliamne. Some even recognized each other from their time spent among the ilvir forests and embraced jubilantly.

At a low clay table sat Rowan, James, Katherine, and Masa, heads bowed in eager conversation.

"So you say you've heard from our holvi friends? How do they fare?" asked Rowan.

"They left Bristendine. Maria, my daughter-in-law and Lady Elect of Dragon's Hill, wrote of their spirited song and their hope for the unity of faiefolkr. Little did I think we would meet their friends so soon," he responded, raising a toast.

The curious clear liquid burned with a sweetness that caught in Katherine's throat, and she coughed, laughing.

"I see you don't know the nectar of the agave," Lord Masa chuckled, pouring her another drink and squeezing the tart juice from a hard skinned fruit over it. "It is always a pleasure to introduce our customs to strangers."

"Your magic is incredible," she replied, looking at the half-formed mounds of buildings raised from the red mud and sandstone. "You can build this without a blessing? How?"

He smiled, and tweaked his mustache. "We listen to the land when she speaks," was all he offered.

The hum of conversation lulled, and then broke with the sharp sound of a winding horn. Katherine looked up in surprise. In the middle of the square a band had formed, alongside lines of dancers with legs twining gracefully and skirts flying wildly. Katherine giggled and blushed as Lord Masa stood and, bowing, begged her hand for a dance. They took off, leaving the magistrate and the squire to watch bemusedly from the table.

"So much for the rivalry between Dragon's Hill and Wheelspoke," Rowan mused aloud to James, leading off hints from the earlier conversation.

"Hmph. Both towns are in the highest favor of Bahamut. The paladins from each have always fought each other or married each other- or both. But this goes a little deeper than that," the squire replied, swirling the drink Katherine left behind. "I think Lady Arianna's decision to stand with the guild and rebuff the refugees is what they despise the most right now."

"Can you blame him?" Rowan asked fairly, with a raise of one silver eyebrow. "Seems like she threw her neighbors to the wolves for a bit of extra power."

"Lady Arianna knew the guild was after her son," James countered gruffly. "She had the choice to either stand with them, denouncing both him and her neighbors, or watch her city burn like the rest of the realms. Lord Masa had the same choice- and he chose wrong. He thought the strength of Dragon's Hill's devotion to Bahamut was stronger than the guild's. So when the guild demanded they obey its rules, instead of following their own lore, they laughed in its face. Lot of good it did them," he sighed angrily, at the sight of the ruins around them.

"I don't know. You can always rebuild a town. But you can't so easily rebuild trust between neighbors, or the love of the devout for their god." Rowan, reclining against the table, spoke softly and considerately, not looking at James. "Ljotebroek should count themselves lucky we survived as long as we did. We owe our thanks and our city to that durgirn woman and her friends. But even were we not so lucky, I think knowing we had each other to fall back on and rebuild with would mean more than the effort to do so."

"How many had to die for you to prove that point, though?"

James' tone was quiet, but he clutched the drink in his hand so tightly the glass whined in protest.

Rowan looked taken aback. "Are you saying they should've given up their freedom? For a promise of safety?" He questioned, keeping his voice light.

James, brow still furrowed, sighed and downed his drink.

"I don't know. All I know is this... this idea of noble sacrifice, it's just an idea. And it failed. They're dead and we're here," he closed his eyes, hiding the depths of their burning pain from Rowan's keen gaze, "cleaning up after them."

With a shrug, he got up and disappeared into the camp. The calm night wore on, the revolving figures illumined by the glow of the lanterns and the milky clouds of stars above.

Dawn of morning shone bright on the army as they continued, with forces grown by those of Dragon's Hill. They covered the remaining leagues with stalwart determination and, before long, the imposing gates set in a seamless wall of white marble rose before them.

Lord Masa and Katherine advanced, addressing the

sentries barring their way. "We speak for the united army of Beausun. We seek audience with the Grand Masters of Golden Eye and Tooth and Claw, to beg their alliance in facing the undead scourge that plagues our realms."

Katherine spoke imperiously, her soft musical voice unflinching, even adamantine in the face of the impenetrable guards. She waited as they turned in through the gate to consult with the magistrate of passage. Only the horses' restless whinnies broke the silence that stretched uncomfortably, and Katherine began to feel uneasy. Finally the guards returned.

"The magistrate must consult with the Noble's Council first. We have strict orders," he said uncomfortably, especially chagrined at the look on Katherine's mottled face, "to bar entry to any town seeking asylum without first converting to the unified sect of Sanct Germain and Bahamut."

Katherine turned an incredulous expression toward Lord Masa, who peered searchingly at the guard. "*Estas loca? Que es* 'unified sect'? Since when have Sanct Germain and Bahamut agreed on anything?" he demanded.

"Afraid we can't tell you that," the guard responded calmly. "You're free to wait, and your party can find shelter outside the walls. Once we have confirmation from our magistrate, we'll come escort your leaders in."

As Katherine and Lord Masa made their way back to the party, she shook her head dazedly. "A unification of Sanct Germain and Bahamut? But... are the guilds and the Noble's Council uniting under both gods? I don't understand!"

"It smells foul. I don't like it," Masa responded, his face a thundercloud. "Why would Lianor remain barred? They should be sweeping the plains for vengeance and glory, not hiding like cowards."

Katherine nodded uneasily, not eager to share the tale among their party. She knew what dwelt beneath the stone towers of Golden Eye. A unified guild sworn to restore the realms of Faie was one thing. A unified guild under the thrall of a daemoric cult in league with the Lich King, was another entirely.

James and Rowan, when confronted with the news, agreed it was fishy. But what could they do, other than wait?

The sun had begun to set behind them before a Lianor guard rode out to the encampment. Katherine noted he was fully armed and armored, and she felt her heart sink.

"Your army is ordered, by the nobles of Lianor, to disband and return from where you came," he spoke imperiously to the gathered group.

"What? Why? We don't even get an audience with the magistrate?" replied Rowan loudly.

"No. It appears your party is in thrall of the traitor McKenna and her Abyssal host," he said, hand on the pommel of his sword. "There is nothing the magistrates need hear from that devious woman's followers."

The announcement struck the party dumb. "McKenna's... Abyssal... her what now?" gasped Katherine. She'd heard the rumors the guilds had spread, about Katarin's opening of the Doors of Death and McKenna's mysterious powers. But to outright declare her the source of the horde's advance was as new as it was absurd.

"The monk from the mines of Mount Oer has been found responsible for the horde's march-" a gasp of outrage from the group forced him to raise his voice threateningly, "and any who ally with her declare themselves enemies of the goodly realms of Lianor and of those who follow the light of Sanct Germain and Bahamut," the guard replied firmly.

"Say that to our faces, ye scoundrel!" rumbled a voice from the back of the crowd, and a small scuffle broke out as the durgir forced their way to the forefront of the gathered party.

James' own hand flexed, and she placed a staying hand on his elbow. "You know the rule - don't shoot the messenger," she hissed at him urgently.

"Durgir? And holvir, too?" spat the guard, wheeling his horse around. "You keep odd company, heroes of Beausun. But you are not welcome here, and I order you to leave on pain of death," he swore uprightly. Then, spurring his horse to action, he bolted back toward the gates, leaving the dumbfounded party in his wake.

"Huh. That went… well." Katherine blinked several times, as the figure slowly vanished in the distance. She turned to Lord Masa, a look of mute inquiry upon her face.

His own glowed with wrath, mirrored in the faces of James and Rowan beside him. She felt a sinking feeling of dread as she scanned their party, the crestfallen and baffled faces reflecting the disappointment of each.

"We should return to Dragon's Hill. When María and Charlot return, we can figure out where to go from here. Perhaps we can convince the durgir of Bristendine to listen to us, but I… I little expected this," Lord Masa gave the signal for the party to pick up and march back toward the plains.

"If McKenna ever returns… she's going to have quite the rude welcome," muttered Katherine under her breath.

Behind them, the bright walls of Lianor shimmered, impassable, implacable, imperious.

XIII

LIFE

Hazy, late afternoon light descended over the savannah that rested between Beausun and Naijor. Though the golden vista rolled unvaryingly before them, it bore little other comparison to the idyllic, yet monotonous pastures of the realm of death. McKenna felt a surge of joy to be again walking on the plane of the living. An early moon rose to meet the sun, its crescent waxing as solstice rolled closer.

Sethisto's words echoed in her head, directing her steps and those of Seth's towards the holvi village they departed from that unknown time ago. To ascertain exactly how much time had elapsed, and get as much of an understanding of the Lich King's position as possible, they decided to venture first among the Padfoot tribe, arming themselves with better knowledge than that which they had after their sojourn in pasture.

It was heavenly just to walk with Seth again. Though the dangers of the land had not lessened, to face them as a pair gave McKenna almost greater happiness than she could endure.

"I still can't believe you met my father," Seth mentioned as they walked along a narrow track skirting the dead woods.

"I couldn't either. He kind of... popped out of nowhere," laughed McKenna, recalling the queer experience of listening to an amorphous ball of light bully her and her sister into obedience as they tried unsuccessfully to make sense of the strange realm. "He was so forgiving, though, and so kind. He said he'd met my sister too, at a joust of some sort," she continued.

"Sethisto T'ssama revelled in jousts in his early days. To back a horse and pit his strengths, and the strength of his god, against all the goodly women and men he encountered was his absolute delight," reminisced Seth. "When I was initiated he gave most of that up, only participating in some of the more traditional events of our town. I guess he didn't want to steal the limelight from his son."

He stared off into the horizon, and McKenna could see again the golden castle, the rising stands, the cheering crowds. That ache of misgiving tugged at her, but she shrugged it off.

"Jousts. I read about so many of those, the histories of tourneys and rivalries, but I guess I just never… got it," she said, twirling her guisarme to sweep away the grain that rose before them.

"The paladins of Sanct Germain are all a bunch of bookish snobs. Few had any might worth competing with, though they did boast some excellent marksmen. To be honest, they probably view the burly and boisterous followers of Bahamut with scorn. But for all that, our guild and our following has simply grown so much quicker than theirs," he responded with a lopsided grin. "Their lack of power and marked disdain didn't stop them from accepting our challenges. But the guilds have grown and changed so much in the past few decades…" he trailed off, staring across the vast expanse of empty grassland toward the civilization that lay beyond, "their motivations are beyond me now."

His words recalled McKenna to her studies of the rival aesir gods. Sanct Germain, patron of lawful magics, religious incantation, and ceaseless clerical devotion to study; and Bahamut, patron of the sword and shield, the might of man, the spark of ingenuity and innovation that catalyzed the swift ascension of the short-lived race from meagre subsistence to a great and thriving population. While Bahamut boasted a larger following scattered across the plains of Beausun, the most elite and noble aesir families, safe in the strongholds of the coastal towns, belonged to Sanct Germain.

It made sense that Bahamut's flagship guild would turn to such indefatigable evangelism. What they couldn't come up with in gold, they could compensate for by sheer numbers alone.

"I don't know why it has to be like that," he commented in answer to her unspoken musings. "And when Sanct Germain's Guild of Golden Eye, too, is known for its own folly of trusting and guarding that evil Cult of Naszer. There's plenty of room for both of them in the world," Seth sighed, thinking of the curious town of Ljotebroek, free of any kind of religious fanaticism. "I guess you could say you told me so, after all. The gods should be more involved with those who invoke their names to acquire great power and justify their actions."

The durgirn monk, certain in her own devotion to Malfaestus, couldn't answer him. She simply grinned and squeezed his hand. "We'll focus first on the undead horde and destroying the Lich King. The guilds are playing themselves false in this battle, and are now shown for what they are to all faeifolkr. They owe the realms an apology, and a better example. And I can think of no better hero to set that example than you."

He rolled his eyes, trying not to smile. But the monk could sense a shadow in the paladin's heart, one she still hadn't the courage to confront. Luckily, they were now in sight of the Padfoot village, and all thoughts of her partner's discontent fled quickly when they realized...

"It's empty?"

No sounds, no song- the roads, normally pattered by tiny feet and chickens, lay bare in the dying light of day. The pair hurried forward, weaving the streets in search of anything, anyone.

Finally, they reached the center of the village, the very square where they had once been entranced by dancers and shared their own poignantly sweet moment. The large, open space was gone, replaced by a tipsy wooden structure filled with a soft, nearly inaudible hum. McKenna and Seth looked uneasily at one another and stepped together past the curtain swung before the door.

The inside was dark- much darker than they thought the crude structure had any business being. Cracks of light and smoky candles cast an orange hue, dim and faded. Every holvi of the tribe knelt upon squares of black cloth, their foreheads touching the ground. From their throats came the source of the humming sound. Each one sang as softly as they could, weaving the magic of song in place of cries of agony. Upon a dais, surrounded by the thorny, brittle flowers one found swaying amidst the grasses of the savannah, reposed a small, wizened figure.

"It... it can't be," whispered McKenna.

The Padfoot Pasha clung to life. She could, with the

celestial power of her heritage, sense his faint aura, held aloft by the songs of his kin. None dared to intercept or intervene in her approach; they all focused on the depth and power of their mournful dirge. At the soft touch of her hand on his forehead, he opened his bleary eyes and a smile crossed his lips.

"You came back," Oyewolo whispered to her. "Did you save the paladin?"

"I did, good Pasha," she said, stepping aside so Seth could join them. The Padfoot leader closed his eyes again, the smile still on his features.

"I am glad you returned. You are both sorely needed. You spoke true. Our bright stars returned to us, accepting the gift of our blessing, before setting off to spread the word of the Lich King's rise."

He frowned and winced slightly. The singing shifted tune, from a slow melancholy song to something softer, more hopeful, more forgiving. He smiled again.

"They do not want to let me go. But I have been here long - much longer than I should have. The sight of my village facing such a fearsome foe makes me hate to quit them. But when the Faie Mother beckons, none can ignore her call."

"Do you have a soul?" McKenna asked.

The question was blunt, but she knew he would take no offense.

He didn't. "No, child. I have no spirit to accompany to the realm of death. My spirit, such as it is, lives on in the magic of my kind. You promised to watch over them, to guide them in a world that defies and disregards them. Do you mean to keep that promise?"

No bitterness or distrust marred the soft tones of his voice, simply a fervent longing that McKenna thrilled to. A beard quest, the Lich King, her demigodhood- none of these guided her so much as her desire for justice and peace for the holvir throughout the realms.

"Of course I do," she said firmly.

"Then I can be at peace," Wole sighed.

One by one the holvir stood, holding hands and chanting in a language more ancient than the gods. They sang of hope, of truth; of the life and the blood and the light that guided their race. And one by one they offered release to the ancient one who lay before them. McKenna turned to Seth, her own wordless grief mirrored in the tears that flowed down his face. They turned and withdrew from the building, leaving the tribe with their dead.

Slowly, the holvir began to file out and prepare for the ceremony where they would mourn and celebrate their Pasha's life. Dismantling the small wooden structure, they turned it into a pyre upon which they reverently laid Oyewolo's body, and around it the open square filled with food and music and dancing, much as it had done the night the pair had first visited the tribe.

As a token of the honor and respect Oyewolo had for them, the holvir presented each of the heroes with a gift. To replace her tattered pelt worn since first leaving the mines, they gifted McKenna a beautiful embroidered tunic and soft, malleable leggings that suited the monk's martial capabilities without the hindrance of cumbersome armor dividing her from her god. And for Seth, they dropped a pile of golden apples into his lap before hurrying out of the path of a knickering, cantering horse- Kurya, gold and sprightly as of yore. The surprised paladin embraced the steed with affection and disbelief, and both thanked the holvir with fervor.

That evening brought forth the loudest song, the lightest dance; the brightest fire, and the most bountiful feast. As darkness fell, they carried Wole's body on a litter through the streets he had watched over with fairness and love. Finally, they approached the bonfire, and with a mighty song that echoed throughout the savannah, offered him to the devouring flames that brought warmth and light to their whole village. McKenna and Seth sat upon the dais during the ceremony, accompanied by a woman bearing the new mantle of Pasha to the Padfoot tribe.

Contrary to her predecessor, Lulann brimmed with life and vigour. Aware that her visitors knew nothing about the politics behind their changes in leadership, she sat them down and shared with them the story and the history of their tribe. Lulann was a painter. Her artwork covered most of the buildings in the village, and her renown among the tribe rivalled that of Ginni and Tjena's. It was her knowledge that first qualified her as their new Pasha. Her charisma carried the rest.

"Though I didn't quite understand Wole's trust of you at the outset," she said as she feasted with them on the dais, "I can understand now how fairly he judged you. We have suffered much, and none have ever offered to help us before. Let alone actually make good on their word."

"Ginni and Tjena are my best friends," replied

McKenna, "and nothing should prevent them from making a place in this world as accepting as mine is."

Lulann studied her for a moment, her sphinxlike smile not meeting her hard black eyes. "Many have made pets of us. That doesn't mean they treat us like faiefolkr."

Shock drained McKenna's face of blood. "Pets? No- that's not true at all! Ginni is my friend."

"*Our* friend," corrected Seth quietly, with just as unfathomable an expression on his face as Lulann had on hers. "The measures holvir have had to take to live safely in aesir societies... it's appalling. We know that, and I have lived it, and contributed to it myself. Whether you believe us or not- and you don't have to," he added fairly, seeing the wrinkle between her brows and above her bitter lip, "since we've given you no reason to yet- we mean what we say. It is not enough for just aesir to unite against our enemy. We have to make it right by all who live on Faie."

"And I will stand by that promise until death," added McKenna firmly.

Lulann smiled incredulously, but didn't argue. She turned the subject instead, to talk of the tales of the horde and its advance. "You have been gone a long time. Though holvir do not walk the realms of death, even we understand it is not a short journey to make. However, you baffled the Lich King more than you realize."

"So he hasn't struck yet?" asked Seth.

"No. He never meant for Atosa to survive his rise. Since she did, he cannot wield the full might of the undead army he has built. She defies him at every step. But it is a short-lived stalemate," sighed the holvi. "Unless Atosa joins with her sister, it is only a matter of time. His advance is inevitable."

"Atosa is trying to ally with Sh'nia?" McKenna replied incredulously. "Isn't she the reason this started in the first place?"

The holvi pressed her fingers to the bridge of her nose impatiently. "You mustn't underestimate the dire necessity of unity, good monk. It's not about who started it. Faiefolkr are at war," she insisted, "and the horde is the symptom, not the disease."

Seth sighed quietly under his breath. "So the gods are paying attention after all."

"Yes. But they are still very proud, and have little patience with these sisterly squabbles. They see only the homage paid to them by their faithful, nothing more. Why fight the sisters' battle for them? they think. So Atosa must somehow bridge the gap with her sister. But luckily, she has ambassadors who will speak for her."

McKenna raised her eyebrow at Seth, who shrugged. "We just came from the realm of death. Which heroes could you be referring to-"

She gasped, clapping her hand to her mouth in sudden realization. "Ginni and Tjena? My mother sent holvir to Gamorre?"

"Your mother has more faith in my kind than even you, it seems," chuckled Lulann bemusedly.

"It's not faith in them we lack, Pasha. It's faith in the world at large, who have so ignored them," countered

Seth. The elder simply shrugged.

McKenna wondered if she should try to reach her mother, gain greater insight into this willful war among the pantheon that left the races of Faie in the lurch. She leaned back, contemplating the constellations in the heavens above.

"I must warn you of other rumors, though," Lulann leaned in, and a true spark of terror kindled in the depths of her black eyes. "It is said that since the Lich King cannot build his army of the undead, he chose to rely on more sinister and chaotic powers."

Her words confused McKenna, until she caught a look at Seth. The paladin had gone rigid, white; with fury or fear she couldn't really tell. The faint scar across his cheek burned lividly against the pallor of his face.

"Do you mean…" she began to clarify.

"Daemor. The Lich King is summoning daemor." McKenna had never heard the paladin's voice so shaky before. He took a ragged breath, and tried to shake the sensation imposed by the monstrous word.

"Yes. So far, we think he is unsuccessful. Or biding his time until he is truly ready to strike. Summoning a daemor horde is no simple feat, and controlling one nearly impossible. But we are only holvir, with only whispers of the energies of Faie to guide us. You will have to venture to the eastern realms, to the homelands of your kind, to find out more."

The pair nodded in understanding, turning their attention back to the bonfire throwing sparks high into the air. The tribe still danced and sang around it, continuing to do so until the sun died on the horizon and the moon peeked her shining silvery face into the inky sky above.

Night had fully descended before the tribe sought sleep. McKenna, restless and unable to find composure in the face of everything they'd experienced, watched in wakefulness. The lights of the holvi village had all faded and a full moon, rising slowly through the midnight sky, cast its glow over the encampment. Her head down on her knees, the monk watched its stately progression and hove a sigh from the very depths of her soul.

The events of the day had shaken her, Seth's disquiet not the least of it. She wondered if her mother had ever faced such an inscrutable dichotomy before.

Suddenly, the translucent form of the goddess appeared, taking form with McKenna's thoughts.

"Mother!" she cried, jumping up and embracing the goddess. Atosa laughed, stroking her daughter's tall head.

"I see you've found something decent to wear, finally," the goddess laughed as she inspected the monk from head to foot.

McKenna laughed, recalling the fur of the dire panther in which she'd originally been clothed. "You left me with durgir. They have some… odd customs."

"That seems to be an understatement."

McKenna sighed, remembering those lonely and wonderful days spent wandering the valleys surrounding Mount Oer, before the advent of her journey had truly begun. She turned back toward her mother. "What brings you here?"

"You did. Or rather, the draw of a soul needing guidance. What lays you low, sweet?"

McKenna cast a look over Seth's bedroll, curled up as it was around the remnants of their fire.

"There is a... darkness in him. I can't describe it."

"Where there is light, there is always darkness," her mother muttered under her breath, with another smile.

McKenna's brow contracted, and she smiled quizzically. "Your sister tell you that one?"

Atosa stifled a laugh. "How did you know?"

"She's a child of light, isn't she?" McKenna said as she stared at the point on the horizon below which the sun had disappeared. "It just sounds like something sanctimonious enough for her to say."

"My sister has never pretended to be perfect," sighed Atosa, "that was only my projection."

"She would be eager to recognize the darkness within, though," insisted McKenna. "Does that absolve her of the responsibility to cast it out?"

"I am no darkness needing to be cast out, McKenna," Atosa responded in a tone of warning, "and none know that better than Sh'nia."

They both turned to regard the recumbent form that lay before the dim embers. "Think twice before condemning others. Until you know the nature of the purpose his darkness serves, and the lessons he's learned in facing them himself. We cannot always escape that which haunts us, despite the steps we take to banish them."

"But he's so strong, so bright, so… so good, Mother. Is it… am I not doing enough to show him?"

"It is not up to you, child. You do what you can by loving and believing in him. But the darkness we take with us belongs only to ourselves. We hide it from each other, certain that should anyone else see the festering fears that devour us, we will encounter nothing but their condemnation."

Atosa gazed deeply into her daughter's face. She sensed a similar anxiety, common in mortals. The constant fear that they were impostors to their own achievements; simply pretenders to any throne or mantle wrested from the cold clutches of this world.

"No hero is absolved of this, no matter their accomplishments or their strengths," she hesitated, trying to put into words that which separated mortal from deity. "He will not let that doubt defeat him, and neither should you."

She put a hand on McKenna's hair, and the monk again hove a sigh from her soul. "Is this what feeds the Lich King then? Our own self-deceit? Our hubris?"

The goddess looked out to the stars, to the moon still lighting the night sky. "Perhaps. The Lich King draws his power from the restlessness of the death. The idea that when we die, we leave behind a life unfinished. But one must live the best one can, regardless of what the voices in their heads try to tell them. Those are the voices of liars. It is deceit, and this evil influence from beyond; the voices of wicked things jealous and fearful of mortal goodness, terrified of the light and adamantly denouncing it to save its own wretched self. You, together, must stand fast against that evil. Stand fast against these wretched foes both within and without, and they will not prevail against you."

She waved a hand toward Seth. "This man has fought so much. More than just against himself. To do so takes its toll on any mortality. Yet, daughter, remember," she said, cupping McKenna's face in her hands, "he chose to return with you. No matter what happens, he trusted you with his life. And that trust will save him, when nothing else can."

The monk nodded, lacing her fingers with her mother's. They sat like that for a minute, quietly, until the dawn began to break above the horizon.

When McKenna opened her eyes, tucked into the bedroll beside Seth, her mother had gone.

XIV

AMBASSADORS

Early morning light shone through the dewdrops that fell from the canopy overhead. As the sun rose before them, the two holvir tucked and twisted in the salute grown familiar to them as any ritual they'd learned during their sojourn in Gamorre. It began with bending almost in half to touch their fingertips to the ground, then tilting their faces so the sun's light could bathe them in its glorious glow.

So many times had they greeted the day like this. First stretching, saluting, then kulning; their miraculous voices blending with the harmony of the ilvir's as they sang the sunrise shining off the superfluous trees and brightly coloured glass domes that made up this glorious city.

Ginni straightened first, shifting the stone beads strung around her neck and shaking out the caftan of soft knitted wool so it draped more easily over her diminutive figure. She paused to regard her partner, who stretched their arms before them, cracking their joints blissfully and shaking the fingers so skilled at plucking their unique stringed instrument. Tjen tousled their shock of chestnut hair, then smoothed the wrinkles from the leather skins strapped under their embroidered vest. They offered the bard a bright grin and exhaled, peering with hooded eyes at the cresting sun.

"Reckon it's time to hit the road yet?" they asked nonchalantly, as Ginni chirped and hummed at the large raven that had accompanied them during their time spent in the glass temple.

"It's been time, Tjen, but you know what the Moon ilvir are like. No solstice, no seance," she sang, cooing at the raven as she hopped bashfully side to side, preening her feathers.

"We've said this at every solstice for too many moons now," Tjen grumbled, offering a crumble of bread to the coquettish bird. "Now that Grand Master Mistmoon has stepped down, we have to take our chance."

Though the holvir had grown fond of their temporary new home, the quest that brought them there stayed foremost in their minds. Assisted by Siberne and High Druid Master Llen, their story traveled to the furthest reaches of Gamorre, inspiring the Sun ilvir to action. But success came far from easy. What dangers the ilvir didn't see, they didn't fear. And their disdain for their Moon-worshiping cousins to the west far outweighed their desire to pit their might against the oncoming undead scourge. Without their support, what chance did the holvir have to summon Sh'nia?

"Before you came, it seemed as if the trees, the animals, had given up living, stopped growing," Siberne said. "This cycle of souls you speak of… such an old myth. In the time of Atosa's mortality, Sh'nia used the forest to collect life. As if death had no place on Faie. Souls would simply pass on to new creatures, new life."

"But Sh'nia needed Atosa to return," argued Ginni. "She couldn't handle both roles on her own."

"What! Says who? Are you telling the truth?" the wide-eyed child turned first to Ginni, then Tjena.

"Of course it… Siberne, what exactly have they taught you here, then?" queried the bard in shock.

"Why, Atosa grew jealous, and angry that her sister could so easily replace her. She demanded for Sh'nia to restore her to the pantheon and she agreed, but her sister never really forgave her."

The holvir stared at the little tiger boy in absolute bafflement. Tjena groaned. "Holvir don't even have gods, and yet we know the truth of yours better than you do."

Siberne looked hurt, and Ginni knelt beside him. He turned to her apologetically.

"How could we be so willfully blind? Our forest," he turned mournfully to the drooping trees, the thinning herds, "is dying. If what you say is true, we have to reunite the sisters," his voice gaining confidence with every word, "if what you say is true, we owe it to more than just our forest to unite them. We owe it to ourselves, and our realms."

The Sun ilvir listened in disbelief and derision at first. The Tale of Two Sisters had long been regarded as a charming bardic melody, but nothing more than a myth.

Ginni stamped her little foot in frustration. "This wasn't even that long ago! Even by holvi standards. Barely two generations have passed since Atosa returned to the pantheon… you can't just rewrite your own history for the sake of convenience."

But they had. And despite their hospitality for the holvir, Ginni knew they still had to overcome the inevitable prejudice that prevented their race from trusting her and her partner.

The forest itself turned the tide. Moons of the inevitable and accelerating creep of destruction passed before they finally acknowledged their only hope lay in reaching their goddess.

"Should you be able to bridge the divide between Sun and Moon ilvir," Master Llen told them, "perhaps the two tribes in tandem could summon the Goddess of Life to fight by her sister's side."

Go to the Sun ilvir of Gamorre, they said, it'll be fine, they said, thought Ginni grumpily as she watched her partner perform the complex salutations. *And now we're going back to the Moon ilvir. Back to where we started. Asafolk don't even like us and yet we're expected to go through all this to solve their problems for them.*

A rustle in the brush turned her attention. Striped ears popped up above the foliage, followed quickly by the lithe form of their Gamorren friend, Siberne. He bore a tray with three bowls and, plopping gracefully to the ground of the little clearing, offered one to each of the holvir .

"Good news, I'm thinking? The sun has spoken well to you?" he said, tail flicking merrily as he slurped the hot soup pooled in the bowl.

"Good news for us, bad news for you, Siberne," replied Ginni, as she blew on the bowl to cool it. "Unless High Druid Llen changed his mind and will let you go?"

SIberne's ears drooped, and he bit his lower lip. "No. Unchanged and unchanging. He's afraid the sight of a sunchild will put the Moon worshipers into a panic and prevent your meeting."

Tjen whistled as they blew on the hot soup, raising an eyebrow toward Ginni, who understood as well as words what the holvi meant. "I guess we have to take his word for it. The Moon ilvir have never rebuffed us before. They kinda like us, actually. To be fair, we've never travelled alongside their sworn enemies though. That might set up their hackles."

"But don't think that means we don't want your company," offered Tjen as the druid's ears remained flat. "We'll be back as soon as we can, with an army for you to lead. It's time the ilvir stopped hiding from the rest of the world. You all have so much to offer, so much we can share with and benefit from one another."

Siberne sighed, then a corner of his mouth twitched into a smile. "You're right. You're always right. And as long as I'm here, I can keep telling your story, keep the Sun ilvir from going back on their word. Will you take Cajwa with you?" he said, stroking the striking plumage of the dire raven as she cawed softly, pecking at Siberne's empty bowl.

"I don't think we have a choice, do we, sweetest?" trilled Ginni, kissing at the bird. She cawed and flapped her wings, ruffling the holvi's curly locks.

"No, you really don't." Siberne smiled with his whole face this time, standing and opening his arms toward the holvi pair. They both stepped in for an embrace and the raven hopped around the little trio, cawing and kicking up dust.

The preparations for their departure, thankfully, took

less time than they thought. With solstice still a tenday away, they felt confident they could make the trek in a couple short days and arrive just before preparations. This first solstice without Grand Master Mistmoon presiding gave them the perfect opportunity, since they hoped the master nominated in her place would be more receptive to the idea of a union with the Sun ilvir.

"Anything to get those refugees out of their forests, you'd think, right Tjen?" Ginni quipped, as they marched through the rolling jungles toward the temperate forest to the west.

"Sounds like the refugees are leaving of their own accord, if what María and Charlot of Dragon's Hill said is to be believed," Tjen offered in response.

Cajwa cawed from above them where she circled, scouting ahead for any divergence or dangers in the quiet wood.

Suddenly, a groan from Ginni's stomach disturbed the silence in which they'd been walking. The holvi sighed, casting a pout at Tjen. "Can't we stop for a snack? I'm starving!"

"You had two breakfasts. Even Cajwa doesn't eat as much as you do."

"But that was ages ago!" she whined.

"Ugh, fine. You're such a little goblin, I swear."

"I'm nothing like a goblin!"

"You're not *like* a goblin, you *are* a goblin. You can't be a simile when you're a metaphor."

Ginni stuck her tongue out at her partner, then took a seat on a log and cautiously unwrapped a parcel of rations provided by Master Llen. First offering a piece to Cajwa and then to Tjen, she bit happily into the spicy soft rice wrapped in aromatic flat leaves. As they travelled, the ambiance in the forest slowly shifted from wild, feral hot jungles to the tepid, mystical, mist-woven woods of Meliamne. Ginni was sure they'd crossed the border ages ago, though the lack of habitation slightly unnerved her.

"I guess Siberne wasn't kidding. Meliamne ilvir really want nothing to do with Gamorre. They won't even settle near the border. This place is completely abandoned, it looks like."

"Well, it wasn't always," mumbled Tjen through a mouthful of rice.

"How can you tell?"

They pointed through the mist, at a silhouette disguised in the gloom. "Because I don't think stone temples like that build themselves."

As a breeze shifted the rolling clouds, Ginni could make out the distinct shape of a small cairn. It was nearly overgrown with lichen and moss, but clearly hand-built to honor some obscure god or forest spirit. Tucking the leaf-wrapped snacks back into her pack, she stood and ventured over to investigate.

"I dunno, Ginni, remember the last time we ended up too close to something clearly Celestial?" said Tjen warily, keeping their distance.

"I'll go first. I feel like it… we should see what it is.

Like it's important. Besides, it's your turn to take care of me when something inevitably goes wrong," she joked lightly, but stepped softly and with greater respect.

The shrine, small as it appeared, still offered an opening easily large enough for the holvi to squeeze in and investigate inside. Shaking a canister of liquid light, a gift from the Sun ilvir, she held the glowing object aloft to study the runes carved along the wall. "Tjen. Tjen, you really need to see this."

Mumbling under their breath, they joined their inquisitive spouse, contemplating the wall before them first skeptically, then incredulously as the words unfolded and the ritual on the wall became clear.

"I can't believe it. It's the Song of the Two Sisters," Ginni breathed, stroking the runes reverently.

Word for word, it was the very song passed down generation after generation by the holvi bards, almost lost forever to the rest of the realms and forgotten by all but themselves. The story of the unity, then the rupture, and then the ultimate forgiveness of the two sister goddesses, spelled out in runes and carved into the wall of this forgotten temple.

But the essence of the song carved into the walls went deeper. The accompanying translations, and the soft, nearly completely effaced paintings that adorned the temple's crumbling pillars showed a unity beyond that of the goddesses, but of the mortals who worshipped them.

"This temple… this whole, I don't know, No Man's Land I guess… it used to be populated by Sun AND Moon ilvir. They used to live together. And it looks like one day they just…"

"Stopped. How strange," finished Tjen.

"We should go. Before something ominous happens," whispered Ginni, making her way back toward the entrance.

"Like what? You go deaf or something?"

"Shh! Don't even joke about that!"

As the sun began to set, they found themselves once more on the outskirts of the great canopy that hosted the Guild of Moonbow. Ginni could even guess the same guards manned the posts. Nothing daunted, they stepped forward, hailing them with cheery grins.

"Good to see you still work here," Ginni curtsied at the bemused assassins, while Tjen bowed. Cajwa perched herself on their shoulder, fixing a beady eye on the guards.

"Good to see you've… returned," replied the guard in a measured tone. "Do you know who it is you seek this time?"

"Yes, actually. Your new nominate for Grand Master, if you don't mind!" Ginni spoke heartily, with a flourish of her facile hands.

The stoic aesir could only stare. "You've learned nothing, then. Do you have an audience?"

"Well… we want one. Can't we get one? We're really on a very important mission, after all," continued Ginni.

"How important is 'important'", spoke a calm tone

from behind them.

"Again?!" whispered the other guard to his partner, at the sight of former Grand Master Mirai Mistmoon's timely appearance behind the holvir. "How do they keep doing that?"

The holvir swiveled in place, dropping into deep obeisances before the powerful ilvi. "A pleasure to see you again, Master Mistmoon. It's been a long time," sang Ginni.

A soft expression lit the sorcere's face. "Indeed it has. Are you here to perform at the solstice?"

"We would be honored, though that isn't exactly why we're here. Could you possibly get us an... what did he call it? Oh! An audience!" She smiled charmingly at the guards, who stared back in bewilderment, "With your nominate for Grand Master? I would love to share our news with you both, if you're interested." Ginni rose from her curtsy, and linked arms with Tjen.

"I'm always interested. Whether I find any value in it is another story. But come," she snapped her long fingers, and the guards fitted a key from their massive ring into the oaken panel, opening a portal that glowed a silvery green.

As they proceeded through the portal, curious sounds and smells filled the air around them. Ginni and Tjen stared in amazement as the chambers resolving around them filled, not with runes of power and magic spells, but all manner of machinery, bubbling concoctions, and bright panels of light reflecting curious scenes. A tall, stocky figure ambled about the space, swathed in an enormous black apron lined with lavender ruffles. Master

Mistmoon cleared her throat, but the figure either could not or chose not to hear.

"Illene. Illene of Silverden, you have guests," she rose her voice slightly.

"Illin. It's Illin, Grand Master. Err, former Grand Master," huffed the figure, waving a plume of smoke from a boiling cauldron out of his face. Illin stepped forward, and Ginni and Tjen bowed discreetly, unsure of how to address the mage.

"Holvir? Oh, how quaint. You shouldn't have, Master Mistmoon. Hello there, you," they said, stooping towards Ginni and Tjen with their hand outstretched.

"Ginni, Master Illin," she stammered.

"And Tjen," responded her partner, peering curiously at the ilvi. He had a long mane of silky black hair and a rounded, plump physique. Underneath the apron, instead of the silken robes that commonly adorned Guild of Moonbow members, he wore a soft fitted sleeveless top tucked into linen drawstring pants. A square jaw, set in a curious expression, inspected them from head to foot.

"Ah, Tjen. But not always?" the Master said, raising an eyebrow in mutual understanding with the holvi.

"Sometimes Tjena," they replied with a cheeky grin.

"I like that. I like them. Thank you for bringing them here, Master Mistmoon. Uhm, that is… why did you bring them here, exactly?" Master Illin scratched his head, staring curiously at them all.

"They asked for an audience with the nominate for

Grand Master. That would be you, Master... Illin," spoke the Master, catching herself determinedly.

"Yes, always Master Illin. Shame you still want me to be Grand Master though. Should've been Katarin," he sighed, waving a hand towards the boiling cauldron and reducing the heat below it.

Tjen coughed, and both their and Ginni's eyes stared widely at Illin. Was he serious?

"Oh, I know all about that possession stuff. And the fact she's stuck in Pasture. Trust me, none of her novitiates will let us forget it," he said ruefully, interpreting their gazes. "You two are the ones blighted by the Lich King then, am I right? And the ones who woke him, too? Is that why you're here? Seems a bit strange, turning yourselves in, even if I wanted to punish you, which I don't."

"Master Illin, I suggest you let them tell you themselves why they are here. And as I have been invited to listen, I will make myself comfortable and do so." Master Mistmoon cut off the rambling mage and took a seat gingerly on a wooden chair, leaning against her palm and studying the holvir intently.

"I think we'd rather sing it to you. We're better at that," Ginni said modestly, and Tjen strummed their instrument to accompany the ballad sung first to the united army of Beausun, then to the mixed society of Bristendine, and then to the Sun ilvir of Gamorre. At the end, they tacked on a few improvised stanzas to explain their visitation from Urtha, their time spent in the jungles to the east, and the temple they found in the wastes between the two realms. As they finished, Grand Master Mistmoon peered intently at them but offered no immediate comment.

Master Illin tapped his chin thoughtfully. "So, making sure I got this. All of it. You say Atosa needs Sh'nia's help to defeat the Lich King? And that we should do it because…"

"We've done it before," murmured Master Mistmoon, still gazing keenly at the holvir.

"Yes, that. What did they mean by that? What temple are they talking about?" continued Master Illin.

"The Temple of the Two Sisters. It's been a long time since your early studies… and you wouldn't have continued to learn about it, as it is an old part of our history that we choose to continue to ignore. But I suppose," Master Mistmoon studied a rune inked onto her hand idly, "now that holvi bards, infamous for their inability to keep their mouths shut, do, we would do well to face our past and learn from it."

She stood, and bowed her head to the surprised holvir. "There is a story you will hear tonight, at the celebration of the solstice and at Master Illin's own ascendance to Grand Master. I wish you would sing your ballad, so all may hear, and judge for themselves. If I'm not speaking out of turn," she said, acknowledging Master Illin's precedence with a nod.

"Until that ring goes on my finger, you're still the boss, Master Mistmoon. Let the holvir have the stage," he shrugged, then set about cleaning up the practices they had interrupted.

Seeing she wasn't getting any more of an answer from the churlish mage, Mistmoon simply shrugged and turned her attention back to the holvir. "You're welcome to stay here, or go preview the festivities. You two seem to know your way around." With another courtly nod, she vanished.

The Master watched her leave with a perplexing expression on his face. Tjen looked at him for a moment before musing aloud, "You know that expression, 'someone else's problem'?"

Illin shook his head free from reverie. "Yes actually. I'm beginning to think I understand it now, too," and shared a hearty laugh with the bard. He continued to bustle about the chamber, tucking stacks of books back onto their shelves and wiping clear some of the glowing screens. Tjen plucked at a few strings of their instrument surreptitiously. The noise suggested a lively cleaning song, almost inspiring the sounds of the room to bubble and fizz and hum along. Illin caught himself whistling to the tune, before suddenly whipping around and studying the holvir keenly.

"Quite catchy. Anyway, I'm glad she left you here, because I do want to talk to you," the mage said, clearing piles of documents from two spindly metal chairs and grabbing a steaming kettle. "Please, do join me for some tea."

"Oh, just hot water for me thanks, and a bit of lemon," waved Ginni, perching amiably on the offered seat. Tjen took the one opposite and held out a mug, gratefully accepting the aromatic drink. "In honor of your hospitality, we'll let you talk first."

Illin nodded, taking a seat on a tall stool near their little table. He hunched toward them not ungracefully, and Ginni could sense the dichotomy that ruled the mage's movements. "I love my aunt, but I don't think she's particularly good at listening to me."

Tjen snorted into their cup of tea. "Your uh… your aunt??"

"Yes, of course. Sorry, silly me, I thought everyone knew that. Yes, my illustrious, and exceedingly powerful and convincing, aunt. Who nominated me, of all people, to lead the Guild of Moonbow. Could you imagine? I can't turn her down, of course, and honestly at this point I'm just surprised none of the other Masters have had me assassinated yet."

Tjen had luckily put their cup down at this point, and sustained the blow with fortitude. Ginni wasn't so lucky, emitting a sharp "ouch!" as the hot liquid she spilled stung through her caftan. While she patted herself feverishly, Tjen leaned in toward Illin, fixing him with a keen look. "There are a lot of things to unpack here. Let's start with the first thing. Why can't you turn her down?"

Illin shrugged. "She's Grand Master. She has a right to elect the most fitting replacement to stand for her when she chooses to retire. It just wouldn't be honorable. I'm sure she picked me for a good reason, because honestly, nepotism doesn't suit her. She saw my reaction, but it didn't change her mind… so, why bother?"

"Huh. That's… fair. I guess. Yet she seems to struggle with your identity?" Tjen pushed, but with an unmistakable tone of compassion in their voice.

"Yeah. That. In her defense, I'm a mage, and she's a sorcere. She hasn't been involved with any of my training, or novitiate. In fact, there have been about three decades between the last time I saw her before joining the guild, and a dozen or so years since I ascended... and came out. She hasn't had much time to adjust to her niece becoming her nephew, I think."

A heated murmur from Ginni met the silence after Illin's statement, and the mage raised an eyebrow at the holvi. "Sorry. Do go on."

Illin shrugged. "Holvir don't take a lot of time to adjust to anything. You don't have much of it to begin with. I understand."

Tjen plucked their instrument again, accompanying their next words with a soothing, soft melody. "And about the... assassination. You're just, you're fine with that? Being a sitting target for all these other power-hungry mages and sorceres?"

A loud caw out the window. Cajwa came and perched on the sill, eager to be involved. Illin's face lit up. "A familiar! But I didn't think holvir had any magic. Yet you have a familiar, how darling."

"Cajwa's not a familiar. She's just a friend," corrected Ginni.

Illin eyed her beadily. "You're followed by a dire raven, and you think she's just a friend. Your kind are so mysterious. Anyways, what was I saying... oh yes, assassination. Well. To be honest, I do think the more... morally questionable members are keeping low profiles. Katarin's possession and defection was a huge blow, and a gigantic loss of face to some of the factions within our guild. Not to mention the death of that assassin. Onyx Blade nearly disintegrated. But luckily, they're such a loose jumble of miscreants, it was easy enough for their Altenette and our Grand Master to strike a deal and keep them in check. They owe the Grand Master one for that, I think. She could've thrown them out instead. So keeping in her good graces is key… and killing her nephew, not to mention her nominate, would definitely go against the grain, don't you think?"

The holvir nodded, sipping their drinks in silence. Despite the mage's erratic behavior, they could easily see what it was that set him apart from the powerful, but narrow-minded, masters of the Guild of Moonbow.

"Alright, now it's your turn. We've asked plenty of questions. You said you had some for us?" Ginni settled back into her chair, stroking the soft feathered head of Cajwa, who perched up next to her.

"I do. I have so many. So many that you'd probably miss the solstice, and we definitely can't do that. Are you sure I should start now? Or let you surprise me during your performance?" replied Illin, with a smile.

Ginni and Tjen looked helplessly at one another. Ilvin politics were so strange.

"Fine, fine. I'll start. There's another reason I didn't want to talk in front of Master Mistmoon. Listen, we owe the Sun ilvir a lot more than just an apology. And she has never, ever, under any circumstances wanted to admit to that. I'm surprised she even listened to you, let alone gave you an opportunity for an audience." Illin looked out the window, at the moon rising above the treetops, and sighed. "We Moon ilvir… we've dug our own graves, drawn our own lines. The Lich King is almost as much our responsibility as it is Atosa's, and we're just too ashamed to admit it. And too fearful that our power isn't great enough to stop him."

Illin's eyes glowed in the moonlight. Every line of his posture denoted a calm, empathetic mien Ginni had never seen in any Moon ilvi before. She stood up and put a hand on the mage's knee, and another over her heart.

"Your aunt may not be strong enough to face this threat. But she knows you are. That's why she picked you, I'm sure of it. The ilvir of Gamorre want your help too. We've lived among them for a while now, and though it took us that long to come to an understanding, we truly believe they miss you, their closest cousins. There's no pride in this world anymore. We can't afford it, Illin. Our kin are dying, and we need to face it together."

Illin put his hand over the little holvi's fingers, and wiped a tear tracing from their smoky blue eyes. "You sure have a way with words."

Tjen snorted. "We're bards. It's what we do."

That drew a laugh from the quirky Master. With a cheeky grin directed at the holvi, he donned a heavy woolen cloak and snapped, opening a portal to the woods beyond.

XV

MORNING

"Arya. Psst. Lady Arya."

"Urrrrghhhhh."

"Are you kidding me? That always works… Arya, wake UP!"

Arya felt the yank of the sheet from her curled form and an ice cold hand on her leg.

"AGH! Stop! Stop! I'm awake, I'm awake… ugh, but at what cost," she groaned, slapping a pillow over her head.

"I swear to the gods, why are you like this in the morning? What is wrong with you?" Layne muttered, wiggling her frigid toes against Arya's bare stomach. The girl gasped and smacked her friend with a pillow.

"I'm AWAKE! What do you want, you harpy," she moaned, propping her head on her hand, bleary eyes unfocused in Layne's general direction.

"I guess that's as good as I'll get. I need you to listen- I've got a letter."

"A letter?"

"Yes, you know, those things people far away like to

write to each other?"

"Layne."

She giggled, then shook the paper out. "Anyways, you need to hear this."

"Who even writes to you? I thought your family ignored you."

She winced. "They do. This is from María. I haven't heard from her in a while, but she tries to check up on me from time to time. I guess she just got back from a trading mission to the durgir in Bristendine. Listen to what she says."

Layne read the contents of the letter, recounting María and Charlot's encounter with the holvir and a fairly accurate copy of their song. Arya, still fuzzy from sleep, tried to focus on what her friend was saying.

"McKenna... McKenna went through the where now?" she slurred, lifting herself up in an ilmaurtish stupor to lean against Layne's shoulder and try to make sense of the words on the page.

"Through the Doors of Death. It was something about restoring her love's breath... taken by the Lich King, or whatever."

Arya blinked, then suddenly rocketed out of bed.

"Layne. Layne. Layne Layne Layne Layne Layne." she stammered, dancing in place. "I was right. She did it. Layne, she went through the Doors of Death to save my brother. Layne what if she succeeded."

"Can you stop saying my name?" the girl replied with a begrudging smile. "I'm right here."

"Okay-but-you-don't-understand-I-need-to-say-your-name-because-I-absolutely-love-you-this-is-exactly-what-I-wanted-to-hear-please-we-need-to-go-on-a-quest-Layne-we-need-a-quest," blabbered Arya all in one breath.

"Okay, *loca, calmate.* Why would we go on a quest?"

Arya rolled her eyes, then stuck a hand out to catch her balance. Layne gripped her arm bemusedly. She hadn't seen her friend act like this in forever.

"We're graduating to Master, right? We can go on a quest. If we get a quest, we can leave and find Seth. If we find Seth…"

"Then what?" a hard edge sparked the words from her mouth.

Arya blinked, then frowned at her friend. "You know, I can be excited about my brother being alive without implying I want him to come back to the guild," she replied, her own voice whetted with suppressed anger.

Layne huffed, rolling her eyes. Arya bit back a retort, then draped herself apologetically in her friend's lap.

"Layne. I made a promise. I just… I just want him back. I just want to see him. And once we complete our quest," she said, wrapping her arms around Layne's waist and resting her chin on the girl's rigid collarbone, "we'll come back here and ascend to Masters. I promise, Layne."

The empty plinth. The rotting Guild. Their sullen faces. *He can unite them. He's a child of prophecy. It's what he was meant to do.*

The girl tried to look stern, but failed under the influence of Arya's impulsive caresses. She brushed the girl's hair from her forehead and smiled. "Alright, fine. It's time we get out of the stupid library cleaning pool anyways."

"Yessss!!" cried Arya, jumping up and careering around the room in delight.

Only he can bring the blessing of Bahamut back to us. I just have to find him. How could he not want it. He has to want it.

Several hours later found the two in audience with Elgitha. Arya's heart beat in her throat to see how infirm and aged the glorious paladin had become in the few short years since she initiated into the guild. She swallowed and knelt before her Grand Master.

"Grand Master Elgitha," she began, and Layne knelt beside her. "Together, Layne Riquelme and I, Arya T'ssama, have trained and served for the glory of the goodly god Bahamut. Before we ascend to the great honor of Master, we humbly beseech a quest, to prove our spirit and our prowess for the glory of our god."

It was an old formality, but Arya stubbornly determined to uphold the traditions of her guild to the highest regardless of the consequences. Elgitha smiled gently, placing a hand on each of the girls' heads. "You two have served both bravely and well. With the power vested by our god, I do grant you your quest."

She leaned back, tuning her ear to the whispers of the heroes of old. In the lands to the west of Lianor, refugees attempting to return to their homes still faced occasional bands of the ilmaurte. Together, the two would quest to clear the pass between Wheelspoke and Ljotebroek from the scourge.

"And when you return," Elgitha said, a glimmer in her eye, "please seek me out."

Arya nodded, and out of the corner of her eye spotted Master Gareth shift annoyedly in place. She bit her lip to avoid smiling, and the two bowed out of the great hall.

Gareth eyed them viciously, then cast a glance at Clint, who slouched listlessly at attention. *Lady Astore and her hellish army better work fast.*

The novitiates chose not to ride, instead hopping along a caravan headed west for Wheelspoke. Arya tensed as the signposts counted down the distance between her and her hometown.

"Calm down, Lady Arya, your mother's not going to pop out from behind a bush and order you home," Layne jeered, elbowing her friend every time she winced.

"You don't know my mother," grumbled Arya, burrowing deeper into their perch on the back of a rumbling cart.

Another sign, a grim pointed finger. Her toddler feet pattering toward the racks of wooden weapons stuffed in a shed in the garden. A youthful, boyish face closing the door behind him- even then, proudly bearing the insignia of a chosen of Bahamut. She grabs for the practice weapon hanging loosely from his grip. He flinches, but after a furtive look toward the closed doors of the conservatory, kneels and holds it out to her.

"Go on then, Arri," he whispers, closing her fingers over the hilt. Proper grip, thumb turned out to prevent breaking under a sudden parry, loose enough to maneuver quickly but surprisingly strong for a child her age. She sets her face in a grim mockery of Seth's own, plants her feet shoulder width apart, struggling to lift the long blade gracefully. She is steady, he notes with candor.

A voice calling in the distance startles her, loud, imperious, compelling. She looks away quickly and loses her footing, toppling over into an ignominious heap.

"Don't want Lady," she whispers to him, silver eyes pleading with gold.

He bites his lip. What can he tell her?

"-Thank the gods for that," a different voice said at her shoulder. Arya shook her head, clearing it from its reverie, focusing again on Layne's words. "Besides, isn't she happy you're a paladin? Restoring the honor of your name, and all that?"

Arya bit her lip, a hereditary trait shared by sister and brother. "Not really. Seth was always the golden child. I was just supposed to fold my hands and be a Lady," wrinkling her nose in disgust. Layne laughed outright, nearly tumbling off the seat.

"I can't even imagine. You're good at directing and stuff, but your chicken scratch is appalling. If you wrote a memo, you'd start a war."

"Oh, thanks for that, Miss Calligraphy. Show me how

to read a map again?"

The hopelessly directionless novitiate just rolled her eyes, and clapped a hand to Arya's knee. "Fine, fine. Doesn't matter anyways as long as I've got you to follow. You point me where to shoot, and I'll shoot."

Arya leaned into her, watching the sun overhead. Three long years spent as far away as she could get. Signs pointed, familiar faces passed on the road, leading her home. *Home, is that it?* She shook her head, feeling the pressure of her partner against her.

No. This is home.

Sunset found them on the dusty banks of a dry riverbed, the preface to the pass between Wheelspoke and the realms to the north. Even from this distance, Arya could see the ragged encampments of refugees along the banks, huddled masses fearful of leaving the carefully guarded borders of Wheelspoke but unable to beg for safekeeping within its barred gates. Arya fumed internally, knowing the stalemate between her city's religious prejudice and the safety of those faiefolkr thrown to the mercy of the horde.

They disembarked from the caravan, waving off the folk who travelled with them, and made their way toward the largest of these encampments. Small fires surrounded by grim figures and ragtag children chasing each other through the brush met their gaze. They approached the largest gathering, seeking some form of authority figure.

A man stepped forward at the approach of the armoured girls bearing the sigil and the blessing of Bahamut. He seemed surly, yet either unwilling or unable to try repelling the two. "If you're coming from that town yonder, we've heard the lot of words can be used to scare up new converts. We want none of it," he started, crossing his arms over his chest.

Arya sighed, and puffed a lock of short hair from her face. "We are not evangelizers. We're on a quest, to rid this pass of the ilmaurte and allow you your freedom to return to your homeland. Are you the leader of this band?" she asked, holding out her wrist facing upwards- a universal gesture of goodwill and mutual respect.

He accepted this, and a relieved smile cracked the churlish expression on his face. He exposed his wrist in recognition and they grasped one another briefly. "Argus Delf, at your service. Surely then, you're a sight for sore eyes, though you seem a bit..." he trailed off.

"Young?" Layne shot back, twirling her crossbow on her index finger.

"Hmph. Green is more like," he responded.

"We've fought the horde before. We are paladin novitiates of Tooth and Claw, on a quest to earn our rings and ascend to Master. You are in good hands, I promise," Arya flicked her friend's spinning crossbow and she dropped it. Argus laughed outright, then beckoned them forward.

"At some point, we belonged to Garden Gate, Illusen, and Norreland," he waved a hand as he named off several smaller towns that could be found in the north along the border of Bread Basket, Mount Oer's vast valley. She raised her eyebrows in surprise. They all were Bahamut worshippers, and had some form of representation within her guild.

He caught her train of thought. "The durgir are our friends, child. If we closed our gates to them, our towns would collapse. No durgir, no trade. The guild," he spat, "that sits in its ivory towers-"

"More of a stone cathedral, really," muttered Layne as she flicked a speck of dirt from beneath her fingernails.

"-came to us and demanded we give 'em up. What would you do, then?" he challenged. "We said no. Then when the horde came…" he winced, covering his face with his hands. "We didn't stand a chance. Even the durgir couldn't come fast enough. Swept off the map in an instant, we were. Of all you see here, we've lost twoscore more for each survivor."

This gave Arya pause. The durgir easily could've housed all three cities with room to spare in their vast mines. How could the horde have advanced so quickly?

"What of Dragon's Hill? Have you seen any of them?" interrupted Layne, peering into the faces of those around them.

Argus sized her up, then smiled. "Aye, you would be then. Should've recognized that red hair anywhere. 'Sfar as I know, after your magistrates left to beg the aid of Bristendine, the rest of the townsfolk decided to try to go home. It appears they have… curious talents that annoyed our ilvin hosts," he wrinkled his nose.

Layne laughed at that. "Ah yes, I bet those devout magicians just loved being outwitted by a bunch of charlatan asafolk."

The citizens of Dragon's Hill boasted a power similar

to that of the despised holvir. They were deeply attuned to the land, and the land's inherent magics, and claimed the ability to whisper any shape from the ground. From pottery to colourful wooden statues to magnificent and imposing architectural structures that defied gravity, the masters of Dragon's Hill were well known to the realms at large. They also practiced sleight of hand, using their abilities to transform objects from one thing to the other, and some of the even more practiced could make objects, regardless of size, vanish. Arya had a sneaking suspicion her friend's attunement to Faie's energies were responsible for her superb marksmanship. Why bother aiming, when you can just will the ground to move your target, or whisper to the wind to move your bolt?

The strangest part, though, was despite the town's deep and ancient devotion to Bahamut, their curious magic had nothing to do with the dragonish god. Which probably, Arya assumed, explained why they didn't employ the same evangelistic tactics as the other devout towns. They simply didn't have to prove anything to anyone.

"Well, at any rate," cut in Arya, keen to resume the track of their initial conversation, "we thank you for your welcome, and are eager for any news you can give us of the dangers that lie ahead.

Argus nodded, and sitting with them before the fire outlined what his scouts had discovered. The undead horde's slowed advance unfortunately hadn't decreased their numbers. They seemed to find the pass the best place to lie in ambush for any enterprising travellers, and so far made it completely impossible to travel any farther north.

"What I don't understand, though," he said, his

forehead wrinkled in consternation, "is what's directing them. They seem, I dunno, conflicted like. Not the same as when they chased us from our homes."

Layne and Arya exchanged glances. The rumors they had heard were just that, only rumors. To spread them might endanger McKenna, or even the towns who rallied against the advance. But the girls were fair, and knew that to withhold information from anyone with the same agenda invited discord and distrust they couldn't afford.

"Well, seeing as you've suffered from evangelists, I guess I can offer you the truth as we know it," she began, her stormy grey eyes trained unblinkingly on his face.

His face softened, and she continued.

"There are rumours of an unknown daughter of Atosa, who managed to journey through the doors of death and return unscathed. But there are rumors too that a Lich King is responsible for this horde. With which rumor lays more truth, we can't begin to say. But…" she trailed off, certain that the woman who had listened to her, who had respected her, and whose spirit seemed to match her own, could never be responsible for these atrocities, "we, the two of us, are questing specifically to prove the innocence of the former, and the existence of the latter. McKenna is my friend," she said heatedly, the fires of determination lighting her conviction, "and though you may hear much to the contrary, I believe she, like us, is fighting against this evil."

Argus nodded, unwilling to contradict the woman's undeniable fervor. "All I can say is, Lich or goddess, the horde is torn and the land is too. And us… we just want our homes back," he said simply, staring into the vista.

She laid a hand on the man's arm. He felt the sincerity in her, and the compulsion of her conviction. "The Guild of Tooth and Claw has much to answer for. None know it better than us."

Encountering traces of the ilmaurte took less time than they thought. The next morning, after hiking about halfway up the dry riverbank, Arya began to feel the sap of energy and discordant hum of evil that preceded the scourge. Layne nocked a blessed bolt to her crossbow, keeping a flask of holy water on her hip.

"What can we do? What if there are too many? We should've thought this through, Arya..." hissed Layne, keen senses attuned to the danger.

"I have an idea," the girl responded, as she crouched with her palm pressed flat to the riverbed, "but I don't think you're going to like it."

Layne pondered her for a moment, then her jaw dropped. "Are you crazy?! You're absolutely crazy. Not even Elgitha herself would have enough power to-"

"Hush. It's all we've got, and I can do it, I know I can," she responded fiercely.

Hours in the library studying the lore and maps of Faie had indeed given the woman more of an edge than any could have guessed. She knew this riverbed, though drained dry of its lifeblood for a century, originally made its meandering course all the way back to the great Naijor Desert and the river Styckes that bordered it. Styckes water was famous for its magical properties. Not the least of which, for its ability to wake the dead.

"If I can summon the water of the Styckes here,"

she said aloud, continuing to trace runes in the pebbly sand with the finger bearing her signet ring, "it will have enough power to sap the souls from the ilmaurte and bear them back to the Doors of Death. At least, that's what the orgir use it for."

"Orgir," mouthed Layne. "Well, I sure hope you know what you're doing, and that you have the blessing to do it- because here they come!"

Half a league away, advancing slowly through the shimmering haze of heat that rose from the dry riverbed, shuffled the demented and ghastly forms of the undead horde. As they began to approach Layne shifted her crossbow and fired at the leadmost ilmaurte, each strike of the blessed bolts immobilizing them where they stood. Muttering under her breath and twisting her wrist with a jerk, the ground shook and a small chasm appeared between them.

"Layne, you're perfect. Keep them off for a few minutes longer," Arya whispered a slow, solemn prayer, chanting as she stroked the sand more vigorously. The runes began to glow, then ripple.

Her partner whipped the battle axe from its strap on her back, dousing it too in the holy water. Taking keen aim, she hurled it into a tight knot of undead, who vaporized in an instant. With a smirk, she channeled her energy to return the axe in time to swing it into another creeping monster advancing toward her.

"Now, Layne! Jump onto the bank!" Arya shouted, before punching the ground with all her strength.

The red haired paladin leapt to safety just in time. From the chasm she'd cracked in the ground, a frothing geyser bubbled, then exploded- filling the wash with silvery waves capped with white foam. Arya, focused on channeling the river toward the ilmaurte, braced herself for the impact.

I sure hope this works, she thought, as the deluge swept her away.

—

"Arya! Arya, Lady Arya, wake up!"

Ugh. Morning already?

"Arya, come on, I know you're in there, just get up!"

But I'm sleepy...

"Arya," spoke quite a different voice. "Arya, it's okay. Just open your eyes."

No need to tell her twice. They sprang wide open at the sound she thought she'd never hear again.

Her brother, speaking her name.

She shot up and launched herself at him, knocking the paladin from his crouched position. He laughed and tousled her hair, gripping her in an adamantine embrace.

"You-came-back-I-knew-you'd-come-back-I-can't-believe-you're-back-I'm-so-happy-to-see-you-and-McKenna-and-oh...hey, where's McKenna?" she rattled off in her breathless way, before looking up and peering around.

"Right here, spitfire," waved the monk, who dropped

to a knee beside her to give her a fierce hug. "We missed you too."

"Thank you. Thank you so much," was all she could say, tears pooling in the corners of her eyes as she squeezed her arms around the monk's torso.

She heard the sound of a throat clearing from behind her and looked around. Layne was staring at her with an eyebrow raised. Arya hastily got to her feet and tugged the paladin towards her brother.

"Seth, McKenna, this is Layne. She's a novitiate, like me," she said breathlessly.

Seth blinked, then narrowed his eyes. "Novitiate? Novitiate of…"

He trailed off as he saw the signet ring on Arya's right forefinger. Layne cleared her throat again.

"Novitiates of Tooth and Claw. Paladins, on a quest to earn our ascension to Master," she finished pointedly, keeping close to Arya's side.

"A paladin? What! That's amazing news, Arya, I'm so proud of you! I knew you could… ah…" McKenna's words died at the sight of Seth's face. She pursed her lips and continued. "I knew you could do it. And a Master so soon! Truly, I can think of none more deserving."

Seeing Arya wasn't likely to respond, Layne jumped in again. "Well, I mean, we're both head of our ranks. But Lady Arya's the favorite. We expect her nomination to Grand Master any day now-"

"Layne!" hissed Arya, her face white. "Do you

mind?"

"What? It's true," she replied simply, holstering her crossbow.

McKenna eyed Seth, who still hadn't said a word. She rolled her eyes and addressed the women with a smile. "Well, it's a pleasure to meet you, and always good to see you again, Arya. As you're on a quest, I suppose we should keep to our own road." She put a hand on the woman's shoulder, letting her amber eyes speak the words they hadn't time to share. "Let us hope we meet again in the middle."

Seth jolted upright. "I... Arya. Congratulations," he stammered, not quite meeting her gaze. Arya nodded jerkily, then turned her face away.

Together, he and McKenna, finding purchase on boulders sticking out of the swiftly moving river, crossed back to the other side, hopping quickly upon the back of Seth's golden mount. Arya winced, afraid to look at her partner.

"What in the world was that all about?" Layne demanded, turning her by the shoulder to look down into the girl's grey eyes.

"I don't know. Honestly, Layne," she replied softly, gripping the hand that rested on her. "I knew he would be... surprised, but I didn't expect him to feel..."

"Betrayed?" offered Layne, an edge to her voice.

Arya simply nodded, unable to describe the look in her brother's face any other way. She knew why he left the guild. She knew why Elgitha let him go. But maybe he didn't. Did he think she intentionally tried to usurp him?

So much for making him come back. He must hate me even more than he hates them.

"Arya. Lady Arya. Look at me," Layne shook her softly, then cupped a hand to her chin. "You promised. You chose this path, and you forged it yourself. You don't owe him anything."

The girl blinked, then sighed, slumping into her embrace. It was so much easier to rest on Layne than it was to live up to her brother.

"Fine. You're right. You're always right," she said, resting her chin on the taller girl's collarbone and smiling up into her face. "Are you sure you don't want to be Grand Master instead?"

"As if. Now stop looking at me like that, or I'm going to have to do something drastic."

"Like what?"

"I dunno. Kiss you? You nearly died, after all."

"I did NOT! I had everything perfectly under control."

Layne gave her a strange look. "So… you wouldn't say no, then?"

Arya rolled her eyes, pressing harder against Layne's chest. "Why would I say no?"

The tall paladin leaned down and planted a soft, furtive kiss on the tip of Arya's nose.

"That's all?" she said, eyes dancing in merriment.

"For now. Until you really almost die."

"Mean!"

XVI

MORTALS

The daemor genirae stalked around the summoning circle, inspecting each rune for accuracy. Though the Lich King himself demanded the servitude of the abyssal creatures, daemor are chaotic and swear no fealty, pay no homage to any being but themselves. And while Lady Astore could walk and mate freely with the daemor on his own home plane, the beast chafed at this sudden reversal of power and control.

Finally he paused, smothering the might of his daemoric rage that pulsed and dragged at the summoning energies of the sacerdhossa. She took a ragged breath, the monster's own fiendish grin mirrored in her dark visage.

"You will march in thrall of the Lich King," she ordered, the power of her voice echoing through chamber, through hallway, through corridor into the ears and essences of every daemor who walked out of the gate. "You will hear him and obey. To defy even his lightest wish will result in banishment from this plane and the delight of the scourge to which you would otherwise lay waste."

He bowed, not breaking eye contact with the woman. She nodded, and with a crack he vanished to seek his army and deliver the orders of the proposed march.

Astore paused, looking around at the small group

before her. A sacerdho lay dead. Faltering in his casting, the daemor with whom he linked powers shad sucked the very life from his frame. She waved an impatient hand and two lesser mages carried off his body. The remaining sacerdhossa approached her silently and bowed, then swept the remnants of the summoning circle and the brazier's dying embers away.

Summoning and sustaining a daemor is no simple feat. To let the beasts of the arcane Abyss walk free upon the land demands a strain on the magic of the people who do so, links their life force to the creatures they command. Lady Astore, with her own daemoric heritage, had never before summoned more than one greater daemor genirae. But in thrall of the Lich King's insidious persuasions, she and the three other high sacerdhossa and sacerdho chanted day and night for the entire solstice, bringing forth the might of a hellish daemoric army. Led by Makarh, the infernal beasts clambered out of the brazier, filling the bowels of the cult of Naszer and the underground labyrinth in which they hid.

"We have done powerful work this evening, Lady," spoke one, the curtain of black hair swept back from her pale cheeks aggressively accentuating the lines of her face. "You have now summoned two daemor genirae successfully to this plane. The Lich King will be most pleased."

"Sacerdhosa Aurum speaks truly," her twin sister, Agaz, agreed. "The sacerdho was not ready. But with yours and Cleric Qu'lan's powers combined, our army will be unstoppable.

"True," Astore whispered, still motionless before the empty brazier. She felt the tug of daemoric energy battling with her own mortality, and marshalled them into strict order. "True," she said again, louder, holding out her arms toward her acolytes. "I eagerly await the descent of the horde. Undead, daemoric, together at last to wipe those atrocious sisters and their petty squabbles off the map. What are the weaknesses of men to the greatness of this power?"

The two women nodded in agreement. "How long?"

Astore paused. To move too soon would test the strength of their powers, to move too slowly would invite discord amongst the chaotic ranks. "Until the end of the third solstice," she said. "Until then, we must continue to build our strength."

Aurum and Agaz nodded again, and silently withdrew from the chamber.

The insidious whispers of the Lich King filled the chamber, but she remained impervious as ever. "Don't you have a guild Master to manipulate?" she hissed, before vanishing through the smoking portal to the Abyss beyond.

--

Upon a wooden platform built outside the doors of the Guild Hall of Golden Eye, Master Gareth Achor stood beside Master Beltainne Diavolo, a tall, angular, snide looking man whose visage clearly showed his boredom for the proceedings before him. After the death of the Guild of Golden Eye's own Grand Master the preceding solstice, its Masters and Clerics simply hadn't bothered to raise a new one, opting instead to accept the timely unification proffered by Tooth and Claw. Their own power waned in the face of their rival guild's growth, and they were eager to cover up their loss of control over the

Cult of Naszer. But Cleric Qu'lan's savage threats paled in comparison to the greater of debts that mounted and coffers that stood empty.

"Make this quick, will you," muttered Beltainne, shifting uncomfortably in his dress robes.

The grim populace staring them down made the cleric nervous. He had heard of the attempt by the army of Beausun to enter, and based on the incongruous and angry faces swimming before him, he assumed the citizens of Lianor somehow knew as well. *The efficacy of cloaking their actions in the face of the horde with excuses of piety and devotion begins to wear off,* he thought, wiping the sweat from his brow and eyeing the Master Paladin from the corner of his eye, who stood motionless at the podium.

"Good people, blessed by the grace of Bahamut and Sanct Germain. We gather here today, for a mighty purpose," the big man boomed suddenly, silencing the crowd. "Our gods have spoken. For too long we have been at odds, fighting each other for the favor of gods who would have us love one another. To be aesir is to be mighty, to be good, to be blessed by the strongest and best Faie has to offer!"

A cheer, from the paladins and novitiates surrounding the huddled citizens, rose slowly and died quickly.

"We heed the wisdom of our mighty guides. They tell us to unite in the face of this sinister daughter of Atosa who would upset the balance of life and death, who would threaten our mighty race with the weaknesses and trickery of holvir, durgir, and orgir! Together only can we prove an unstoppable force capable of destroying the undead scourge and the woman who wields them. As such, before our people today, we announce the unification of the Guilds of Tooth and Claw and Golden Eye. Together, we are strong!"

The cheer rose again, with greater defiance this time. Those who were skeptical or nervous chimed in, with little conviction, but fear of alienation. The guilds were all-powerful in the city; their nobles having long given up most semblance of power or control in exchange for protection, ease, and gold.

"Those heretics out on the plains, they who deny our gods, shut their ears and their eyes to the advance of evil, must be made to see our light. They will join us, or perish. There is no other option. Out there, they say they are our equals. We have no equals!" He smashed a fist to the podium, the echoing drum reverberating throughout the square.

A low hiss emanated from a hooded figure in the crowd. Too low for anyone to notice, though their companion elbowed them and raised their red eyebrows fearfully.

"Where did Master Gareth come up with this tripe?" muttered Maria in *Besonne* under her breath to Charlot, who stood beside her.

"It sounds like what we've always been taught, doesn't it? Just close enough to what our history tells us to remain nearly indistinct from how evil it truly is," Charlot agreed, his eyes flashing at the sight of the golden dragon emblazoned on the Master's spotless white tunic.

Tears filled Maria's eyes at the sight. She could only hope the gods weren't listening.

As the impassioned Master wound up his speech, the crowd began to disperse, citizens shuffling away quickly to muse and gossip about what they'd just heard. Master Gareth's son Clint, leading a troupe of squires and novitiates, advanced toward the wooden podium to lead the Masters back to the guildhall. Gareth muttered something to Clint, who nodded and broke away toward the high gate set into the wall surrounding Lianor. An eerie hush descended upon the stone streets, once so full of the cacophony of chattering citizens. Not a single civilian remained in the open to accost the procession, which moved with dignity and with purpose down the city's main road.

Halfway along it lay two massive, impressive buildings. On one side, a tall structure- twin ivory towers of equal height- cast its shadow across the company. Bridges crossed between them, thirteen in total, leading up like the rungs of a ladder to the topmost floors. A dome of sparkling crystal rested between them, bearing the crest of Sanct Germain- perfectly balanced scales weighing an eye on one side and a hand on the other.

Across the road mirrored an equally imposing monolith. The Cathedral of the Golden God, not quite so tall, but made of brick coated in a thin layer of hammered gold. Its long arcade faced the road, with the bell tower rising in the back, topped with a facade of stained glass depicting the serpentine figure of Bahamut.

No one really knew what possessed the original Grand Masters of the Guild of Tooth and Claw and the Guild of Golden Eye to build their strongholds so near each other. Rumor had it the nobles were much more important back then, demanding the two live in peace- or at least an armed neutrality- and enforced the close quarters to make sure they did so. A lesser-known story went round that it had simply always been that way, that the two guilds' cooperation in their earliest histories led to the building of Lianor in the first place.

Very few people chose to tell THAT version, though. It got lots of dirty looks from any patron of either guild, and was a good way to find oneself banned from the taverns nearby.

Probably the most accurate explanation was that there simply wasn't enough space anywhere else in the city to house such massive structures. Nobles around the city had their manors and their high-rises, sure enough, but aside from the mighty Noble's Council in the center of the city, and the actual wall surrounding Lianor, most of the other narrow brick buildings were small, unassuming, and patently incapable of hosting the two most powerful and influential guilds in the realms.

Citizens liked to watch the occasional spat in the streets between novitiates, eager to distinguish themselves among the others in their guilds by "taking down those snobs a peg or two" or "giving the churlish louts a lesson in manners, for pity's sake". But thankfully the nobles, well aware of the powder keg of dissent threatening to blow at any moment, hosted any number of jousts and melees and feats of skill and strength for the guilds to blow off steam in a less dangerous way.

It had worked for a century, regardless of how the history books reported them.

"So, remind me again why this unification is so important to you, Master Gareth," drawled Beltainne, as he reclined in an upholstered chair at the end of a long dining table. They had toasted to their guilds' success, the honors of their gods, and endured all manner of long-winded protocol until almost all the attendant guild members had snuck out of the chamber or fallen asleep at their post. The third carafe of wine rested nearly empty on the table. With a firm glance at his page, sending the boy scurrying for more, Master Gareth tilted the remaining drink into his guest's glass with a hearty salute.

"It's important to all of us, Beltainne. Our realms are on the brink of disaster. We must face it together, or face destruction," he droned, with much the same tone as during his speech.

"Oh, come off that. You don't expect me to be so easily persuaded. Our guild is weak and nearly penniless. You could sweep us off the map at any point," spat Beltainne, his nonchalance dissolving into anger. "Why even bother? What do you have to gain?"

Gareth smiled to himself, swirling the remains of the wine within his own glass. With a start, Beltainne realized he was alone in the man's chambers. The silence of his entourage shifted his petulant swagger into a feeling much more akin to fear.

"It's not your guild I want, Beltainne, but you're so thoughtful to ask. You see, you put your faith in the wrong gods, my friend," he said with a lurid grin as the sharp, obsidian claws of a daemor suddenly bloomed from the cleric's chest.

Beltainne choked through a mouthful of blood. "But this is madness!" he groaned, as the realization dawned on him. "Our unification was supposed to drive out this hellish cult!"

He slumped to the floor, revealing the pulsating form of Razan. The daemor watched the man die impassively, stepping back slightly to avoid the touch of blood pooling from underneath his corpse.

"Hellish, did you hear that, Gareth?" pouted a sultry voice from the shadows. "Finally that pompous fool is dead."

Lady Astore stepped from the shadows; literally, shadow-walking through the darkness and past her son and the body of the murdered cleric. She raised her skirts to avoid the gore, swaying seductively toward Master Gareth.

"How else would you describe yourself, Astore?" grumbled Gareth. He thrust his chin out toward the novitiates who appeared at their master's signal, and they stepped forward to drag the body from the chamber.

"Listen to the pot calling the kettle black. Your squires did not even flinch at their screams," she replied, drawing out a handkerchief from between her breasts to wipe from them a spot of bright red blood. Gareth tried to ignore her, but as always, her mesmerizing, lascivious beauty entranced him. "Our daemor will feast well in the labyrinth tonight."

She snapped her fingers and Razan melted into the shadows. Suddenly the two were alone in the chamber, something Gareth became poignantly aware of. Whispers began to emanate from the very walls, crowding the masterful paladin's thoughts. He hissed under his breath and Lady Astore's eyes went wide, as she smiled that repulsive sadistic grin.

"Of course you want me. Who doesn't?" She said

lightly, swaying in place, the silken slide of her robes against her skin the only sound in the empty chamber. "You wouldn't have me as an immortal. What makes you think possessing this pathetic creature will change my mind?"

"Don't make me compel you," he whispered, his daemoric tones completely overriding the paladin's own voice.

"What part of this isn't compulsion? But alright, if you insist," she hissed. Her lilac eyes glowed red for a moment before utter darkness swallowed the chamber whole.

XVII

COURAGE

The road grew ever more familiar as the monk travelled along it, though so much time had passed between then and now. Their respite among the holvir of Padfoot helped to adjust them back to the realm of the living, though both knew they had little time to spare. As soon as they were able, she and the paladin returned to the road, deciding they should head to Ljotebroek before marching straight into Lianor and the unknown.

"You're on the right path, then," one of the blacksmith's apprentices had told them. "The united army of Beausun, what they're calling themselves, left for the same road as you. Follow them, we'll hold our own here."

It worried the monk to see how numb the encounter with Arya left Seth. She hesitated to broach the subject, knowing the paladin's reserve would prevent him from sharing his thoughts until he was ready. So they continued along, sometimes in silence, sometimes politely strained conversation, following the trail of the goodly army through the windswept plains.

After crossing Styckes, they stopped only briefly for a quick meal of the dried fruits and bread the Padfoot tribe generously provided them. Fresh from the realm of death, neither hero needed much sleep. And they feared to remain in one place for too long, as ilmaurte still roamed unchecked.

"I should try to use the mirror on the next group we see," she murmured, with a hunk of bread in one hand and the mirror in the other. "Send some souls Katarin's way. Would be a shame to leave her behind with nothing to do."

Seth nodded curtly, absently popping a handful of dried stonefruit into his mouth. Without warning he leaned against her, hiding his face on her shoulder.

"Penny for your thoughts?" she offered, softly stroking the black hair tucked behind his ear.

"No," he grumbled, but didn't move.

"You know you're proud of your sister. So why the hesitation?" she said, preferring to lance the boil as swiftly as possible.

He flinched, but she wouldn't let him go. The dread aura that haunted him- she would face it and she would fight it, no matter the cost. He saw the adamantine edge to the eyes locked upon him and sighed bitterly.

"She doesn't know what we fight for. Or what we fought against," he winced, shuddering under McKenna's keen glare.

"She's just as capable a paladin as you-" began McKenna. Seth cut her off sharply.

"That's not it. Paladins... guilds... faith. Our whole lives revolve around this stupid lie, the manifestation of godliness in chaos. The truth of guilds... of the culture that our whole society is built from, it's nothing like the noble cause she seeks. The young novitiates..." he trailed off. "They fight in these crusades against evil, against daemor or the other races or each other. And they either end up turning against our gods, or they die. What do we even know about the gods that we defy in our imitation? We're just mortals."

The quiet whispers of souls tugged at McKenna's spirit, the memory of her decades in the mines, her journey through the doors of death. Mortal? Was she even?

"I'm sorry. I don't expect this to make any sense to you," he sighed. "You're so sure, you walk so strongly in the light of Malfaestus. You have all the time in the world to live in his glory. Meanwhile, we have mere decades before our lives are done. What must asafolk do to live on?" He eyed her beseechingly.

Suddenly she understood. The spectre that walks beside him wasn't his own inadequacy. It was the clarity with which he saw the weaknesses of others who shared his heritage, whose freedoms he championed and whose lives he put before his own. She realized with a start, he was right. His whole life revolved around achieving the status of near godliness within the parameters of the society in which he lived, and yet their very feckless selfishness mocked him, mocked his great effort, his noble daring. With only one life to live, why make the ultimate sacrifice to achieve a greatness none would recognize, or even appreciate? What set Arya apart from any other on that road?

McKenna recalled the comment Layne made before Arya cut her off. "She said she would be Grand Master. Is that… was that what you wanted? Before you left?"

He sighed again. "It's what I was meant to be.

My entire life, every moment of my training... of my devotions, my quests. All of it centered around becoming Grand Master of the Guild of Tooth and Claw. I had no other purpose."

Suddenly she remembered Katarin, the words she spoke with her sister echoing in her head. "Maybe it's good that Arya's taking up the mantle, then. I think that... maybe, those who go before us know less than they imagine about what is best for their children, for the people we will become. Ultimately, no one but ourselves can know how to best live our lives. They can only make suggestions based on their own experiences."

"So because Arya grew up with expectations of her becoming a Lady, she's better off a Grand Master? That doesn't make sense," he replied.

"No," she said firmly. "It's because Arya knew what she wanted, regardless of what anyone else told her. That's what makes her a perfect Grand Master. She is beholden to no one, only her own strength and her own resolution. Like me," she spoke candidly, ignoring the tension in his hunched form. "I got to choose my own path. My sister didn't, and it nearly destroyed her."

He shrugged noncommittally, his face tinged pale, expressionless and blank. To watch his sister grow up beside him, to have protected her for so long, and then watch as she too was thrown into the maw of the beast that demanded every sacrifice, had to be nearly impossible to bear.

But endure it, he must. It wasn't his decision to make for her. Not knowing how to share such pain, all McKenna could do was drop beside the quiet paladin and wrap her arms around him, offering every inch of her to hold him up.

"I can't face this darkness for you, Seth. But I can face it with you. You have to trust her. You have a new path now," she smiled, lacing her fingers with his, "and you never have to go back to where you were, to what anyone expected you to be. It will take time to grow, and heal, and find your place. But however you choose to advance, you have my faith to go with you."

He kissed her forehead, unable to respond in words. Suddenly she needed him with a fire she'd never felt before, and the desperation with which he grabbed her and pulled her atop him spoke his own burning desire. They met, wild, ferocious; poured into one another the passions unlocked by their brush with death and the unspoken commitment to one another regardless of the road ahead.

Mortal indeed. There are no beings like these that know their truest needs.

She looked down into his golden eyes, seeing them slowly relax into acceptance, and lightly kissed his brow. With a grin, she suddenly stood and took a running leap for the sparkling river that ambled lazily along beside them.

"Come on, it's not even that cold," she cried, its reflection sparkling in her amber eyes. She laughed at the petulantly crossed-legged figure seated on the bank, refusing to dip even a toe into the refreshing waters.

"You're insane. That's Styckes water, you can't just… you can't just swim in there!" he stammered, unable to take his eyes off her lithe form stroking languidly up and down along the current.

"So? I'm a demigod of death. I've been through pasture and back, remember?" Cackling, she slapped a hand on the river's surface, splashing him. He yelped, then growled.

"You sure you want to play this game, monk?"

"As sure as I am you'll lose it, paladin."

Sighing and slipping back out of his breeches, he took a deep breath and dove gracefully under the crystal clear water. He surfaced next to her, blinking the drops from his own golden eyes.

She'd never get tired of staring into them. The memory of how they looked when first he spotted her across Hanthor's smoky tavern came in stark contrast to the limpid, joyful gaze that caressed her now.

Learning to love on an adventure comes with perilous pitfalls. What part of adoration can be traced to mere situation, after all? But she knew this went deeper than that. She knew the righteousness within him, mingled as it was with the world-weary heart that thought it had seen the worst in people, found its match in her naive spirit ready to empathise with any who offered her their trust. That their senses of humor, and their shared ability to face the daunting perils this world offered with a grin instead of a complaint, brought them mutual solace.

"You're right, it's actually not cold," he said, interrupting her reverie as they both tread water along the shoreline. He watched his hands for a moment, as though waiting to see them disappear, and she giggled.

"I already dragged your soul back once. I think the

river knows better than to take it again before it's ready," she said, lacing fingers with his. He smiled and planted a kiss on her knuckles.

"I'm lucky you came to get me. You're right, I wasn't ready to go," he murmured, his voice low. Before she could respond, he pulled her forward into a tight embrace, kissing her first softly, then with the desperation she felt when she'd watched him fall.

They floated like that for a moment, the golden glow of a late afternoon sun shining off the water and glistening on their skin, like gemstones set against the light. Pausing to reach into her innate powers, she thought she could sense the current's slow moving passengers- the souls of the ilmaurte that Arya had freed, flowing lazily along until they reached Pasture and then, hopefully, ascension. Any of those souls could have been theirs. But they were still here, together, ready to face what came next.

As the sun sank into the horizon, they reclined before a campfire. McKenna massaged her long fingers against Seth's scalp, wringing out the water and braiding his long black hair as her durgirn foster parents had taught her to braid their beards. Their closeness soothed her. The relaxed lines of his shoulders, glowing in the firelight; beads of water reflecting crimson flame, and the warmth of his skin against hers. She pressed a soft kiss into the crown of his hair, and he tensed and sighed.

"McKenna?"

"Yeah?"

"I love you."

She paused, then resumed braiding. "I love you too. I thought, you know, plucking you from the realm of death made that kind of obvious."

He turned under her touch, locking eyes with a ferocity that matched his kisses. Taking both her hands in his, he slid a copper ring off one of his fingers and touched it to the tip of her ring finger. She held her breath.

"This was my father's. It was his father's before him, and his father's before that, on and on like we asafolk like to do. He didn't want to pass it to me. He loved my mother, but he didn't think I'd want a family when I had a guild instead. Arya stole it," his eyes twinkled, "right off his finger, because I dared her she couldn't. And if you don't… want it," he hesitated, his deep voiced flexing with emotion, "if you don't want to marry me, I can give it back to her instead."

Slipping the ring onto her hand was effortless. It rested at the root of her finger like it was meant to be there, and she knew nothing would ever take it off. He wrapped his arms around her, clinging to her like a lifeline, and she pressed herself into his protective embrace.

"So… that's a yes, then?"

"That," she said with a smile and a kiss, "is absolutely a yes."

He placed his arms around her and breathed deeply, drinking in the scent of her skin and hair. *Like some flower unknown in this realm or the beyond,* he thought, *So familiar, yet unlike anything else. Positively intoxicating.*

"The road to Lianor is not so dangerous as what we'll find at the end of it." He spoke the words with a softness she rarely saw him express. In his voice she could hear conviction, though heavy with the weight of his memories. "But you're right. I'll not abandon my sister, or her ideals, to their mercy. I swear it, McKenna," he knelt before her, the hand holding hers pressed to his heart, "where you lead, I will follow."

"I wager we can hold our own against any manner of folk, fair or foul," She replied, grinning before blessing his lips with a gentle kiss and breaking free from his grasp in one graceful movement. "In any case, now you're stuck with me, and we have ilmaurte to fight. So let's go."

Lifting him to his feet, they mounted Kurya again, taking off down the road with their backs to the setting sun.

Halfway through the next day, they spotted the unmistakable signs of an army's march.

"Uhm… are they coming toward us?" Seth squinted into the vista, sure the figures were growing, not shrinking, as they approached.

"That doesn't make any sense. Come on, let's see who we can find," replied McKenna, and the two galloped for the crowd.

Of course, James spotted them first. With a whoop and a fist pumped high in the air, he dismounted his own steed and enveloped the paladin in a hug so tight he nearly disappeared. Both were laughing and shining eyed as they broke apart.

"So much for being dead! You barely gave me enough

time to even mourn you." The squire's voice broke as he kept a hand clapped to Seth's shoulder.

"I couldn't let you get too far ahead of me, could I? Where's Katherine?" he responded, peering into the crowd.

James rolled his eyes. "She and the Lord of Dragon's Hill are mounted up at the rear, supposedly to make sure we aren't attacked from behind. Considering they can barely pay attention to anything other than each other, I doubt how well that's going."

"Lord of Dragon's Hill, huh? Masa Riquelme? They've joined your enterprise?" His eyes roved the goodly company as McKenna jubilantly reunited with Pabble and the durgir of Clan Hammardin. "Durgir and holvir too? You've been busy, friend!"

"Yes, but unfortunately the best we can say is that we're all together," James scowled darkly.

"Lianor won't budge?"

"Worse. I'll tell you when we've made it back to Dragon's Hill. For now, it's the safest spot to remain 'til we figure out what we can do."

Twilight set upon the party before Seth and McKenna could be filled in on the exploits of the army of Beausun and the shocking news of the unified guilds.

"How could Tooth and Claw and Golden Eye even begin to unify? What did Elgitha have to say about that?" asked Seth, hand clamped tightly on a frothy mug.

"We don't know. They wouldn't even let us talk to

the magistrate of the guard, let alone enter and speak with the Grand Masters," replied Katherine, who sat across from them beside Lord Masa.

"Didn't you say the Cult of Naszer is under Golden Eye? If what Lulann told us is true, and they've summoned daemor along with the Lich King…" McKenna trailed off, unwilling to finish the sentence.

"That's exactly what we're afraid of. A unification would make it that much easier for the Lich King to manipulate the guilds and the strength of Lianor's army. How they're going to explain a host of evil daemor is another story." Lord Masa inspected McKenna's open expression. "You say this holvi Pasha knew of a summoning?"

"She'd heard rumors. And if there's one thing among the many holvir are good at, it's listening," affirmed McKenna. "It seems he's unable to control them just yet, not until he's ready to strike."

"A daemor legion is almost impossible to wield," added Seth. "He was probably waiting for the unification of the guilds before launching a secret strike. Make it look like an external attack on Lianor by an unknown force, manipulate the guilds and the nobles from the inside, and assume power. But once they're on this plane, daemor are unstoppable and uncontrollable. If he released them too soon, before usurping power, the realms would turn on Naszer."

Sethisto's words echoed in McKenna's head. *I'd wager to bet the gods will bring you back just when you're meant to.* She chuckled to herself. The spirit had been right.

A bustle outside of the town square attracted the

table's attention. Sounds of cheers precluded a crowd, making their way toward them. An attractive brunette, alongside a tall, lanky man with fiery hair and a swagger, waved cheerily at the assembly. Lord Masa shot up from his seat and enveloped the two in a warm embrace.

"Mi hija! Mi hijo! Ustedes han regresado sano y salvo!" He kissed both heartily on the cheeks, then led them toward the group at the table. "Honored guests, my son and his wife, Charlot and Lady Maria. Every day I thank the gods who blessed me with a dutiful daughter-in-law…" he trailed off, and a pained expression crossed his face.

"And a dutiful daughter, who misses you both very much," Maria said pointedly, frowning both at him and Charlot. Charlot rolled his eyes, but Lord Masa at least had the decency to drop his.

"Riquelmes. Honestly." She held out her hands toward McKenna and Seth, peering interestedly at the monk and the runes inked on her skin. "You must be the durgirn child of the goddess we've heard so much about. Your friends sing your praises well."

"You met Ginni and Tjena? How are they?" McKenna and Seth both spoke at once, eagerly.

"We met the holvir in Bristendine. Their road lay south, to Gamorre, but they made certain to inspire as many as they could to take arms against the scourge in defense of you, goddess-child."

"In my defense? Whatever for?" McKenna turned to Seth, the confusion on her face mirrored in his own.

"You've been gone too long, McKenna," spoke

Katherine, her voice whetted with anger still at the blindness of the guild's prejudice. "Your exploits, as the unknown daughter of Atosa with control over the ilmaurte and access to the realm of death, has put you in a particularly unfavorable position."

Maria nodded, taking a seat next to the dazed monk. "It's true. We have heard similar tales. They hide their own sins behind a curtain of mystery, which they accuse you of drawing. They say the horde's advance has slowed in the three years you spent in the realm of death. But now you are back, they warn anyone that to ally with you is to bring down the wrath of the gods."

Seth frowned. "Bahamut blessed her himself. I was there. How can the gods be so blind?"

McKenna couldn't help but giggle. "What?" his eyebrow shot up.

"You sound like me. What was all that about 'the petty squabbles of mortals are beneath them'?"

"It's not mortals we're dealing with anymore, though," broke in Katherine. "The gods can turn a blind eye for only so long."

A hush descended on the party. Without Sh'nia, the pantheon refused to come to their aid. Would the little holvir be enough to rouse the Sun ilvir and summon her?

Maria's voice broke the silence. "This place was beautiful once. Women danced in the streets, men and children sang songs, played games, told stories. Our people have belonged to the pantheon since before they even were immortal, and yet…" she looked around at the assorted company, crestfallen at how little they numbered, a reminder of how many they lost.

"We lost our way, we turned our backs on gods who then turned their backs on us. We let men speak for us who would watch us die if it meant their coin remained untouched and power unchallenged. They say, 'Gods don't listen'. Gods play their games with the lives they've made, then claim divinity, that we cannot achieve such heights as we are simply mortal, simply souls, simply fodder for the eternal game. But what game is this?" she gestured violently, throwing her arms wide. "What cruel rule allows us to see the board for what it is, see our place upon it, and see the moves we could never make and the moves that instead will be made for us? We see enough to know that we play ourselves for fools, enough to know that those we play with are stuck in the same abysmal trap."

She paused for breath, a breeze stirring the chocolate curls that brushed her cheek. "We may not have divinity. But we have our will. If we didn't, we wouldn't be so miserable, and if we didn't, we wouldn't be so blindly hopeful, and if we didn't, we wouldn't be able to see the lies for what they are. We'd be far too busy burying our heads in the sand, in our foibles and weaknesses, knowing what's best for us, wanting what we can't have."

As she looked them over, a fierce light bloomed in her fiery brown eyes. Each person her gaze lit upon felt that fire warm their own determination, their own courage, to fight.

"I have a will of my own, and I choose to make a stand. My will may be bound, like that of so many of yours, but I will not let my history determine my future. My courage is not drowned in fear. My desperation to right this eternal wrong will never outweigh the uncertainty of the outcome. And none of that," she finished breathlessly, "will keep the weight of mithril from my hand and the blood of my enemies from watering the soil!"

At her speech, a great silence, and then a great cheer, rang through the courtyard. Maria smiled, then whistled blithely. At her cue, the musicians from before struck up a rousing tune, to remind the company they were yet still living, and whole, and had the strength to fight another day. The colorful lanterns and bright moon in the sky gave off a glow that couldn't even begin to match that of their spirits.

XVIII

BLESSED

Her steps fell heavier than they did before. Light heart, hope and promise, brought her to this quest. And now, if she were being honest with herself, all Arya felt was the loss of her brother all over again.

Rogue. My brother is a rogue. Why do those words hurt worse than his death?

The rock she clipped with an angry foot sailed into the brush, startling a flock of affronted quails who tittered and scattered before a concerned Layne. Her heart faltered at the unexpected emotional outburst. It just wasn't like the reserved Arya.

"The refugees shouldn't be far," she offered, when the silence stretched on beyond endurance.

The flow of the fresh river forced them onto uneven banks, and each picked their step with care. Styckes water *did* things, or so the legends told, and neither girl wanted to take the risk of another plunge. Arya shrugged her shoulders in response, face turned away, silent and otherwise unresponsive.

Refugees. He turned his back on them, just like he turned his back on us.

An unsettling aura emanated from her, the conflict of her age-old devotion and the disappointment she believed she had no right to feel. How could she dare to judge him? He was the child of prophecy; he was the chosen one, and she was just a pretender. A lucky charlatan, in the right place at the right time, granted this opportunity simply to fill the space he left vacant. It was his duty to finish what he started, to assume the place he'd been destined for since birth, and the longer she pretended she could fill it for him...

Suddenly she stopped dead in her tracks. Layne, a few paces behind her, had stopped too; long enough for the aura that had arrested them both to descend, and fill the hearts of each with mortal dread.

"That's not just ilmaurte," Layne whispered, color draining from her face along with every calm, hopeful thought as the shifting energies became clear.

A pulsing black miasma grew on the horizon. Another host of undead, waves of heat and spray from the roaring river blurring their numbers. Something more marched with them, something with a shape and an energy foreign to the two paladins who, with martial readiness, prepared to meet their foe.

"Come on, we have to face it- whatever it is," cried Arya, the spark of light returning as she saw the despair in Layne's face.

Nothing should ever dare to make her look like that. Listen to me, wallowing in some kind of self-pity. She's worth more than that.

Together, they raised their arms against the deadly host, meeting in battle with a cry to Bahamut and a determination to prevail.

"Ugh, this is infuriating. Where are they even all coming from?!" raged Arya, as she fired bolt after blessed bolt into the advancing scourge, eviscerating them in their tracks.

They had their backs to the river, standing on a small jetty that curled like a crooked finger into the oily black water. A ridge of sandstone obscured the host as it shambled listlessly towards them. But it served the double purpose of driving them in nearly as straight a line as possible towards the warriors, who stood ready to sweep them from the thin dirt path along the river's banks and into its rapids below.

"Lots of people have died in the past few years. The Lich King can really just take his pick at this point," replied Layne with a grunt as she shifted the ledge upon which a group of ilmaurte crawled, sending them careening into the swiftly moving water. Her ground-moving powers, unlike most magic, seemed to grow stronger with use. Throwing her battle axe with all her might at a knot of undead, splitting them up into two smaller groups, she pushed one half to the side and into the river with a subtle tremor. The other half, she simply dumped into a hole and buried with a clap of her palms. Before the scourge could regain its forward momentum, her axe whistled through the air- blasting through the heads of two and the spine of one, sending pieces of undead monster flying into their brethren.

"I wish McKenna were here. She's definitely not summoning the ilmaurte, but I bet you she could take them out." The paladin wiped a line of sweat from her brow and, whispering a short prayer, summoned a blessing that struck another line of ilmaurte into the turbid ravine. The clouds, hovering on the line of sandy cliffs that bordered the ravine, seemed to glow gold with the power of her paladin magic. The anxiety in her heart, that wore the aspect of her brother's face, disappeared in a wave of devotion for the glorious golden god who granted her his might in battle.

I want this. I want this more than anything. More than his redemption. Bahamut bendiga.

"We're supposed to be doing this on our own, Lady Arya. We'll be fine- oh."

Arya turned at the sound of her friend's breathless gasp. On the horizon, a black, shifting cloud had risen. And with it marched a beacon of Abyssal light.

No, there weren't just ilmaurte. There was something else.

"A daemor genirae," whispered Arya.

Razan's lurid form bloomed from the heart of the black, unnatural storm cloud that spread over the prairie. The daemor genirae led a host of imps and ilmaurte, advancing across the plains with ease.

Arya couldn't understand it. How could a genirae get here?

"It looks like… they're coming from Lianor. How is that possible?" seethed Layne, as the two ducked into a trench the paladin formed in the ground.

"I don't know," Arya was breathing heavily, wracking her brains for everything she'd ever learned about daemor. "The sorceres of Meliamne can summon daemor, but they would never, ever release them. And besides, Meliamne is behind us! How could they have crossed to Lianor without going through Wheelspoke?" Arya replied confusedly, twisting her rings.

"Wherever they're coming from, they're definitely marching here. We have to stop them, Arya, they'll kill every single refugee in their path!" Layne's green eyes glimmered almost golden with the light of her god, as she whispered a prayer and stroked the runes along her wrists.

"Well, you know what you owe me if we fail," muttered Arya, with a crooked grin. Layne stared at her intently, then without warning leaned down and kissed her fiercely.

"Wait! We're not dead yet!" laughed Arya, twining her fingers in the girl's fiery hair.

"You think I'm going to wait til we're both stuck in Hel to kiss you? When I've been waiting for so long already? You're crazy, Lady Arya," replied Layne breathlessly, leaning in for another.

"I love you," Arya whispered against the softness of her mouth.

"I love you too."

They embraced, and a pulsing light began to glow around the two of them. Shrouded in the blessings of their god, and the strength of their loyalty and devotion.

The oncoming scourge of the Abyss didn't stand a chance.

Razan's bloody, obsidian gaze narrowed at the Celestial brightness. With a hiss, he released the horde to strike, scores of imps and undead heading directly for the two seemingly defenseless paladins.

"We need to run them into the river. Layne?" Arya, her gaze shining with love, looked over to the paladin at her side. Her friend's own reflected their shared passion, and she nodded.

Charlatan magicians, they called them. Amateurs, phonies, untrained and uncouth in the mysteries of real magics. What illusion, what trickery, those Dragon's Hill folks. A soothsayer at her mother's elbow- both near death, though neither knew it then- that bound this child of fire and golden prairie at once to the god of the sky above and the ground upon which her people found their power. A twist of arm, a flick of wrist, and from the ground a shelf of impenetrable rock.

No one came close to the latent power Layne- Elena Riquelme, the second daughter and second child of prophecy of Dragon's Hill- possessed over her town's heritage. With a flash of those green eyes, she flexed her right arm, as though gripping the roots of the realms in her muscled hands and lithe fingers. A dexterous twist, and a *Besonne* chant that called upon the divine Faie Mother herself, flowed from the depths of her soul and the tips of her fingers into the sand and stone beneath their feet.

The rumble of dirt that closed on the wave of monsters could fell a building. While the imps and lesser daemor could simply fly over her summoned impediment, the ilmaurte were forced to stagger closer to the riverbank, or be crushed utterly under the wave of rock that rolled from beneath them.

Now, Arya's turn. She knelt and stroked runes in

the sand with the same dexterity and accuracy as before, when she had summoned the waters from Styckes to flow again. With a shout, she struck her palm across them, scattering the sand and dust into a cloud.

The water at the bank frothed. A wave, matching the cloud of dust, swept up and doused the ilmaurte where they stood. One by one, the swirling vortex sucked them into the river. Daemor hissed as the blessed mist stung them, overspray splashing onto the horde.

"Look out!" screamed Layne, shoving Arya to the side, as a bolt of energy struck the ground where they stood.

"Mortals. Why waste your time," hissed a voice above them. Layne shot bolts wildly at his hovering figure, but he simply dodged them effortlessly.

"Who are you? Where did you come from?" she shrieked, still hunched protectively over Arya, calling down an oath that bloomed into a golden dome. Arya used the cover to begin chanting a powerful summoning.

I bet Arya could do it.

A tattered scroll, the vellum wiped clear. An ancient oath struck from the annals of time by the Masters who feared the truth of its power. She murmured under her breath, willing the words to form. If Bahamut truly blessed her, honored the bearer of a family name that sang his praises for generations, now would be the time to show it.

"I could ask you the same, but it doesn't matter. You're dead," he replied, releasing another bolt of energy at the girls.

Layne shouted, lifting her axe over her head, and the golden light flexed, repelling the daemor's blast. It bounced into a crowd of chattering imps, obliterating them instantly.

"Disgusting. As though the gods even know what true power is," the daemor spat, then dove toward Layne with his talons outstretched. Two bolts fired in succession drove him off course, followed by the sweep of battle axe.

Layne screwed up her concentration, eyes widening as she caught the cadence of the spell Arya cast.

"Are you sure about this?" she yelled, drawing the divine protection spell tighter around them as Razan recoiled from the flat of the battle axe's blunt attack, eager for another strike.

"No," Arya replied with a grin. "But... you're still going to help me do it."

I just kissed her for the first time and I'm about to bury her. Typical, Layne thought to herself. With a flick of her wrist she opened the sand around the paladin and shut it quickly, then stood to face the daemor.

Please, Bahamut, whispered Arya. *I am not my brother.*

Suddenly the ground around her became hot. Stiflingly hot. A glow tore through the darkness, and fire seared the flesh within it. It hurt so badly Arya didn't even realize she was in pain. With a roar, she burst from the ground, leaping into the air on newly made wings of gold.

"*Bahamut bendiga...*" Layne whispered, ducking a

blow from the daemor.

Arya's entire form glistened with bright scales. Her arms ended in talons longer than the daemor's own, and her mouth filled with sharp, elongated teeth- and fire.

Lots of fire.

The dragon girl roared, releasing a molten blast over Layne's head. The paladin ducked and Razan barely managed to dodge, sustaining a blistering burn that scorched his daemoric wing. He shrieked, then fled back towards the oncoming army.

With a blinding flash, Arya released another searing stream of fire into the advancing horde. Incinerating imps, daemor, and undead, a single blast nearly managed to obliterate the entire legion. Layne fired bolts at the remaining troops, pushing them closer and closer toward the purifying waters of the rejuvenated river, still in thrall of Arya's first oath. It swept them away with little more than a murmur, souls left to float peacefully toward Pasture, toward a salvation the Lich King tried to deny them.

Their numbers finally began to dwindle, and the clamoring army turned in pursuit of their injured leader. Soon, only the scorchmarks the dragon girl left on the rocks remained.

She came to a landing beside Layne, who tensed. "That is one hell of a blessing, Lady Arya."

The dragon chuckled. "One day, you'll have to stop calling her that. Though I think secretly, she likes it."

Layne's eyes widened in fear. "B...Bahamut? It's you?

Then where…"

"We're both here, don't worry. The T'ssama girl has a fierce spirit of her own even a god couldn't subdue. I thank you for guarding my champion, Layne Riquelme. Both body, and heart."

The paladin, pulse racing in the hand placed over her chest, bent a knee in reverence. The dragon sighed, exhaling warm breath over her, stirring her red hair and releasing a medley of sound from the clanking of her metal armor.

Without a word, the avatar stepped backwards, dipping quickly into the river. Layne rose and scrambled toward the bank. There, floating and gasping, was Arya.

"That… that was weird. Please don't let me do that again," she sputtered, spitting a stream of water onto the shore.

Layne laughed helplessly, then tugged her partner out of the river.

"I'll do whatever you want, if you promise to learn to aim that firebreathing!" she joked, running her fingers through Arya's wet hair.

"You're a redhead. Aren't you fireproof?" Arya returned cheekily, kissing the paladin's wrist. "Come on, let's go home. We have a guild to fix."

The normally bustling thoroughfares that crisscrossed through the plains and gave Wheelspoke its name stood perilously empty. Though circumventing the valley in which lay Arya's hometown, they still expected to see the normal traffic that populated the well-travelled highways.

They grew concerned, wondering where all the traders and travellers went.

"It's nearly solstice. We should be tripping over envoys to Lianor. What's going on?" mused Layne out loud, when they were within sight of the massive walled city.

"Hmm. I think we're about to find out," replied Arya, squinting at a plume of smoke rising in the distance.

Its source proved difficult to find. The small campsite, half hid in the brush and far off the main road, would've gone completely unnoticed had lesser people than they sought it. Nothing daunted, Arya and Layne held out their wrists as they advanced towards the figures huddled around the small, smoky fire.

"Gods, it's paladins! We're sorry, we're sorry, we're leaving right now!" cried the closest, throwing up his hands in surrender.

"No no! It's okay! All peace," Arya spoke with authority. The man and his partner shook, but slowly extended their wrists in salute. Tapping each briefly, the women took a seat, looking with concern at the campers. Arya noted with surprise the somewhat fine garb each were robed in, suspiciously unmarked, but unlikely to be found on any less than a noble or a guild Master. "Are you refugees?"

"Well, we weren't, until a few days ago," the man's partner, a diminutive blonde under a huge hood, muttered angrily.

Layne peered curiously at her, noting her accent and fine, noble features. "Aren't you from Lianor?

What's going on, where is everyone? I've never seen the countryside so abandoned in my life."

She shrank into herself slightly, then drew back her hood. On her neck, a set of scales tattooed in mottled black and silver ink gleamed in the firelight. Arya gasped in sudden recognition. Only the Masters of Sanct Germain chose to brand themselves with their god's symbol. She and Layne dropped into half-bows before the high ranking mage- Ignithe, Cleric of Golden Eye.

"Oh, please don't- especially not paladins of Bahamut, I can't stand that ceremony," Ignithe said, waving her hand at them. "Are you coming back from a quest then? How long have you been gone, exactly?"

Arya and Layne looked at each other, and shrugged. "A tenday at most, give or take a couple days. We've been a bit… preoccupied, and haven't really kept track," Layne replied in a measured tone.

"Lucky you," chimed in the woman's companion, whom Arya also recognized as her apprentice Severn, a thin, dessicated man with a fringe of sandy hair. Though unassuming, she knew he possessed incredible magical abilities granted by the God of Justice- Sanct Germain, patron deity of Golden Eye.

"I'm not sure I understand," Arya said deferentially, turning an inquisitive look to the cleric. "Has something happened in Lianor?"

"Something happened, alright. The guilds," Ignithe took a deep breath as Severn sucked air through his teeth, "defying gods, and logic, and whatever else, have proposed unification."

Confusion settled on the brows of both paladins.

"Unification. Of the... of Golden Eye and Tooth and Claw?" Arya's eyes were the size of coins, while Layne simply gaped wordlessly beside her. "Like, a truce? A pact?"

The woman sighed, the sigh turning into a hiss of anger. "No. It is no simple truce. Our gods aren't good enough for the masses any more, it seems. So our Masters proposed a merger between Golden Eye and Tooth and Claw," her voice took on a pitched mocking tone, "'presenting a unified front of Lianor to face the horde.'"

Layne's jaw dropped. "A WHAT?! How is that possible? Grand Master Elgitha would never agree to that. No offense, but Sanct Germain and Bahamut have never been... close."

"Call a scale a scale. They're eternal, fearsome rivals. Why do you think we're out here, instead of in there?" A coy half grin accompanied her words.

"As far as we're concerned, the gods have absolutely nothing to do with this," affirmed Severn, the devotion on his brow clear to the paladins. "No, it is asafolk who are responsible," he said mournfully, closing his eyes as though in pain, "Asafolk who wield holy might and flout the gods who blessed them with it."

"So, not all the Masters agreed then. That's... terrifying," returned Layne. Arya could read the distress in her face. How could Elgitha let this happen?

"As for your Grand Master, I don't know what side she's on. No one's heard from her in days. Before we left, rumors spread that she was ill; confined to her quarters with only a couple close attendants. But don't worry," she said hastily at the expression on the women's faces. "She's definitely not dead. Everyone would know if she was, silent gods or no. But she wasn't at the unification ceremony. It was that pompous what's-his-name… Gavin Ichor?"

Arya groaned so loudly it disturbed a crow overhead, who cawed annoyedly and took flight. "Master Gareth Achor?"

"That's the one! I do hate that man. Always slinking around with Cleric Qu'lan… hate him too," she seethed, fingers clawing at her fine robes.

"Don't worry, you're not the only one. But we can handle him, once we get back. We'll get to the bottom of this, I promise," Arya leaned toward the woman and her companion. "Where will you go in the meantime?"

The woman tapped her cheek thoughtfully, studying them for a moment. "We heard another rumor. That an army of refugees and liberated towns has formed on the plains. They call themselves the army of Beausun. We hoped we could follow their tracks and join them. They're trying to face the horde, after all, and any Master worth their god," she shrugged, and put a hand on her apprentice's shoulder with a trusting smile, "should be doing the same."

A unified guild, and a unified army. Such things were completely unprecedented in the realms' modern history. A wave of remorse flooded Arya's thoughts. *He knew, didn't he. He knew the path the guild headed down, despite what he did for them. No wonder he left. No wonder he won't come back.*

She remembered the daemor genirae, and the legion of imps and ilmaurte, and shuddered at the thought of such a foe facing any of their kindred. Layne laced her fingers through Arya's reassuringly. Anything they must face, they would face together.

"We wish you luck and gods' speed on your journey, then, friends," Arya said, standing and sweeping a nod at the pair.

"And you, fair paladins. May your god bless your entry back into Lianor. You'll need it, and more," Severn replied cryptically.

They all turned to face the high walls of Lianor, glowing in the fading light; a monument to aesir determination. A living testament to the power and ingenuity of the asafolk, of glory, of greatness.

And a reminder of all that meant.

XIX

UNITY

Tjen noted with some surprise that, though the bard's mouth was open, not a single sound came out.

The Red Solstice Sing of Meliamne celebrated all the wonder and achievement of their people and their realm. Led by their great Choirmaster, the night of revelry centered around powerful seances of song that summoned as much magical energy from the turn of the season as possible.

On this night, even the xenophobic ilvir of the Moon could sense the stirring of great events reverberating throughout the realms. The refugees huddled still beneath their great bowery towers, their goddess' silence pierced their devotions. And the Guild of Moonbow, the undisputed heart of their realm, had been rocked to its core by intrigue.

Grand Masters do not usually step down from hard-won pedestals.

"You all knew the whole time?" Tjen asked incredulously, staring around at sheepish faces turned away from the holvir and each other. Their partner, jaw dropped in disbelief at the display they'd just witnessed, squeaked in agreement. The song's notes still reverberated in the sky, dripped from the trees, sparkled in the stars. The song of the Moon ilvir and their mourning for the loss of their Gamorren cousins' faith.

"Many of us lived through it. These buildings," the former Grand Master, Mirai Mistmoon, swept a stately arm at the forest vista interwoven with lifeless towers of metal and stone, "you think they came from our own ingenuity? We erected them in spite," she sighed, folding her hands across her chest, "to separate us further from the ilvir of Gamorre. What need had we of their magic of life? Their goddess, who so challenged and belittled the glory of ours?"

"Where do we start," muttered Ginni under her breath.

"For over a hundred years we have been estranged from those who were once closer than family," she continued. "Our hubris, our jealousy- our mortal expression of the grudge between the two sisters- pushed us from one another, and in that emptiness and anger we sowed the seeds of discord that blossomed into a Lich King and hellish legion of undead."

"Stubbornness, spite, pride," Ginni ticked each off the tip of a finger. "Sounds so… aesir, if you ask me.

Illin chuckled. "Is this your way of asking if we've learned our lesson?"

Ginni turned to the mage, eyes narrowed, hands on her hips. "I think you'll have to answer that with a lot more than just words."

The chastened crowd looked at her sullenly, affronted that a holvi would dare challenge their Grand Master so flippantly. Illin simply laughed again.

"We heard you, child." He stood, and suddenly a

hush descended upon the gathered company. His figure, discordant as it appeared to his identity, issued an almost harmonious balance of confidence, the truest security in one's being. Ginni stole a look at Mirai, who watched with a proud light glinting in her imperious eyes.

"Those who choose to stay, are free to stay. This is your home, your god, your neighbors, your family. None fault you for their protection. But I go," he said, conviction rising with every word, "I go to unite our people."

He turned to the holvir, a puzzled look of deep, almost ancient sadness on his soft face. "How do we apologize to someone who doesn't want to hear it? How does one begin to... to resolve such a dispute? Rooted in misconception, buried in spite, and manured with misgivings and determination to persevere, in the insistence that this is simply the new status quo?"

The bard began to wish Urtha could be here to solve this. *Figures*, she thought to herself, *the races most persecuted are the ones they turn to in distress.* She took a deep breath, trying to frame a response that unified criticism with compassion.

"We do what we can to feel accomplished, to mature and grow within ourselves and be proud of who we are," she sang, her spoken words flowing with all the magic of her holvi voice. "There will always be mornings where we wake in tears, in gasps of strife over memories of one failure, of a single point of contention for which we may never find closure. It's stupid. It's painful."

She could almost cut the tension with a knife. The warble of song infused with her voice stood as the only thing separating her words from violence.

You are not "just" anything, Urtha's words echoed in her head. Swallowing, she continued in spite of the growing hostility, knowing that even should they turn on her, she must speak.

"We can't expect everyone to love us. We have to expect that there will always be people, good people, who despite our own goodness will despise us for a weakness we cannot control. Or worse, could, but didn't. Nothing will change that. It doesn't make them worse than us. It just makes us mortal, and not gods."

A single shaft of moonlight filtered through the canopy above. It glowed on flesh and raised ire, cooling the passions lit by this challenge thrown by such a despised creature. Mortal. To live, and to die. Not be forced to endure the eternity of an uncaring universe. None of them lived in a vacuum. Nothing earned or achieved done in solitude.

The holvi's words were uncomfortable. But then, they were truth.

"Remember your heroes are mortal too. Nothing in the whole wide world can save us from this except ourselves. Face our wrongs, acknowledge them, and grow from them. That… that's all I can really say," she finished lamely.

She was a holvi, after all. Holvir had no magic.

Ilvir, glowing in a spell of moonlight untouched and unrecognized for a century, however, do.

Silver runes blossomed as though lined with a fae fire on pale skin. An ethereal sound echoed across the platform, blooming flowers starred the boughs above, and the holvir could only stare in awe as the Moon ilvir appeared to experience some kind of ethereal transformation beyond anything they'd ever witnessed. A haunting melody filled the air and the moon seemed to grow brighter; bright enough they had to shield their eyes for a moment.

When the brightness faded, Atosa stood before them.

"About time," she smiled, placing a faintly glowing hand upon Ginni's coppery tresses. "My daughter beat you by almost a tenday."

"McKenna? She's back in the land of the living? Did she…" Ginni trailed off hopefully, while Tjena clasped their hands in delight. The ilvir surrounding them gasped, then dipped low into bows, kneeling before their beloved goddess and the unexpected holvir who summoned her.

"Yes. She saved the paladin. They ride for Lianor. My champions, thank you for taking my quest on her behalf. None could succeed but you." She looked around at the gathering of Moon ilvir, lined as they were with the soft moonlight.

Their faces had grown longer, their skin nearly translucent, their ears aggressively tapering to animalistic points. In place of the marks born by the Sun ilvir mimicking the animal life they lived among, their skin showed constellations matching the night sky above. Each had a long, thin hand over their heart and their head bowed before her.

"Ah, that's much better," Atosa crowed happily, placing a finger under Illin's angled chin.

The Grand Master smiled, humbled by her recognition. "The holvir were right. In our arrogance, our spite, we began to lose ourselves. Now, before our goddess, we are whole again. The magic of Faie emboldens us like never before," he sighed happily, holding his arms out wide to the people of Meliamne.

"The ilvir were... were turning aesir? That's weird. That's weird, right?" Ginni looked frantically at her own fragile fingers and diminutive limbs, as though expecting some kind of similar transformation. *Phew. Still holvi.*

"In a way, I guess you could say that," Illin replied. "Beloved Goddess, we made a promise to right our wrongs, to help restore peace to Faie. We hope... we mean to find..." he faltered, hesitating to bare the truth before the enigmatic deity.

"My sister? I sure hope you do. That's why I sent them here in the first place," she replied, putting a hand on each of the holvir's shoulders. "And I'm here to make it easier for you. The longer I spend on this plane, the more souls the Lich King can steal from Pasture. I-"

She stumbled suddenly, braced against falling by the steadying hands of Ginni and Tjena.

"My lady? What's the matter?" Ginni asked concernedly, her lilting voice singing in an attempt to restore the goddess's nerve.

She winced, her face screwed up in pain, the agony of death as it was torn from her careful guardianship by the Lich King's powerful might.

"We must go quickly. He moves," she gasped,

drawing a ragged breath. "I can… open a portal to Gamorre, send you through. But you have to sail," she closed her eyes again, bracing against the pain. "You have to sail for the north. You cannot ride, you'll be too late. I cannot protect you… you have to summon my sister. You have to have her blessing to make the crossing through the seas."

Illin and Ginni exchanged nervous glances. No one sailed the untamed sea that pushed on the border of Faie. They didn't even name it. Across that great expanse, only once had any ship made land. A contingent of asafolk, lost amid the endless swells, ran aground below White Face, the cliff upon which Lianor stood.

The nobles of Lianor tried to return home many times. All had failed.

"I… yes, my lady. Send us quickly, and then return to Pasture. We promise, your sister will come to your aid." Illin bowed again, and Atosa walked toward the trunk of the tall tree upon which they perched, pressing her palm against its bark. It glowed softly, then the outline of a translucent door appeared.

"This will last until you are ready to depart. Thank you, my champions," and like Bahamut, bowed to the surprised mortals, then faded in a sparkle of stardust.

"Did that just…" Tjena blinked at Ginni, who stared open mouthed at Illin. "A goddess. She just bowed. She bowed to us."

Illin's face was inscrutable. Ginni opened her mouth to question it, but for the second time that day found herself completely speechless.

With surprising rapidity, the envoy of Moon ilvir presented themselves before the gate. Shouldering her pack, Ginni straightened and without a backwards glance, stepped through into the forest that waited beyond.

—

"For time eternal in realms of Faie
Two sisters guard as night and day,"

The ilvir tribes shifted uncomfortably, but could not turn their eyes from one another. So like, and yet so unlike.

"You guard the realms of death and life
Charge not this land with undue strife"

The holvi's voice carried through the clearing, above the canopy, in the throats and howls and chirrups and cries of elf, and animal, and all beyond.

"Rule and guard us side by side
Heal your bitter, deep, divide"

The sun hovered yet above the horizon, glowing and pulsing with otherworldly strength. Holding her arms above her head, and grasping the hand of the tigre-striped Sun ilvi to her right, Ginni let forth a kulning cry that lifted itself on the wind and echoed throughout the jungle. The cry was mimicked by Tjen's powerful instrument; Siberne's throaty roar; the silvery chants of the Moon ilvir and the crystal clear cries of the Sun ilvir.

The sun went out.

A sudden silence descended on the gathering, falling

harder than the darkness. Followed by a coldness that seemed to cling closer than death itself.

Where there is light, there is always darkness.

Where life may lead, death will always follow.

And with a crackle, and a spark, and a slow, brilliant flame that glowed brighter and brighter with each breath, the sun returned.

She had a flashing white grin set in warm, dark flesh; burnished bronze coils of wiry, wavy hair; a soft, statuesque, rounded figure that spoke of motherhood, and vigor, and vitality clothed in gossamer folds that draped picturesquely from her frame.

Sh'nia, the Goddess of Life, stood before them, a hand on her hip, kind eyes of mellow ochre smiling at all who bowed at her feet.

"It's about time I get summoned as a mortal," she laughed, and her laugh burst forth in flowering trees and the cries of baby animals that tumbled out of the forest. The familiars of the Sun ilvir, that stood at attention with almost as much devotion as their soulful masters, yelped and bounded in joy at the sound.

"And who have I to thank?" She continued, putting a finger to her dimpled chin and swiveling in place to take note of the holvir, the Grand Master of Moonbow, and the Sun ilvi, who stood motionless as she surveyed them.

"G-Ginni, your uh... your goddessness? O Great and Blessed Lady, Sh'nia?" she stammered. No wonder holvir and gods didn't mix.

Sh'nia laughed. "Ginni Willow, and Tjen Oak, of the Padfoot tribe. Your life was granted by your Faie Mother," she nodded, then turned to regard Siberne. "And Siberne, of the Tigre. You... received your blessing late," she sighed, with a sorrowful look. "I hope you do not resent me for that."

Siberne shook his head, and though she didn't understand the statement Ginni could tell he meant his denial. Only pure, fervent devotion and love appeared in his face as he stared at his beloved goddess.

"Good. Because I would have to beg your forgiveness, and that is something," she laughed again, "that I am not very good at doing. Much easier is it for me to grant forgiveness of my own, which I do freely, to all my people, even those who departed from me."

As she said this, she turned toward the contingent of Moon ilvir, who still watched her both quietly and warily. Stepping down from the grassy mound upon which she'd alighted, she walked up to Illin, who had his head bowed and eyes firmly fixed on his own feet.

"But I will not sit here and pretend," she said, lifting his chin much like her sister had, "that I did nothing to drive you away. I have been waiting long to heal the breach between myself and my sister, watching as the divide grew ever wider, between both ourselves, and our beloved flock. It is our duty to love you, as we would love each other, and for that I am thankful, and most deeply, humbly sorry," she cast her own eyes to the ground and dipped her head before the Grand Master, "for what I have done, and failed to do in the aftermath."

Grand Master Illin seemed slightly off put by the vision of a goddess bowing before him, but with great presence of mind, simply inhaled and smiled gratefully.

"Your sister begged us just as prettily to help her. We would be remiss to ignore your plea. Will you join us, and Atosa, and defeat the scourge that threatens all of Faie?"

Sh'nia didn't answer in words. With another flashing glow, that momentarily dazzled all the mortals surrounding her, she too let forth a torrent of song- a kulning cry that plucked the very fibers of the life within everything that heard it. A song that promised glory, a song that promised victory, a song that promised peace.

"Yes," she sang, and the cheer that followed could be heard all the way to the peaks of Mount Oer.

—

"Has there… Always been a river here??"

The holvir blinked at one another, then turned back towards what was unmistakably the mouth of a frothing river floating directly into the sea before them. Their guide, glowing in anticipation of the upcoming battle and prospect of reuniting with her sister, pondered the new feature with a puzzled expression on her dark face.

"That hasn't been there for a long, long time. Someone has unlocked the river Styckes. Someone who absolutely should not have the power to do so."

Ginni squinted into the vista, and shrugged. "Must have been McKenna then, right?"

Sh'nia nodded absently, but Ginni knew the goddess remained unconvinced.

The soaring cliffs, breaking from what had once been endless fog and unrelenting ocean, soothed the spirit and fired the morale of their ilvin company. Their course was kept by the Sun ilvir in the day and navigated by the Moon ilvir at night. Ginni quickly lost count of the number of each they'd been at sea. Such cooperation had almost certainly reduced their overall travel time, but the little bard still worried about the fate of her friends.

The sight of Sh'nia standing beside her atop the prow of their ship filled Ginni with a glorious confidence and purpose the holvi had never experienced before. *We're just holvir. We're holvir who travel and sing and are barely tolerated by the world at large. And despite that, we summoned two of Faie's most powerful deities.* The thing was unbelievable. Yet there the goddess stood, smiling with a fierce joy at the water, the sky, the cliffs alongside her.

The stories never mentioned Sh'nia getting a chance to be mortal. She really must have been a little jealous of her sister. The immortals wouldn't love their worshipers so much if they didn't envy and admire them, too.

She dropped from her station atop the prow of the ship and made her way towards the figures huddled at the helm. Siberne stood poised over a map beside Grand Master Llen, and under a shade held up by two lesser mages reposed the exhausted Master Illin. As they approached, Tjena flicked an expert finger along their instrument and Ginni, catching the tone, hummed a soft melody. Illin started up, then rubbed his eyes sleepily while smiling at the approaching holvir.

"I know, I know, can't fall asleep yet..." he mumbled, his hand hovering lightly over the map as it glowed.

"That's kind of the opposite of true, actually, but we

know you won't sleep until you find her," chided Tjena, taking a seat beside the Master.

Each moon the ilvir of both realms, Meliamne and Gamorre, had gathered together to sing, lending their aid to Atosa in her battle with the Lich King over the souls suspended in limbo and to heal the rift between their people and their deities. As their fervor and their magic grew, Master Illin had begun to enchant a map that would lead them as swiftly and as close as possible to the goddess, while avoiding the perils of the open sea and the swirling, vicious surf. Their passion paid off, but the spell took its toll on their newly elected leader. He rarely left the bridge, not even to sleep. Even the apprentices lending their energy to the mage looked spent.

We're so close. We'll make it. We've got to.

"Looks like this river may prove a godsend after all. That's Lianor up on White Face over there," she pointed at the stately city shining above them to the north, "So we should just take the river inland. We're bound to run aground at some point, and find out if the united army ever reached the city."

Siberne nodded, and the ilvi manning the helm steered them for the river's mouth. As soon as they crossed from the saltwater of the sea to the fresh water of the blessed river, the Moon ilvir at the bridge began to perk up.

"Well, this is curious," Illin said, yawning vigorously but blinking brightened eyes. "What did you say this river was?"

"Uhm, Sh'nia said it's Styckes."

"Styckes? How is the realms is that possible?" He looked overboard at the clear amber water sparkling below. "Styckes is leagues away."

"Styckes linked all the realms, before they were settled by mortals," Sh'nia, who had silently joined them, replied. "As my sister and I assumed our immortal roles, channeling the spirits of life and death ourselves, the river began to dry up. It hasn't met the sea in centuries."

"Hmm. Wonder if the river senses all those undead and is trying to bring them home," mused Illin.

"Could be. Regardless, I don't recommend trying to refresh yourselves in it. The draw of Styckes is nearly irresistible, and we need all your souls very much attached to your bodies for the coming battle."

She drew herself up suddenly, illuminating everything on the deck with otherworldly brightness. Ginni felt the hairs on her neck prickle, and looked around to seek out the source of the goddess' unexpected distraction. Nothing she could see, but without reason she began to sing, filling her heart and soul with song. The tone spoke of hope, of strength, and of joy for battle, longing for home.

Her song drowned out the shrieks of daemor as they rose in the sky, blotting out the sun.

"By the gods. It's him. It's…" Siberne trailed off, swallowing hard.

There, on the vista outside the gates of Lianor, surrounded by a host of evil beasts and ilmaurte, stood the Lich King.

XX

DIVIDED

A low breeze rifled through the trees overhead as the women made their way back to the road. A bank of clouds rolled over the hills from the north, cast in a fiery glow on the horizon from the setting sun. Lianor's high wall shone bright, dimmed only by the black gate set into its front. They marched purposefully toward it, each proudly bearing the crest of the Guild of Tooth and Claw on their armor.

"Hail! Open the gates, for paladins returned from their goodly quest," shouted Layne, her voice carrying through the stone and metal. A guard leaned forward and scrutinized them for a moment.

"State your name, and your guild," he yelled down.

Arya's eyebrows shot up. She stared at Layne, who looked equally puzzled. "What ceremony is this? We are paladins of Tooth and Claw, on a quest granted by Grand Master Elgitha herself. Where is Kelshin Darley, the magistrate of the gate? Who are you?" Layne shouted back.

Crossing her arms, Arya remained mute, investigating the high gates and openings along it. Several shadowy faces peered out, then scurried away as she noticed them. Something wasn't right.

Finally the gates swung open, and the paladins

strode forward. They stood firm at the entrance, not even flinching when the heavy metal slammed shut behind them.

We just faced a daemor, Arya thought to herself. *Some uppity guardsman isn't going to cow me.*

The magistrate of the gate rushed forward, her wheeled chair clattering over the stones. She reached the paladins breathlessly, waving her hands and panting as she spoke.

"Sorry… so sorry… new protocol… not used to heroes… please forgive him… Elric!" she shouted sternly. "Elric, get yourself down here right now."

The guard shambled down, and it took every ounce of Arya's reserve not to laugh. The tiny magistrate ordered the giant guard around like a kitten barking at a mastiff. "Elric. Are you blind. Look at them," she pointed fiercely at the crests on the paladins' armor. "Do you see that? Can you see? I better not have someone blind manning the gate."

His reply was surly. "Sorry, magistrate. So many going, not many coming through, not since that motley army of miscreants. I thought they come back."

Arya distrusted the shifty look he gave the magistrate. But surrounded as she was by so many hostile-feeling eyes, she didn't interrupt.

"I didn't hire you to think. I hired you to guard. Do your job next time, or I'll send you back to stock duty. Now," she turned toward the pair, waving off the chastened soldier. "Again, I am *so* sorry about that. Come with me, Masters," Kelshin gestured for them to follow, which they did, dragging their feet and desperate for the solace and comfort of the barracks deep within the hallowed halls of the Cathedral. Leading them through a small portal set into the wall, they follow Kelshin as she dexterously rolled up an fictile corridor before finding themselves in a cozy chamber with a view of the outskirts of Lianor's suburbs.

"I know you girls are exhausted. But listen to me," the breathlessness was gone from the magistrate's voice. She suddenly sounded stern, almost to the point of fear. The tone raised prickles on the hairs of Arya's neck. "You can't go back to the guild, not the normal way. I'm not sure how to say this... but you've been put on probation. Indefinitely."

Something akin to a startled squeak escaped Layne's throat, followed by a noise much more vicious. The magistrate's eyes widened. "Please don't shoot the messenger. I can-"

Arya put a reassuring hand on Layne's knee. "Sorry about that, Magistrate Kelshin. We've had... a very long quest."

I'm so tired.

"We've heard bits and pieces of what's been happening, and we don't want to get you in any more trouble. Please... can you get us back into the guild?"

She nodded without a word, and beckoned for them to follow her. The passages through the wall were tight, but blissfully empty. It irritated Arya to no end. She had just completed her quest to ascension, after three long years of nonstop toil and training, and now stood merely moments away from achieving the dream she'd cherished since childhood. Yet here she was, sneaking through the city like some kind of petty criminal. How the mighty have fallen.

"Calm down, Lady Arya. You just turned into a dragon like, two days ago," whispered Layne, gripping her hand tightly. "We have Bahamut's blessing with us. Master Gareth won't know what hit him."

"Oh, you bet he won't," she growled under her breath.

But the guild doesn't belong to Bahamut anymore. The guild belongs to him.

They reached the end of a long hallway, in front of a massive oaken door. Kelshin fumbled with her keys for a moment, muttering to herself, before fitting a long rhoditum key into the lock. She pushed the door open and sighed in relief.

"Phew! I was worried they'd changed the locks. You can go from here. I suggest, if you're feeling quick enough, that you should seek Grand Master Elgitha's chambers. She's…" the magistrate sighed, wiping a furtive tear from under her glasses, "she's very ill. Her divine aids won't let anyone but themselves near her. But I know she'll see you. Please, girls," she pled, gripping Arya's hands tight, "this madness has to end. Our city, our realm, is on the brink of collapse."

Startled, but determined, they both nodded and wordlessly made their way through the darkened catacombs that laced the foundation of Lianor. Though quiet, and empty, both women felt a deep unsettling gloom pervade the hallways, as though they had been recently occupied by vile and unholy beings. But finally they faced a familiar portcullis, and slid under the bars into the underground level of the Cathedral.

Several lucky staircases later, they found themselves stepping lightly down a quiet corridor. The narrow hallways, devoid of ornament as they were, began to look familiar. Though Arya hadn't many opportunities for a tête-à-tête with the Grand Master, she still remembered clearly the ascent from the barracks to her chambers.

If they'd had time to notice, the absolute stillness of the space would have struck them as eerie. Luckily, even without the general clamor to disguise them, the women knew how to walk silently, masking the natural shifting of their movements, armor, and weapons to deaden any sound.

The effort seemed almost wasted. The corridors lay empty, haunting even, devoid of the sound of jovial challenge and bond of brethren that once ignited them. No guards marched the hallways, no huddled knots of novitiates whispered in corners. Even the few civilians who made the hallowed halls of the Cathedral of the Golden God their home had disappeared. Finally they found themselves before the door to the Grand Master's suite, standing ajar and lit by candlelight. The sound of voices coming up the spiral staircase froze them upon the threshold.

"...pesky Dragon's Hill traitors. We should just raze the whole town," the voice was saying. Layne's eyes went wide, and Arya whispered another oath to blend them into the shifting shadows cast by the dim candlelight. Two figures strode into view, and both girls tensed in recognition.

"Yes, Father," Clint's lethargic tones grated on Arya's

ears. "We can ready troops on your command."

"It's your command, boy. You keep forgetting that. Elgitha isn't a fool. She's dying, and that T'ssama brat can't show her face within a dozen leagues of here without ending up in prison. She has to nominate you, you're her only choice at this point," Master Gareth grumbled, before pounding his fist loudly on the stone doorway. A veiled figure appeared almost instantly.

"We're sorry, Master Gareth. She's still asleep, we can't wake her-" the girl spoke softly, but firmly; Yuun, Elgitha's youngest, but most imposing, divine maiden. Arya commended her reserve in the face of the livid Master.

"She can't avoid us forever, dammit. When will she rise?" he demanded angrily.

"We've had to sedate her for the time being. She's troubled by visions, and it's hindering her recovery. Even if she were to see you, it would be with eyes unfocused, and you wouldn't get any viable answers." She looked pointedly at Clint, her meaning clear. *You can't force a nomination from an impaired Grand Master.* "Send the boy tomorrow evening and perhaps she'll be well enough for an audience," Yuun's tone was calm, despite the increasing choler of Master Gareth.

He humphed, then jerked his head toward Clint and disappeared with heavy footsteps back down the stairs. Once Arya was sure they were out of earshot, she recalled the spell and stepped before the girl.

"Arya! And Layne! Oh, I'm so glad to see you!" Yuun cried, her cornflower blue eyes glowing in relief.

"Shhh, not so loud. Is it true? Is Elgitha…" Arya trailed off, unable to finish.

The girl lowered her head, shaking it softly. "There's no hope. But she'll see you now, I think," replied the girl, gesturing them into the room and closing the door.

Elgitha's powerful aura emanated throughout the chamber. A wide stained glass window filtered multicolored light into the space, infusing the recumbent Grand Master with an ethereal glow. Both Arya and Layne knelt beside the bed in silence, the eyes of each full of unshed tears.

Stirring slightly, the woman brushed a withered hand across Arya's cheek. "My child. You have returned. Ah, and I see," she smiled, and sighed happily, "you have found the blessing of Bahamut."

"She found something, alright," Layne's tone, though usually flippant, had a subdued and reverent quality as she addressed their Grand Master. With one hand on Layne's shoulder and the other on Elgitha's, Arya took a deep breath.

"We have completed your quest. We're sorry… so sorry it took so long. But we're back, and we mean to make it right. I… I mean to make it right," she spoke waveringly.

He gave up on our god. He gave up on our family.

"Of course you do, child. Will you accept this, then?" Elgitha whispered, wiggling a thin golden band of interlocking golden scales off her finger.

"I…"

Arya hesitated for a moment, feeling the draw of the band, the weight of its power, and of its responsibility, resting upon her. None more qualified than she stood to assume it. After ruling for half a century, seeing the rise and fall of all the Masters who came before and after her, Elgitha had seen within the T'ssama girl a spirit and a fire that matched her own, and matched that of the god they all worshipped.

So young. But then, I was young too. She's a different sort from her brother. She'll lead like he never could. I hope she learns that, one day.

"I will, Grand Master."

The divine maidens who tended to Master Elgitha in her illness formed a semicircle around the paladin and her partner. An eerie hush descended over the tableau, and the sunlit patterns of the glass window sparkled across the Grand Master's bedspread. Their voices rose; a consecration, recognized by both mortal flesh and immortal spirit. Arya felt the same warmth she had when the dragon's avatar shared her body, and she checked her arms frantically to make sure she hadn't erupted in scales.

A sigh of relief escaped her. Still flesh.

Elgitha slid the band onto Arya's finger, to rest above her brother's signet ring. She tensed suddenly.

Seth had returned. This was his ring. This was his honor.

The chosen one, the child of prophecy. A rogue and a callous deserter. Am I really any better?

The Grand Master read her thoughts. "Arya T'ssama. You are now my nominate for Grand Master. When my soul crosses to Pasture, the Guild of Tooth and Claw will bow to you. You belong in no man's shadow," she whispered, echoing the words Layne used so long ago. She felt her partner choke back a sob, and tense under her grip. Both turned their gaze to Elgitha, who smiled and shut her eyes- the imperious soul of the noble woman finally at rest.

A low, keening wail broke from the divine maidens, filling the room with a passionate and heartbreaking melody. The sound spiraled like the effervescence of sparkling water, singing through the empty halls, pouring and flowing through the rafters and the stone floors of the Cathedral, spreading next through the streets of Lianor then on to the farthest reaches of all the realms, touching the heart and spirit of any and all who shared her love of the Golden God, the great dragon Bahamut. As it echoed throughout the stronghold, each member of Tooth and Claw broke into a heartrending cry that resounded far and wide. Bright tears tracked down the cheeks of each, tears to shine their Grand Master's noble soul into the afterlife.

"Arya, you must come with me," Yuun tugged Arya's sleeve urgently. "We are all witnesses to Elgitha's nomination, but the guild is in peril. We have to get you to the throne room as swiftly as possible. Everyone knows Elgitha is dead. They have to know you are our Grand Master now, too."

Kneeling and still dazed with grief, Yuun's words barely registered in Arya's mind. Probably because it was currently occupied by thoughts like *"I'm the nominee for Grand Master of Tooth and Claw"* and *"Grand Master Elgitha just died right in front of me"* and, finally, *"I'm the Grand*

Master of the Guild of Tooth and Claw."

A shy smile hovered in the corners of Layne's mouth that still quivered in its grief. The paladin clearly shared her partner's thoughts, and an almost insufferable "I told you so" had written itself across her freckled brown face. Layne caught Arya staring and sucked in a breath, wrinkling her nose in an effort not to grin.

"Don't say it," Arya whispered.

"I'm not saying anything!"

"You just did."

"That doesn't count!" Layne put her hands on Arya's face, forcing the woman's silver eyes to meet her emerald ones. "Are you ready?" she said, suddenly serious. Almost subconsciously her thumb stroked itself along the high planes of Arya's cheek, and they smiled at one another before sighing and rising to follow Yuun.

Together, they passed through a hidden panel and down a tight spiral staircase. Elgitha must have had her own passage to the throne room.

How handy, the paladin thought to herself. *I'll have to get used to that.*

The throne room was empty, but they knew it would only be a matter of time before the guild members would descend, eager to learn whether or not their dead Grand Master managed to nominate anyone before her passing. Slowly, they were flanked by the divine maidens, who silently stood in rows beside the throne. Arya hesitated. How could she sit there?

"You must, Grand Master Arya," urged Layne. "If you don't, think of who will take it."

"But..." she stammered.

Did she earn this? Did she truly deserve this? She looked down at the rings on her finger, clenching and unclenching her fist.

"He... I betrayed him. How could I take his place? How could I do it?" she whispered, trembling, turning a teary face to Layne.

A rogue and a callous deserter. A daughter meant for a Lady. I don't deserve this.

A golden glow outlined her partner. That shining light glinted in Layne's eyes again, kindling every inch of her figure. "What are you saying?"

"I... I can't take this, Layne. I can't do it. He..." she choked, agitated beyond speech. *The throne of the Golden God. I'm not even a child of prophecy. How could I take it?*

"Arya, they're making me fight my own family!" Layne hissed. "You heard Master Gareth. Elgitha didn't choose Seth to lead. She chose you. If you don't accept that nomination, our guild is doomed."

Arya had never seen such an expression on that face before. Suddenly she gasped, then clutched the ring to her heart. She felt again the warmth of Bahamut's blessing. She felt again the softness of Layne's skin, the shiver of lips against hers. Throwing back her head, she sat upon the golden throne, just as the doors burst open and a flood of people swarmed in.

"Arya T'ssama! What is the meaning of this?" boomed a voice from the crowd.

A low hum filled the room, and the pale divine maidens formed a row in front of the throne. "We are witnesses to Elgitha's natural death. In her final moments, she named Arya her successor. You should bow before your Grand Master," Yuun spoke with fierce authority, those mild blue eyes kindling with the light of Bahamut's highest favor, but falling dim on the man who had so long been out of it.

"Traitors! Accomplices!" shouted Master Gareth above her voice. "You said just this evening that Elgitha wasn't fit to nominate anyone! Why should we trust you?"

"Clearly we were wrong. She holds the ring," Yuun leaned back and held Arya's hand forth, displaying the golden band resting upon her finger. "Were it not placed here willingly by the active Grand Master, her arm would be burned off. You know this just as well as everyone else."

Master Gareth narrowed his eyes. "I see no proof other than that of your traitorous witchcraft. Elgitha's nomination remains unconfirmed. As the highest ranking member of the guild upon her passing," his voice thundered through the hall, daring any to question him, "I alone possess the power to nominate the next Grand Master- and that shall be my son, Clint Achor."

A phalanx of warriors flanked the surly paladin, who listened with eyes downcast to his father's bold-faced contradiction. Their faces were grim, set to defend the path they'd followed now for years.

A challenge to a nomination. Unprecedented, but not unexpected in these changing times.

"I demand the arrest of Arya T'ssama, traitor to our goodly guild!"

The divine maidens, and few lower ranked members of the guild who remained behind to watch the spectacle, wavered in place. A bold challenge. The energies emanating off Master Gareth were powerful, compelling, assured. Their god lay silent as ever.

Arya's heart sank at the sight of the novices, ranged as they were beside the overbearing Master who had for years directed and dictated every waking moment of their lives and their novitiates. By most standards, she was almost entirely an outsider. Though she came from a noble family, though her own brother and then she herself had accomplished the arduous climb to Master, most of those before her had been raised within the hallowed halls of the Cathedral since childhood; raised and trained and drilled by this very man. Suddenly she realized accepting her nomination was only the first hurdle. She had to convince far more than just herself that she deserved this role.

They brought their arms to bear. Could she fight them? Slay her own brethren, here, upon the throne of the Golden God?

A whispered spell emanated from Yuun's thin lips, one Arya recognized. With a milky shimmer, the sounds of the hall and the motion of those within it ground to a halt.

"You know the truth of these madmen, Arya. You know who is controlling them, and you know you stand no chance at a fair trial. You must leave," she said, with tears in her eyes, "Grand Master, and find the source of this hellish blight that curdles the goodly spirit of our ranks."

I can't do anything, honestly. I can't even breathe. What a mess.

Layne's warm fingers laced through hers, tugging her toward the door through which they'd come. Back to the streets. Back to ignominy.

So much for glory.

A dull buzzing thrummed through the city. Those few who walked the streets did so in tight knots, fear and unease twisting every face, bowing every figure. Something wasn't right. While a Grand Master's passing did affect all the worshipers of their shared god, it was a cleansing grief, not a source of terror. But what caused this panic?

"Arya…" Layne stopped dead in the middle of the street, pointing a long finger toward a black cloud rising in the sky above the city.

Crackling with lurid red and green energy, they realized without a shadow of a doubt the ominous presence heralded evil beyond any the realms had ever experienced.

And it was moving straight for Lianor.

The shriek of sirens and clangor of bells did nothing to drown out the cries of the populace, citizens trapped within the high walls watching in horror as a legion of blackness enveloped their fair city. White walls dimmed to grey, shining streets were shadowed in sludge; the sky a roiling green, red, and yellow pulsing like the very plane of the Abyss had opened above them.

A man encumbered with the bundle of a child nearly floored Arya as he dashed breathlessly around the corner, intending, like many, to seek refuge and asylum of the guild's glorious fortress.

"Master, please," he shook, his eyes rolling at the spectres that spun evilly above them. "Sanctuary!"

She gripped the man's arm, her own despair overwhelmed by his. Sanctuary. She was Grand Master of the guild behind her. She couldn't even grant sanctuary to a dog.

"The guild has been... compromised," she hissed through gritted teeth. She set him gently aside and stood upon the stone arcade raised several steps from the street. Ragged figures, noble and civilian alike, watched in awe as the woman flashed in her fury.

"Nobles, hear this," she spoke clearly, her clarion voice carrying to the furthest reaches of the haggard crowd. "Your own halls are safest now. For the love you hold of your city- the faith you have for your gods- the charity you hold for your neighbors, your friends," she begged, "open your doors to them. This scourge threatens to devour us from within, and we must unite to fight it!"

"Says who?" shouted a voice from the masses. "Who do you speak for then, craven Master unwilling to open the doors of your stronghold?"

A paladin's power rests in the bond of their oath with their god. A truly divine paladin could summon a blessing, a benediction; a flash of light maybe, or a holy song.

Arya simply turned into a dragon. She'd had enough.

The look on Layne's face bore a surprising similarity to one of superior smugness. As Arya again felt the warmth of a union between her soul, and her god's, wash over her she realized that the paladin was right all along. No one bore the blessing and the recognition of Bahamut's favor like Arya did. Not her brother, not the children of prophecy, not even Grand Master Elgitha herself. Kneeling on the flagstones, Layne twisted her wrist to lay the back of her hand flat over her heart, saluting the dragon girl who shone above the crowd.

And slowly, many of those who had lived long in Lianor, seen the rise of the great Guild of Tooth and Claw, and knew the blessing of the god it stood for, knelt with her- despite the confused and fearful looks of some of the others who had gathered for sanctuary, and recognized not the avatar of the Golden God that hovered above them.

"You have watched the guilds turn on you, grasp each soul they can devour, inch by deathless inch!" she roared, her voice blended with that of Bahamut's, insistent, compelling, and above all, honest. "You have long turned a blind eye, believing that they who speak with such devotion could be too big to fail. You watched as they single-handedly destroyed the realm of Beausun, leaving a swath of destruction that defied even the undead scourge! You know it," she pointed a scintillating claw at the source of the dissent, "you ignore it, and now you challenge it! Seek, then, the safety of your oppressors, so much as they would grant you," sweeping her arms wide at the aloof Tor Savant of Golden Eye and the stately

Cathedral of Tooth and Claw.

The crowd shifted uncomfortably. Layne noticed that the daemor swirled harmlessly above the thin sheen of a protective dome erected, she hoped, by the magistrates of the gates. A fairly capable mage in her own right, Kelshin's magic could only hold so long against such terrible power. It was only a matter of time before the full might of the scourge reached them. Only a matter of time before they failed.

Arya doubted the power of her words. Convincing a crowd of anything was hard enough. Pleading with a crowd of fear-crazed, impotent civilians, who hadn't even lifted a finger to challenge the inevitable creep of authoritarian control imposed by the guilds, was simply impossible.

Lucky for her then that divine intervention always proves more persuasive.

A vivid crack rent the protective sphere into fragments. Just before the daemor descended, a bolt of molten energy struck the twin towers of Tor Savant, setting the building ablaze.

The terrified gathering hove a great gasp in unison. Bricks smashed to the ground at their feet, massive slabs of marble hurtling through the air along with dust, debris, and daemor. Everything was pandemonium and the fragile asafolk stood in helpless terror, holding their collective breaths.

The man who had collided with Arya looked upon her in terror, the lines of his face slowly settling to a grim determination. Behind her rose the Cathedral of the Golden God, lit by the blaze of its rival, scintillating in shadow and in light. Its doors, closed, despite the cries of those who stood on its very threshold.

"Go, then!" he yelled, and as though his voice broke a spell holding the party in place, they scattered, hopefully, thought Arya, toward the stronghold of the Noble's Council in the center of the city.

"You want a way to prove your nomination?" Layne yelled over the din, drawing forth her bow and loosing blessed bolts one after the other at daemor and imps pursuing the fleeing populace. "Take these hellbeasts down with me! We can't save anyone inside, not while Gareth is in control. We'll have to… I don't know, find a way back in and defeat him. But first," and she grabbed Arya's forearm, kissing her fiercely on the forehead, "we defeat… this. Come on, Dragon Girl."

The warmth of her love, and the warmth of Bahamut's blessing, melted the cold reserve and layer of fear of inadequacy that had suffocated the girl since her childhood. Throwing back her head in a wild roar, she loosed a stream of golden fire that incinerated a kvetchling to nothing, not even ash.

They were left with the roar of flame, the screech of daemor, and the sparkling window of glass high, high above.

XXI

MARCH

The monk wrenched to wakefulness, heart throbbing, chest heaving. She felt Seth rustle groggily up next to her, placing a calming hand on her thigh. His concerned face swam into view, focusing blearily on hers.

"It's beginning," she rasped in a hoarse whisper. The cry of a thousand souls, draining from the everywhere; summoned into being against their will, against even the laws of magic that arranged their realms.

They hastened out into the town square, dawn's light glowing on the horizon a vivid, unappealing yellow. Several of their night's watch yawned and waved halfheartedly, their own faces falling as they saw the expression on hers.

"No good news from the other side, then?" sighed Michelle Magi, as she passed a dish of bright green leaves wrapped around a curious yellow fruit toward McKenna. She took a bite, expecting sweetness, yet surprised by its savor.

"I'm afraid not. Hazy though. Maybe," she ran a fingernail along the bezel of the mirror kept tucked at her side, "I'll try getting a more direct view."

Michelle raised a curious eyebrow at the monk, but didn't inquire further. Planting a soft kiss on Seth's forehead as he ate mechanically, still in thrall of the vestiges of sleep, she took off for the edge of the town, hoping for silence to summon her sister's spirit.

"McKenna. Nothing good, I'm assuming?" her sister's violet eyes fixed on hers, trying to gauge the expression within them.

"I'm that easy to read, huh?" she mused aloud, and Katarin smiled. "Could you feel it too?"

"I saw it," the sorcere replied in a whisper. "Working with the orgir. We'd gathered a group together to perform a blessing and without warning the souls simply vanished."

McKenna felt her throat go dry. "Vanished? From Pasture too?"

"Yes. Gone in an instant." Tears sparkled in anger and despair. "We tried- worked as fast as we could, to help as many ascend as were able, but… there were thousands of them."

Thousands of souls. Souls turned undead, an army marching for Lianor, joining the legion marching for the destruction of the realms. Pressing the tips of her fingers to her forehead, the woman hove a sigh that threatened to turn into a sob. "Katarin, I… there's something else you should know."

She told her sister about the cult of Naszer, about the daemor horde, and about the fate Seth had warned for Razan. Her face turned pale, but resolute.

"He was mortal. I know he was. Above all else," she spoke with passion, where once fear tinged the hardness of her voice, "he loved these realms, protected them and all those under him. I know there's the soul of faiefolkr in there. We just have to reach it."

Silence met her words. The edge of fear McKenna woke with slowly ebbed, as the love she felt for her own paladin filled her in its place. There is nowhere so far a mortal could fall, she thought to herself, that they could not be brought back by the loyalty of those who loved them.

"I trust you, sister." McKenna touched the glass softly, its cold surface still managing to commune a measure of warmth between the two women. "If anyone can reach him, it's you. I'll do my best to give you that opportunity."

Katarin gave her a watery smile in return, then both looked off into the distance as a discordant twang struck the essence of each. A rumble of death, where death should not be.

"Have you heard from our mother lately?" Katarin broke the silence, swallowing her own reverie.

"No. I'd hoped you would have news of her. She sent my friends, the holvir Tjen and Ginni, to the Sun ilvir to wake her sister. But we have no way of knowing-"

A high, piercing note echoed throughout the town's adobe walls- a horn, sounding from the peaks that lay between them and Lianor.

McKenna blanched, then turned toward her sister. "Those are battle horns. Sister... he marches now."

Katarin paled, but nodded. The glass went blank and McKenna stood as Seth approached her.

They considered one another for a moment, drinking in the sight of the other, a reflection of their love, loyalty, and joy. How could she face it? The man who stood before her, dead once already, revived by her hand. Could she stand to lose him again? *Should we run? Dive into the mines and bury ourselves alive, where no Lich nor daemor could ever find us?*

He studied her eyes, flecks of fool's gold glowing deep in amber pools of fire. It hadn't been so long ago that he was called the shame of his guild, nor since he had fallen to his death. *If not for her, if not for the woman beside me, I'd have been only that- a dead man with disgrace for a legacy*, he reflected. *I owe her everything I am today.*

He leaned forward, slowly grabbing the hand that bore his ring, lacing his fingers through hers. She closed her eyes and sighed, smiling at the touch, feeling his courage steal into her soul with each caress. The words went unspoken. Certain things just tend to go without saying, and they knew, with greater confidence than anything they'd known before. It awoke a fire within each, a spirit and energy untested and unbound.

To fight, perhaps to die, with or without one another paled in the face of this one great and noble truth. Love stood as a reflection of their deepest, truest nature, the very joys of living, the stuff of vigor and of grace.

An air of rapidity and earnest devotion permeated the town, wrapped every living member of the goodly company in an almost glowing shield of determination and fortitude. They could almost smile. They could almost laugh. They faced death itself, and yet they knew the strength of gods, and that which is greater than even gods, fought on their side. No foe could face such a challenge and be victorious.

"Any word from your mother?" Katherine, wrapping bundles of herbs and bottling brews and potions, asked McKenna as she approached the party.

"No. I can only hope she's got through to Ginni and Tjena, and that when we crest the peak we see our friends on the other side," she replied, leaning over to help pack. "My sister saw the souls summoned by the Lich King - he has an army of hundreds alongside however many daemor who managed to claw their way out of the Abyss."

"They don't stand a chance. We have so much more to fight for," Lord Masa, who had carried a load of weapons and magic portents to the caravan and was coming back for more, interrupted. "We fight for our families. We fight for our lives. We fight for our homeland. They, what do they fight for?"

"Death. Destruction. Despair. You know, the usual," James muttered caustically, dodging an upbraiding smack from Katherine.

"The goddesses will come. Together they can face the Lich King. And while they fight, we can slay the daemor and ilmaurte where they stand. Lianor will not fight for us," Maria chimed in, her powerful tone captivating her audience. "We must prove we are worth protecting, that we can stand under one banner and protect our brothers, for the good of every soulful being that walks these realms."

"Aye to that, lass," chimed in one of the Hammardin durgir with a twinkle in his cairngorm eye.

They marched through the mist-filled dawn; the road flat, quiet, yet thrumming with an energy that seemed from Faie itself. McKenna sensed the discordance, the vile creatures not of this plane that sapped the strength from the realms and stomped upon its goodly land. In the distance rose a pillar, deathly black, lit occasionally by lurid green and yellow streaks that screamed through the atmosphere.

"Is Lianor… already taken?" Katherine asked breathlessly as they came into view of the walled city.

"I can't tell. But if we were right, about the cult of Naszer being the true force behind the guild's unification, I wouldn't be surprised if they took the opportunity to finally strike," replied James through gritted teeth.

"Look! The river Styckes, it's… flowing? And what's that coming up… is that… a ship?"

McKenna, Seth, James, Katherine, and the Riquelmes of Dragon's Hill all stared into the vista unrolling before them. A deep fog had descended around the city, but a brightly burning light flared within its morass, highlighting the slowly moving current of Styckes and the faint but unmistakeable outline of a fully rigged ship. A shiver ran through McKenna as she recognized the divinity from which that light shined.

"It's Sh'nia. The Goddess of Life."

Sh'nia's glow grew stronger, pushing back the pillar of darkness that hung ominously over the open field. A late moon hung in the sky behind her, pale in the face of the still-rising sun. The party watched in fascination as the moon began to disintegrate, dimly glowing motes of light answering the call of the sun's divine brightness. A softly twirling vortex, eddies of golden light and silver glow, began to intermingle above the ship floating up the river.

"Atosa. The two divine sisters, joined once more in harmony and unity," breathed McKenna, awestruck at the sight. She lept behind Seth, who sat astride Kurya. "We should ride for that ship. If it brought Sh'nia, those aboard are our allies, no matter what face they wear." With a thrust of his saber, Seth led the troops down the slope toward the riverbank below.

"Seth! McKenna! By the gracious Faie Mother herself, you're alive!"

A small, singing figure launched itself laughingly at the pair. McKenna nimbly dismounted, sweeping the little holvi into a fierce embrace.

"Alive, and ready to die again, it looks like," sighed McKenna into Ginni's hair as she smiled on Tjena, running a hand along their cheek. "I see you brought friends."

The ilvir had begun to disembark from the ship to mingle among the army that marched from the prairie. Squinting into the vista, McKenna thought she saw robed figures approaching, and tensed at the sight.

"Mages? Masters from Lianor?" She asked Seth in confusion, who studied them through narrowed eyes.

"Yes. But if they are who I think they are, they could have caused a lot of damage by now if they were foe and not friend. James," he beckoned to his squire, who hefted his mighty shield in an instant, "we'll go investigate."

They departed to intercept the approaching figures. McKenna turned back to Ginni, who had been joined by Masters Illin and Llen, along with Siberne and the inquisitive Cajwa.

"Right, so, you can all probably tell this is McKenna..." trailed Ginni leadingly, and pointing to each of the ilvir in turn. "Illin, newly nominated Grand Master of Moonbow... High Cleric Llen, of the Gamorren Sun Ilvir... and this is Siberne. We kind of, uh, saved his life on accident. So he repaid us by leading us to Gamorre and introducing us to, well, everybody else!" She finished breathlessly, grasping the ilvi's hand and giving it a reassuring squeeze.

"McKenna," Grand Master Illin bowed his head in homage, with a smile twinkling in his eye. "We've not met, but I knew your sister well."

"Grand Master, I see," replied McKenna with a spark in her own. "Were I not completely convinced Katarin has no ambition to return from Pasture, I'd almost be inclined to question that. But I'm glad to meet you," she said, turning a bright face on the gathered party, "all of you. And I thank you for coming to our aid, and bringing my mother and her sister together."

"You have the holvir to thank for that!" chimed in Siberne, with an adoring smile at Ginni.

"Hush. If this were a competition of heroism, McKenna would most certainly win," insisted Ginni.

"I'm not so sure about that." The monk's grin brought out a wrinkle on the bridge of her nose, but the expression didn't last long. Seth and James returned, the robed figures striding purposefully behind him.

His look was one of determination, and not of fear, and that alone quelled the anxiety rising within her. As they approached, McKenna stepped back in a line with the ilvir and the holvir, offering as much protection as she could give.

"More allies," assured Seth once within shouting distance, and she breathed easy. One of the figures, a pale woman with a sheet of shimmering hair, drew down her hood and raised her wrists in greeting. A thin man beside her did the same, as did two others who huddled beside them. Further behind, a woman being pushed in a wheeled chair by what looked like two plain guardsmen waved, flashing a surprisingly youthful grin from her lined face.

"Allies? From Lianor, I'm guessing?" McKenna took stock of their fine robes and noble, almost dainty features. Though the hems of their clothes were muddy and dusty, and all struggled to catch their breath from their haste, she could see other clear markings that bespoke their origin from the walled city.

"Yes. Rogues, like myself," he replied with a debasing grin, "who forwent the gods of their ancestors to stand among ruffians and heretics and face the Lich King."

"Speak for yourself, Paladin," replied Ignithe. Sweeping her sheet of silvery hair into a leather thong, she pulled it back from her face to reveal the tattoo of scales on her neck. "We still believe in the gods. It's time for them to prove they believe in us now, too."

Severn nodded beside her, his gaunt face set in lines of determination. The two other clerics, both bearing mantles of lesser stations but still proudly wearing the scales of Sanct Germain, said nothing, standing in mute devotion behind the Master cleric.

"Yeah, what she said," agreed Kelshin, who'd finally caught up to the rest. "Gods or no gods, guilds or no guilds, this has gone far enough."

As she spoke, the shimmering dome above Lianor shivered and fractured into a trillion motes of sparkling light. Kelshin grimaced.

"I didn't think that would hold without me. But I can't hide behind marble walls forever, and neither should they."

"What happened to the guilds? Is it true they united?" Seth asked urgently, as the army's horns began to wind and the troops gather on the field of battle.

"It's true. And it is just as true," replied Ignithe, as she began to invoke a complicated ritual, assisted by the deep chanting of her apprentice and the complex rune drawing of the novices, tracing glowing figures of ancient magic in the air before them, "that they housed within them this unspeakable evil."

"The paladins... the novitiates..." Seth's face was white, and his voice shook, "know you their fate?"

"The city is nearly empty," she said mournfully. "Those with an ounce of courage are standing here beside you, ready to fight. And the rest," her mouth set in a grim line, "better be hiding in the Noble's Council.

With a determined nod, the rest of the gathered mages and ilvir hastened to join the army. Seth looked back to McKenna, and she could see his fear for his sister written clearly across his face.

"You have to trust her. If she's in there, you know she's doing all in her power to save the city." McKenna spoke softly, stroking his cheek with her calloused palm.

He sighed, but didn't speak. Another loud clap of daemoric power rent the sky; shaking the ground and the air itself.

"We have a war to fight," he answered finally. "Let us go meet it- come what may."

She took his outstretched hand and smiled.

"Come what may."

XXII

WAR

The lifting mist, burning off under the pressure of all the conflicting magics, revealed the singing clerics and masters of Bahamut and Sanct Germain who had joined forces with the legion.

Almost the goodly army began to wish it stayed. The horrific view struck fear deep into their hearts even as they advanced toward it.

A black mass, writhing and hissing, of daemor and ilmaurte spawn awaited them upon the plain.

"Well, we couldn't expect anything less, could we now?" sighed Kelshin to Ignithe, who nodded in agreement, her brows knitted in concentration as she infused her prayer with greater strength. Kelshin took the woman's lead and bowed her own head, weaving her hands this way and that in a salute to Bahamut that shone upon the imps, who shrieked as the sparkles of light arrested their momentum and froze them to the ground. With a deep harmonic prayer, Lord Masa and Severn, raising their voices with lesser priests plucked from the homeless wanderers, struck down the daemor one by one.

Seth had advanced with caution, seeking no lowly foe to slow his advance. The thick vortex surrounding Makarh became clearer as the army around him dispersed to battle the soldiers on foot. Wheeling Kurya into a breakneck canter, he plowed through the lesser beasts that separated him from his mighty foe. He wheeled to a stop some distance from the daemor, knowing he could not alone win such a fight. Knowing despite the disgrace that drove him from his guild, without his god, he had not the strength to conquer.

"I seek the guidance from my master," he whispered, rubbing the vacant space where the signet ring his sister wore had rested, "Bless this battle, Bahamut. Bless your warrior who fights in your honor."

"I will do more than that, Champion," boomed a voice above him.

Bahamut- scales reflecting a thousand sunbeams, his dragonish form lithe and deadly- descended beside him. His own god, doing battle on the Material plane.

Seth choked back a response, simply bowing before the golden dragon. Bahamut breathed on the prone paladin, his warm sigh granting Seth a strength and heroic might he'd never felt before.

"Together we will destroy this blight upon your land, banish him to where he came from for a thousand years and more," growled the god.

Makarh's advance hadn't even slowed. He paced eagerly toward the challengers, a thick, oozing daemoric energy snatching at Seth's spirit. He met the paladin's vicious strike with a smile, and Seth could feel the scar upon his cheek burn as the claws that carved it sliced again toward him. He parried them with another slash of saber, and another, and another.

"They send you again to face me. Has your kind no

greater champion?" Snarled Makarh.

"Probably. But why waste the effort? I've already destroyed you once," replied Seth quietly.

The clearing around them grew still. The imps and kvetchlings accompanying their master spread, seeking foes more easily defeated than this blessed champion. The cries of each army grew dim, though in truth they were not at any great distance and they fought with vigour and with heart against the malevolent evil spread through their realm. Those lesser daemor who chose to stand against Seth were almost instantly struck down and annihilated by either a blast of Bahamut's mighty breath or a swipe of his vicious claws. Imps were no match for a god.

Lips peeling back from the genirae's teeth in a vicious smile, Makarh swung each of his four arms in strike after strike aimed at tearing the upright paladin from his mount. The summoning that brought him to the Material plane had imbued him with the power controlled by the Cult of Naszer; his swings unerring in their accuracy, potent in their strength. Though able to dodge most of them, the ones that struck Seth's saber sent shockwaves up the paladin's arm, and more than once he almost dropped his blade.

But Kurya's flawless footwork compensated for the paladin's speed. The horse could outmatch any mere daemor, blessed as he was with Celestial grace and agility. Seth need not even guide the beast, so attuned was his spirit to outwitting the daemor's antagonistic Abyssal energy.

Makarh, frustrated by the enchanted steed, let loose a blast of daemoric energy, encircling their battleground with the same kind of strange plane-altering power that he had used the first time he battled Seth. The paladin watched as the sights and sounds of the field dimmed, blotted out by a heavy inky fog lit occasionally by a livid red glow.

Almost immediately he could feel the draining effects of the spell. Kurya, a Celestial creature by nature, began to fade as the fog severed them from the influence of the Celestial plane.

"I am not afraid to fight you alone," spoke Seth with courage, as he dismounted and dismissed the noble mount.

"Unwise. You shouldn't seek to fight me at all, when instead you could join me," purred the daemor, before whipping a lightning fast sting at the paladin with his tail. Seth brought up his blade to block the strike, the weight of it pushing him several inches. His boots dragged in the dirt, and the shock of the blow reverberated throughout his wiry frame. *The daemor is stronger here in this space. It must be some pocket dimension meant to parallel the Abyss.*

Prayers to Bahamut would not work here. Seth had to either force the daemor to call down the spell, or break the dweomer himself. Neither would be easy. The monster's well of arcane energy, drawn as it was from both his ties to the Abyss and the sacerdhosse who commanded his presence, seemed almost limitless.

He paced slowly along the inner ring of the enchanted space, moving with deliberation. The spells of his mithril armor, imbued as they were with the strength of his devotion, absorbed the impacts of projectiles hurled by the impatient daemor. Moving into a stance almost meditative in its fluidity of motion and low impact of its strikes, he began to dance around the daemor, moving again too quickly for it to avoid every hit.

Makarh laughed at the impotence of the strikes, simply healing each cut almost as it formed upon his adamantine flesh. No wound lasted longer that the time it took to cut open a new one, the monster's regenerative abilities not even impeding his ability to attack.

But Seth didn't care. Staying just out of range of those swinging fists and the bolts of energy tossed haphazardly at his quickly moving form, he continued to land hit after hit, every single muscle strictly disciplined to move exactly as he commanded it. He even began to increase his pace again, hitting the daemor faster and faster until his blade was a silver blur, the melody of mithril making itself heard among the din. As Makarh continued to heal those superficial wounds, the bubble of blackness that enveloped them began to fade, slightly, almost imperceptibly.

Too late to discover the paladin's strategy and frustrated with his opponent's impenetrable dexterity, Makarh attempted the same attack as before, grabbing at the paladin as he dove within range with all four arms. Seth accepted the crushing blow, focusing all the remaining vestiges of holy blessings he possessed upon the daemor's source of arcane energy.

It worked. Just before Makarh managed to squeeze the life from his very body, the planar pocket dissolved, bringing them back to the battlefield. Surging with restored magical energy and the blessings that had gone dormant, Seth's armor repelled Makarh's attack and broke his grip, wrenching free and retreating back outside the daemor's range.

"You may have escaped this, but the Abyss has a stronger hold than even I. We will have your soul eventually," snarled Makarh.

Seth didn't bother to respond. He knew where his soul would go upon death.

They met again with fury, Seth summoning Kurya again and mounting the steed to even the odds against the monstrous entity they faced. The glorious horse seemed to be the only help Seth would get against the daemor genirae. Though the blessings and oaths he carried with him normally remained stalwart, no new magic flowed through him from the god who stood behind him in this fight.

As the battle raged on, Seth noticed the dragon did little more than even the balance between the two opponents. Though an immortal deity, Bahamut too was limited by the laws of the Material plane, and the blessings called from him by the legion on the plane reduced his presence. The Guild of Tooth and Claw may have strayed from the path laid by their patron deity, but there were still many goodly folk in that space who prayed heartily and earnestly for the blessings of their god.

James, astride a powerful warhorse and leading a phalanx of confused, but eager soldiers, glowed with the power of an oath a mere squire shouldn't normally have the capability to call. A gathering of clerics, tucked under a shelf of rock built from the strange powers controlled by the asafolk of Dragon's Hill, maintained the energy of a shielding force that kept a host of hissing creatures at bay and emitted flashes of brightness and magical energy that distracted and paralyzed them. The magic of the gods emanated throughout the battlefield, and in Bahamut's limited mortal form, it took all the dragon's concentration to even manifest this physical presence.

But Seth didn't understand. Did his god believe in him?

A sinking feeling enhanced the pressure of Makarh's pure daemoric energy. It would be easier, so much easier, to submit to the violent and unstoppable beast. Bow to his will, become his thrall, succumb to this king of monsters. The sight of the goodly legions doing battle upon the plains, nor even the image of his glorious god beside him, could lift the agony weighing like a millstone upon Seth's heroic spirit.

It would be easier to succumb, as he thrust his sabre with a dextrous twist toward the daemor's throat.

Makarh coughed a mocking laugh, slapping the halfhearted attack wide.

Easier to bow to his almighty will, as the pounding hooves and shrieking whinny of Kurya drove the embattled paladin closer, to make another strike.

He drew a breath, composing himself, martialing thought and muscle to respond. One strike, two. Leaping from Kurya's back, he could feel the gravel beneath his boots. He found purchase for a lunge, then a dive, then a roll, as the daemor's swift movements matched his every strike. The battlefield shrank within his view, but this was another bout with the novitiates. Lunge, thrust, block, retreat. Just another spar with McKenna. Striking down the daemor's swinging tail simply a dodge from Laghrusse. He could almost smile as he heard the ring of mithril. Almost.

The spark could die within you, hissed a malevolent voice. *That which guides you, ties you to these weak and baseless gods that toy with mortals. Why be their pawn, to such feckless glory? Why not instead swing your arm for the unparalleled might of the Abyss? Why not?*

Why not?

Seth could taste blood in his mouth. The grit of battle working between his teeth, the chafe of leather and buckle inside his thighs, the weight of a pommel- his nameless saber. It glistened with a shine of shame, no drop of daemor blood to dim its brightness despite his unwearying strikes, his relentless offense. Better to just drop it. There was no truth left to discover. There was no life worth saving. He who had once turned his back on his family's legacy, his guild's loyalty, his god's might, his father's unshriven soul-

A golden stream of fire blasted past him, enveloping the poisonous aura crackling with black energy that struck at the prone fighter.

Bahamut looked upon him, offering nothing but a gaze. What did those expressionless gold eyes have to say? Why would the dragon choose to save him- he, a worthless nobody who had abandoned his deity not once, but twice. Walked away from salvation. How could he be worth anything?

A tail, armored in mithril scales and rigid with spines the length of a holvi's arm, slashed viciously toward the daemor, landing a hit upon the brutal fiend and finally drawing forth his blood.

"You are a warrior, son."

The words echoed in his mind. The ghostly army, souls summoned by McKenna fighting desperately on the Material plane to drive back the horde that would keep them from their final rest, surged around him. Their faces were blurred in the dappled sunlight, brighter for the clouds that glowed in white fury. Even if his father were beside him, freed from Pasture, freed from doubt and despair that caused his death and the guilt that defied his ascension, the souls' features were completely unrecognizable.

Yet the words remained. They hovered in the air like a benediction, like a guide.

His god would not fight this battle for him. But his god would never abandon him. His god loved him- outcast, uncertain, unstable as he was. Any who flew the banner of Bahamut, no matter how often or how long they may need to drop the standard, lived with his blessing and his eternal love. And that love brought power. And that love brought strength.

And in a singing slice of mithril, that love brought the daemor's head to fall beside his rigid body.

With another blast of golden fire, Bahamut's lethal breath disintegrated the remains of the unholy monster, banishing it for a thousand years from the Material plane back to the Abyss. As the imps of the surrounding area sensed the shift in daemoric presence, they shrieked and chattered and attempted to flee a similar fate. The legion under Beausun's standard surged forth triumphantly, slaying every fiend in its path. The shock of so many creatures evacuating the Material plane rippled across the field. The goodly masters who stood with Beausun, chanting in unison, channeled the unleashed energy into a driving attack aimed at the heart of Naszer's sacerdhosse. As their prayers reached a fevered pitch, the unholy ring began to stumble, gasping as the daemoric life leaching from them left them vulnerable.

Agaz crumbled first. Her twin hadn't even time to watch her fall. The attack burned the eyes from her skull before she, too, collapsed in a heap to the floor. Qu'lan lasted a moment longer. And the great Lady Lilithen Astore watched them disperse to ash before feeling the vicelike grip of Makarh's claws reach from the pyre and drag her whole through the doors of the Abyss.

And with that, the insidious Cult of Naszer was no more.

--

Beyond the safety of the rock wall, Ginni and Tjena peered into the dim dust that settled over the battlefield. Katherine crept up next to them, followed by Masa and the other clerics. A calm, haunting melody warbled from the holvi's throat. It reached the farthest corners of the clearing, filling its listeners with the essence of bright, golden light. They sang back to her- kulning of Sun ilvir, silver melody of Moon ilvir, thundering clamour of duergi, lively trill of holvir, and soulful cry of asafolk.

Covered in mud and dirt, McKenna dragged herself from the trenches where hid the remainder of the Beausun army. The air had filled with an acrid smoke, otherworldly bile from the Abyss flooding the open plains. With a flash of her amber eyes she summoned a measure of purification, channeling the crystal clear waters of Styckes as a mist to dispel the toxic fog. Those who'd succumbed to the seeping miasma felt themselves stir, the souls departing tugged back to bodies ready to fight again. McKenna passsed through these, the warriors and simple folk who had been so ready to die to restore peace to their land. With this goodly army she knew they would prevail, and her aura shone brightly among these souls restored from untimely death.

The demigoddess advanced slowly, drawn toward a livid black and red form that crackled with energy. She knew her target and, twirling the guisarme imbued with all the great power of her blood and her heritage, quickened her pace to meet it.

Her heart sank slightly as she saw the daemoric gaze painted across that still somewhat familiar face. Was it possible a measure of the man her sister loved lived still within that monstrous frame?

He smiled evilly, promising a fate worse than death should she choose to do battle with him. Worse still were the troops of ilmaurte ranged before him, their unholy visages twisted in pain and fear and anger, the reanimated corpses that bore souls stolen from beyond the Doors of Death. She would restore Razan to himself. But first, she would restore the balance of life and death that he manipulated.

Whispering a prayer first to Malfaestus, and then to her mother, the runes along Laghrusse's shaft began to crackle and glow. A mixture of magic, blessings of both gods, rippled through the weapon and the markings lining McKenna's own skin. But her confidence was a gift granted by no god. Within her lay a magic she had developed and nurtured herself. That confidence painted a smile upon her face as she began to reap the undead, culling their ranks with ease, almost dancing among their creeping, clawing forms. Sweeping wide swaths of cleansing destruction among them, every strike of Laghrusse severed the dweomer animating the corpses and binding the soul within them in one fell swoop. The air, once thick with poison and mist, now filled with the shivering ephemeral residue of tetherless souls that were loathe to leave the battlefield, and to leave the presence of the goddess who had granted them such freedom.

A ring of daemoric fire burst to life around the mutilated corpses, preventing the advance of the remaining horde toward the sure destruction that lay in wait for them. Razan, watching the wholesale obliteration of his troops, swooped down to intercept the demigoddess instead.

"Another round then?" hissed the creature, as he leapt out of range of the spinning polearm into the sky.

"Let's hope you don't run away like last time," she replied calmly. A good sign- he remembered their battle.

"What other memories lie locked within you, assassin?" she shouted at him, drawing down a spell that tethered the fluttering daemor to the ground below.

That ought to even the playing field, she thought to herself, picking her steps carefully, knowing her frustrated opponent would soon throw himself into an attack.

He moved quicker than she anticipated. With a blinding flash, he somersaulted in midair and dove, talons ringing against the adamantine weapon raised just in time to parry. The weight of the rush knocked McKenna back a step, and Razan took the moment to shoulder her, throwing her to the dirt as she lost her balance.

Within range of the long weapon, Razan pressed his

advantage, grappling with the monk and striking with taloned fist, spined tail, and bared teeth with as much speed as he could manage. His tail found purchase in the soft skin between her ribs, slicing into flesh and loosing a spray of vibrant red blood.

McKenna shrieked, but managed to draw back her palm and strike the daemor in the chest, the hit packing enough power to stop the daemor's breath. Wheezing and stunned, McKenna was able to roll out from underneath him and regain her footing, shakily.

"Malfaestus... that hurt," she winced, drawing her palm across the wound. *My spell should've stopped that...* she thought to herself, before realizing her flesh had already begun to knit of its own accord again.

"My strike was aimed at your dweomer, Monk," Razan rasped, getting to his own feet. "You should know better than to try and pit Celestial magic against Abyssal, especially with your own loyalties so... conflicted."

"Oh, you're doing that thing again," she groaned, remembering with clarity the assassin's propensities to talk circles around his foes.

"What? What thing?" The daemor's tone had warped slightly; what once was a guttural groan possessed a genuine quality of curiosity.

Now we're getting somewhere. She was right- he's got some mortality in him after all.

"Remember? That thing where you put words into someone else's mouth? And then blame them - HEY!"

McKenna dodged a lightning fast strike from the

daemor's tail, diving into a roll and scooping up the guisarme she'd dropped.

"I wasn't done talking," she complained as she thrust the weapon at him, aiming for the dexterous limb.

"I was done listening," he seethed, using it again to parry her blow.

Not if I have anything to say about it.

"Razan, come on," McKenna spun around the pole of Laghrusse again, using it to vault her up to a ledge of rock. "As much as I love our... conversations... there's someone else waiting to hear from you."

He pivoted in place and tried to take flight after her, but couldn't break through her spell cast to tether him to the ground. He picked up a boulder and hurled it at her, exploding it next to her head.

But the shrapnel simply bounced off. "Your body may be Abyssal, but no rock can hurt me," she chided, tossing one of the pebbles idly. "I'm a daughter of the durgir, after all. Unlike my sister.." she paused to duck another exploding rock, "you know, Katarin? Lucky her, she got to live with ilvir."

At the mention of the Moon Princess, Razan went rigid. McKenna hoped it would be enough to hear her name. And for a moment, she was almost right.

Only for a moment. "You'll find out what it's like to be a creature of the Abyss," he snarled, eyes flashing red as he hurled yet another projectile at her.

Maybe if I show her to him. Have to be closer for that,

though...

Leaping from her perch, she landed lightly next to the daemor. The sight tore at her heart in a way that even Seth's death hadn't. Sacrificing himself for the sake of her sister's mind; did he know this would be the result? To watch a Celestial entity parade around with his heart and tear down the pantheon, while finding his soul trapped in the despised form of an Abyssal immortal?

"This shouldn't be your fate," she cried softly. "The gods owe us more than this."

The gods that moved them all- the pantheon of magic that imbued Faie with its life, spirit, and celestial strength- how could they allow such a perversion of every goodly thing? Ringing within her own body and blood were the blessings of two, reigning over separate spheres and guiding flocks of hopeful and devout believers who followed completely different paths. Her existence was a dichotomy; a fusion of the otherworldly spirit above and Faie's strength below.

Did he, too, walk two planes? Did the strength of the ancestry of his blood really outweigh the essence of his mortality, that which made him faiefolkr, that which gave him life?

She began to hum a durgirn mining song, meant to regulate the cadence of miners as they struck the stone one after the other. Rhythmic and gravelly, she felt the magic dispel itself along her flesh, soothing the fervor within her mind and heart.

We may be divided. But we choose our path regardless. I know he didn't choose this.

"Razan," she hummed, the power of her voice compelling the man within to listen and subduing the beast without. "There is no conflict within me anymore. I am whole, or I guess, as whole as any mortal can truly be. This doesn't have to end for you. Not like this."

Empowered by the durgirn song and the blessings of Malfaestus, McKenna walked slowly toward the livid figure that bore Razan's tormented soul. There was no tension in her stance, only a calm surface that told no tale of the surging tide below. She continued to sing softly. First the durgirn mining chant, then a holvi healing ballad, then the celestial cry of her heritage as she held out the mirror before her. The sounds of battle died down around them, surrounded as they were by the energies of the afterlife.

Amber eyes met crimson glare. Each stared the other down, unflinching, resolute. But her strength was greater than his. Razan broke their gaze, drawn to the call of the mirror and the reflection of the violet eyes and moon bright hair of the woman he'd loved within it.

"What do you see when you look into a mirror?" whispered the apparition, Katarin's immortal soul calling out to his.

McKenna finished the spell, raising a hand toward the daemor and crying out in Celestial, "Your self."

With a piercing yell that tore the sky and vaporized a dozen nearby daemor, Razan began to glow along with the mirror. Each black and crimson vein crossing his flesh shone with a pure, crystalline brightness. Motes of light, souls of the dead released on the battlefield, surrounded him, whispering and singing to the true aesir soul locked within the daemor's Abyssal form.

Suddenly a deathly hush descended. Among the clouds, where battled Atosa and Sh'nia with the Lich King, a darkness dimmed the brightness of day. Like a meteor, the combatants crashed to the ground below.

Drawing a ragged breath, the Lich King stood facing his general, the restored spirit of Razan searing in its purity. Razan reached out and thrust his taloned fingers into the chest of the disgraced god, and with another cry that shook the heavens wrenched forth the beating heart within it.

"This belongs to someone, and I intend to return it," hissed Razan, as the Lich King shuddered and stumbled in place.

Atosa and Sh'nia took quick advantage of the monster's weakness. McKenna, knowing in a split second what they intended to do, quickly shielded her eyes as they assumed their immortal forms, the bright and cosmic celestial power obliterating the darkness of the heartless Lich King.

Sh'nia and Atosa turned toward the demigod, who stood motionless still with her hands clenched tightly to the mirror's bezel. The glass lay smooth and empty. Above it hovered a beating heart, held aloft by a pure white soul.

She smiled. The soul nodded deeply, and with a flash of a rust coloured eye, vanished.

--

They fought daemor after daemor, standing alone in the empty streets. The Cathedral stood ominously quiet.

They won't even pretend to send troops to battle? Are they so wrapped in rotten corruption they can lay dormant at such a time as this?

"Barely a hundred of us," swore Layne, as though she read Arya's mind. "A hundred novitiates remaining in a guild that spent the last half decade sweeping the realms. They never expected to face this. They thought they could control it."

She hissed in alarm as an imp, sneaking through slices of her fierce battle axe, dug its spiny teeth into her side. She wrenched the creature from her and sent it flying, blessed bolts chasing after it.

"We can't just sit here and fight them in the streets, Layne," replied Arya through gritted teeth, the vestiges of her divine blessing draining her strength as it slowly faded. The weight of her signet ring grew heavy.

I'm the Grand Master of this bloody guild. I will not let them take it from me.

"Say that out loud, Lady Arya!" yelled Layne, reading the expression that crossed the paladin's face as her rings dug into her clenched fist, her eyes clearer than the thunderous clouds resting above the cathedral that towered behind them.

Arya could sense without even trying the pulsing, daemoric aura emanating from both it and the ivory towers that lay in flames across from them.

"This is my destiny!" she screamed, runes inked along her skin alight with the fire in her eyes. "I will not let them take it from me!"

Considering how difficult entering the keep was earlier, Arya grew almost annoyed at the ease with which they entered the space now. She turned down a familiar hallway- the grand entrance that lay before the imposing golden doors of the throne room. Without warning, the ground beneath them lurched, and shook the very brick and stone upon which they stood apart.

If they knew how the battle waged outside, they'd be more hopeful. If they knew the labyrinth that housed the insidious cult of Naszer disintegrated below them, they'd have had more faith.

Mortals cannot read the minds of gods.

"I call a spell of divine protection!" echoed from the mouths of both women before the walls collapsed. A dim golden light reflected off the clouds of dust, and Arya stood without flinching as chunks of rock gave way before an onslaught of daemor, led by an imposing figure she recognized all too well as the imperious and dread shape of the man who had thrown her guild into such chaos.

Master Gareth, eyes glittering evilly in thrall of the Lich King and bolstered by the daemoric spells cast upon him by Naszer's vile sacerdhossa.

Layne's own protection spell lifted out of sight somewhere beyond the crumbled hall. Arya heard the harsh crunch of an axe pulverizing the bones and breaking the putrid flesh of daemor.

"On your own now, you filthy wretch," Gareth seethed, and she watched in horror as his features distorted, stretched, and shredded into the monstrous form of a Lich.

Bright teeth flashed in her clenched jaw, the lines of her face stretched taut in a wordless scream of defiance. The heat radiating from her figure challenged the dread darkness emanating from his. He raised a hand against his cheek, drawing forth a grimace, transforming to a smile.

"Child. You think you can outwit me?"

Her silver eyes sliced with her blade through the air. The clarion ring of screeching metal whetted by blood slammed against her ears, clawed at the senses overwhelmed by rage. The ferocity of her strikes could fell giants. Their speed could defy wind wraiths.

The haunting specter only yawned.

Staccato thuds echoed in her ears. Was it her heartbeat? she thought dully. No. A flash of bright red hair, a freckled arm extended past the threshold, a crossbow in its grasp. The shriek of daemor as they evaporated into smoke and sulphur. Daemor. In the guild hall ruled by Elgitha, in the heart of the most beautiful and powerful gathering of goodly folk that Faie had ever seen.

Daemor.

"You vile, repulsive beast," she roared, each word lending strength to the arms that struck at him. "You cowardly uncouth heathen. You defy the glory of my ancestors, you pile obscenities at the altar of my god, you step your fetid feet upon hallowed ground."

Thud of quarrel. Hiss of blade. The imps hadn't even

the moment needed to scream before being swept away to the banishment of the Abyss.

Her heart felt as empty as the stone walls surrounding her. Her limbs grew heavy with the crackling pressure of a daemoric void. Where was her god? Where was her blessing?

She dropped her blade in a rage and slammed her palms together. The hall rang.

She didn't need it.

Every evil creature within the high walls of Lianor vanished into smoke with the power of her oath.

Master Gareth stumbled in place, eviscerated by the vacuum of Abyssal power suddenly flooded by her divine blessing. He saw the woman advance toward him, turned tail, and fled to the throne room.

With a smirk, and a choke, Arya collapsed onto the stone floor.

Layne broke through the barrier and dashed toward her, a lifeless heap by her rapier. The paladin's eyes rolled back in her head, and her hands glowed, covered with blisters and singed with ash.

"Arya! Arya T'ssama, Grand Master of the Guild of Tooth and Claw, Almighty Blessed of Bahamut, if you are a warrior, if you are a woman, you will open your eyes!"

Five more minutes. Just five more blessed minutes.

"ARYA!"

Stop crying, Layne. I'll get up. I promise.

Layne muttered oath after oath over the recumbent figure, shrieking, shaking in horror and disbelief. She refused the specter of death that hovered over the body of the person she loved more than life itself. She defied it with hands outstretched.

She felt fingers lace through her own.

"A... Lady Arya?"

The paladin smiled. "I'm gonna kill you if you don't stop calling me that."

Layne choked back a sob, placing a quivering hand on the girl's cheek. Then she laughed, and Arya, sitting up weakly to wrap her arms around the woman, laughed too. Their lips met, a flood of power drowning even the divine blessing in a torrent. What meant danger, what meant daemor- their vitality, their very mortality, conquered all.

Pulling themselves to their feet, they advanced slowly along the path of the fleeing Master. At the sight of each footprint burned into the flagstones, Arya made a mental note to have Clint clean them later.

The throne, tall, imposing, lay at the end of the long hall. At one time, not so long ago, to enter this hall would be done with reverence, with piety, and with grace. To advance upon the one that reposed in it, a blessing and a moment of great honor.

Arya advanced with knives, thrown one by one, each hitting their deadly mark at the writhing figure.

"You threw our guild into torment."

Thud.

"You challenged the might of our god."

Thud.

"You summoned a daemor legion and sunk the health, the dignity, of our Grand Master."

Thud.

"You sit upon my throne," she said, drawing forth her glimmering rapier and pointing it at the bleeding man's throat. "The throne I earned by my own greatness, and not with lies and intrigue and the cursed, vile manipulations of a Lich King. You sought to elevate yourself above the law we all dedicate our lives, our arms, and our hearts to uphold."

He whimpered, the mind wracked with pain from the Lich King's intrusions unable to resist, or defend, against the woman he had so persecuted. He couldn't even plead for mercy, for quarter, that she in no way would have been obligated to give. He might as well be dead.

With a vicious slice of her rapier that carried its clarion cry throughout the hall, he was.

The paladin dropped to her knees before the throne, tears welling in the pools of her silver eyes. She held up her hands to a shaft of light that split the gloom, alighting first on the signet ring and then the nominate ring, both given to her by the Grand Master whose last words rang in her ears.

"You belong in no man's shadow."

Blood pooled at their feet, peppered across their armor and clinging desperately to the edge of Arya's blade. She turned to Layne, grabbed her by the collar, and as the moment of mutual desire and desperation crossed the eyes of each, kissed her with a ferocity that defied even the heat of battle. Axe and blade clanged to the floor. A shaft of light, glowing through the curtained windows set high into the impassive stone walls, lit them with a fiery splendor.

"Grand Master Arya?"

"Yes?"

"Please don't make me scrub this grout."

XXIII

DEATH

Their palls were draped in cloth of silver and gold. Flowers pillowed noble heads, smiling in death. As they were paraded through the pitted streets of Lianor, their fellow warriors looked on with tears in their eyes and bright smiles on their mournful faces.

There can be no war without death. There can be no light without darkness.

His hair, darker than his children's. The strength and the charm of his expressive brow, the conflict and pride in his people both laid to rest with his hands crossed one over the other. Masa Riquelme would find honor in Bahamut's Eternal Joust, honor in death, as so he had lived in life. His daughters and sons bore his coffin, marching in a step that seemed almost like dancing.

Their father had loved to dance- and so they would dance him unto his very grave.

Michelle Magi's five sisters carried the pall bearing her body, surrounding Yori, nearly heartbroken in his grief. Though none of them had spoken to him since their sister's defection, they recognized him as their brother upon her death. She, too, lay as though in a pleasant dream, the cacophony and discord of her life brought to a swift and silent end. The blacksmith's wife did not fear death, or the promise of an afterlife she had never truly believed in. But she faced both for the sake of the land she loved, and the home she built, and with her sacrifice had saved them all.

On a cart drawn by Kurya, flanked by two solemn rows of men and women from Wheelspoke, lay James Intelior's mighty form. Marching silently behind him, and carrying the massive shield that had so often protected him in battle, went Seth- head bowed, eyes dry in an agony that matched the squire's for his own death. Naught but a day had separated them before. And now James would find the Eternal Joust, await a reunion that came too late for them both.

Many more made up the long queue of the solemn procession. Not all were heroes. Most were simply mortals, caught in a battle between forces of power they could never, and had never, aspired to. Their coffins were no less decorated, and the grief brought by their departure no weaker. They passed along the stately boulevard that led from the gates of Lianor to its heart- the vaunted square that stood surrounded by the burned husk of Golden Eye's Tor Savant, the shattered stained glass facade of Tooth and Claw's Cathedral, and the smoke- and shrapnel-marred gallery of the Noble's Council. Many who had originally appeared only to watch instead joined the procession, shouldered the burden of the dead among their saviors, the nobility of their tears brought by the humility of their hearts.

No, not all were heroes. But it did not change the fact that they died so others could live.

Arya stood on a dais raised above the crowd, the same dais from whence Master Gareth had declared the unification of the two guilds before the same crowd that now milled below for a much different, but no less momentous, purpose. As Grand Master of that unified guild, she now commanded power over all Lianor, and she meant to honor that distinction to the best of her ability.

Because ultimately, she meant to divest herself of it as quickly as possible. She had no intention of being Lady of Lianor for long.

She did not stand alone on the dais. McKenna stood beside her, along with Ginni and Tjena, Siberne, Illin, and Katherine.

"I really, really wish Urtha were here," mourned Ginni. "The orgir deserve a place among the heroes. They're responsible for saving all the souls, after all."

"Hmm. I don't think the orgir would want that, really," mused Tjena. "They seem perfectly happy drawing a line between them and the rest of us mortals. As long as they're treated with respect, and no longer dismissed out of hand…"

Ginni shrugged noncommittally, then smiled as Siberne grabbed her hand, wrapping his limber tail around her waist. "I am thinking an envoy to the orgir would be more in keeping. They called on their ambassador for a reason, and if I'm not mistaken, she has much to report."

He eyed her meaningfully, and she blushed. "Ambassador. That was just- that's just a temporary, I mean, it's not like-"

"Give yourself some more credit, Ginni," mused Illin calmly from behind her where he stood with Tjena. "We wouldn't be standing up here together were it not for you two."

She subsided into a blush, burying her face into Siberne's thigh. He laughed and stroked her curls, watching with a bright, but somber, gaze at the procession that approached them.

"So many," he sang under his breath, "so many to defeat this hellish blight."

"They knew what they faced," spoke McKenna, though she felt a stab as she saw Seth in the crowd. "Without them we would be nowhere; struck down one by one. To live forever in the shadow of their sacrifice would be a disservice to their memory. They would have us be joyous," she smiled, as she recalled the exchange she had with her mother on the boundary of the great chasm of Naijor, "and celebrate what they managed to achieve. Death is no darkness that needs be cast out. It is a glory we all are blessed with, and only our manner of dying defies its inevitability."

Those beside her nodded. She was the daughter of Death, after all. None would know better than she its mysteries and its power.

All they could do was watch as the square filled with unassuming wooden boxes, holding the bodies of those whose souls floated along Styckes and into the glories of Pasture.

"They died so we may live," Arya's voice rang out from the dais, crystal clear and echoing in the packed streets. "We will not forget their names, nor their faces. We will mourn them, and be thankful for those shepherds who guide their souls into the afterlife."

She means the orgir, Ginni thought in sudden shock.

The Grand Master and Lady of Lianor is thanking the tribe of Kumbo.

Some muttering met her speech, but most were too bowed by grief to be dismayed by it. They no longer resented the mysterious people who acted as guides for souls, no longer regarded them as thieves and agents of death, who stole the breath of life from mortals not yet ready to let go of the Material plane.

That's not how it worked, they realized, at the sight of so many noble faces who welcomed death with open arms and hearts willing if it meant the salvation of their brethren. Perhaps death was not their enemy after all.

"And we will celebrate, too," she added, throwing her arms wide. "For there is much to celebrate in this golden hour. People of Faie! Look at who stands among you!"

The high planes of ilvin faces raised towards the light; the diminutive figures of holvir posed shyly as their neighbors turned to regard them with newfound awe; the wiry bristles of durgirn beards twitched as their mouths broke into wide grins, hearty cheers, and grasped hands.

"These people fought for us. They died for us, too. They hid not from the scourge that threatened us, though they owed us less than nothing, met with naught but acrid spite or thoughtless negligence from people who thought we were better than they are. They knew how wrong we were, and yet," she continued breathlessly, "they fought beside us anyways. You see these people who do not look like you. They die like you. They live like you. It was our own hubris and our own arrogance that sought to drive them away. We owe them more than we can ever repay, and yet," her eyes flashed and she almost laughed, "we had better start trying."

On the dais stood aesir, holvi, ilvi, and duergi. United in a common purpose, as the mortals of Faie were always meant to be. In the glistening sky above, they could sense the blessings of deities that, finally, recognized the devotion of their flock.

No shining light or prophetic song heralded their acknowledgment. Ginni realized, with something of a smirk, that perhaps divine intervention just wasn't all they professed it to be.

Mortals won this war. It was time for mortals to celebrate it.

—

Drink flowed with abundance. Long tables, some pulled from the wreckage of the guild halls, some improvised from rubble and debris, overflowed with people, hearty food, and cacophony of song. The somber caskets lay upon the dais, so that the heroes could have one last round of revelry with their family and their friends.

McKenna could sense them; the few who clung to the living, in hopes they would forgive them for being dead. Their souls shimmered in the air, plucked at the fibers of her being. She would watch over them for now, let them have their final night, before dismissing them into the mirror and the Pasture beyond.

She felt arms slip around her torso and a face bury itself into her shoulder.

"Penny for your thoughts?" She asked quietly, stroking the black hair that brushed Seth's cheek.

"You're going to need a lot of pennies," he replied ruefully, with a grin. "But honestly... for once, I feel pretty calm. Nothing desperate or dire nagging at every word or thought."

"Hmm. That is a change. I don't know if I'll be able to get used to it," she teased lightly. "If you're suddenly the optimistic one does that mean I have to practice my brooding?"

He laughed and kissed her cheek. "You'll never, ever outdo me in brooding, McKenna, that's a promise. But," he looked her over concernedly, with a hand to her chin, "that doesn't mean that I intend to leave you alone with your own struggles. Spill it, my love," he insisted, as she dropped her eyelids and hove a small sigh she couldn't fully repress. "You know I'll read it in your face anyways."

"This isn't over, Seth. We may have defeated the Lich King, but the damage he's done... it's gone deep. There's still so much death out there," her eyes were filled with tears, at the plight of the wandering, homeless souls and the castaway refugees, holvi and aesir alike, "and... I have to fix it. I have to."

"And you think you'd face it alone?" he asked bluntly.

"W-well..." she stammered, looking around at the gathering, spotting Arya and Layne with their arms around one another and the dim outline of the battered Cathedral in the distant gloom, "this... this is your home, isn't it? You're no longer an outcast, and your guild... don't they need you?"

He took a deep breath, following the line of her gaze, then breaking it to stare into the gathering dusk and the few stars that shone against the brightness of the torches and glowing lights of the party. "Home is where you are," he said quietly. "And I mean that, McKenna. I mean that with every bit of me. I may have been somebody else before," he said, again rubbing the root of his finger where once rested his guild's signet ring, "and, maybe I should feel responsible for being that person still, for picking up the pieces of the life I shattered in an attempt to escape. But I don't," and his eyes were lit with a fire of conviction that, despite what she knew him to possess, bespoke a greater fervor than any he knew before. "I'm not only responsible for who I was. I am responsible for who I am. And who I am is someone who can do great things for my own sake- not for the sake of any god, or guild, that demands I do things for them. I want to do great things for faiefolkr," he continued, his golden eyes alight at the sight of the goodly gathering, "and I want to do great things for myself... and for you," he finished, taking her hand- the one that bore his copper wedding ring- and rubbing it worshipfully against his cheek.

"You don't have to do anything for me, Seth. We're in this together. Come what may," she grasped his hand, trying to communicate with touch all the desire and honor she felt for the man before her, "our adventure is only beginning."

They kissed passionately, feeling the firelight flicker on their faces, hearing the songs and sounds of merriment that seemed to assure them, for the time being, they had chosen the right path.

"Now, somebody once said they could beat me in a drinking game..."

"I stand by that."

"You're going to regret it."

—

Humming under her breath, sandwiched tightly between Tjena to her left and Siberne to her right, Ginni watched the revelers with bright, but thoughtful, eyes. Suddenly she felt an elbow dig lightly at her side, and turned to see Siberne regarding her with a quizzical look.

"Something on your mind, my friend?" He asked, leaning in to speak quietly and avoid the general notice of those seated around them at the table.

"Always, Siberne. The intricacies of my inner thoughts are an unthinkable mystery," she replied with a quirky grin.

He just shook his head and laughed. "You're hopeless. Are not you worried then, about what's next?"

"No. Worrying about what's next is for people who have too much time on their hands. Me, I get to simply enjoy what's now," she said happily, watching in delight as Illin and Tjena sang together over full cups of mead, "and what's now is a bounteous feast, the glory of song, and a hope," her eyes shone as she saw the mingled races that shared the board, "that it will continue into tomorrow."

The sunchild couldn't answer in words. But he, too, felt the draw of the moment- the warmth of her beside him, the brightness and purity of her candid smile.

"You brought our people together, and yet you expect

no reward," he said after a moment of chummy silence. "I can only hope the people of Faie mean to honor their intent to treat you better in return."

The little holvi shrugged. "Activism really isn't my bag, Siberne," she replied in a low tone. "I just ended up a part of something bigger than me. Which, you know," she gestured to her tiny stature, "isn't exactly difficult, considering."

"Again, you think you so little of yourself," the boy shook his head with a furrow in his brow. "But if this can't prove to you your value, then I don't know what will."

"A dance would be a good start," she replied mischievously, nodding over at the figures twirling to Dragon's Hill's brassy horn players.

"A... a what?"

"Oh, sweet summer child," she replied, tugging him to his feet as she realized the Sun ilvi had never initiated into the mysteries of a lively *Besonne* jarabe, "are you in for a treat."

—

Arya's voice echoed off the stone buildings, their smooth surfaces amplifying her voice better than any bardic spell.

"I can't believe you two are getting married!! Mother is going to flip her-"

"Err, are we 'getting' married?" Seth turned quizzically to McKenna, who smacked him on the arm.

"I mean, we kind of ventured from the realm of death, battled our way through hordes of ilmaurte, destroyed two daemor genirae and a Lich King, and thwarted a plot to destroy the greatest guild in all the realms... together. If that ain't married, I don't know what is!" she laughed in return.

He smiled and kissed her, ignoring Layne's whoops of delight and Arya's mimed gagging. As he laced fingers with the monk, he felt the ring resting right where he placed it.

Gods and men have witnessed us. We need no celebration.

His sister wouldn't be so easily dissuaded. "Well, fine then. As Grand Master of the restored Guild of Tooth and Claw and, err, deranked Guild of Golden Eye..."

"We really need a better name," muttered Layne.

"Guild of whatever we want to call it- I hereby call a tourney, to celebrate the greatest hero of our realms, and extend the strongest performers a novitiate and welcome to our ranks!"

Those within earshot of the young Grand Master, once they had fully absorbed her declaration, gave a vigorous cheer. Arya blushed, tilting her chin with a smile toward her compatriots. Layne pounded her battle axe against a rounded shield, and repeated the proclamation for all to hear.

"A tourney! A tourney! For the glory and greatness of our gods!"

As her voice rang through the embattled square, it

carried with it the hopes and joy of the people who had fought to preserve them.

The sounds of merriment carried through the still summer night. Arya wandered along the arroyo lazily with Layne, enjoying the sweet solitude after so long a period of strain and danger. The water bubbled merrily over the rocks, low and clear- entirely unlike the stormy day when it had nearly swept the novitiates into its turbulent rapids and over the cliffs of White Face. Suddenly, she felt her hand being tugged on by her friend and turned.

"Hm? Layne wh-"

The tall, crop-haired paladin stared at her with an intensity that made Arya blush.

"I... Arya, I love you. I don't want that to be something... we only say when we think we're going to die," she stammered, blushing hotly to the roots of her fiery red hair. "It's something I want to be able to say to you every morning when I wake up in your bed, and every evening before I fall asleep in it. I love you! Those words aren't even good enough!"

Taking the girl's hands in her own, Arya pulled her close, close enough to feel the heat of her bright red face; close enough to taste the passion on her lips; close enough to feel the desire that electrified their shared embrace.

"You're right. The words aren't good enough," agreed Arya, when they finally broke apart. "We're going to have to come up with something better."

Layne nodded dizzily. The Grand Master's reserve, when once broken through, had unleashed a torrent of emotion and passion she felt to her core.

Arya's storm cloud eyes danced and she bit her lip, then smiled. "But before it goes without saying, I love you too. Every morning, every evening, and every boring moment in between."

They laced their fingers together and turned to look at the glow of the celebration, leaning on one another for support and comfort.

"*Te comandarme,* Lady Arya."

"You have got to stop calling me that."

Thank You For Reading!

Looking For More Iron Breaker Books?

www.ironbreakerbooks.com

www.ingramcontent.com/pod-product-compliance
Lightning Source LLC
LaVergne TN
LVHW090719280125
802306LV00004B/57